ALSO AVAILABLE FROM ELLE KENNEDY

The Campus Diaries:
The Graham Effect

Briar U Series:
The Chase

The Risk

The Play

The Dare

Off-Campus Series:
The Deal

The Mistake

The Score

The Goal

The Legacy

A full list of Elle's contemporary and suspense print titles is available on her website, ellekennedy.com

THE
RISK

BRIAR U

ELLE KENNEDY

Bloom books

Published by Bloom Books, an imprint of Sourcebooks
P.O. Box 4410, Naperville, Illinois 60567-4410
(630) 961-3900
sourcebooks.com

Originally self-published in 2019 by Elle Kennedy Inc. This is an updated, edited version.

Cataloging-in-Publication Data is on file with the Library of Congress.

Printed and bound in the United States of America.
WOZ 10 9 8 7

1

BRENNA

My date is late.

Now, I'm not a total bitch. Usually I'll give guys a five-minute window. I can forgive five minutes of tardiness.

At seven minutes, I might still be somewhat receptive, especially if the lateness is accompanied by a heads-up call or text informing me he's going to be late. Traffic is an evil mistress. Sometimes she screws you.

At ten minutes, my patience would be running thin. And if the inconsiderate ass is both ten minutes late *and* didn't call? Thank you, next. I'm walking right out the door.

At fifteen minutes, shame on me. Why the hell am I still at the restaurant?

Or, in this particular case, the diner.

I'm sitting in a booth at Della's, the '50s-themed diner in Hastings. Hastings is the small town I'm calling home for the next couple of years, but luckily, I don't need to call my father's house "home." Dad and I might live in the same town, but before I transferred to Briar University, I made it clear I wouldn't be moving in with him. I already left that nest. No way am I flying back to it and subjecting myself to his overprotectiveness and terrible cooking again.

"Can I get you another coffee, hon?" The waitress, a curly-haired

woman in a white-and-blue polyester uniform, eyes me sympathetically. She looks to be in her late twenties. Her nametag reads "Stacy,"
and I'm pretty sure she knows I've been ditched.

"No, thanks. Just the bill, please."

As she walks off, I pick up my phone and shoot a quick text to
my friend Summer. This is all her fault. Therefore she must face my
wrath.

ME: He stood me up.

Summer answers instantly, as if she's been sitting by her phone
waiting for a report. Actually, forget "as if." She totally has. My new
friend is unapologetically nosy.

SUMMER: OMG! NO!!

ME: Yes.

SUMMER: What. a. dick. I am so so so so sorry, Bee.

ME: Meh. Part of me's not surprised. He's a football player.
They're notorious douchecanoes.

SUMMER: I thought Jules was different.

ME: You thought wrong.

Three dots appear, indicating she's typing a response, but I
already know what it will be. Another long-winded apology, which
I'm not in the mood to read at the moment. I'm not in the mood for
anything but paying for my coffee, walking back to my tiny apartment, and taking off my bra.

Stupid football player. I actually put makeup on for this jerk. Yes,
it was just supposed to be an evening coffee date, but I still made an
effort.

I bend my head as I rummage around in my wallet for small bills.
When a shadow falls over the tabletop, I assume it's Stacy returning
with my check.

I assume wrong.

"Jensen," drawls an insolent male voice. "Got stood up, eh?"

Ugh. Of all the people who could've shown up right now, this is the last one I want to see.

As Jake Connelly slides into the other side of the booth, I greet him with a suspicious scowl rather than a smile. "What are you doing here?" I ask.

Connelly is the captain of the Harvard hockey team, AKA, THE ENEMY. Harvard and Briar are rivals, and my father happens to be the head coach of the latter. He's coached at Briar for ten years, winning three championships during that reign. *The Age of Jensen*—that was the headline of a recent article I read in one of the New England papers. It was a full-page write-up about how Briar is killing it this season. Unfortunately, so is Harvard, all thanks to the superstar across the booth from me.

"I was in the neighborhood." There's an amused gleam in his forest-green eyes.

The last time I saw him, he and a teammate were lurking in the stands of Briar's arena, scoping us out. Not long after, we kicked their asses when our teams played each other. Which was tremendously satisfying and made up for our loss against them earlier in the season.

"Mmm-hmmm, I'm sure you just *happened* to be in Hastings. Don't you live in Cambridge?"

"So?"

"So that's an hour away." I give him a smirk. "I didn't know I had a stalker."

"You got me. I'm stalking you."

"I'm flattered, Jakey. It's been a while since someone was so besotted with me that they drove to a whole other town to track me down."

His lips slowly curve into a smile. "Look, as hot as you are—"

"Aw, you think I'm a hottie?"

"—I wouldn't spend the gas money to come here just to get my balls put through the wringer. Sorry to disappoint." He runs a hand through his dark hair. It's a bit shorter now, and he's rocking some scruff that shadows his jaw.

"You say that as if I have any interest in your balls," I answer sweetly.

"My metaphorical balls. You wouldn't be able to handle the real ones," he drawls. "*Hottie.*"

I roll my eyes so hard I almost pull a muscle. "Seriously, Connelly. Why are you here?"

"I was visiting a friend. This looked like a good place to grab some coffee before I drive back to the city."

"You have a friend? Well, that's a relief. I've seen you hanging out with your teammates, but I assumed they have to pretend to like you because you're their captain."

"They like me because I'm fucking terrific." He flashes another grin.

Panty-melting. That's how Summer described his smile once. I swear, the chick has an unhealthy obsession with Connelly's chiseled good looks. Phrases she's thrown around to describe him include: hotness overload, ovary explosion, babelicious, and mackable.

Summer and I have known each other only a couple of months. We pretty much went from strangers to best friends in about, oh, thirty seconds. I mean, she transferred from another college after accidentally setting part of her sorority house on fire—how could I not fall hard for that crazy girl? She's a fashion major, a ton of fun, and is convinced I have a thing for Jake Connelly.

She's wrong. The guy is gorgeous, and he's a phenomenal hockey player, but he's also a notorious player off the ice. This doesn't make him an anomaly, of course. A lot of athletes maintain an active roster of chicks who are perfectly content with 1) hooking up, 2) not being exclusive, and 3) always coming second to whatever sport the dude plays.

But I'm not one of those chicks. I'm not averse to hookups, but numbers 2 and 3 are non-negotiable.

Not to mention that my father would skin me alive if I ever dated THE ENEMY. Dad and Jake's coach, Daryl Pedersen, have been feuding for years. According to my father, Coach Pedersen sacrifices babies to Satan and performs blood magic in his spare time.

"I have lots of friends," Connelly adds. He shrugs. "Including a very close one who goes to Briar."

"I feel like when somebody brags about all their friends, it usually means they don't have any. Overcompensating, you know?" I smile innocently.

"At least I didn't get stood up."

The smile fades. "I wasn't stood up," I lie, except the waitress chooses that moment to approach the booth and blow my cover.

"You made it!" Relief fills her eyes at the sight of Jake. Followed by a gleam of appreciation once she gets a good look at him. "We were starting to get worried."

We? I hadn't realized we were partners in this humiliation venture.

"The roads were slick," Jake tells her, nodding toward the diner's front windows. Rivulets of moisture streak the fogged-up panes. Beyond the glass a thin stripe of lightning momentarily illuminates the dark sky. "Gotta be extra careful when driving in the rain, you know?"

She nods fervently. "The roads get really wet when it's raining."

No shit, Captain Obvious. *Rain makes things wet.* Somebody call the Nobel Prize judging committee.

Jake's lips twitch.

"Could I get you anything to drink?" she asks.

I shoot him a warning glare.

He responds with a smirk before turning to wink at her. "I would *love* a cup of coffee—" He squints at her nametag, "—Stacy. And a refill for my sulking date."

"I don't want a refill, and I'm not his date," I growl.

Stacy blinks in confusion. "Oh? But…"

"He's a Harvard spy sent here to get the goods on Briar's hockey team. Don't humor him, Stacy. He's the enemy."

"So dramatic." Jake chuckles. "Ignore her, Stace. She's just mad that I was late. Two coffees, and some pie, if you don't mind. A slice of…" His gaze travels to the glass cases at the main counter. "Oh damn, I can't decide. Everything looks so tasty."

"Yes you are," I hear Stacy mumble under her breath.

"What was that?" he asks, but his slight smile tells me he heard her loud and clear.

She blushes. "Oh, um, I was saying we only have peach and pecan left."

"Hmmm." He licks his bottom lip. It's a ridiculously sexy move. Everything about him is sexy. Which is why I hate him. "You know what? One of each, please. My date and I will share 'em."

"We most certainly will not," I say cheerfully, but Stacy is already hurrying off to procure some stupid pie for King Connelly.

Fuck.

"Listen, as much as I enjoy discussing how your team is trash, I'm too tired to insult you tonight." I try to tamp down my weariness, but it creeps into my voice. "I want to go home."

"Not yet." The lighthearted, somewhat mocking vibe he's been giving off hardens into something more serious. "I didn't come to Hastings for you, but now that we're having coffee together—"

"Against my will," I cut in.

"—there's something we need to discuss."

"Oh, is there?" Despite myself, curiosity pricks at my gut. I cover it up with sarcasm. "I can't *wait* to hear it."

Jake clasps his hands on the tabletop. He has great hands. Like, really, really great hands. I've got a bit of an obsession with men's hands. If they're too small, I'm instantly turned off. Too big and meaty, and I'm a bit apprehensive. But Connelly has been blessed with a winning pair. His fingers are long but not bony. Palms large and powerful but not beefy. His nails are clean, but two of his knuckles are red and cracked, probably from a skirmish on the ice. I can't see his fingertips, but I'd bet they're callused.

I love the way calluses feel trailing over my bare skin, grazing a nipple...

Ugh. Nope. I'm not allowed to be thinking racy thoughts in the vicinity of this man.

"I want you to stay the hell away from my guy." Although he punctuates that by baring his teeth, it can't be classified as a smile. It's too feral.

"What guy?" But we both know I know who he means. I can count on one finger of one hand how many Harvard players I've fooled around with.

I met Josh McCarthy at a Harvard party that Summer dragged me to a while back. He initially threw a tantrum when he found out I was Chad Jensen's daughter, but then recognized the error of his ways, apologized via social media, and we got together a few times after that. McCarthy's cute, goofy, and a solid candidate in terms of FWBs. With him living in Boston, there's no chance of him smothering me with affection or showing up at my door unannounced.

Obviously, he isn't a long-term option. And that goes beyond the whole my-father-would-murder-me matter. Truth is, McCarthy doesn't stimulate me. His sarcasm skills are severely lacking, and he's a bit boring when his tongue isn't in my mouth.

"I mean it, Jensen. I don't want you messing with McCarthy."

"Jeez, Mama Bear, retract those claws. It's just a casual thing."

"Casual," he echoes. It's not a question, but a mocking I-don't-believe-you.

"Yes, casual. Would you like me to ask Siri to define the word for you? Casual means it isn't serious. At all."

"It is for him."

I roll my eyes. "Well, that's him, not me."

Yet, inside, I'm troubled by Jake's frank assessment. *It is for him.*

Oh boy. I hope that isn't true. Yes, McCarthy texts me a lot, but I've been trying not to engage unless it's something sexy. I don't even respond with "LOL" when he sends me a funny video link, because I don't want to lead him on.

But…maybe I didn't make our fling status as clear as I thought I did?

"I'm tired of watching him walk around like a lovesick puppy." Jake shakes his head in aggravation. "He has it bad, and this bullshit is distracting him at practice."

"Again, how is that my problem?"

"We're smack in the middle of the conference tournament. I know what you're doing, Jensen, and you need to stop."

"Stop what?"

"Stop fucking around with McCarthy. Tell him you're not interested and don't see him again. The end."

I mock-pout. "Oh, Daddy. You're so strict."

"I'm not your daddy." His lips curve again. "Though I could be if you want."

"Oh gross. I'm not calling you 'Daddy' in bed."

Proving she's the master of bad timing, Stacy returns as those words exit my mouth.

Her step stutters. The loaded tray she's carrying shakes precariously. Silverware clinks together. I brace myself, expecting a waterfall of hot coffee to scald my face as Stacy lunges forward. But she recovers quickly, righting herself before disaster strikes.

"Coffee and pie!" Her tone is high and bright, as if she hadn't overheard a thing.

"Thanks, Stacy," Jake says graciously. "I'm sorry for my date's potty mouth. You can see why I don't take her out in public much."

Stacy's cheeks are flushed with embarrassment as she scurries off.

"You traumatized her for life with your filthy sex fantasies," he informs me before digging into his pie.

"Sorry, Daddy."

He snickers mid-bite, a few crumbs flying out of his mouth. He picks up his napkin. "You're not allowed to call me that in public." Mischief dances in his green eyes. "Save it for later."

The other slice—pecan, from the looks of it—sits untouched in front of me. I reach for the coffee instead. I need another hit of caffeine to sharpen my senses. I don't like being here with Connelly. What if someone sees us?

"Or maybe I'll save it for McCarthy," I counter.

"Nah. You won't do that." He gulps down another bite of his pie. "You're breaking it off with him, remember?"

Okay, he really needs to stop issuing orders about my sex life as if he actually has a say in it. "You don't get to make decisions for me. If I want to date McCarthy, I'll date him. If I don't want to date McCarthy, I won't date him."

"Okay." He chews slowly, then swallows. "Do you want to date McCarthy?"

"Date, no."

"Good, so we're on the same page."

I purse my lips before taking a slow sip. "Hmmm. I don't think I like being on the same page as you. I might be changing my mind about the dating scenario... I should ask him to be my boyfriend. Do you know where I can buy a promise ring?"

Jake breaks off a flaky piece of crust with his fork. "You haven't changed your mind. You were over him five minutes after you had him. There're only two reasons why you're still screwing him—either you're bored, or you're trying to sabotage us."

"Is that so?"

"Yup. Nothing holds your attention for long. And I know McCarthy—he's a good kid. Funny, sweet, but that's his downfall right there. 'Sweet' won't cut it with a woman like you."

"There you go again, thinking you know me so well."

"I know you're Chad Jensen's daughter. I know you would take any opportunity to mess with my players' heads. I know we're probably going to be facing off with Briar in the conference finals in a few weeks, and the winner of that game gets an automatic bid to the national tournament—"

"That auto-bid will be ours," I chirp.

"I want my boys sharp and focused on the game. Everyone says your dad's a straight shooter. I was hoping the same thing could be said for his daughter." He tsks in disapproval. "And here you are, playing games with poor, sweet McCarthy."

"I'm not playing games," I say irritably. "We hook up sometimes. It's fun. Contrary to what you believe, the decisions I make have nothing to do with my father or his team."

"Well, the decisions I make are for my team," he retorts. "And I've decided I want you to stay the hell away from my boys." He swallows another mouthful of pie. "Fuck, this is excellent. You want some?" He holds his fork out.

"I'd rather die than put my lips on that fork."

He just laughs. "I want to try the pecan. You mind?"

I stare at him. "You're the one who ordered the damn thing."

"Wow, you're cranky tonight, Hottie. I guess I would be too if I got stood up."

"I didn't get stood up."

"What's his name and address? Want me to go rough him up a bit?"

I grit my teeth.

He takes a bite of the untouched dessert in front of me. "Ah fuck, this one is even better. Mmmm. Ohhh, that's good."

And suddenly the captain of the Harvard hockey team is groaning and grunting in pleasure as if he's acting out a scene from *American Pie*. I try to remain unaffected, but that traitorous spot between my legs has other ideas, tingling wildly at Jake Connelly's sex noises.

"May I go now?" I growl. Except, wait a sec. Why am I asking for *permission?* Nobody is holding me hostage here. I can't deny I'm mildly entertained, but this guy also just accused me of sleeping with his guys to ruin Harvard's chances of beating Briar.

I love my team, but not *that* much.

"Sure. Go if you want. But first text McCarthy to tell him it's over."

"Sorry, Jakey. I don't take orders from you."

"You do now. I need McCarthy's head in the game. End it."

I jut my chin in a stubborn pose. Yes, I need to define things with Josh. I thought I'd stressed the casual nature of our involvement, but evidently he's reading a lot more into it if his team captain is referring to him as "lovesick."

However, I also don't want to give Connelly the satisfaction of siding with him. I'm petty like that.

"I don't take orders from you," I repeat, tucking a five-dollar bill under my half-empty cup. That should cover my coffee, Stacy's tip, and any emotional distress she may have suffered tonight. "I'll do whatever I want with McCarthy. Maybe I'll give him a call right now."

Jake narrows his eyes. "Are you always this difficult?"

"Yes." Smiling, I slide out of the booth and slip into my leather jacket. "Safe drive back to Boston, Connelly. I've been told that the roads get really wet when it's raining."

He chuckles softly.

I zip up my jacket, then lean forward and bring my mouth inches from his ear. "Oh, and Jakey?" I swear I hear his breath hitch. "I'll be sure to save you a seat behind the Briar bench at the Frozen Four."

2

JAKE

It's nine thirty-ish when I get home. The two-bedroom condo I share with my teammate Brooks Weston is nothing I could ever afford on my own, even with the sweet rookie contract I signed with the Oilers. We're on the top floor of the four-story building, and our place is ridiculous—I'm talking chef's kitchen, bay windows, skylights, a massive rear deck, even a private one-car garage for Brooks's Mercedes.

Oh, and it's rent-free.

Brooks and I met a couple of weeks before the start of freshman year. It was at a team event, a "get to know your teammates before the semester starts" dinner. We hit it off immediately, and by the time dessert was served, he was asking me to move in with him. Turned out he had a second bedroom in his Cambridgeport condo—for free, he insisted.

He'd already received special permission to live off campus, a perk of being the filthy rich son of an alum whose donations would be sorely missed if the school didn't keep him happy. Brooks's father pulled a few more strings, and I was given a pass from the dorms, too. Money really does pave the way.

As for the rent issue, at first I'd balked, because nothing in life is free. But the more I got to know Brooks Weston, the more apparent it became that for him? *Everything* comes free. The guy hasn't worked a day in his life. His trust fund is huge, and he gets whatever he wants handed to him on a silver platter. His parents, or one of their minions, secured this condo for him, and they insist on paying the rent. So for the past three and a half years, I've been given a glimpse into what it's like to be a rich boy from Connecticut.

Don't get me wrong, I'm no mooch—I tried to give him money. Brooks won't have it and neither will his parents. Mrs. Weston was aghast when I raised the subject during one of their visits. "You boys need to focus on school," she'd clucked, "not worry about how to pay the bills!"

I'd choked back laughter, because I've been paying bills for as long as I can remember. I was fifteen when I got my first job, and the moment I held that first paycheck in my hand, I was expected to contribute to our household. I was buying groceries, paying for my cell phone, gas, our cable bill.

My family isn't poor. Dad builds bridges and Mom's a hairdresser, and I'd say we are solidly between lower and middle class. We were never rolling in the dough, so experiencing Brooks's lifestyle first-hand is jarring. I've already secretly vowed that once I'm settled in Edmonton and hitting all the incentives in my NHL contract, the first thing I'm going to do is write a check to the Weston family for the three years and counting of unpaid rent.

My phone buzzes as I kick off my Timberlands. I fish it out of my pocket and find a text from my friend Hazel, who I had dinner with earlier in one of Briar's fancy dining halls.

HAZEL: You make it back ok?? It's raining like crazy out there.
ME: Just walked thru the door. Thanks again for the grub.
HAZEL: Anytime. See you Saturday at the game!
ME: Sounds good.

Hazel sends a couple of kissy-face emojis. Other guys might

read more into that, but not me. Hazel and I are completely platonic. We've known each other since grade school.

"Yo!" Weston shouts from the living room. "We're all in here waiting for your ass."

I shrug out of my wet jacket. Brooks's mother sent a decorator over when we first moved in and made sure to purchase everything that guys don't think about, like coat racks and shoe racks and dish racks—apparently men don't give much consideration to racks, outside the tit variety.

I hang up my gear in our separate entryway and then duck through the doorway that leads to the main room. The condo has an open-concept layout, so my teammates are scattered in both the living room and dining area, and a few have taken up residence on the stools at our kitchen counters.

I glance around. Not every guy on the roster has shown up. I'll let it slide, considering I called this meeting last minute. On the drive home from Hastings, I was stewing over Brenna's taunt about the Frozen Four and worrying about how she's distracting McCarthy. Which led to a mental investigation of all the other distractions that might be hindering the team. Since I'm all about action, I sent a mass text: Team meeting, my place, now.

The majority of our starters—nearly twenty of us—fill up the space, which means my nostrils are greeted with the combined scent of various body washes, colognes, and the BO of the assholes who decided not to shower before they came.

"Hey," I greet the guys. "Thanks for coming."

That gets some nods, several "no probs," and general grunts of acknowledgement.

One person who doesn't acknowledge me is Josh McCarthy. He's leaning against the wall near the brown leather sectional, his gaze glued to his phone. His body language conveys a hint of frustration, shoulders stiffening ever so slightly.

Brenna Jensen's probably still tugging him around by the cock. I battle my own sense of frustration at the notion. This kid shouldn't even be wasting his time. McCarthy is a sophomore and he's decent looking, but no way does he belong in Brenna's league. The girl is a smoke show. Hands down, she's one of the hottest women I've ever laid eyes on. And she's got a mouth on her. The kind that needs to be silenced every now and then, maybe with another mouth pressed up to it...or a dick sliding between her red lips.

Oh fuck. I push the thought aside. Yes, Brenna is gorgeous, but she's also a distraction. Case in point: McCarthy hasn't even lifted his head since I entered the room.

I clear my throat. Loudly. He and the other handful that were still on their phones swivel their heads toward me. "I'm gonna make this fast," I tell the room.

"You better," Brooks drawls from the couch. He's wearing black sweatpants and nothing else. "I left a chick in my bed for this."

I roll my eyes. Of course Brooks was banging somebody. He's always banging somebody. Not that I'm one to talk. I've had my share of girls over at our place. I feel sorry for our downstairs neighbors, having to deal with the parade of footsteps marching up and down the stairs. Luckily for them, we don't throw many parties. Hosting a party sucks balls—who wants their house to get trashed? That's what the frat houses are for.

"Aren't you special," Dmitry, our best defenseman, cracks to Weston. "I left my bed too for this meeting. Bed, period. Because I'm goddamn exhausted."

"We all are," a junior left-winger named Heath pipes up.

"Yeah, D, welcome to the tired club," mocks Coby, one of our seniors.

I cross the room toward the kitchen, where I grab a bottle of water. Yeah, I hear them. This last month has been intense. Every Division I conference is balls deep in their tournaments, which means a solid month of the most competitive hockey you'll ever see. We're all vying for auto-bids into the national tournament, and, if that fails, hoping for a good enough record to be selected to the finals. Entire seasons are on the line here.

"Yes," I agree, uncapping my bottle. "We're tired. I can barely keep my eyes open in class. My entire body is one big bruise. I live and breathe these playoffs. I obsess over strategy every night before bed." I take a slow sip. "But this is what we signed up for, and we're so close to reaping the reward. This matchup against Princeton will be the toughest one we've faced all season."

"I'm not worried about Princeton," Coby says, smirking arrogantly. "We already beat them once this year."

"Very early in the season," I point out. "They've picked up steam since then. They swept the quarterfinals against Union."

"So?" Coby shrugs. "We swept our series, too."

He's right. Last weekend we played some of the best hockey we've ever played. But we're in the semifinals now. Shit just got real.

"This isn't best two out of three anymore," I remind the guys. "This is single elimination. If we lose, we're out."

"After our season?" Dmitry says. "We'll get selected to the national tourney even if we don't make it to the conference finals."

"You'd bet our entire season on that?" I challenge. "Wouldn't you rather have that guaranteed bid?"

"Well, yeah, but—"

"But nothing," I cut in. "I'm not gonna hang our hopes on the *possibility* that our season might be deemed good enough to move forward. I'm gonna bet on us kicking Princeton's ass this weekend. Got it?"

"Yessir," Dmitry mumbles.

"Yessir," some of the younger guys echo.

"I told you, you don't have to call me sir. Jesus."

"You want us to call you Jesus?" Brooks blinks innocently.

"Not that, either. I just want you to win. I want *us* to win." And we're so damn close I can practically taste the victory.

It's been…fuck, I don't even know how many years it's been

since Harvard won the NCAA championship. Not during my reign, anyway.

"When was the last time the Crimson won the Frozen Four?" I ask Aldrick, our resident statistics guy. His brain is like an encyclopedia. He knows every piece of trivia there is to know about hockey, however miniscule.

"1989," he supplies.

"'89," I repeat. "That's almost three decades since we called ourselves national champions. Beanpot games don't count. Conference finals don't count. We keep our eye on the ultimate prize."

I conduct another sweep of the room. To my irritation, McCarthy is checking his phone again, and not at all discreetly.

"Seriously, do you even know what was being done to my dick when you texted about this meeting?" Brooks gripes. "Chocolate syrup was involved."

A few of the guys hoot.

"And all you wanted was to give us the speech from *Miracle*? Because, yeah, we get it," Brooks says. "We need to win."

"Yes, we do. And what we *don't* need are any distractions." I give Brooks a pointed look, then direct the same sentiment at McCarthy.

The sophomore is visibly startled. "What?"

"That means you, too." I lock my gaze to his. "Stop playing games with Chad Jensen's daughter."

His expression turns stricken. I don't feel bad about outing McCarthy to whoever didn't know, because I'm pretty sure everyone and their mother already knew. He wears his hookup with Brenna like a badge of honor. He's not sleazy about it by engaging in locker-room talk, but he also can't shut up about how beautiful the girl is.

"Look, I'm not one to usually tell you guys what to do with your dicks, but we're talking about a few weeks here. I'm sure you can keep it in your pants for that long."

"So nobody is allowed to hook up?" a junior named Jonah pipes up, aghast. "Because if that's the case, then I'd like for *you* to call my girlfriend and tell her that."

"Good luck, captain. Vi's a sex maniac," Heath says with a snicker, referring to Jonah's longtime girl.

"And wait a sec—didn't you leave the bar with a hot redhead the other night?" Coby demands. "'Cause that doesn't sound like you're practicing what you preach, bruh."

"Hypocrisy is the devil's crutch," Brooks says solemnly.

I smother a sigh and hold up a hand to silence them. "I'm not saying no hookups. I'm saying no distractions. If you can't handle the hookup, don't do it. Jonah—you and Vi fuck like bunnies and it's never affected your performance on the ice. So keep fucking like bunnies for all I care. But you—" McCarthy receives another stern look. "You've been screwing up in practice all week."

"No, I haven't," he protests.

Our goalie, Johansson, speaks up. "You missed every shot on goal during the shooting drill this morning."

McCarthy is dumbfounded. "You *stopped* all my shots. I'm getting shit because you're a good goaltender?"

"You're our top scorer after Jake," Johansson replies, shrugging. "You should've gotten a couple of those in."

"How is it Brenna's fault that I had an off day? I—" He stops abruptly and glances at his hand. I assume his phone buzzed with a notification.

"Christ, you're proving Connelly's point," a forward named Potts grumbles at McCarthy. "Put your phone away. Some of us want this meeting to be over so we can go home and crack open a beer."

I swivel my head toward Potts. "Speaking of beer... You and Bray are officially banned from all frat parties until further notice."

Will Bray balks. "Come on, Connelly."

"Beer pong's fun, I get it, but you two need to abstain. For fuck's sake, you're starting to get a beer belly, Potts."

Every set of eyes in the room homes in on his gut. It's currently covered by a thick Harvard hoodie, but I see the dude in the locker room every day. I know what's under there.

Brooks makes a tsking noise at me. "I can't believe you're body-shaming Potts."

I scowl at my roommate. "I'm not body-shaming him. I'm simply pointing out that all those beer pong tournaments are slowing him down on the ice."

"It's true," Potts says glumly. "I've been sucking."

Someone snorts.

"You're not sucking," I assure him. "But yeah, you could afford to lay off the beer for a couple weeks. And you—" It's Weston's turn. "Time for abstinence on your part, too."

"Screw that. Sex gives me my superpowers."

I roll my eyes. I do that a lot around Brooks. "I'm not talking about sex. I'm talking about the party favors."

His jaw instantly tightens. He knows precisely what I mean, and so do our teammates. It's no secret that Brooks like to indulge in a recreational drug or two at parties. A joint here, a line of cocaine there. He's careful about when he does it and how much, and I suppose it does help that coke only remains in the blood for forty-eight hours.

This is not to say I tolerate that shit. I don't. But telling Brooks what to do is about as effective as talking to a brick wall. One time I threatened to tell Coach, and Weston said go ahead. He plays hockey because it's fun, not because he's in love with the game and wants to go to the pros. He could give it up in a heartbeat, and threats don't work on someone who isn't afraid to lose.

He's not the first to dabble in the occasional drug, and he won't be the last. It does appear to be purely recreational, though, and he never does it on game day. But the after-party? All bets are off.

"If you get caught with it or fail a piss test, you know what happens. So congratulations, you're officially going clean until after the Frozen Four," I inform him. "You feel me?"

After a long, tense beat, his head jerks in a nod. "I feel you."

"Good." I address the others. "Let's focus on beating Princeton this weekend. Everything else is secondary."

Coby flicks a cocky grin in my direction. "And what are you giving up, captain?"

My brow furrows. "What are you talking about?"

"You call a team meeting. You tell poor McCarthy he can't use his dick anymore, you take away Weston's party favors, and you deprive Potts and Bray of their beer pong championship title. What are *you* going to do for the team?"

A hushed silence falls over the apartment.

For a second I'm speechless. Because is he for real? I score at least one goal a game. If someone else scores, it's usually with my assist. I'm the fastest skater on the Eastern Seaboard, and I'm a damn good captain.

I open my mouth to retort when Coby starts to laugh.

"Bruh, you should've seen your face." He grins at me. "Relax. You do plenty. You're the best captain we've ever had."

"Aye, aye," several of the guys call out.

I relax. But Coby does have a point. "Look, I won't apologize for wanting us to be focused, but I am sorry if I'm being harsh on you guys. Especially you, McCarthy. All I'm asking is for us to keep our heads in the game, can we do that?"

About twenty heads nod back at me.

"Good." I clap my hands. "You can all take off now. Get some sleep and bring your A-game to morning skate tomorrow."

The meeting adjourns, the group dispersing. Once again, our neighbors are forced to suffer through the footsteps, this time the heavy stomps of two-dozen hockey players thudding down the stairs.

"Dad, may I please go back to my room now?" Brooks asks sarcastically.

I grin at him. "Yes, son, you may. I'll lock up."

He flips up his middle finger as he dashes toward the bedrooms. Meanwhile, McCarthy lingers by the front door, waiting for me.

"What am I supposed to say to Brenna?" he asks.

I can't tell if he's angry, because his expression reveals nothing. "Just tell her you need to concentrate on the tournament. Tell her you guys will get together after the season."

They'll never get together again.

I don't voice the thought, but I know it's true. Brenna Jensen would never condone being "put on hold" by anyone, let alone a Harvard player. If McCarthy ends it, even temporarily, she'll make it a permanent split.

"Briar has won three national championships in the last decade," I say flatly. "Meanwhile, we're over here, winless. That's unacceptable, kid. So tell me, what's more important to you—getting mindfucked by Brenna Jensen or beating her team?"

"Beating her team," he says immediately.

No hesitation. I like that. "Then let's beat them. Do what needs to be done."

With a nod, McCarthy walks out the door. I lock up after him.

Do I feel bad? Maybe a little. But anyone can see that he and Brenna aren't destined to be together. She said as much herself.

I'm simply speeding up the inevitable.

3
BRENNA

"WHERE HAVE YOU BEEN? I CALLED YOU THREE TIMES, BRENNA."

My dad's brusque tone never fails to raise my hackles. He speaks to me the way he speaks to his players—curt, impatient, and unforgiving. I'd like to say that it's always been this way, that he's been barking and growling at me for my entire life. But that would be a lie.

Dad didn't always snap at me. My mother died in a car accident when I was seven, which thrust my father into a maternal role as well as a paternal one. And he was good at both. He used to speak to me with love and tenderness on his face and in his voice. He'd pull me onto his lap and ruffle my hair and say, "Tell me how school was today, Peaches." His nickname for me was "Peaches," for Pete's sake.

But that was a long time ago. Nowadays, I'm just Brenna, and I can't remember the last time I associated the words "love" or "tenderness" with my father.

"I was walking home in a downpour," I reply. "I couldn't pick up the phone."

"Walking home from where?"

I unzip my boots in the cramped corridor of my basement apartment. I rent it from a nice couple named Mark and Wendy, who both travel quite a lot for work. Add to that my separate entrance, and I can go weeks without having any interaction with them.

"From Della's Diner. I was having coffee with a friend," I say.

"This late?"

"Late?" I crane my neck toward the kitchen that's even tinier than the hallway and glance at the clock on the microwave. "It's barely ten o'clock."

"Don't you have your interview tomorrow?"

"Yes, so? Do you think me getting home at nine thirty means I'm going to sleep through my alarm?" I can't keep the sarcasm out of my tone. Sometimes it's difficult not to snap at him the way he snaps at me.

He ignores the taunt. "I spoke to someone at the network today," he says. "Stan Samuels—he runs the master control booth, solid fellow." Dad's voice becomes gruff. "I told him you were coming in tomorrow and put in a good word for you."

I soften a little. "Oh. That was nice of you. I appreciate that." Some people might feel awkward about calling in favors to get ahead, but I have no problem using my father's connections if it helps me secure this internship. It's hyper competitive, and although I'm more than qualified—I've worked my ass off to be—I'm at a disadvantage because I'm female. Unfortunately, this is a male-dominated field.

The broadcasting program at Briar offers official work placements for students in their senior year, but I'm hoping to beat everyone to the punch. If I can land a summer internship at HockeyNet, there's a fair chance I'll be able to continue working there for my senior placement. That means an advantage over my peers and a potential job when I graduate.

My end-game has always been to become a sports journalist. Yes, HockeyNet is only a decade old (and the originality coffers must've been running low the day they chose their name), but the network covers hockey exclusively, and when it launched, it filled a deep void in the sports coverage market. I watch ESPN religiously, but one of the major complaints about it is its lackluster hockey coverage. Which is egregious. I mean, in theory, hockey is the fourth major sport in the country, but the bigger networks often treat it as if it's less important than NASCAR or tennis or—shudder—golf.

I dream of being on camera and sitting with those analysts at the big boys' table, breaking down highlights, analyzing games, voicing my predictions. Sports journalism is a tough route for a woman, but I know my hockey, and I'm confident I'll slay my interview tomorrow.

"Let me know how it goes," Dad orders.

"I will." As I cross the living room, my left sock connects with something wet, and I yelp.

Dad is instantly concerned. "You all right?"

"Sorry, I'm fine. The carpet's wet. I must have spilled something—" I stop when I notice a small puddle in front of the sliding door that opens onto the backyard. It's still raining outside, a steady pounding against the stone patio. "Crap. There's water pooling at the back door."

"That's not good. What are we dealing with? Runoff directing water into the house?"

"How would I know? Do you think I studied the runoff situation before I moved in?" He can't see me rolling my eyes, but I hope he can hear it in my voice.

"Tell me where the moisture is coming from."

"I told you, it's mostly around the sliding door." I walk the perimeter of the living room, which takes about, oh, three seconds. The only wet spot is near the door.

"All right. Well, that's a good sign. Means it's probably not the pipes. But if it's storm-water runoff, there could be several culprits for that. Is the driveway paved?"

"Yeah."

"Your landlords might need to consider drainage options. Give them a call tomorrow and tell them to investigate."

"I will."

"I mean it."

"I said I will." I know he's trying to be helpful, but why does he have to use that tone with me? Everything with Chad Jensen is a command, not a suggestion.

He's not a bad man, I know that. He's simply overprotective, and once upon a time he might've had reason to be. But I've been living on my own for three years. I can take care of myself.

"And you'll be at the semifinals on Saturday night?" Dad asks briskly.

"I can't," I say, and I'm genuinely regretful about missing such a vital game. But I made these plans ages ago. "I'm visiting Tansy, remember?" Tansy is my favorite cousin, the daughter of my dad's older sister, Sheryl.

"That's this weekend?"

"Yup."

"All right, then. Say hello for me. Tell her I look forward to seeing her and Noah for Easter."

"Will do."

"Are you spending the night?" There's an edge to the question.

"Two nights, actually. I'm going up to Boston tomorrow, and heading back Sunday."

"Don't do—" He halts.

"Don't do what?" This time, it's my tone taking on that sharp edge.

"Don't do anything reckless. Don't drink too much. Be safe."

I appreciate that he doesn't say, "Don't drink at all," but that's probably because he knows he can't stop me. Once I turned eighteen, he couldn't force me to abide by his curfew or his rules anymore. And once I turned twenty-one, he couldn't stop me from having a drink or two.

"I'll be safe," I promise, because that's the one assurance I can give with confidence.

"Bren," he says. Then stops again.

I feel like most conversations with my father go like this. Start and stop. Words we want to say, and words we don't say. It's so hard to connect with him.

"Dad, can we hang up now? I want to take a hot shower and get ready for bed. I have to wake up early tomorrow."

"All right. Let me know how the interview goes." He pauses. When he speaks again, it's to offer some rare encouragement. "You got this."

"Thank you. Night, Dad."

"Night, Brenna."

I hang up and do exactly what I told him—take a scalding-hot shower, because the twenty-minute walk in the rain chilled me down to the bone. I'm redder than a lobster when I emerge from the cramped shower stall. My little bathroom doesn't have a bathtub, which is a shame. Hot baths are the absolute best.

I don't like sleeping with wet hair, so I do a quick blow-dry and then rummage around in my dresser in search of my warmest PJs. I settle on plaid pants and a thin long-sleeve tee with the Briar University logo on it. Basements tend to be cold as a rule, and my apartment is no exception. I'm surprised I haven't come down with pneumonia in the seven or so months I've lived here.

As I get under the covers, I pop my phone out of its charger and find a missed call from Summer. I have a feeling she'll call again if I don't respond, probably five seconds after I fall asleep, so I preemptively ring her back before she can ruin my good night's sleep.

"Are you mad at me?" is how she greets me.

"No." I curl up on my side, the phone balanced on my shoulder.

"Even though I set you up with Jules and vouched for him?" Her voice ripples with guilt.

"I'm an adult, Summer. You didn't force me to say yes."

"I know. But I feel terrible. I can't believe he didn't show."

"Don't worry about it. I'm not the least bit upset. If anything, I dodged a bullet."

"Okay, good." She sounds relieved. "I'll find someone even better to hook you up with."

"You most certainly will not," I say cheerfully. "You're officially relieved of your matchmaking duties—which you bestowed on yourself, by the way. Trust me, babes, I have zero issues when it comes to meeting men."

"Yes, you're good at meeting them. But dating them? You suck at that."

I'm quick to protest. "Because I'm not looking to date anybody."

"Why not? Having a boyfriend is awesome."

Sure, maybe when your boyfriend is Colin Fitzgerald. Summer is dating one of the most decent guys I've ever met. Intelligent, kind, astute, not to mention hot as fuck.

"Are you and Fitzy still obsessed with each other?"

"*So* obsessed. He puts up with my crazy, and I put up with his dorkiness. Plus, we have the best sex ever."

"I bet Hunter loves that," I say dryly. "I hope you're not a screamer."

Hunter Davenport is Summer and Fitz's roommate, and he was recently rejected by Summer. She agreed to go on a date with him, only to realize her feelings for Fitz were too strong to ignore. Hunter didn't take it well.

"God, you have no idea how hard it is to try to be quiet when Fitz is doing his magical magic to my body," Summer says with a sigh.

"Magical magic?"

"Yes, magical magic. But if you're worried that Hunter is lying in bed listening to us and weeping inconsolably, don't be. He's got a different girl over here every night."

"Good for him." I snicker. "I bet Hollis is green with envy."

"I'm not sure Mike's even noticed. He's too busy mooning over you."

"Still?" Dammit. I was hoping he was done with that.

I briefly close my eyes. I've committed some asinine acts in my life, but hooking up with Mike Hollis is high on that list. We were both drunk out of our minds, so all we did was share a sloppy make-out session and I fell asleep while giving him a hand job. It definitely wasn't my finest moment, nor was it all that memorable. I have no idea why he'd want a repeat.

"He's smitten," Summer confirms.

"It'll pass."

She giggles, but the humor dies quickly. "Hunter is being a jerk to us," she admits. "When he's not screwing anything in a skirt."

"I guess he was really into you?"

"Honestly? I don't think it's about me. I think it's about Fitz."

"I can see that. He wanted to fuck Fitz," I say solemnly. "I mean, who doesn't?"

"No, you brat. Fitz straight up lied when Hunter asked if he had a thing for me. Hunter views it as a betrayal of the bro code."

"The bro code is holy," I have to concede. "Especially among teammates."

"I know. Fitz says there's a lot of tension at practice." Summer moans. "What if affects their performance in the semifinals, Bee? That means Yale will move on to the finals."

"My dad will straighten them out," I assure her. "And say what you will about Hunter, but he likes to win hockey games. He won't let a beef over some girl—no offense—distract him from winning."

"Should I—"

A buzz in my ear mutes her question.

"What was that?"

"Text message," I explain. "Sorry, keep going. What were you saying?"

"I was wondering if I should try to talk to him again."

"I don't think it'll make a difference. He's a stubborn ass. But eventually he'll put his big-boy pants on and get over it."

"I hope so."

We chat for a while longer, until my eyelids grow heavy. "Summer. I'm going to sleep now, babes. I've got that interview in the morning."

"Okay. Call me tomorrow. Love you."

"Love you, too."

I'm about to turn off the bedside lamp when I remember the text. I click the message icon and narrow my eyes when I see McCarthy's name.

> Hey, B. It's been really awesome chilling with you, but I need to take a step back for a while. At least till playoffs are over. Gotta focus on the game, you know? I'll give you a call once everything settles down, k? xo

My jaw falls open. Is this a joke?

I read the message again, and, nope, the content doesn't change. McCarthy actually ended it.

It appears that Jake Connelly just declared war.

4

BRENNA

I CAN USUALLY HOLD MY OWN IN MOST SITUATIONS. I'VE NEVER suffered from anxiety, and nothing really scares me, not even my father, who's been known to make grown men cry with one look. That's not hyperbole—I saw it happen once.

But this morning my palms are sweaty and evil butterflies are gnawing at my stomach, and it's all thanks to this HockeyNet executive, Ed Mulder, who's been off-putting from the word *go*. He's tall, bald, and terrifying, and the first thing he does after shaking my hand is ask why a pretty girl like me is applying for a job *behind* the camera.

I hide a frown at the sexist remark. One of my TAs at Briar, Tristan, used to be an intern here and he warned me that Mulder is a total jerk. But Tristan also said none of the interns report directly to Ed Mulder, which means I won't need to deal with him past this interview. He's just one obstacle I have to get through to strike internship gold.

"Well, as my cover letter stated, I eventually want to be an on-screen analyst or a reporter, but I'm hoping to build experience behind the scenes, too. I'm majoring in Broadcasting and Journalism at Briar, as you already know. Next year I'll be doing a work placement at—"

"This isn't a paid internship," he interrupts. "You're aware of that?"

I'm caught off-guard. My palms feel slippery when I wring them together, so I place them on my knees. "Oh. Um. Yes, I'm aware."

"Good. I find that while male applicants come in knowing the details, the female ones often expect to get paid."

He's gone from vaguely sexist to obscenely so. And the comment doesn't make much sense, either. The job posting on the HockeyNet site clearly specified this was an unpaid internship. Why would men expect one thing and women expect another? Is he suggesting that the women didn't read the posting correctly? Or that we can't read at all?

Beads of sweat break out at the nape of my neck. I'm so off my game here.

"So. Brenda. Tell me about yourself."

I gulp. He called me Brenda. Should I correct him?

Of course you should correct him. Screw this guy. You own him. Confident Brenda—I mean Brenna—rears her spectacular head.

"Actually, it's Brenna," I say smoothly, "and I think I'd be a good fit here. First and foremost, I love hockey. It's—"

"Your father is Chad Jensen." His jaw moves up and down, and I realize he's chewing gum. Classy.

I answer in a careful tone. "Yes, he is."

"A championship-winning coach. Multiple Frozen Four wins, right?"

I nod. "He's a great coach."

Mulder nods back. "You must be proud of him. What would you say is your biggest strength, aside from having a semi-famous dad?"

I force myself to ignore the snide note in his inquiry and say, "I'm smart. I think on my feet. I thrive under pressure. And most of all, I genuinely love this sport. Hockey is—"

Annnd he's not listening to me anymore.

His gaze has shifted to the computer screen, and he's still chewing his gum like a horse chomping on some oats. The window behind his desk provides a fuzzy glimpse of the reflection from his monitor...is that a fantasy hockey lineup? I think it's the ESPN fantasy page.

He suddenly glances at me. "Who's your team?"

I wrinkle my forehead. "My college team or—"

"NHL," he interrupts impatiently. "Who do you root for, Brenda?"

"Brenna," I say through gritted teeth. "And I root for the Bruins, of course. What about you?"

Mulder snorts loudly. "Oilers. I'm a Canadian boy, through and through."

I feign interest. "Oh, that's interesting. Are you from Edmonton, then?"

"I am." His eyes flick back to his screen. In an absent-minded tone, he says, "What would you say is your biggest weakness, aside from having a semi-famous dad?"

I swallow an angry retort. "I can be impatient at times," I confess, because there's no way I'm doing that cheesy bit about how my biggest weakness is that I care too much or work too hard. Gag.

Mulder's attention is once again diverted to his fantasy hockey team. Silence falls over the spacious office. I shift irritably in my chair and examine the glass case against the wall. It displays all the awards the station has won over the years, along with signed paraphernalia from various pro hockey players. There's a lot of Oilers merch in there, I note.

On the opposite wall, two big screens are showing two different programs: an NHL highlights reel from this weekend, and a Top Ten segment counting down the most explosive rookie seasons of all time. I wish the TVs weren't on mute. At least then I could hear something interesting while I'm being ignored.

Frustration climbs up my spine like ivy and tightens around my throat. He isn't paying a lick of attention to me. Either he's the worst interviewer on the planet, a rude jackass, or he's not seriously considering me for this position.

Or maybe it's D) all of the above.

Tristan was wrong. Ed Mulder isn't a jerk—he's a mega asshole. But unfortunately, good, hands-on internships at big networks like HockeyNet don't come along every day. It's slim pickings out there in the internship market. And I'm also not naïve enough to think that Mulder is a special case. Several of my professors, both male and female, warned me that sports journalism isn't the most welcoming field for women.

I'm going to face men like Mulder during my entire career. Losing my temper or storming out of his office won't help me achieve my goals. If anything, it'll "prove" his own point in his misogynistic head: that women are too emotional, too weak, too ill equipped to survive in the sports arena.

"So." I clear my throat. "What would my duties be if I got this internship?" I already know the answer—I practically memorized the job posting, not to mention my CIA-worthy interrogation of Tristan the TA. But I might as well ask some questions, seeing as how Mulder isn't interested in returning the favor.

His head lifts. "We've got three intern slots to fill in the production department. I'm the head of that department."

I wonder if he realizes he hadn't answered the question. I draw a calming breath. "And the duties?"

"Highly intensive," he replies. "You'd be required to compile game highlights, assemble clips packages, help to create teasers and B-roll. You'd attend production meetings, pitch ideas for stories..." He trails off, clicking his mouse a few times.

AKA, the perfect job for me. I want this. I *need* this. I bite the inside of my cheek, wondering how I can turn this disastrous meeting around.

I don't get the chance. There's a loud knock on the door, and it flies open before Mulder can respond. An excited-looking man with an unkempt beard thunders into the office.

"Roman McElroy just got arrested for domestic abuse!"

Mulder dives out of his leather chair. "Are you fucking shitting me?"

"There's a video of it all over the Internet. Not of the wife-beating, but the arrest."

"Have any of the other networks picked this up yet?"

"No." Beard Man is bouncing up and down like a kid in a toy store, and he can't be a day younger than fifty-five.

"Which talking heads do we have on set?" Mulder demands on his way to the door.

"Georgia just got here—"

"No," the boss interrupts. "Not Barnes. She'll try to give it some sort of feminist bullshit spin. Who else?"

I bite my lip to stave off an angry retort. Georgia Barnes is one of the two female analysts at HockeyNet, and she is *amazing*. Her insights are topnotch.

"Kip Haskins and Trevor Trent. But they're doing a live segment right now. *The Friday Five.*"

"Screw *The Friday Five*. Have Gary write up some copy, then get Kip and Trevor to debate the fuck out of it and break apart the arrest video frame by frame. I want a whole segment on this McElroy thing." Mulder skids to a stop in the doorway, suddenly remembering my existence. "We'll finish this on Monday."

My mouth falls open. "I'm sorry—what?"

"Come back Monday," he barks. "We're dealing with a monster exclusive here. The news waits for no man, Brenda."

"But—"

"Monday, nine o'clock." With that, he's gone.

I stare at the empty doorway in disbelief. What the hell just happened? First he opened the interview with a bunch of sexist comments, then he didn't listen to a word I said, and now he's abandoning me mid-interview? I understand that a professional hockey player being charged with abusing his wife is big news, but…I can't come back on Monday. I have classes. Tristan warned me about Mulder, but the man was even worse than I'd expected.

I angrily gather up my purse and coat and rise to my feet. Fuck that. I'm not returning on Monday. I'm not letting that asshole—

Dream internship, I remind myself, then repeat the phrase over and over again in my mind. ESPN and HockeyNet are the two biggest sports networks in the country. And ESPN isn't hiring.

Therefore…

I guess I'm skipping school on Monday.

Rochelle, Mulder's cute blonde receptionist, glances up from her desk when I walk up. She officially reschedules the interview, and I leave the HockeyNet building with the worst feeling in the pit of my stomach.

For the first time in ages, it's not raining, so I arrange for an Uber and stand outside by the curb. I call my cousin while I wait. "Hey," I say when Tansy picks up. "My interview's over."

"Already?"

"Yup."

"How did it go?"

"It was a total disaster. I'll tell you about it later. I just ordered an Uber—can I still head to your dorm?" The plan was for me to hang out there alone while Tansy is in class.

"Yeah, I left my key with my RA. She's in room 404. Knock there first and get the key. I'm in 408."

"Cool." I glance back at the high-rise I just exited, with its sparkling windows, glass lobby, and massive white-and-red HockeyNet logo. A sigh slips out. "I hope you're ready to get lit tonight, because I need to drink the memory of this interview right out of my head."

"I hate you so much. How do you always manage to look so good without even trying?" Tansy gripes later that evening.

We're in her suite at Walsh Hall, one of the Boston College residences. Tansy shares it with three other girls, and bunks with a chick named Aisha, who's away for the weekend visiting her parents in New York. Aisha is a girl after my own heart, because she transformed her desk into a vanity. I would've done the same thing to my desk at home, if I had one; I've always preferred doing homework while sprawled on my bed or couch.

I grin at Tansy's reflection in Aisha's huge mirror, then continue applying mascara to my upper lashes. "I'm putting on makeup," I point out. "How is that not trying?"

She makes a grumbling noise in her throat. "You call that makeup? You put on a dab of concealer and a bit of mascara. That doesn't count as trying."

"And lipstick," I remind her.

"And lipstick," she concedes. She rolls her eyes at me. "You know colors other than red exist in this big, beautiful world, right?"

"Red's my color." I purse my lips at her, then smack them together in an air kiss. "My friend at Briar says it's my trademark."

"It totally is. I can't remember the last time I saw you without it. Maybe Christmas morning?" She pauses. "No, wait, we both wore red lipstick that day. It matched our Santa hats. I looked awful, though. I remember that. I can't pull off red lips."

"We have the same complexion, Tans. You could absolutely pull it off."

"No, I mean swag-wise. You need to possess a certain amount of swagger to rock the red."

She's not wrong. It's a look that requires confidence. Ironically, it's what gives me confidence. I know it sounds absurd, but I feel invincible every time I slather on some crimson lipstick.

"I can lend you some of my swagger if you want," I offer.

Tansy's nose scrunches up as she grins. The silver stud in her left nostril catches the light and seems to sparkle. "Aw thanks, Bee. I knew there was a reason you're my favorite cousin."

"Well, the others aren't exactly prime candidates for that honor. Leigh and Robbie are too preachy about religion. And don't get me started on Alex."

We both grimace. Alex is our uncle Bill's daughter and she's incredibly annoying.

I hear the chirp of an incoming message. "Hey, can you check that?" I left my phone on Tansy's desk, and she's closer to it.

She reaches over from her bed. "Someone named GB says he misses you. He used about a hundred u's and five, no, six, heart emojis. Oooh, and it's the *red* heart. That means he's serious. So. Who is GB and why haven't you mentioned him?"

I sputter with laughter. "GB stands for Greenwich Barbie. That's what I call my friend. Summer. She's a hot rich girl from Connecticut."

"Liar. I've never heard you mention a Summer," Tansy accuses.

"She transferred to Briar at the beginning of January." I stick the mascara wand back in the tube and twist it closed. "This chick is insane, like in a good way. She's hilarious. Always up for a party. I can't wait for you to meet her."

"Are we seeing her this weekend?"

"No, unfortunately. She's performing her girlfriendly duty and supporting Briar at the semifinals against Yale tomorrow night. Her boyfriend is on the team."

"Why does she miss you?"

"We haven't hung out since last weekend. And yes, I know a week is not a long time at all, but in Summer years that's a decade. She's melodramatic."

My phone chirps again.

"See what I mean?" I chuckle, tucking my mascara and lipstick into the small makeup case I brought with me. "Pass me my phone, will ya? If I don't text her back, she's liable to have a panic attack."

Tansy checks the screen. Her shoulders stiffen slightly. "It's not Summer," she informs me.

I knit my brows. "Okay. Who is it?"

There's a long pause. Something shifts in the air, and suddenly a cloud of tension settles between us.

Tansy studies me, wary. "Why didn't you tell me you were still in touch with Eric?"

5
BRENNA

THE TENSION SEEPS INTO MY BODY, TURNING MY SHOULDERS TO stone and my spine to iron. And yet my fingers feel like jelly, and I begin to tremble. Luckily, I'm finished putting on mascara; otherwise, I would've poked an eyeball out.

"Eric messaged?" I'm bothered by how weak my voice sounds. "What does it say?"

Tansy tosses me the phone. My gaze instantly lowers to the message. It's brief.

ERIC: Call me, B. Need to talk to you.

Uneasiness trickles down my spine like drops from a leaky faucet. Shit. What does he want now?

"What does he want?" Tansy speaks my thoughts, only she sounds far more distrustful than I am.

"I don't know. And to answer your question, we're not in touch."

That's not entirely true. I hear from Eric two or three times a year, usually when he's high as a kite or drunk off his face. If I don't pick up, he keeps calling, over and over and over, until I do. I don't have the heart to block his number, but the heart I do possess splinters each time I answer his calls and hear how far he's fallen.

"Did you know my mom ran into him, like, six or seven months ago? It was around Halloween."

"Really? Why didn't she say anything about it over the holidays?"

"She didn't want to worry you," Tansy confesses.

A heavy breath gets stuck in my throat. The fact that Aunt Sheryl thought I would be worried tells me the state Eric was in when she saw him. "Was he high?"

"Mom thinks so."

I exhale slowly. "I feel so bad for him."

"You shouldn't," Tansy says frankly. "He's the one who chooses to keep indulging in that lifestyle. His mom got him a spot in that super-expensive rehab in Vermont and he refused to go, remember?"

"Yeah, I remember." I feel bad for Eric's mother, too. It's so frustrating trying to help someone who refuses to admit they have a problem.

"Nobody is forcibly pouring booze down his throat or making him do drugs. Nobody is holding him hostage in Westlynn. He can leave town anytime. *We* did."

She's right. Nothing is keeping Eric in Westlynn, New Hampshire, except for his own demons. I, on the other hand, fled to Boston right after high school graduation.

There's nothing wrong with my hometown. It's a perfectly nice place, meeting the small-town requirements of tranquil and quaint. My dad and his siblings were born and raised in Westlynn, and Aunt Sheryl and Uncle Bill still reside there with their spouses. Dad waited until I moved out before he relocated to Hastings, Massachusetts. Before that, he made the hour-long commute to Briar so that I could continue to attend school with my cousins and friends. I think he's happier in Hastings, though. The town is five minutes from campus, and his house is a roomy old Victorian with a ton of charm.

My ex-boyfriend chose to stay in our hometown. He spiraled

after graduation, falling in with all the wrong people and doing all the wrong things. Westlynn isn't overrun with drug dealers, but that's not to say you can't find drugs there. You can find drugs anywhere, sadly.

Eric is stuck. Everyone else has moved on, and he's still in the same place. No, he's in an even worse place these days. Maybe I shouldn't feel sorry for him, but I do. And our history makes it hard to write him off entirely.

"I don't think you should call him."

My cousin's stern words jolt me back to the present. "I probably won't."

"*Probably* won't?"

"Ninety percent won't, ten percent might."

"Ten percent is too high." She shakes her head. "That guy will only drag you down if you let him back in your life."

I blanch. "God, don't even worry about that happening. A hundred percent chance it won't."

"Good. Because clearly he's still obsessed with you."

"He was never obsessed with me," I say in Eric's defense.

"Are you kidding me? Remember when you got mono junior year and couldn't attend school for a couple of months? Eric had a total meltdown," she reminds me. "He called you every five seconds, skipped class to go see you, freaked out when Uncle Chad told him to stop coming over. It was intense."

I avert my eyes. "Yeah. I guess it was a tad dramatic. What do you think of this top, by the way?" I gesture to my ribbed black crop top. It ties around the neck and the back, exposing my midriff.

"Hot AF," Tansy declares.

"You know you saved no time by saying AF instead of 'as fuck,' right? Same amount of syllables," I tease, all the while battling relief that she accepted my change of subject so readily.

I don't like dwelling on that time in my life. Truth be told, thinking about Eric is as exhausting as it was actually dealing with him back in the day. One thought of him, and I feel as if I just climbed Everest. My ex is an energy vampire.

"I speak internet lingo," Tansy retorts. "The one true language. Anyway, you look hot, and I look hot, so let's go out and show everyone how hot we are. You ready?"

I swipe my purse off her roommate's bed. "Ready AF."

———————

We end up at an Irish pub in the Back Bay area. It's called the Fox and Fiddle, and populated primarily by college students, judging by all the younger faces. Sadly, there's a conspicuous lack of hockey attire. I spot one or two maroon-and-gold jerseys, the colors of the Boston College Eagles. But that's it. It makes me long for Malone's, the bar in Hastings where all the Briar hockey fans congregate.

Tansy checks her phone as we walk inside. We're meeting her boyfriend here. Or maybe it's her ex-boyfriend? Fuck buddy? I never know when it comes to her and Lamar. Their on-again/off-again relationship has the head-spinning quality of riding a Tilt-O-Whirl.

"No text from Lamar. I guess he's not here yet." She links her arm through mine on our way to the bar. "Let's order shots. We haven't done shots since Christmas."

There's a huge crowd waiting to be served. When I catch the eye of one of the bartenders, he signals that he'll be a minute.

"I really wish you went to BC with me," Tansy says glumly. "We could do this all the time."

"I know." I would've loved to attend Boston College with her, but they rejected my application. I didn't have the grades back then; my relationship with Eric pretty much torpedoed my ability to concentrate on school. I went to community college instead, until I was able to transfer to Briar, where I don't have to pay tuition since my father works there.

"Sweet. They're showing the Bruins game." I gaze up at one of the monitors mounted from the ceiling. A blur of black and yellow whizzes by as the Bruins go on an offensive attack.

"Hurray!" Tansy says with mock enthusiasm. She doesn't give a crap about hockey. Her game of choice is basketball. As in, she only dates basketball players.

I try to flag down the bartender again, but he's busy serving a group of chicks in teeny dresses. The pub is surprisingly packed for ten thirty at night. Normally, people are still pre-drinking somewhere else at this time.

Tansy checks her phone again, then types something. "Where the hell is he?" she mutters.

"Text him."

"Just did. He's not answering for some rea—oh wait, he's typing." She waits until the message appears. "Okay, he's—oh my God, you have *got* to be kidding me."

"What's wrong?"

Irritation flashes in her dark eyes. "One sec. I need to call him and figure out what the *hell*."

Oh boy. I pray there isn't trouble in paradise, because I know Tansy can sometimes get fixated on her boyfriend slash ex-boyfriend slash fuck buddy. I'm still not sure.

What I do know is that I was looking forward to a fun weekend with my favorite cousin, especially after my dreadful interview this morning. Holy shit did that suck.

I watch the Bruins game as I wait for Tansy. Neither of the two bartenders comes to take my order, which is probably a good thing because my cousin stomps back in a huff.

"You won't believe this," she announces. "The stupid idiot got the bars mixed up. He's at the Frog and Fox near Fenway. We're at the Fox and Fiddle."

"Why does every bar in this city have the word *fox* in it?"

"I know, right? And I can't even be too mad at him, because it's an honest mistake." She blows out an aggravated breath. "Anyway, he's there with a bunch of friends and he doesn't want to move his whole group over here when you and I can just hop in a cab and be there in ten minutes."

"He has a point."

"You don't mind leaving?"

"Nope." I ease away from the bar. "Let me hit the ladies' before we go."

"Cool. I'll order the car. Meet you outside?"

"Sounds good."

Tansy exits the pub, while I amble toward the restrooms. Despite the Friday-night crowd, there's no line for the ladies' room. I walk in to find two girls in front of the mirror, chatting loudly as they fix their makeup. I nod in greeting and duck into a stall.

"If you want to go to the Dime, then let's go to the Dime," one of the girls is saying.

"I told you, I don't want to."

"Are you sure? Because you keep blabbering on about Jake Connelly and his amazing tongue."

I freeze. I swear my pee stops midstream like some sort of magic trick.

"We've got nowhere else to be tonight," the first chick says. "Let's just hit the Dime so you can see him. Maybe you guys will hook up again…"

"Unlikely. Connelly doesn't do repeats." The second chick sounds dejected. "Going there is pointless."

"You never know. You said he had a good time, right?"

"He was getting a BJ. Of course he had a good time."

I press my lips together to fight a smile. Aw, listen to that. Jakey got some the other night. Good for him.

Except then I remember the stunt he pulled with McCarthy, and I'm no longer smiling. I quickly resume peeing, eager to leave the bathroom so I don't have to listen to this shit anymore.

A wistful sigh echoes from beyond the stall. "You have no idea how hot it was."

"Actually, I do. Because you can't shut up about it."

"He's *such* a good kisser. And when he went down on me, he did this thing with his tongue, like…I can't even describe it. It was sort of like…a kiss and a swirl."

Discomfort forms in my gut. I've had my share of dirty conversations with my girlfriends, but these chicks are going into a lot of detail. And they know they're not alone in the bathroom. They *saw* me come in.

"I'm surprised he returned the favor. Guys that good-looking don't usually give a shit if the girl gets off. A lot of them would take the blowjob and bail."

I flush the toilet and noisily exit the stall. "'Scuse me, need to get in here," I say airily, gesturing to the sinks.

They step aside but keep talking. "Well, he wasn't like that at all," Jake's chick assures her friend. "He wanted to get me off."

This time, I pay closer attention to their appearance. The friend is a tall brunette. The one Jake hooked up with is short, with auburn curls, huge boobs, and enormous brown eyes, resembling a very sexy deer.

Is that Connelly's type? Hot Bambi?

"Then let's go to the Dime," the brunette insists.

Hot Bambi bites her lower lip. "I don't know. I'd feel weird showing up at his favorite bar. I mean, we hooked up four days ago. He probably doesn't even remember me."

I run my soapy hands under the hot water. Four days and she's concerned he's already forgotten about her? Is that how little she thinks of herself? Maybe I ought to chime in and advise her not to bother tracking him down. Jake would eat someone like her alive.

"Fine, I guess we're staying here," the friend says on their way out. "We should find a…"

Their voices trail off as the door swings shut. I dry my hands with a paper towel and ponder what I just heard. So. Four days ago, Jake and his amazing tongue got some Hot Bambi action. Talk about hypocrisy.

Where does he get the nerve, telling me who I can hook up with and ordering McCarthy to dump me? Here he is, oral-sexing hot deer women and spending his Friday night at some bar, likely trying to pick up. Meanwhile, poor McCarthy is sitting at home, unable to jerk his own dick without asking Connelly's permission.

Screw that.

Fortitude straightens my shoulders as I go outside to find my cousin. She's by a parking meter on the sidewalk, standing at the back door of a sporty black sedan. "Ready?" she calls when she spots me.

I join her at the car. "Yes. But change of plans. We're making a quick stop first."

6

JAKE

The Dime is my favorite place in the city. It's the epitome of a dive bar. Cramped. Dark. The pool table's missing three balls, including the eight ball. The dartboard is cracked in half. The beer tastes watered down half the time, and the food is covered with a layer of grease that congeals like a rock in the pit of your stomach.

But despite its failings, I love it. The place is small, which means larger groups usually venture elsewhere. And the clientele is mostly male, so it's the perfect spot to visit when you're not looking to hook up.

That doesn't stop Brooks, of course. My roommate can find a chick anywhere. Take him to a convent and he'd seduce a nun. Take him to a funeral and he'd be banging the grieving widow in the bathroom. Or hell, on the casket. Dude's a slut.

Right now, he's at a corner table making out with our waitress. Only two servers are working tonight, and Brooks has his tongue in one of their mouths.

The other one, an older dude with a beard and glasses, keeps clearing his throat pointedly. She keeps ignoring him. When he calls, "Rachel, your table's waiting," she breathlessly unlatches her lips from my teammate's and waves her coworker off. "Can you handle it? Tips are yours."

I'm assuming she doesn't want the job anymore and this is

her way of quitting, because there's no way she's escaping without punishment. The other waiter and the bartender keep exchanging sullen looks, and I'm pretty sure one of them already phoned the manager.

While Brooks is in the corner feeling up the waitress, the rest of us are enjoying the Bruins game and listening to Coby Chilton complain about the two-beer limit I've enforced. He can bitch about it all night, for all I care. We're playing Princeton tomorrow afternoon and nobody is allowed to show up to a game hungover. Hell, I forbade Potts and Bray from going out tonight altogether. I don't trust the beer pong duo.

"If you could bang any hockey player, dead or alive, who'd it be?" Coby asks Dmitry. Since a second ago he'd been talking about beer, the change of subject is jarring.

"What?" Dmitry sounds extremely confused. "You mean like a female hockey player?"

"And when you say 'dead,' do you mean I'm fucking her corpse or am I doing her when she was alive?" Heath pipes up.

"Nah, I'm talking NHL. And none of that necrophilia shit." Coby's expression conveys horror.

"Wait, you're asking us which *dude* we'd fuck?" a senior D-man demands.

I swallow a laugh.

"Yeah. I'd pick Bobby Hull. I like blondes. How 'bout you guys?"

"Hold up. Chilton," squawks Adam Middleton, our most promising freshman. "Are you gay?" The eighteen-year-old glances around the table. "Has he always been gay and I'm just finding out? Did y'all know?"

"You *wish* I was gay," Coby shoots back.

The freshman's eyebrows crash together. "Why would I wish that?"

"Because I'm a great lay. You're missing out."

"What is happening right now?" Adam asks me.

I press my trembling lips together. "No clue, man."

"I heard a bunch of chicks debating this shit in Harvard Square the other day," Coby explains, polishing off his second (and last) bottle of Sam Adams. He rolls his eyes dramatically. "They were choosing the lamest dudes. Tyler Seguin! Sidney Crosby!"

"I'd do Crosby," Dmitry pipes up. "I wouldn't even need to picture some girl to get hard. I'd just think about his stats line."

As laughter breaks out at the table, I feel my phone vibrate in my pocket, and pull it out.

HAZEL: Whatcha up to tonight? I'm home and bored.

I shoot a quick text back, telling her I'm out with the boys.

HAZEL: Use condoms!

I laugh out loud, drawing the attention of Coby. "What are you giggling about over there?" He scowls. "You better not be chatting up a girl. You banned hookups, remember?"

"I banned distractions," I correct.

And so far it's been working. McCarthy was in top form at morning skate, proving that his flirtation with Brenna Jensen was the cause of his recent bout of sucking. He didn't come out with us tonight because he wanted to stay home and watch all the available game tape from Princeton's season to prepare for tomorrow. See what happens when you eliminate pesky distractions?

"Also, I'm not chatting up a girl," I add. "I'm texting Hazel."

"Oh nice, tell her I say hi," Coby orders.

Hazel was my "date" for a team event last year, so most of my teammates know her. Coby, in particular, took an immediate liking to her. Granted, Coby takes a liking to anyone with tits. And to blondes, apparently, regardless of gender.

"Are you ever gonna give me her number?" he gripes.

"Nope. You're not allowed to mess around with my friends." I don't want Chilton anywhere near Hazel. He's a major player, and he'd break her heart. She's too inexperienced to handle someone like him.

To be honest, I don't think she's ever had an actual boyfriend. I assume she hooks up, because she's an attractive, twenty-one-year-old woman, but I've never seen her with a man. In the past I wondered if maybe she was a lesbian, but I haven't seen her with any women, either, and I've definitely caught her checking out dudes before. I think she just doesn't have much game. And Coby has too much of it.

A loud wolf whistle cuts through the rock music blasting in the bar. It comes from the direction of the pool table. The two men standing there have abandoned their game to gape at the entryway.

I follow their stares and...*da-yum*.

Brenna Jensen is marching across the room. And she looks good enough to eat.

She's wearing high-heeled leather boots, a short skirt, black leather jacket. Her chocolate-brown hair is loose around her shoulders, and her full lips are blood red.

Another dark-haired girl trails after her. Also pretty, but Brenna holds all my attention. Her dark eyes are on fire, and every molecule of heat is aimed directly at me.

"Connelly." She reaches our table, baring her teeth in a mocking smile. "Boys. Fancy meeting you here. Mind if I join you?"

I pretend to be completely unfazed by her arrival. Inside, suspicion coils like a rattlesnake in my gut. "Sure thing." I gesture to the sole empty chair. "Afraid there's only one seat, though."

"It's okay, we won't be staying long." She addresses her friend. "Want to sit?"

"Nah." The girl is clearly amused by all of this. Whatever *this* is. "I'm gonna call Lamar. Come grab me when you're done." She moseys over to the bar, phone already glued to her ear.

"It's so hot in here," Brenna remarks. "All the bodies crammed in this shoebox are generating some serious heat." She unzips her jacket.

What she's wearing underneath makes everyone's eyeballs pop out of their sockets.

"Aw fuck," I hear Coby mumble.

The crop top bares her flat, smooth belly, and it's cut low enough to showcase some impressive cleavage. She's also not wearing a bra, so I can see the outline of her nipples, two hard beads straining against the ribbed material. My cock stirs behind my zipper.

She appraises my teammates before focusing on me. "We need to have a chat, Connelly."

"Do we?"

Her gaze sweeps over the table again. Each guy, even the lowly freshman Adam, receives a thorough examination. To my displeasure, the longest scrutiny is awarded to Coby, whose tongue has fallen to the Dime's sticky floor.

"Have a seat already," I say darkly.

"Don't mind if I do." Flicking up an eyebrow, she saunters to Coby and settles directly on his lap.

He makes a choked noise. Part surprise, part joy.

I narrow my eyes at her.

She smiles. "What's wrong, Jakey? You told me to have a seat."

"I think a chair would be more comfortable." There's an edge to my tone.

"Oh, but I'm super comfy right here." She wraps a slender arm around Coby's neck and rests her hand on his broad shoulder. He's six-four and two hundred and forty pounds, making Brenna appear tiny in comparison.

I don't miss the way his hand curls around her hip to keep her in place.

"Jensen," I warn.

"Jensen! Hey!" Brooks, coming up for air, finally notices Brenna's arrival. "When did you get here? Is Di Laurentis with ya?"

"No, Summer's back in Hastings."

"Oh. That sucks." Shrugging, he resumes the game of tonsil-hockey he's playing with our soon-to-be-unemployed waitress.

"So here's the thing," Brenna says. She might be in Coby's lap, but she only has eyes for me. "You ordered Josh to break up with me."

I raise my beer bottle and take a slow sip, contemplating what she said. "Break up, eh? I thought you weren't dating."

"We weren't. But we had a good arrangement going. I liked him."

It's strangely frank of her. Most women probably wouldn't enjoy admitting how much they liked the person who just dumped them. I experience a weird tug in my stomach at the notion that she might've actually been into McCarthy.

"I liked the way his hands felt on me," she continues in a throaty voice, and suddenly every man at the table is eating up her every word. "I liked his lips…his fingers…"

A strangled cough comes from Adam the freshman. I silence him with a deadly glare. He gulps down some beer.

"I guess you'll have to find other hands and lips and fingers to keep you occupied," I tell her.

When Coby opens his mouth, I glare at him before he can volunteer his body parts. His mouth promptly slams shut.

"I told you, you don't get to make decisions for me," Brenna says coolly.

"I didn't make any decisions for you. McCarthy made up his own mind."

"I don't believe that. And I don't appreciate you interfering in my life."

"I don't appreciate you interfering with my players," I retort.

My teammates' heads swing back and forth from me to Brenna.

"Are we really going to have this argument again?" she asks in a bored tone. Her index finger trails down Coby's arm.

His eyes glaze over.

Shit. Brenna is not only smoking hot, she's also magnetic as hell.

And her perfect ass is currently pressed up against the crotch of a hockey player who's full of pent-up aggression and anticipation for tomorrow's semifinals.

"Did you come here to yell at me, Hottie? Because that's not going to bring poor, sweet McCarthy back." I'm goading her. Mostly because it's fun to see her dark eyes smolder with anger, like two hot coals burning in a fire pit.

"You're right. I'm not going to get McCarthy back. So I guess it's time to find a replacement." Her fingertips reach the hand that Coby placed on her hip. She laces their fingers together, and I frown when I glimpse her thumb rubbing the inside of his palm.

I think he might actually groan. The music muffles the sound, but his tortured expression tells me he's not unaffected. I glower at him. "Focus, man. She's just playing a game."

"It's not a game. I think your boy here is hot." She tosses her silky hair over one shoulder and slants her head to meet Coby's appreciative gaze. "What's your name?"

"Coby." Gravel thickens his voice.

Oh fuck. We're in trouble. He's looking at her as if she's already naked. Hell, I think everyone in the bar is.

"I'm Brenna," she coos. "It's so nice to meet you."

"So nice," he echoes, visibly gulping.

Brenna grins at me, and then unlaces their fingers and slides her palm up Coby's beefy chest. She presses it to the Harvard logo that's decaled onto his gray sweatshirt, her palm flattening over his left pec. "Your heart's beating so fast. Is everything okay?"

"Everything's just fine." He's completely under her spell. From beneath heavy eyelids, he admires the curves of her body. Then he shifts in his chair, probably because he's sporting a massive hard-on.

"Focus on me, Chilton," I order. "Don't let her lure you to the dark side."

"Don't listen to him, Coby. I mean, do you *really* want Connelly to run your life? He's such a buzzkill. Who likes a buzzkill, right?"

She snuggles closer to him. "So what do you like to do other than play hockey? Do you like to dance?"

"Love it," he mumbles. His gaze is glued to her chest.

I know for a fact he's got zero moves. "Coby, don't fall for this. She's not interested."

They both ignore me.

"We should go dancing sometime. We'll have so. Much. Fun." She strokes his pec before gliding her hand up to his bearded chin. She strokes that, too. "I'd bet having our bodies so close like that would make your heart beat even faster."

Adam starts coughing again. Beside him, Dmitry looks utterly captivated. They all do. Brenna has that effect on men.

I scowl at Coby. "She's teasing you. This is payback for my perceived crimes against her."

Brenna smirks defiantly. "Actually, I happen to find Coby incredibly appealing."

"I'm sure you do," I drawl. To the dumbass whose lap she's on, I offer more encouragement. "You can do this, man. Crawl out of the darkness."

When he finally speaks, the words are strangled, as if they're being pried out of his mouth by force. "Sorry, Jake. I think I love her."

She laughs, easily sliding off his lap.

Coby shoots to his feet, too. "We should go dancing tonight," he says eagerly.

I sigh. "Weak bastard."

With a sigh of her own, Brenna gently touches my teammate's arm. "Sorry, babes, but Connelly was right. I was playing you."

He gawks at her. "For real?"

"For real. I was manipulating you, and I apologize for that. You were an unwitting pawn in this little chess game between me and your captain."

Coby looks so disappointed I have to choke down laughter. I don't feel sorry for him, though. I did warn him.

Brenna turns to me. "See how easy that was?" She shakes her head irritably. "The only reason I'm not crying over this McCarthy thing is because it was a temporary arrangement. But let this serve as a warning to you, Connelly. Stay out of my life. My love life, my sex life, my life in general. You have no right to force someone to break up with me. That's just childish."

"And what you did right now wasn't childish?" I challenge.

"Oh, it was. I don't deny that. I absolutely stooped to your level, because I was trying to prove a point. If you mess with my life, I'll mess with yours. Keep accusing me of distracting your guys, and guess what, I'll start doing it. And based on what I just saw, it won't be difficult at all." She pats Coby on the shoulder. "Again, I'm truly sorry for involving you. For what it's worth, I think you're wicked hot, and I have this friend—Audrey—who I kind of want to set you up with. You're exactly her type."

Coby's expression brightens. "Really?"

Brenna holds up her phone. "Smile. I'll text her a pic of you and see if she's interested."

I watch in total disbelief as Coby actually stands there and poses for a picture. He flexes his biceps, for fuck's sake. And then, to add insult to injury, he says, "Thanks."

The idiot is *thanking* her. Christ. My teammates are unbelievable.

Brenna slides her phone into her purse and seeks out my gaze. "Enjoy the rest of your night, Jakey." She gives me a wink. "And don't forget... If you mess with me, I mess right back."

7
JAKE

I FIND MYSELF IN THE KITCHEN AT THREE IN THE MORNING chugging a glass of water at the sink. I'm not sure what woke me up. Maybe the thunder? It started pouring when Brooks and I got home from the bar and hasn't stopped since. Not even a lull.

Or maybe it's guilt that jolted me out of my slumber. I'd never admit it to Brenna, but…I do feel bad about sticking my nose in her business. When she'd confessed to liking McCarthy earlier, I can't deny I felt like a total jerk.

"Oh!" a female voice squeaks. "I didn't realize anyone else was up."

I lift my head in time to see a shapely figure skid to a stop about six feet away. Either the shadows are playing tricks on me, or she's wearing nothing but a thong. She takes a few steps forward, a curtain of blonde hair swinging behind her. The kitchen light flicks on, and yup, she sure is topless. Her tits are on full display for me.

"I'm sorry," she says. "I thought I'd be alone in here."

Yet for all her protests, she doesn't make an effort to cover up.

And since I'm a man, I can't help but stare at her chest. She's got nice boobs. They're on the small side, but cute and perky, with pale-pink nipples that are currently puckered from being exposed to the air.

But the coy twinkle in her eyes puts me off. Although I hadn't heard anyone come in, I assume Brooks invited her over. And since she's practically naked, I assume she and Brooks aren't exactly pulling an all-night study sesh in his bedroom. Which means she definitely shouldn't be looking at me like that.

"You're crashing with Brooks tonight?" I ask as I rinse out my glass.

"Mmm-hmmm."

I wrinkle my forehead. "When'd you get here?"

"Around midnight. And before you say it, yes, it was a booty call."

I resist the urge to shake my head. Brooks Weston is something else. Making out with one chick all night, and then booty-calling another.

"Do you mind getting me a glass? I don't know where anything is." She licks her lips. "I'm thirsty."

She's thirsty, all right.

I open the cupboard, grab a drinking glass, and hold it out. Her fingertips brush my knuckles suggestively as she accepts it. "Thank you."

"No prob." I withdraw my hand. "You look cold," I say with a pointed glance to her nipples.

"Actually, I'm feeling really hot right now." She giggles. "And you're looking it."

"Looking what?"

"Hot."

I try not to raise my eyebrows. This chick is bold. Too bold, considering whom she came to see tonight. "Weren't you just with my roommate?" I nod toward the corridor.

"Yeah? So?"

"So you probably shouldn't be telling some other guy he's hot."

"Brooks already knows what I think about you."

"Does he." An itchy feeling crawls up my spine. I don't like the idea of people discussing me. And I seriously hope I'm not part of whatever kinky games the two of them play behind closed doors.

She pours herself a glass of water from the filtered dispenser in the fridge. Then she stands there and drinks, topless, no care in the world. She's got a gorgeous body, but something about her rubs me the wrong way. It's not the brazen attitude. I *like* outspoken girls. Girls who bust my balls. Like Brenna Jensen—she's the very definition of bold, and she doesn't make me want to sprint out of the room.

This girl, on the other hand...

"What's your name?" I ask warily. I don't know where the distrust in my gut is coming from, but her presence is unnerving me.

"Kayla." She takes another long sip, propping one hip against the granite counter. She's completely unfazed by the fact that she's wearing teeny panties and nothing else. "We met before," she tells me.

"Did we?"

Visible displeasure darkens her eyes. Yeah, I don't imagine this is a girl who likes being forgotten. But I genuinely have no recollection of meeting her, ever.

"Yes. At Nash Maynard's party?"

"You go to Harvard?"

"No. We talked about that at the party, remember?" she says tightly. "I'm at Boston University?"

I draw a blank. There's a black hole in my memory where this alleged interaction is supposed to be.

"Babe," a sleepy voice drifts from the hallway. "Come back to bed. I'm horny."

I give her a dry smile. "You're being summoned."

She grins back. "Your roomie's insatiable."

"I wouldn't know," I say with a shrug.

"No?" She finishes her water and places the glass in the sink. Curiosity gleams in her expression as she studies my face. "You and Brooks have never...?" She lets the question hang.

"Nah. I don't swing that way."

She tilts her head thoughtfully. "What if there's a girl in the middle to act as a buffer?"

Annnd we're done here. It's too late and I'm too tired to be discussing threesomes with a strange girl in my kitchen. "I don't do that either," I mutter on my way past her.

"Pity," she tells my retreating back.

I don't turn around. "Good night, Kayla."

"Good night, Jake." A teasing lilt.

Jeez. So many invitations in one measly encounter. She would've let me bang her on the counter if I'd made a move. If I were into threesomes, she'd have me and Brooks banging her together.

But neither notion appeals to me.

I go back to bed and make sure to lock my door, just in case.

———

Early the next morning, I make the trek to see my folks. This requires a quick ride on the Red Line, followed by a not-so-quick one on the Newburyport/Rockport line, which takes me all the way to Gloucester. It'd be faster to borrow Weston's car and drive up the coast, but I don't mind taking the train. It's cheaper than gassing up the Mercedes, and it provides me with quiet time to reflect and mentally prepare for today's game.

Our entire season rides on this game.

If we lose…

You won't lose.

I heed the self-assured voice in my head, tapping into the confidence I've been cultivating since I was a kid playing Pee Wee hockey. There's no denying I was talented from an early age. But talent and potential mean nothing without discipline and failure. You need to fail in order for the win to mean something. I've lost games before, games that counted for rankings, trophies. Losing is not supposed to crush your confidence. It's meant to build it.

But we won't lose today. We're the best team in our conference, maybe even the best in the entire country.

The train rolls into the station around nine o'clock, and since it's actually not raining this morning I decide to walk home instead of Uber'ing it. I breathe in the crisp spring air, inhaling the familiar scent of salt and fish and seaweed. Gloucester is a fishing town, the country's oldest seaport, which means you can't walk five steps without seeing a lighthouse, a boat, or something nautical. I pass three consecutive houses with decorative anchors hanging over the front doors.

The two-story house where I grew up resembles most of the other homes lining the narrow streets. It has white siding, a sloped roof, and a pretty front garden that Mom tends to religiously. The garden in the backyard is even more impressive, a testament to her green thumb. The house is small, but it's just the three of us, so we've always had more than enough room.

My phone rings as I'm approaching the porch. It's Hazel. I stop to answer the call, because she's supposed to show up this afternoon for the game. "Hey," I greet her. "You still coming to Cambridge later?"

"Never. I'd die before betraying my school."

"Oh shut up. You don't even like hockey. You're coming as a friend, not a fan."

"Sorry, yes, of course I'm coming. It's just fun to pretend we have a massive rivalry. You know, a forbidden relationship. Well, friendship," she amends.

"There's nothing forbidden about our friendship. Everybody knows you're my best friend and nobody cares."

There's a slight pause. "True. So, what are you up to right now? If you want, I can drive up early and chill with you until the game."

"I'm about to walk into my folks' house. Mom's cooking up a special game-day breakfast."

"Aw, I wish you'd told me. I would've joined you."

"Yeah right. That would have required you waking up before eight o'clock. On a Saturday."

"I totally would've done that," she protests.

"'The world doesn't exist before nine a.m.' That's a direct quote from you, Hazel." I chuckle.

"What are we doing to celebrate after you win today? Oooh, how about a fancy dinner?"

"Maybe? I'm sure the boys will want to go out partying, though. Oh, and I've got somewhere to be around ten. You can come with if you want."

"Depends what it is."

"Remember Danny Novak? His band's playing in the city tonight. It's their first gig, so I promised I'd be there." Danny was a teammate of mine in high school. One of the best stick handlers I've ever seen, and that dexterity with his hands serves him well as a guitarist, too. He never could choose what he loved more, hockey or music.

"What kind of music do they play?"

"Metal."

"Ugh. Kill me now." Hazel sighs. "I'll let you know later, but right now it's a tentative no from me, dawg."

I snicker. "I'll see you later, okay?"

"Yup. Tell your parents I said hi."

"Will do."

I hang up and walk through the unlocked front door. In the small entryway, I toss my hockey jacket on one of the iron coat hooks, which are shaped like—what else—anchors. "Mom?" I call as I unlace my boots.

"Hi, baby! I'm in here!" Her greeting wafts out from the kitchen, along with the most enticing aroma.

My stomach growls like a grumpy bear. I've been looking forward to this breakfast all week. Some guys don't like to pig out on game days, but I'm the opposite. If I don't eat a huge breakfast, I feel sluggish and off.

In the kitchen, I find Mom at the stove, a plastic red spatula in hand. The hunger pangs intensify. Fuck yeah. She's making French toast. And bacon. And is that sausage?

"Hey. That smells fantastic." I saunter over and plant a kiss on her cheek. Then I raise my eyebrows. "Nice earrings. Are those new?"

With her free hand, she rolls the shiny pearl on her right earlobe between her thumb and index finger. "Aren't they pretty? Your father surprised me with them the other day! I've never owned pearls this big before."

"Dad did good." Rory Connelly knows the secret to a healthy marriage. Happy wife equals happy life. And nothing makes my mother happier than shiny baubles.

She turns to face me. With her dark hair pulled back in a sleek ponytail and her cheeks flushed from the stove, she appears way younger than fifty-six. My folks had me when they were in their mid-thirties, so she's constantly referring to herself as an "old mom." She definitely doesn't look it, though.

"Hazel says hi, by the way. I just got off the phone with her."

Mom claps happily. "Oh, tell her I miss her. When is she coming home for a visit? She wasn't here for the holidays."

"No, she was at her mom's this year." Hazel's parents got divorced a few years ago. Her dad still lives in Gloucester, but her mom is in Vermont now, so she alternates holidays with them. "She'll be at the game today. Are you guys coming?"

"I'm afraid not. Your dad won't be home in time, and you know I don't like driving on the freeway alone."

I hide my disappointment. My parents have never been too invested in my hockey career. Dad was always too busy with work to attend any of my games, and Mom just plain wasn't interested. When I was little, it hurt my feelings. I'd see all my friends' families in the stands, mine would be nowhere in sight, and envy would flood my chest.

But whatever. It is what is. That's my attitude about most things. Can't change the past, don't cry over the present, don't stress about the future. It's all pointless, especially regret.

"Well, try to make it to the finals if we're playing in them, okay?" I say lightly.

"Of course. Now stop looming over me and go have a seat, superstar. I'll take care of everything."

"At least let me set the table," I argue, trying to grab plates from the cupboard.

She swats my hands away. "No. Sit down," she orders. "This might be the last time I'll be able to serve you before you have your own staff waiting on you hand and foot."

"Nah, that's not gonna happen."

"You'll be a professional hockey player this fall, honey. That means you'll be famous, and famous people employ household staff."

I made the mistake of showing my folks the paperwork for my NHL contract, and when they saw how much money I'll be earning soon (not to mention all the performance incentives my agent persuaded the club to include) their eyes nearly bugged out of their heads. I can't predict the actual amount I'll end up bringing in, but the value of my contract is around two million, which is definitely on the high end for a rookie.

According to my agent, that's what they give the "projected superstars." Damned if my ego didn't inflate hearing that. My mother liked it too, because that's all she calls me now. Superstar.

"I don't want household staff." But I chuckle and sit down anyway, because if she wants to spoil me today, why not? She's partly right. Next year I'll be in Edmonton, freezing my balls off in the Canadian winters. I'm going to miss Saturdays in Gloucester with my folks.

"Where is Dad, anyway?"

"He's at the job site," Mom answers as she turns off the burner.

"On Saturday?" And yet I'm not surprised. My dad is a superintendent for a construction company that specializes in bridges and tunnels, usually handling city contracts. And city contracts mean tight deadlines and a lot of red tape, which in turn means Dad is always under tremendous stress.

It's the kind of job that gives you heart attacks—literally. He went into cardiac arrest at a bridge site a few years ago, scaring the shit out of Mom and me. I'm surprised she actually let him go back to work, but I suppose he didn't have a choice. He's nowhere near retirement age.

"There was a problem there yesterday," Mom explains. "Don't ask me what, you know I tune him out when he blabbers on about his bridges. All I know is that it's crunch time, they need to finish before the winter, and they're in danger of falling behind because some of the crew are acting like, and I quote, motherfucking morons."

I bark out a laugh. My father has a way with words. "I'm sure it'll be fine," I assure her. "Dad's good at yelling at people. And he enjoys it, so win-win."

Mom starts carrying serving plates to the large cedar table that my dad and I built one summer when I was a kid. I try to stab a piece of French toast with my fork and she swats at my hand again. "Wait until I bring everything. And, truth be told, I don't know if ordering the crew around is bringing your father much pleasure anymore. He's tired, honey. He's been doing this job for so long."

She places a stack of buttered rye toast on the tabletop. "But tell me about you! Are you going to bring home a you-know-what one of these days?"

I play dumb. "A you-know-what? Like, a puppy? A car?"

"A *girlfriend*, Jake. You need a girlfriend," she huffs.

"Oh, I do, do I?" I can't help but tease. My parents have been on my case for a while now about my bachelor status.

"Yes," she says firmly. "You do. You need a nice, supportive girlfriend. Like Hazel—I still don't understand why you won't date Hazel. She's perfect for you!"

Hazel is always the first candidate whose hat Mom throws into the ring. "I'm not going to date Hazel," I say, as I've said about a dozen times prior. "I'm not interested in her that way."

"Fine, then go out with *someone*."

That's always Mom's second option: *someone*. She's dying for me to settle down already.

But that's not in the cards at the moment. "I don't want to," I answer with a shrug. "Hockey's my main priority right now."

"Hockey has been your main priority since you were five years old! Don't you think it's time for some new priorities?"

"Nope."

She shakes her head in disapproval. "You're in college, Jake. You're young and handsome, and I just don't want you to one day reflect on this time in your life and regret not having someone special to share it with."

"I don't have regrets, Mom. Never have."

Although if I'm being totally honest, I am feeling regretful about something.

I can't seem to shake off the guilt over my interference with Brenna and McCarthy. Sure, it's not as if they were engaged to be married, but she's right—I did ask him to dump her. That was a dick move. I wouldn't want someone dictating my sex life, either.

I'd hoped the guilt would simply fade away, but it hasn't. It was gnawing on my insides last night, and it's still chewing at me this morning.

Game day, a stern voice reminds me.

Right. Today's game against Princeton is all that matters right now. We need to win.

We *will* win.

The alternative is not an option.

8

BRENNA

"I can't believe you're abandoning me." I glower at Tansy, but deep down I'm not surprised.

I had desperately hoped that she and Lamar wouldn't ruin this weekend for me, but as my father likes to say, hope is for fools. *Work hard and make your own dreams come true,* he always harps, *and then you won't have to hope for a damn thing.*

"It'll only be for an hour or two," my cousin promises.

"Yeah right," I scoff from her roommate's bed. Once again, Aisha proved herself to be my hero. Somehow, she replaced the standard-issue mattress that came with the dorm room with one of those memory foam ones that make you feel like you're sleeping in a cloud. I dove right back under the covers when Tansy and I returned from our afternoon of lunch and shopping. That's how comfy this bed is.

"I'm serious," Tansy insists. "I'm just going over there so we can talk about what happened last night."

"Oh, you mean how the two of you screamed at each other like maniacs in front of the entire bar?"

Yeah. That was fun. Tansy and Lamar started arguing almost the instant we arrived at the Frog and Fox. It was one of the most impressive snowball progressions I've witnessed in a while.

They kissed hello, she teased him about getting the location wrong, he grumbled that *she* gave him the wrong bar name, she denied it, he insisted, she said it wasn't her fault his dumb ass couldn't read a text message, he said, "Why are you acting like such a bitch," and there you have it—the Apocalypse.

Oh, Lamar. You never, *ever* tell your girlfriend she's acting like a bitch. Even if she is.

Lamar's friends and I decided to do a couple of tequila shots. We figured that Tansy and Lamar would eventually tire themselves and rejoin the group, except they never did, and Tansy dragged me out of the bar in tears and we went home before midnight.

I woke up this morning and didn't even have a hangover. As far as I'm concerned, that constitutes a crappy night.

"Come on, Tans, tell him you'll see him tomorrow. You already ruined Newbury Street by texting him the entire time." We were supposed to be shopping and having a blast, and instead I spent the day watching her tapping on her phone. We barely spoke during lunch because he kept messaging her.

"I know, I'm so sorry. It's just…" She peers at me with big, imploring eyes. "We're talking about getting engaged after gradua-tion. I can't ignore him when we're fighting. We need to work it out."

I don't even blink at the word "engaged." Tansy and Lamar have been on and off and off and on so many times that I no longer take their relationship seriously. If you keep breaking up, there's a reason for it. Fun fact: perpetual drama is not conducive to a long-lasting commitment.

I highly doubt an engagement between them is in the cards. And if by some chance it happens, no way does it lead to an actual wedding. I'd bet my meager life savings on that.

But I tamp down my skepticism and say, "Okay, you're talking about getting engaged. That has nothing to do with the fact that your cousin, who you haven't seen in months, came all this way to spend the weekend with you. Last night turned into a sob fest. Today's shopping trip turned into a text fest. And lo and behold, now you're blowing off dinner and the club."

"I'm not blowing you off, I swear. I'll miss dinner, but we're still hitting the club. You can use my meal pass and eat here, won't even cost you anything. Then take a nap or something, and I'll be back in no time, and we'll go to Bulldozer just like we planned."

Bulldozer is the nightclub I've been dying to visit. Despite its crappy name, it's been getting rave reviews, and apparently the music is off the charts.

I have a feeling I'll never get to hear it.

"Please," Tansy begs. "I won't be gone long. Just a few hours."

I love how it went from "an hour or two" to "a few hours."

"And I promise I'll never, ever do this to you again. The next time we plan a girls' weekend I'll come to Briar, and Lamar will stay home, and you and I will have the best time ever."

I swallow a nasty retort. She's already made up her mind, so what's the use in arguing? "Do whatever you want, Tans."

"Come on, Bee, please don't be mad at me."

"Then don't ditch me."

"Brenna—"

My phone goes off. Normally I wouldn't be rude and check it in the middle of a conversation, but Tansy's testing my last nerve, so I grab the phone just to be a bitch.

Except…how lovely. The notification on the screen is even more aggravating than my cousin's bullshit.

"Harvard beat Princeton," I growl.

She eyes me warily. "Is that good or bad?"

I take a calming breath. "If you'd listened to a word I said today, you'd already know the answer to that."

TANSY: I'm heading back soon.

The message comes at nine o'clock, triggering a rush of relief. Finally. She's been gone for three hours.

Earlier, I took full advantage of her dining hall privileges. Had a yummy dinner, chilled with some cool chicks, fended off the advances of a few lacrosse guys. But now the boredom is creeping in, and for the past forty minutes I've been lying on Aisha's bed, mindlessly swiping through Tinder profiles.

I don't use dating apps much, but what else do I have to do right now? I can't call any of my friends—they're all back at Briar, either attending the semifinals game against Yale, or playing in it. I can't watch the game on the New England station because Tansy and Aisha don't have a TV, and I was unable to find a live stream on my phone.

So, chatting with random dudes it is.

Within two minutes of opening the app, I matched with about fifteen guys. And fourteen out of fifteen have already messaged me, an assortment of *heyyy* and *hey sexy*, a handful of heart-eyes emojis, and a "holy shit are you real??"

The last one brings a laugh to my throat. I peek at the guy's profile again. His name is Aaron, he has the lean, lanky build of a basketball player, and a great smile. Rolling onto my side, I message him back.

ME: Sometimes I wonder.

HIM: LOL

ME: I mean, what is real? Are any of us real? Is the sky real?

HIM: The sky's not real. Sorry to break it to you...

ME: OMG. What is it then?

HIM: We're in a dome. It's like a Truman show scenario.

ME: Um. Spoiler alert, dude. I've never seen that movie!

HIM: You should. It's so good. You'd be really into it. I'm a film major so we watch a lot of really cool shit in class.

ME: Sounds awesome. So what's your specialty? Screenwriting? Directing?

HIM: Directing. I'm gonna win an Oscar one day :) Actually, I already make my own movies.

At first I'm intrigued. Until he follows it up with a winky face. Uh-oh.

I decide to keep my response vague, because I sense where this is heading.

ME: That's cool.
HIM: You're not going to ask what kind of movies I make? ;)
ME: I have a fairly good idea.

Two more winky faces appear.

HIM: You're so gorgeous. I love your body. I'd love to feature you in one of my movies.

Although he hasn't officially gone full douche yet, it's only a matter of time, so I kibosh the conversation by typing, Sorry, I'm not interested in being an actress.

HIM: I bet your tits are so sexy. Mmmmmm, and your nipples. I'd love to suck on them and film myself doing it.

Ugh. Why? *Why?*

I unmatch him without delay and stare up at the ceiling.

I am honestly starting to question evolution. We went from cavemen, to Homo sapiens, to this incredible society of great minds—Alexander Graham Bell inventing telephones, Steve Jobs inventing…everything. And now we're devolving. We've travelled back to cavemen, only nowadays we call them fuckboys.

Evolution has come full circle and that's a real bummer.

I groan out loud, willing my cousin to get home already. I can't believe I'm missing the semifinals for this.

At the reminder, I check my phone for an update on how Briar's doing. According to Twitter, the second period ended with

Briar leading 2–1. That's still too close for comfort. Harvard beat Princeton by three goals.

I bet Connelly is mighty pleased with himself. Maybe he's out with Hot Bambi right now, celebrating the win with a follow-up BJ and some kiss/swirl oral action. Goodie for him.

I'm pulling up Tinder again when another text from my cousin pops up.

TANSY: Change of plans. Lamar's coming to the club with us.

My fingers clench around my phone. Seriously? This is our *girls' weekend.* Her boyfriend already ruined every single thing we've done so far, and now she's letting him ruin Bulldozer? I was excited for Bulldozer, damn it.

I call her rather than text, resentment slithering up my throat. "Are you serious?" I demand when she picks up.

"I'm so sorry," Tansy moans. "It's just...we made up, and he asked if he could come, and what was I supposed to say? No?"

"Yes! Yes, you're supposed to say no. Tell him it's not personal. We need girl time."

"Come on, Bren, it'll be fun. I swear."

Right. The way last night was fun? I grit my teeth so hard they begin to throb. I try to relax my jaw with a slow exhalation. I'm tired of arguing with her. "Fine. Are you picking me up or should I meet you there?"

"We'll pick you up. Lamar's driving because he doesn't plan on drinking tonight. I'm going to get ready here, so we'll be about an hour?"

"Whatever. Text me when you're on the way. I'll start getting ready."

I push aside my annoyance and take a quick shower, then dry my hair and style it in loose waves using Tansy's flat iron. I brought a sexy clubbing dress with me, a shimmery black body-con number that reveals a lot of cleavage and a lot of leg. I slip it on and then settle at Aisha's awesome vanity to do my makeup. I put on more than usual tonight; along with my trademark red lips, I create a smoky-eyes look, with winged liner and thick mascara.

After I'm done, I examine my reflection in the mirror, happy with the results. Last night sucked. Today, too. But I have a good feeling about tonight. So what if Harvard is moving on to the finals? Briar will too, and we'll kick their asses. And in an hour or so, I'll be dancing the night away at Bulldozer.

My phone chirps. Good. Here we go. Tansy's on her way to pick me up and—

> **TANSY:** Please don't kill me. Lamar and I are bailing on the club.

The dream is dead. Bulldozer officially slips through my fingers. As anger quickens my pulse, I sink onto the edge of Tansy's bed, at a complete loss for words. Cousin Tansy has officially usurped Cousin Alex. She is, hands down, the worst. Nothing tops this. *Nothing*.

My hands tremble as I respond.

> **ME:** Are you kidding me?
> **TANSY:** I'm so so sorry. It's been SUCH a stressful two days for us and he thinks it would be better for our relationship if tonight was only about me and him. We're going to stay in and watch a movie and reconnect.

Reconnect? They see each other every day! Outrage coats my throat, and my jaw is harder than stone.

> **ME:** Congratulations. You win the worst cousin of the year award, and it's only April.
> **TANSY:** I'm sorry. I feel awful.

ME: No you don't. Otherwise you wouldn't be ditching me.

TANSY: Are you pissed?

ME: Of course I'm pissed. WTF is wrong with you, T?

I'm not afraid of confrontation, and I'm certainly not going to pretend everything is fine and dandy when it isn't. My harsh words clearly have an effect on her, because after several tense moments, she backpedals like crazy.

TANSY: You're right. I'm sorry. I'm being ridiculous. Let me talk to Lamar again and we'll meet you at the club, ok?

My jaw falls open. Is she nuts? Why would that be okay? Teeth clenched, I quickly compose an essay. Thesis statement: fuck you.

ME: No, not ok. And don't bother with the club. Just stay at Lamar's—that's clearly what you want to do tonight anyway, and I don't want to spend time with someone who doesn't want to spend time with me. I'm making other plans, T. I've got other friends in the city, so enjoy your evening and maybe I'll see you tomorrow morning.

Five seconds later, the phone starts to ring.

I ignore it.

————————

My sparkly dress and I end up at a small music venue near Fenway Park. Initially, I try hitting a couple of different bars. I usually have no problem going out alone and talking to strangers, but I'm in such a sour mood tonight that I find myself scowling at anyone who tries to approach me, male or female. I don't want a hookup or a conversation. I want to be left alone.

I decide I need a place where the music is so loud it'll deter any and all overtures.

Bulldozer fits that bill, but I don't feel like dancing anymore, either. I want to order a drink and sulk in silence. Or rather, sulk to deafening heavy metal music, because the venue I wander into is featuring a metal band tonight. Perfect.

The club consists of one main room just big enough to house a narrow stage and a tiny mosh pit. A few standing tables are tucked against a brick wall that's painted black and spray-painted with graffiti. There's a bar on the other wall, but no counter space, so I saunter toward the tables. They're all empty.

Everyone is staring at me as I cross the dark room, probably because I'm dressed for a night out on the town, whereas most of them look like they crawled out from under a boardwalk. Rumpled clothing, greasy hair, and more Pantera and Slayer shirts than I can count. Luckily, the lighting is practically nonexistent, so it's nearly impossible to make out people's actual faces in the shadows. While I feel their stares, luckily I don't have to see them.

"What can I do ya for?" A waiter with black hair that hangs down to his waist comes over to serve me. "Band's about to go on, so you'd better order quick."

"A vodka cranberry, please."

He nods and walks off without asking me for ID. I have it with me, so I wasn't worried anyway. I angle my body toward the stage and watch as the long-haired lead singer bounces up to the microphone stand.

"Hello, Boston! We're Stick Patrol and we're about to FUCK YOU UP!"

If by "fuck us up" he means they're going to play six ear-piercing songs with garbled lyrics and wrap up before I even finish my first drink, then mission accomplished.

I resist the urge to bury my face in my hands and honest-to-God cry.

What the hell was that?

As the singer thanks everyone for coming, I stand there gaping at him. I'm goddamn *agape*.

Their set lasted fourteen minutes. That averages out to about two-and-a-half minutes per song. Aren't metal songs supposed to be a gazillion minutes long? I swear every Metallica track I've ever heard is longer than the *Lord of the Rings* movies.

Fourteen minutes, and then the house lights flicker on and I'm left watching the band dismantle their equipment. Some guy carts an amp off the stage. Another one is rolling up the microphone cords.

Fuck you, Stick Patrol. Fuck them and their dumb name, and fuck my cousin for not adhering to the girl code, and fuck Harvard for winning their game tonight, and fuck global warming for dumping all this unwelcome rain on us. Fuck 'em all.

I drain the rest of my drink in one gulp, then signal the waiter for another.

This is truly the worst weekend ever.

"Wait, did I miss the band?" A beefy guy with a shaved head and two eyebrow rings lumbers over. He glances from me to the empty stage and then back at me. Lust heats his gaze when he notices my dress.

I absently run one fingertip along the rim of my empty glass. "Yeah, sorry. They just finished."

"That's bullshit."

"Tell me about it." And I'm not even a metal fan. I can't imagine actually wanting to see the band only to show up and discover their set is already over.

"Mind if I join you?" He curls his fingers over the edge of my table.

My gaze drops to his hands. They're huge, two big meaty paws with red knuckles. I don't like them, and I don't particularly want company, but he doesn't give me a chance to say no.

He moves closer, resting his forearms on the tabletop. His arms are also huge, and the left one is covered with tribal tattoos. "Are you into music?"

Did he just ask me if I'm into *music*? In general? Aren't most people? "Sure. Of course."

"Who's your favorite metal band?"

"Er, I don't really have one. I'm not into metal. I wandered in here because I wanted a drink."

"Cool."

I wait for him to say something else. He doesn't. He also doesn't leave.

"So, are you a student?" I ask, resigning myself to this conversation. It's not like I have better things to do.

"Dropout," he says flatly.

Um. Okay. I don't care either way, but that's an odd thing to say. "Where did you drop out from? BC? BU? I'm at Briar."

"I went to St. Michael's."

"St. Michael's?" I scan my brain. "I haven't heard of that college."

"High school," he grunts. "It's not a college. It's a high school." He thrusts both thumbs at his own chest. "High school dropout."

Um.

How on earth does one respond to that?

Luckily, the waiter spares me from replying. He appears with another vodka cran and a bottle of Corona for the self-proclaimed dropout. I eagerly raise my drink to my lips.

My companion takes a long swig of his beer. "So what's your name?"

"Brenna."

"Dope."

"Thanks. How about you?"

"No, that's my name—Dope. My name's Dope."

Um.

I swallow a soul-sucking sigh. "Your name is Dope?"

"Well, no, it's actually Ronny. Dope is my stage name." He

shrugs his massive shoulders. "Used to be in a band, we performed GNR covers."

"Oh. Cool. I think I'm going to call you Ronny, though."

He throws his head back and laughs. "You're a ballbuster. I like that."

Silence falls between us again. He sidles closer, his elbow nudging mine. "You look sad," he says.

"Do I?" That's doubtful. The only emotion I'm experiencing at the moment is irritation.

"Yep. You look like you need a hug."

I force a smile. "No thanks, I'm good."

"Are you sure? I'm the hug master." He holds out his beefy arms and arches his eyebrows, like he's Patrick Swayze from *Dirty Dancing* beckoning me to jump up on him.

"I'm good," I repeat, firmer this time.

"Can I try your drink?"

What? Who asks that? "No. But I can buy you one, if you want."

"Nah, I never let a lady treat."

I try to ease away and create a larger space cushion, but he steps toward me again. I don't feel threatened by him, however. He's a big guy, but not menacing. He isn't trying to bully me with his physicality. I think he's just completely oblivious to the *I'm not interested* vibes I'm transmitting.

"Yeah, so I know, my life story is…it's complicated," Ronny confesses, as if I asked for his life story.

Which I didn't.

"I grew up on the North Shore. Father's a deep-sea fisherman. Whore mother took off with some asshole."

I can't. Oh God, I just can't.

Ronny's not a horrible creep or anything. An over-sharer, indisputably, but he seems nice enough, and he's simply trying to make conversation.

But I *can't*. I want this night, this whole damn weekend, to be over already. It's been absolutely horrible. Dismal. I honestly can't see how it could get any worse.

No sooner do I think those words than the universe decides to bitch slap me by bringing Jake Connelly into my field of vision.

Jake fucking Connelly.

My neck muscles snap to attention, going taut with suspicion. What. Is. He. Doing. Here.

"It sucks, you know? You move to Boston, thinking you'll land a sick job, but it's hard 'cause you don't have that diploma."

I'm only half-listening to Dope. I mean, Ronny. Jake holds the majority of my attention. With his faded blue jeans, dark green Under Armour shirt, and Bruins cap, he's the only male in the venue who isn't wearing black or a band shirt. He's also about a foot taller than everyone else.

I grit my teeth. Why do athletes have to be so big and masculine? Jake's body is incredibly appealing. Long legs, muscular arms, sculpted chest. I've never seen him without a shirt, and I find myself wondering what his chest looks like when it's bare. Ripped, I assume. But is it hairy? Smooth like a baby's bottom? My traitorous fingertips tingle with the urge to find out.

He hasn't spotted me yet. He's standing at the edge of the stage, chatting with one of the band members. The guitarist, I think.

I wonder if I could sneak out the door without him noticing. Having Connelly find me here, in this dump of a club, decked out in a glittery, skintight dress… That would be the rotten icing on the past-its-expiry-date cake that this weekend is turning out to be.

"And you know what's harder? The whole online-dating thing," Ronny is bemoaning.

I tear my eyes off Jake. "Yeah, online dating sucks," I say absently, trying to locate the waiter.

"I get all these matches and girls being like, 'Hey handsome, you're so great and sexy,' and then the conversations just die. I don't get it."

Really? He doesn't get it? Because I have a sneaking suspicion why those conversations are dying. Elements of his game are desperately lacking. For example, the casual mentions of his "whore mother" and constantly referring to himself as a "dropout." Sadly, Dope might not be putting his best foot forward, but I refrain from offering constructive criticism. I'm too busy trying to execute an escape plan.

My gaze darts toward the stage. Jake's still engaged in deep conversation with the guitarist.

Crap. Where is that waiter? I need to pay for my drinks and get the hell out of here.

"You're a cool chick, Brenna," Ronny says awkwardly. "Easy to talk to."

I cast another look around at the room. It's time to go. If Jake notices me, he'd never let me live this down. The dress, the location, the company.

Yes. I spot the waiter emerging from the swinging door next to the bar. I frantically wave my arm.

"Sorry, just trying to get the bill," I tell Ronny. "I—"

I stop talking. Because Jake isn't across the room anymore.

Where on earth did he go?

"You're leaving?" Ronny is crestfallen.

"Yeah, I'm getting tired, and I—"

"There you are, babe," drawls a familiar voice. "I'm sorry I'm late."

The next thing I know, Jake strolls up, cups the back of my neck, and lowers his mouth to mine.

9

JAKE

I didn't plan on kissing her. I was merely going over there to save her from the dude she was clearly trying to escape. But her lips are *right there*. Pouty and red and so damn tempting I can't resist.

My mouth brushes over hers in a scant tease of a kiss. I think it teases me more than it teases her, though, and I regret it almost instantly because *fuuuuuck*, I want more. I want tongue. I want it all.

But I can't have it. I came to rescue her, not to make out with her.

I've gone out with Hazel and seen her get hit on by somebody she's not feeling, enough times to be able to recognize an SOS in a woman's eyes. It's a cross between *dear Lord make this stop* and *someone please get me out of here.*

Brenna's eyes were conveying that telltale panic. I couldn't believe it when I spotted her across the room. My first thought, however crazy, was that she followed me here, but I quickly dismissed it. That's not Brenna Jensen's style. Once I got over the shock of seeing her, I noticed her desperately trying to signal the waiter, and I snapped to action.

As I ease my lips off hers, my entire body rebels. My dick yells at me and my mouth demands another kiss. A real one this time. Instead, I come up behind her and wrap both my arms around her slender frame.

"Hey, Hottie," I murmur, bending my head so I can nuzzle her neck. Holy hell, she smells good.

She stiffens for a second before relaxing. "Hey. You're late." She tips her head to meet my gaze. We share a moment of understanding before she turns to our third wheel. "Ronny, this is my boyfriend, Jake."

"Oh." Unmistakable disappointment clouds his face. "I didn't realize... Uh, I'm sorry."

"Nothing to be sorry for," she says lightly.

"Yes, there is." He sends a remorseful look in my direction. "I was chatting up your girl. Sorry, bro."

"All good." I run a hand down her bare arm. It's a playful gesture, but also a possessive one. Translation: she's mine.

His expression takes on a hint of envy. "How long've you been together?"

"About a year," I lie.

"One year too many," she grumbles.

Ronny frowns.

"Ignore her." I trail my fingers up Brenna's arm, and her breath hitches. Hmmm. She likes it when I touch her. I tuck that nugget of wisdom away for future use. "Trust me, she's obsessed with me. Blows up my phone every day telling me how much she loves me. I think psychologists call that love-bombing."

"Oh, don't get me started on love-bombing," Brenna says sweetly. "He writes me a beautiful haiku every night before bed. Usually about my eyes. And my lips."

"And her ass," I say with a wink. My hand slides down her delectable body to squeeze the aforementioned ass. Which is a terrible idea, because it's firm and juicy and feels like heaven in my palm. Almost instantly I'm rocking a semi.

"Wow. You two are...so in love, huh? It's nice to see. This goddamned hookup culture is killing love. Everyone is disposable, you know?" He smiles at us, and it's so sincere I feel bad for lying to him. "You make a cute couple."

I plant a kiss on Brenna's shoulder. Another bad idea. Her skin is hot beneath my lips, and smells so good. "Yeah. We're in it for the long haul."

"Forever and ever," she chirps, beaming up at me.

Ronny polishes off his Corona and sets it on the table. "Well, I won't bother you anymore. But thanks for the chat. Have a good night, you guys."

Once he's gone, Brenna disentangles herself from my arms and puts about two feet of distance between us. A deep scowl twists her crimson lips. "What are you doing here?"

"I could ask you the same thing."

"I asked first."

I shrug. "I'm with the band."

"Right. I'm sure you are. Why aren't you out celebrating your big win with the rest of your Harvard cronies?" Her dark expression tells me precisely how she feels about our win.

"I told you, I'm friends with the band. I went to high school with the lead guitarist."

Speaking of Danny, I turn to make sure he's not glaring at me for abandoning him, but he's involved in an animated discussion with a dude in a Metallica hoodie. When I catch his eye and signal I'll be a few minutes, Danny nods and continues talking.

"Well, you should tell your friend that his set needs to be longer than fourteen minutes," Brenna says. "I blinked, and it was over."

I chuckle. "I know. But this was their first gig, so you can't fault 'em." I signal the passing waiter, who stops at our table. "Could I get a Sam Adams, please? And another of these for my girl." I gesture to her empty glass.

"I don't—" Her protest dies, because the man is already bounding off. "I didn't want another one, Connelly," she mutters.

"It's on me. The least you could do is have a drink with me. I just saved your ass, after all."

She gives me a dry grin. "Is that what you think happened?"

"It is what happened. Your expression was broadcasting 'Get me the hell outta here.'"

Brenna gives a throaty laugh before running a hand through her thick, glossy hair. "I did want to get out of here," she confirms. "Because I saw *you*."

I narrow my eyes.

"It's true. I mean, come on, do I look like the damsel in distress type? You really believe I couldn't have gotten away from that guy all by my lonesome?"

She has a point. A helpless damsel she is not. My stomach twists at the notion that she was trying to escape me and not Ronny. The hit to my ego is unwelcome. "So, what, I don't get a thank you for *trying* to be nice?"

"Is that how you view yourself? As nice?" Brenna winks. "Haven't you heard? Nice guys finish last."

"You still haven't told me why you're here. Wearing *that*." I direct a pointed nod at her dress—and hope my expression doesn't reveal my thoughts on it.

Because, fuck, that *dress*. It's indecently short, and cut so low my mouth runs dry. Where the hell is that beer? I'm dying here. The shimmery material clings to every tantalizing curve of her body, hugging a pair of high, round breasts that a man would give up his firstborn to get his hands on. And her legs... Jesus. She's not too tall—I'd put her at average height, maybe five-five—but the length of the dress combined with her high-heeled boots make her legs appear endless.

"I was supposed to go clubbing tonight," she answers tightly. "But my cousin bailed on me at the last minute."

"Sucks."

"Yup."

Our drinks arrive, and I slug back a huge mouthful to bring much-needed moisture to my throat. Brenna Jensen is way too hot, and I definitely shouldn't be in her presence tonight. I'm still riding the high from this afternoon's victory, adrenaline still coursing through my veins. We destroyed Princeton. Crushed them. And now the universe has placed Brenna in my path, and it's messing with my head, not to mention my intentions.

When I saw her with Ronny, I thought rescuing her from him could be my way of apologizing for the McCarthy thing.

But now that she's standing in front of me in that dress, I'm not thinking about apologies. I'm thinking about kissing her. And touching her. Squeezing that tight ass again. Nah, more than squeezing it.

A slew of dirty images swamps my mind. I want to bend her over this table and fuck her doggy-style. Run my hands down her smooth ass cheeks. Slide my cock inside in one, slow stroke... I bet her back would arch and she'd moan when I did it.

I have to bite my lip to stop a groan. Thankfully, she doesn't notice. She's too busy stirring her drink with a thin plastic straw. She takes a sip, grimaces, and sets the glass down.

"Sorry, Connelly, I can't drink this. I've already had two in less than an hour, and I'm feeling the buzz."

"Where are you staying?" I ask gruffly. "You're not driving back to Hastings tonight, are you?"

"No, but I'll be Uber'ing there."

"That's one expensive ride."

"Eighty bucks," she says glumly. "But it's better than going back to my cousin's dorm."

I whistle. The invitation to crash with me and Brooks tickles the tip of my tongue, but I manage to refrain. That's one of the most boneheaded ideas I've ever had. Besides, she'd never say yes.

I curl my fingers around the bottle and force myself to accept the truth: I'm horny.

I'm still pumped up from the game. My blood's hot and my dick's hard and Brenna is sex on heels. Her presence is shorting out my common sense like a tripped circuit.

When warm fingertips suddenly touch my wrist, I jolt as if I've been electrocuted. I glance down to find Brenna toying with the beaded bracelet I'm wearing. She fingers one of the pink beads, her lips twitching as if she's trying not to laugh.

"Nice bling," she remarks. "Did you ransack an eight-year-old girl's bedroom?"

"Funny." I roll my eyes. "It's my good-luck charm. I always wear it on game day."

"Athletes and their superstitions." She purses her lips. "Guess number two: you held up a Girl Scout troop and robbed them blind."

"Wrong again."

"Guess number three: you're a time traveler from the 1960s and—"

"Sorry to disappoint you," I interrupt with a grin, "but this bracelet doesn't have an exciting origin story. I lost a bet to a teammate freshman year of high school, and my punishment was to wear this for a month straight."

Her tone is dry. "Was it supposed to be a threat to your masculinity?"

"I know, right?" I wink. "Clearly he didn't know me at all. My masculinity is rock solid." And so is my erection, but I'm trying not to focus on it in hopes it'll go away. I twist the pink-and-purple bracelet around my wrist. "I think he did steal this from his little sister, though. I hope she wasn't attached to it, because she sure as shit ain't getting it back."

"Does it have magical powers?"

"Damn right it does. We didn't lose a single game during the month I wore this thing. We swept every series we played. I'm talking four consecutive weekends. And then, when I took it off..." A cold shiver races up my spine.

Brenna looks fascinated. "When you took it off, what?"

"I can't even discuss it. It'll trigger my PTSD."

Melodic laughter spills out of her throat. I can't deny I like hearing it. No, I like knowing that I'm the one who *made* her laugh.

This beautiful, bitchy girl with the prickliest attitude I've ever encountered, who doesn't miss an opportunity to neg me.

"The first game we played AB—after bracelet," I clarify. "That's how I measure time now."

Amusement dances on her face. "Of course."

"Well, we lost. No, we lost *hard*. It was unfathomable how badly we played." The memory still brings the heat of humiliation to my cheeks. "We might as well have bent over and let the other team spank us with their sticks. It was the ass-kicking of the century." I pause for effect. "We got shut out. Eight-nothing."

Brenna's mouth falls open. "Eight-nothing? I don't think I've ever seen a hockey game where a team scored *eight* goals. Wow. Don't ever take that bracelet off, otherwise you'll—" She stops. "Actually..." She smiles sweetly. "Can I borrow it?"

I smirk. "You wish. It's gonna be on my wrist when we're winning the finals. Speaking of which..." I pull out my phone. I've been monitoring the Briar-Yale game all night, but I haven't checked the score in nearly thirty minutes. "Well, look at that, Hottie. Guess who's in overtime."

Her good humor fades. "What's the score?" she demands.

"Two all." I blink innocently. "If I recall correctly, Briar was up a goal until the last two minutes in the third. Looks like your boys choked under pressure and let Yale tie it up."

"I'm not worried. Briar's got this." She shrugs carelessly. "With that said, I'm heading home now. Have a good night, Connelly."

A peculiar pang of disappointment tugs at my gut. I want her to stay. That's so fucked up.

I shift my gaze to the stage, where Danny's still engaged in conversation. "I'll walk you out," I offer.

"Completely unnecessary. I don't need an escort." She pats my arm. "Good night, Jakey."

Despite her dismissal, I follow her.

"I told you, I don't need an escort."

"Yeah, you did tell me that."

She stops at the bar and hands the waiter a twenty-dollar bill. "That should cover his beer, too." She glances over her shoulder. "Say thank you to your sugar mama, Jakey."

"Thank you." I flash an overly lascivious grin. "Daddy loves it when you take care of him."

Brenna sighs. "I hate you."

I trail after her toward the narrow stairwell. "Nah, you don't hate me," I argue.

The club is on the lower level of the building, so we have to climb one flight to get upstairs. Brenna goes ahead of me, which places her ass about two inches from my face. I nearly choke on my own tongue. Christ. I can practically see up her dress.

When we reach the landing, I stop her by resting my hand on her shoulder. "You like me," I inform her.

She slowly appraises me. "On the contrary. I think *you* like *me*."

I shrug. "You're all right."

A smile lifts the corners of her mouth. "Nuh-uh, you think I'm more than all right. You've got a case of the Jensens."

"Come on now. That's just crazy talk."

"So you're saying if I asked you to go home with me right now, you'd say no?" She licks her lips, those sexy red lips, and moves closer.

I lick my lips, too. "I'd say no."

Still smiling, she comes even closer. Backing me to the wall, inch by inch, until her warm, slender body is pressed up against mine and the top of her head is tickling my chin.

"I think you'd say yes," she whispers. She glides her hands up my chest and plants them over my collarbone.

I quirk an eyebrow. "Do you really believe I'm going to fall for this trick? I saw you pull this on Chilton last night, remember? And I'm not as dumb as he is."

"You're a man. All men are dumb." Brenna peers up at me, and damned if she isn't the most beautiful woman I've ever seen. She's bold and fierce, and those qualities combined with her beauty make her a force to be reckoned with.

And yet…I don't miss the way her pulse throbs in the center of her throat. Or how she's breathing a bit faster. She's not unshakeable, this girl. I have the power to shake her up.

"You talk a big game, babe. But if I called your bluff, I think you'd be running out the door."

"Who's bluffing?"

"You are. I think all you do is bluff." I rest my hand on her hip. My grip is loose, careless almost, but it's a very deliberate touch and it gets the desired response.

Heat flares in her eyes.

"If I take my hand and slide it under your dress, what would I find?" I rasp.

The question is meant to shake *her*, but it fucks me right up, too. I'm rock-hard now. I love games like this, the dirty ones where you tease and toy and dare each other until something gives. Until someone breaks.

"What would I find?" I repeat. Ever so slightly, my fingers shift downward to play with the hem of her incredibly short dress.

Brenna doesn't break eye contact. "You'd find me dry as a desert."

"Mmmm. Doubt it. I think I'd find you ready for me." I tug on the stretchy material, finding the spot where it meets her flesh. I rub my thumb over her thigh and enjoy the way her lips part. "What do you say? Should we test my hypothesis?"

Our gazes lock. I brush my knuckles over her skin again. It's impossibly soft, and I'm painfully hard. My cock is a hot spike in my jeans. And then it starts to vibrate.

Rather, my phone does. But it's lodged in my pocket and in such close proximity to my aching dick that the vibrations actually make me shudder with pleasure.

"You gonna get that?" Brenna asks knowingly. Her body is still flush to mine, palms flat on my chest, and I'm sure she feels the erection pressing against her belly.

"No. I'm busy." My hand is still under her dress, inches from paradise.

She jerks suddenly, before reaching into the small purse hanging off her shoulder. Both our phones going off at once? That could only mean one thing…

I drop my hand from her thigh. I have my phone out first, scanning the array of messages that were responsible for all the vibrating. Brenna checks her notifications and releases a victorious squeal that bounces off the black walls in the cramped stairwell.

"Yes," she exclaims. "Fucking *yes!*"

I grudgingly meet her gaze. "Congratulations." Briar beat Yale in overtime. Winning goal courtesy of Nate Rhodes, the team captain.

Brenna's smile lights up her entire face. Then it becomes a smug curve, more smirk than smile, before settling into a wicked grin of challenge.

"So. I guess we'll be seeing you in the finals."

10
BRENNA

DESPITE BRIAR'S VICTORY OVER YALE, I'M STILL DISAPPOINTED with how the weekend turned out. I got home around midnight, courtesy of an obscenely expensive Uber ride, and woke up this morning to about ten texts and three voicemails from Tansy apologizing profusely and begging for my forgiveness. I texted back to say I require at least a full month of groveling before I can grant my complete forgiveness, but since it's hard for me to stay mad at the people I love, I told her we're good and that she owes me a girls' weekend.

Now I'm having Sunday brunch with Summer at the diner, where I fill her in on the weekend from hell. Leaving out the parts involving Jake Connelly, obviously. Summer would snatch onto those bits like a dog with a bone. Except unlike the dog, who'd eventually drop the bone or go bury it somewhere, Summer would discuss and dissect every detail of my Connelly encounters until the end of eternity.

"I'm sorry, but your cousin sounds like a total bitch," Summer says as she munches on a strip of bacon. Her golden hair is arranged in a messy braid, hanging over the shoulder of her white cashmere sweater. She isn't wearing a stitch of makeup, and doesn't need it. Summer Heyward-Di Laurentis is disgustingly stunning. Ditto for her older brother, Dean. The two of them resemble Ken and Barbie, although Summer hates being called the latter. So of course, I do it just to piss her off.

"Eh, she's really not," I answer, referring to my cousin. "But she sure acted like one this weekend."

"She ditched you *both* nights? That's harsh."

"Well, we were together the first night. Kind of. She and her boyfriend got into an epic fight, so I spent most of the time hanging out with his friends."

I skip what came before that—my ambush of Connelly and his teammates at the dive bar. And I don't even dare bring up the concert. I easily could, without mentioning Jake's role in it, but I'm afraid I might slip and reveal something I shouldn't.

Like how warm his lips felt when they touched mine.

Or how he slid his hand under my dress and nearly put it between my legs.

Or the sheer relief that crashed over me when he moved that hand, because if he hadn't, I would've been revealed as a liar. I wasn't dry as a desert, like I'd mocked. I was wetter than I'd ever been. In that moment, I don't think I've ever wanted anybody more.

And that is not good. Not good at all. Jake is too unpredictable. I can never figure out what he's thinking, what he's going to say or do next, and that's unacceptable to me. How are you supposed to protect yourself when you don't fully understand a person's motives?

"I repeat, she sounds like a bitch…" Summer wags a piece of bacon at me. "Just saying."

"It's that toxic relationship she has with Lamar. She didn't used to be this selfish." I pour maple syrup on my second pancake. "I hate saying this, but I really hope they break up."

Summer takes a sip of her herbal tea. "Well, the good news is, you're home now, and I'm going to make sure you finish your weekend off right. Do you want to come to Malone's with us tonight and watch the Bruins game?"

"Definitely." I swallow a bite of my pancake.

"And I can help you practice for your follow-up interview if you want. That's tomorrow morning?"

I nod. "It'll probably be as crappy as the first one."

"Don't say that. Positivity breeds positivity, Bee."

"Did you just make up that saying?"

"Yes. And you know what else?"

"Negativity breeds negativity?" I supply.

"That, too. But what I was going to say is, I've decided I'm lending you my Prada boots to wear tomorrow. The black suede ones my grandmother sent me. They'll bring you good luck."

"Uh-huh. You have scientific proof of that?"

"You want proof? It's called Prada. Fucking Prada, Bee. Nobody can wear Prada and *not* feel invincible."

I still can't grasp how I became best friends with this girl. Summer is the complete opposite of me. Bubbly, girly, obsessed with designer clothes. Her family is filthy rich, so she can afford those designer clothes. But me, I've never cared about labels. Give me my lipstick, my favorite leather jacket and boots, some skinny jeans and a tight dress or two, and I'm good to go. And yet despite our differences, Summer and I just…fit.

"Oh, and I confirmed with Fitz before I got here—he can drive me to campus in the morning, so you're good to borrow my car." Summer drives a flashy Audi, and she offered to let me drive it to Boston tomorrow, sparing me from taking a million trains and buses. At noon I've got a Communication Theory lecture that I can't miss, so I need to return to Hastings as fast as possible.

"Are you sure you don't mind?"

"Not at all." She picks up her teacup.

"Thanks. You have no idea how much time you'll be saving me by—"

"Hi!!!" a happy voice interrupts.

Before I can blink, a whirlwind of brown hair and luminous skin and big, big eyes streaks across my field of vision.

A girl I've never met in my life slides into our booth next to Summer and plops her butt down as if we've all been friends for years.

Summer's jaw drops. "I'm sorry...what..." She drifts off, speechless. A rare state for Summer Di Laurentis.

I sweep my gaze over the newcomer. She's wearing a white, collared shirt with red buttons. Waves of chin-length hair hover over the lacy collar.

"Hello," I say politely. "I'm not sure if you're familiar with the word *etiquette*, but typically it means you can't crash someone's brunch, particularly when they don't know who you are."

"It's okay. You're about to know me." She smiles broadly, flashing a set of perfect white teeth. She's rather cute, actually.

But just because someone is cute doesn't mean they're not insane.

"I'm Rupi. Rupi Miller. And yes, that's a Hindi first name and a completely white-bread last name, but that's 'cause my dad is super white bread. He's really, really bland. He's a dentist, you guys. Like, the *definition* of boring. My mom is awesome, though. She used to be a huge Bollywood star!" Rupi's tone ripples with pride.

Beside her, Summer blinks in confusion. "That's really great..." Her voice trails again.

I bite back a laugh. "Rupi?"

The girl beams at me. "Yes?"

"Why are you in our booth?"

"Oh. Sorry. I talk a lot, I know. Let me start over. I'm Rupi, and you're Brenna Jensen and you're Summer Heyward-Di Laurentis."

"Yes, thank you for informing us of our names," I say dryly.

Summer finally remembers how to finish a sentence. "Don't be mean to Rupi," she chides, and I can tell by her twinkling green eyes that she's warming up to this pushy little girl.

"I'm a freshman," Rupi explains. "I know, that sounds lame, but I swear I'm not. Lame, that is. I'm *so* much fun—you'll find out, I promise. But the thing is, I don't really have a lot of connections with the upperclassmen. Don't worry, I'm not stalking you or anything.

I was sitting over there with my friends when I noticed you guys. That's Lindy and Mel." She points to two girls sitting a few booths down the row. One of them is blushing profusely, while the other gives an enthusiastic wave.

I spare them a look before turning back to Rupi. "Still doesn't explain why you're interrupting our brunch."

"I wanted to put in a formal request," she announces.

"A formal request for *what*?" Summer sputters.

"I want an introduction."

My brow wrinkles. "To whom?"

"Mike Hollis."

I set my fork down.

Summer puts down her tea.

Several seconds tick by.

"Mike Hollis?" Summer finally says.

"Yes. He's your roommate," Rupi replies helpfully.

I snicker.

"I'm aware that he's my roommate." Summer shakes her head. "But why on earth do you want an introduction? To *him*."

Rupi releases a long, dreamy sigh. "Because he's the most beautiful man in the world, and I think he's my soulmate, and I'd like to be introduced to him."

Another silence falls. I'm not one to declare anything a hundred percent, so I'll say I'm ninety-nine-point-nine-nine-nine percent certain that this is the first time in the history of the planet that anyone, at any time, has referred to Hollis as the most beautiful man in the world and/or as someone's *soulmate*.

Summer appears to be as stunned as I feel. But we both recover fast, sharing a telepathic moment that brings a grin the size of Boston to Summer's lips. She pats Rupi's arm and says, "I would be honored to make that introduction."

"Actually, I'll do you one better," I chime in. "I'll give you his phone number, and you can contact him directly."

Summer is quick to second that. "Yes, even better! And when I get home I'll be sure to tell him that the daughter of a Bollywood star is going to be calling him." She winks at me when Rupi isn't looking.

Rupi's brown eyes light up. "Really?"

"Oh, absolutely." Summer pulls up her contact list. "Do you have your phone on you?"

Rupi produces an iPhone in a bubble-gum pink case, and Summer quickly recites Hollis's number. After Rupi finishes entering the digits, she gives us a solemn look. "I want you to know that you're both gorgeous and wonderful and I'm going to be seeing a lot of you once Mike and I start dating."

I won't lie—her conviction is downright inspirational.

"Anyway, I won't take up any more of your time. Just know that I think you're beautiful creatures and I'm *so* grateful for your help!"

And then, as rapidly as she appeared, she bounces out of the booth like a tiny ball of energy.

———

Later that night, I arrive at Malone's at the same time as Nate Rhodes. "Hey!" I exclaim, slinging my arm through his muscular one. "I didn't know you were coming."

I'm a big Nate fan. He's not only a skilled center with a wicked slapshot, but he's also a stand-up guy. A lot of jocks have a reputation for being cocky jackasses. They strut around campus with huge chips of entitlement on their athletic shoulders, "honoring" women with their time and their wangs. Not Nate. Along with Fitzy, he's the most humble, down-to-earth guy I've ever met.

"Yeah, my plans got canceled. I was supposed to meet up with a chick and she bailed."

I give a mock gasp. "What! Doesn't she know you're the captain of the hockey team?!"

"I know, right?" He shrugs. "Probably a good thing she bailed, though. I'm still rocking a hangover from last night."

"That was some game-winning miracle you pulled off in OT," I tell him. "I wish I got to see it in person."

"Most stressful overtime period of my life," he admits as we enter the bar. "For a moment I thought we might actually lose the damn thing." His light-blue eyes scan the main room, which is crammed with sports memorabilia, TV screens, and college students.

"There they are," I say, spotting our friends in a far booth. "Ugh. Hollis is here? Now I'm even more glad you showed up. You'll be my buffer."

"He still trying to get in your pants?"

"Every time I see him."

"Do you really blame him?" Nate gives an exaggerated leer.

"Knock it off. You've never once expressed any interest in my pants."

"Yeah, because Coach would castrate me! Doesn't mean I haven't thought about it."

"Perv."

He grins.

We reach the oversized booth, a semicircular one with enough space to accommodate four hockey players and me and Summer. She's snuggled up beside Fitz, while Hollis sits alone on the other side, his gaze glued to the Bruins game that's already underway.

Hollis shifts his head at our arrival. "Brenna! Come sit." He pats his thigh. "There's room for you right here."

"Thanks, big boy. But I'm good." I slide in next to Summer.

Rather than sit with Hollis, Nate flops down beside me, which forces Fitz and Summer to shift closer to Hollis.

"I don't have a contagious disease, you guys," he grumbles.

I glance up at one of the television screens. Boston is on the attack. "Where's Hunter?" I ask.

Almost immediately the mood shifts. Fitz looks unhappy.

Summer's face holds a touch of guilt, although I don't think she needs to feel guilty. Sure, she and Hunter had a bit of a flirtation, but the moment she realized she had feelings for Fitz, she was honest with Hunter about it. He needs to get over it already.

"I dunno. He's out and about, probably with some chick," Hollis answers. "He's a pussy posse of one lately."

I purse my lips. I hope Hunter's extracurricular activities aren't affecting his performance on the ice. Then again, he scored both goals in the regulation periods last night, and got an assist on Nate's OT goal, so it doesn't seem to be a problem.

"Why don't you two just kiss and make up?" I ask Fitz.

"I'm trying," he protests. "Hunter's not interested."

"He's being a douchebag," Nate admits, which is alarming coming from the captain. It tells me that Hunter's behavior is affecting the team. "Short of an intervention, there's not much we can do. He's playing well, and all the partying and hookups aren't slowing him down during games."

"Yes, but two teammates having beef is not good for morale," Fitz counters.

"So squash the beef," Nate says, rolling his eyes. "It's *your* beef."

"I'm trying," Fitz repeats.

Summer squeezes his arm. "It's okay. He'll calm down eventually. I still think maybe I should move out...?"

"No," Fitz and Hollis say immediately, and that's that. She doesn't bring it up again.

We watch the game for a while. I drink a beer, joke around with Nate, and ignore Hollis's advances. During the first intermission, we discuss the semifinals results.

"Corsen and I watched a live stream of the Harvard–Princeton game," Nate says darkly. "It was such fucking bullshit."

I frown. "How so?"

"Goddamn Brooks Weston. He dished out two of the dirtiest hits I've ever seen. First one was leaping into a Princeton defender from the blindside, drove him headfirst into the boards. It completely flew off the ref's radar, which is unfathomable—like how did he miss that? Second hit was a slash to a guy's knee. Weston took a penalty for that one."

Fitz shakes his head at Summer. "I hate that you partied with him in high school."

"He's a cool guy," she protests.

"He's a goon," Nate says tightly. "A goon who doesn't play fair."

"Then the refs should call him out on it," Summer points out.

"He does it in a way that escapes their notice," Fitz says. "It's a tactic for some teams—purposely fouling other players so that they retaliate and take a penalty. Harvard is really good at it."

"That's why my dad hates Daryl Pedersen so much," I tell Summer. "Coach Pedersen fosters that kind of gameplay."

"Didn't your dad and Pedersen play together back in the day?" Nate asks.

"They were teammates at Yale," I confirm. "They can't stand each other."

Summer looks intrigued. "Why?"

"I don't know the exact details. Dad's not much of a talker."

His players snort in unison. "No shit," Hollis cracks.

I shrug. "I think Pedersen played dirty back then, too, and Dad just didn't like him."

"I don't blame Coach for hating him," Nate mutters. "Pedersen's a total fuckhead. He encourages his guys to be as brutal as possible."

"Shit, people can get hurt," Mike says, and there's such sincerity in his tone that I can't help but laugh. Something about Hollis is very endearing. He's like a big kid.

"Not sure if you know this," I solemnly tell Hollis, "but... hockey's a violent sport."

Fitz chuckles.

Before Hollis can issue a comeback, noise blasts out of his phone.

He's got the most annoying ringtone, a hip-hop track with a bunch of guys shouting nonsense. Suits him to a T, though.

"Yo," he answers.

My attention returns to the Bruins game. Briefly. It's quickly diverted back to Hollis as he provides the most bizarre half of a conversation.

"Slow down…what?" He listens. "Do I have a car? No." Another long pause. "I mean… I guess I could borrow one? Wait, who is this?"

Nate barks out a laugh.

"What's happening right now?" Hollis sounds bewildered. "Who is this? Ruby? What pee? Did we meet at Jesse Wilkes's party?"

Summer makes a strangled sound and covers her mouth.

I look over and we exchange a huge grin. Not Ruby. *Rupi.* The energy tornado from the diner made her move. She hadn't wasted any time, either.

"I don't understand this… Um okay…listen. Ruby. I don't know who you are. Are you hot?"

Fitz snorts loudly. I just roll my eyes.

"Yeah, okay… I don't think so." Hollis is still wholly baffled. "Later," he says, and then hangs up.

Summer's lips are trembling as she asks, "Who was that?"

"I dunno!" He picks up his beer and chugs nearly half of it. "Some crazy chick just called and said to pick her up for dinner on Thursday night."

Summer buries her face against Fitz's shoulder, giggling uncontrollably. I don't have a boyfriend to shield my laughter, so I bite my lip and hope Hollis doesn't notice.

"This is weird, right?" he says in confusion. "Strange chicks don't call you out of the blue and ask you on dates, right? I must've met her before." He glances at Nate. "Do you know a Ruby?"

"Nope."

"Fitz?"

"Also nope."

Summer laughs harder.

"Do you?" Hollis accuses her.

"No," she lies, and I can tell she's making a conscious effort not to look my way. "I just find this incredibly hilarious."

I unhook my teeth from my bottom lip. "So are you going out with her?" I ask as casually as I can muster.

He gapes at me. "Of course not! She wouldn't tell me if she's hot, told me I'd find out Thursday night. So I said I don't think so and hung up. I'm not in the mood to get murdered, please and thank you."

Why do I have a feeling Rupi Miller isn't going to be satisfied with that outcome?

My grin nearly cracks my face in half. Summer was right. The weekend from hell *did* finish off right.

11

BRENNA

"I'M SURE HE WON'T BE MUCH LONGER." THE EMPLOYEE WHO'S BEEN tasked with babysitting me keeps repeating the assurance.

Frankly, I don't care how long Ed Mulder takes. In fact, I've been fighting the urge to leave out of spite. If I hadn't endured nearly two hours of rush-hour traffic this morning to reach Boston, I totally would've said screw it and stomped out of the HockeyNet building, never to return. But I'll be damned if that bumper-to-bumper traffic was for naught.

He's just one little obstacle, says the reassuring voice in my head.

Right. If I can conquer Jerk Mountain, the internship promised land awaits me on the other side. I won't have to report to Mulder. I probably won't even see him again. All I need to do is prove to him that I'm qualified for this position, and then I can forget he exists. Which won't be too difficult to do.

I can't believe I've already been waiting an hour for him. When I walked in at nine o'clock sharp, Rochelle apologetically informed me that Mr. Mulder was currently on an unscheduled conference call. *Super* important, apparently.

Uh-huh. I'm sure that was why I kept hearing bursts of laughter and nasally guffaws from behind his closed door.

After about forty-five minutes, Rochelle went into the office to speak to him. The next thing I knew, an employee named Mischa popped up and announced he was taking me on a tour of the station while we wait for Mulder to finish up.

I follow his tall, lanky frame down the brightly lit corridor. "So what exactly do you do here, Mischa?"

"I'm the stage manager. Which is a lot less glamorous than the title implies. Basically I coordinate the talent, see to the needs of the director, clean up the set, keep the caffeine flowing." He offers a dry look. "Sometimes I get to make small adjustments to the lighting equipment."

"Oooh, you've hit the big-time!"

He grins. "Eventually I hope to become a director, or maybe run master control. That would be the big-time."

We pass a bulky man in a gray pinstriped suit. He's on his cell phone but spares us a brief look as we walk by him. Recognition instantly hits me.

"Holy shit," I hiss to Mischa. "Was that Kyler Winters?"

"Yup. We just landed him as a special commentator. He'll be reporting on the NHL playoffs."

"Do a lot of other former NHLers work here?"

"Definitely. Most of them are analysts or game commentators. We've got some former coaches, too. And then there's the fantasy guys, stats guys, injury experts. And the loud-mouthed opinion dudes, like Kip and Trevor," he says, naming the popular talking-heads duo whose show is probably the most controversial. Both men have strong opinions and aren't afraid to voice them.

"That's a lot of testosterone in one building," I tease. "What's the estrogen situation like?"

He laughs. "Well, if we're talking on-camera, we've got Erin Foster. She usually reports from the locker room. And Georgia—"

"Barnes," I finish.

Georgia Barnes is kind of my idol. She's the one who asks the hard-hitting questions after the games, pulling no punches. She's also smart as a whip and hosts a weekly opinion segment, and while her views aren't as contentious as Kip and Trevor's, I find them a lot more intelligent, if I'm being honest.

"Georgia's awesome," Mischa tells me. "Sharpest wit you've ever experienced. I've seen her verbally cut down men three times her size."

"I love her," I confess.

"We've also got a female director for some of the evening segments, a few analysts, a couple women who work on the crew. Oh, and exhausted assistants like Maggie over here," he finishes, gesturing to the figure barreling toward us. "Hey, Mags."

Maggie is a harried-looking girl with bangs that keep falling in her eyes. She's carrying a cardboard tray of coffee cups, and rather than stop to greet us, she mumbles, "Don't talk to me. I'm late and Kip's gonna kill me." She rushes past without a backward glance.

"Still want to work here?" Mischa teases me.

"I'm a pro at getting coffee," I say confidently. "And I'm never late."

"That's good to hear. Because some of the dudes who work here have hair-trigger tempers. One producer, Pete, fires his assistants every other month. He's already been through three of them this year."

We continue the tour, winding up in the main studio, which is so cool to see. I gaze longingly at the news desk where the analysts sit, but even cooler is the set of Kip and Trevor's show, *Hockey Corner*. The familiar brown leather couch and backdrop covered with pennants and trophies trigger a wave of excitement. How amazing would it be to have my own show one day? My own set?

I force away the grandiose delusions. It's a nice fantasy, but I imagine it'd take years, decades even, before somebody gave me my own show.

The radio clipped to Mischa's belt crackles with static. "Mr. Mulder is ready for her," comes Rochelle's voice.

"See? That wasn't too long of a wait," Mischa tells me. "Right?"

Uh-huh. Right. Mulder was an hour and fifteen minutes late to an interview that wasn't even supposed to be today. Consummate professional.

Mischa walks me back to the production offices, where Rochelle hurriedly ushers me to her boss.

"Mr. Mulder," I say. "It's good to see you again."

As always, his attention is elsewhere. There are several overhead screens mounted on the wall, and one is showing a newscast from a rival network. It's on mute, but the coverage is on Saturday night's Oilers game.

He tears his gaze away from the screen. "Thanks for coming back. Friday was a total shit show."

"Yeah, it seemed crazy." He doesn't ask me to sit, but I do it anyway and wait for him to continue the interview.

"So, your school will be facing Harvard in the conference finals," he says. "What are your thoughts on that?"

"I'm excited to kick their butts."

Mulder's smile is mocking. "With Connelly at the helm? I'm afraid you're destined to lose. You've heard of Jake Connelly, right?"

Unfortunately. "Of course."

Mulder leans back in his chair. "All right, then here's a nice test for you—our interns are expected to be statistics savvy. Tell me, what are Connelly's stats for the season?"

I hide a frown. That's the most generalized question I've ever heard. His stats? What stats?

"You'll have to be a bit more specific," I reply. "What statistics are you looking for? Goals? Assists? Power play goals? Shots on goal?"

Mulder seems annoyed by my questioning. Rather than answer, he shuffles through some papers.

Lovely. This is shitty interview 2.0. I hate this man. He doesn't care that I'm here, and he has no intention of hiring me. But I patiently sit there even though I can tell he's totally checked out.

His intercom buzzes, blessedly breaking the uncomfortable silence. "Mr. Mulder, your wife's on the line. She says it's important."

He rolls his eyes. "It's never important," he informs me. He jams a button with his finger. "I'm in the middle of an interview. Ask her to be more specific."

Ohhhh really? *He's* allowed to ask people to be more specific, but when I do it, it's inexcusable?

After a short delay, Rochelle returns. "She needs to confirm the amount of people to expect for dinner on Friday."

"Important, my ass. Tell her I'll call her after the interview." He hits the button again. "Women," he mutters.

I refrain from commenting, because hello, I'm a woman.

"We have a dinner party this weekend," Mulder explains, shaking his head irritably. "As if I give a shit about any of the details. What do I care what the napkins look like? Or if it's four courses or twenty? I swear that woman obsesses over the most trivial nonsense."

I'm surprised he doesn't follow that up with some progressive commentary about how women are trivial creatures who have teeny pea brains and could never, ever work in a sports environment. The sports treehouse is for men! No girls allowed!

On the big screen, ESPN is showing a clip of the Oilers' Connor McDavid scoring one of the most beautiful goals I've ever seen. Sadly, it's not enough to win them the game.

Mulder whistles loudly, his mood brightening. "That kid is a legend!" he crows.

"He's a generational talent," I agree. "Best thing that's happened to the franchise in decades."

"And next season we have Connelly, too? Yee-haw! We'll be unstoppable."

I nod. "Connelly will bring some much-needed speed to the team. He's one of the best skaters there is."

"Lightning on skates. Lord, Brenna, I've never looked forward to a season more!" He rubs his hands together with unabashed glee.

My body language relaxes. This is the first time Mulder has actually warmed up to me. I'm not particularly thrilled that Jake Connelly is the reason Mulder is thawing, but at this point, I'll take whatever assistance I can get. Jerk Mountain is harder to climb than frickin' Everest.

We discuss Jake for nearly five minutes. I swear, Mulder actually seems to appreciate my opinions. One of my remarks legit causes him to say, "I couldn't agree with you more."

And yet when I try to steer the conversation back to the internship?

Mulder's attention goes back to his computer screen.

Frustration claws at my throat. I just want to scream. I can't figure out if he likes me or hates me. If he wants to hire me or wants me to GTFO.

"Anyway. Thanks for coming in again," he says absently.

Well, there's my answer. Get the fuck out.

"We still have a few more candidates to meet with, but you'll be notified as soon as any decisions are made."

He means I'll be notified that I didn't get the job. At the moment, the likelihood of me landing this internship is about as good as me landing on the actual moon.

Whatever. I swallow my disappointment and try to convince myself that perhaps I'm better off.

"Thank you for your time," I say politely.

"Hmmm. No prob." He's once again concentrating on something other than me.

Yes. I'm absolutely better off. I'd hate working in even the same building as someone like Ed Mulder. The man doesn't give a crap about anything but himself and his precious Oilers. The only time he engaged with me or seemed the slightest bit interested was during our brief discussion about Jake. Mulder's hard-on for Connelly is almost comical—

My step stutters on my way to the door.

An idea forms in my head. It's insane. I'm aware it's insane.

And yet…I think maybe I don't care that it's insane.

I want this internship. I want it so very badly. People have taken far more desperate measures to get a job. In comparison, what I'm about to do is…trivial. You know, just a silly woman with her trivial pursuits.

"Mr. Mulder?"

He glances at the door, annoyance in his expression. "Yes?"

"I…well, I didn't want to mention this before, because I thought it might be a bit inappropriate, but… Jake Connelly…" I hesitate, second-guessing the insanity.

I draw a breath, quickly penning a pros and cons list in my head. There are so many cons. Like, a *lot* of them. The pros don't seem as satisfying as—

"What about him?" Mulder says impatiently.

I exhale in a rush. "He's my boyfriend."

12

JAKE

Morning practice is grueling, but I don't expect anything less from Coach. He was already riding our jocks before we made it into the finals—now all bets are off. We're expected to skate faster, hit harder, take more shots. It's an intense workout, and some of the skating drills we run leave even me breathless, and I'm the best skater on the ice.

Not that I'm complaining. Some guys like to grumble about having to haul themselves out of bed so early. They bitch about the nutrition guides, or Coach's hard-ass nature. I can't deny that Pedersen's got a more physical style of play than I do. Me, I rely on my speed and accuracy rather than brute strength. But in Coach's playing days, he was a goon, and he promotes the same aggression in his players. Brooks is our main enforcer, but lately Pedersen's been pushing the other guys to throw more elbows. He doesn't expect it of me, though. He knows what I can do.

Coach is waiting for me in the hall when I leave the locker room, my hair wet from the shower. He slaps me on the shoulder. "Good hustle out there, Connelly."

"Thanks, Coach."

"You gonna bring that same hustle to the finals?"

"Yessir."

He slants his head. "Briar'll be tough to beat."

I shrug. "Not worried. We got this."

"Damn right we do." His expression turns grim. "But we also can't fall into the overconfidence trap. Jensen had a shit season last year, and he'll be clamoring to make his comeback. I wouldn't be surprised if they're doing two-a-days."

Me neither. Briar is looking much sharper this year. I'm not sure what happened last season, except that ever since Garrett Graham graduated, they've had a tough time finding that offensive breakout. Nate Rhodes is good, but he's not exceptional. Hunter Davenport is almost as fast as I am, but he's still young. He's only a sophomore, with a lot of rough edges that require sharpening. I think next season Briar will be unstoppable with Davenport at the helm. But that's next season. This season is ours.

"I need you to come in earlier tomorrow morning," Coach Pedersen says. "Six thirty, okay? I want you to work with Heath one-on-one."

I nod. I noticed Heath dropping some key passes today. "I'm cool with that."

"Knew you would be." He claps me on the shoulder again before stalking off.

I walk toward the lobby of the arena, where Brooks is waiting for me. The moment I reach him, my phone buzzes with an Instagram notification. I rarely use that app, so I'm about to ignore it when I notice the username.

BrenJen.

As in Brenna Jensen?

Curiosity grabs hold of me. "Hey, go on ahead," I tell Brooks. We're grabbing lunch at the campus café with a few teammates. "I'll meet you guys there. Gotta make a call first."

"Okay." He gives me a weird look and lumbers off.

I load Instagram and open my DMs. The profile picture for "BrenJen" shows a curtain of dark hair and the hint of a profile. But the red lips are a dead giveaway. It's definitely Brenna, and the green dot beside her pic tells me she's online right now.

> Connelly. It's Brenna. Can we meet up?

My eyebrows shoot up to my hairline. I instantly start typing with total disregard to the long lecture Brooks gave me one night about response etiquette. He has a strict rule about waiting *minimum* an hour before replying to a chick, so that she doesn't feel like she's the one with all the power. But I'm way too curious to abide by that.

> **ME:** Did you seriously just slide into my DMs?
> **BRENNA:** Unfortunately. Do you want to meet up?
> **ME:** Are you asking me out?
> **BRENNA:** In your dreams, Jakey.

I smile at the screen, just as Brenna follows up with another message.

> **BRENNA:** I'm in the city and have about an hour before I need to go back to Briar. I was hoping we could meet up.
> **ME:** Gonna need a lot more than an hour for our first time, babe. I mean, foreplay alone will eat up most of that time.
> **BRENNA:** An hour of foreplay? Aren't you ambitious.
> **ME:** Not ambitious. Realistic.

And maybe I shouldn't be trying to lure her into a sexting conversation right now, because the idea of foreplay with her is very enticing.

> **ME:** Why do you want to meet?
> **BRENNA:** Need to talk to you about something. And I'm not doing it on a stupid app, so yes or no?

I'm too intrigued to turn her down. I mean, the daughter of Briar's head coach is trying to arrange a clandestine meeting with the captain of the Harvard hockey team? Who wouldn't be intrigued?

So I type, where and when?

We meet up at a coffee shop in Central Square. Once again, it's pouring outside, and I'm cold and wet when I join Brenna at a small table in the back.

She's holding a coffee cup, wisps of steam rising up from the lip to redden her nose. She gestures to the cup in front of the empty chair. "I ordered you a coffee. Black."

"Thanks," I say gratefully, wrapping my wet hands around the hot mug. My fingers are fucking freezing.

As I take a long sip, Brenna sits there watching me.

I set the cup down. "So," I drawl.

"So," she drawls back.

Damn, she looks cute today. Her long hair is pulled back in a neat braid, and her complexion is devoid of makeup. Or, if she's wearing any, she's opted for a totally natural look. There's a fresh-faced, rosy glow to her cheeks and—holy shit, she's not wearing red lipstick. Her lips are pink and glossy.

I almost blurt out, "What's wrong with your face," but corral the question before it's too late. That is never something you want to ask a chick.

"Are you finally going to enlighten me about why I'm here?" I ask instead.

"Yes, but first you have to promise me a few things."

"Nah. I make no promises, ever."

"Fine. Then I'm out. And at least I get to leave with the satisfaction of knowing I made you come all the way here for nothing." She starts to rise. "Later, Jakey."

"Sit that pretty ass back down," I order, rolling my eyes. "Fine. What am I promising?"

"One, that you'll hear me out until I'm done. And two, that you won't gloat."

The mystery deepens. I lean back in my chair and say, "All right. Cross my heart and hope to die."

"Okay." She blows out a breath. "So I applied for an internship at HockeyNet."

"Nice."

"Sure, it would be. If my interviewer wasn't an enormous dickwad." Brenna's fingers tighten around her mug. "I've had two interviews with him, and he didn't take me seriously either time." She scowls at me. "And before you make some snarky comment about how maybe I'm not qualified for the job—"

"I wasn't going to," I cut in.

"Good. Because I am qualified. I don't think he takes *any* women seriously. Or at least, women trying to break into sports. You should've heard the derisive way he spoke about Georgia Barnes. He acted like she didn't belong at the network. He acted like *I* didn't belong there." Brenna's tone is thick with frustration, but her eyes convey pure defeat. "He's such a dick."

"I'm sorry," I say, and I mean it. I don't think I've ever seen Brenna lose her confidence. I'm surprised she's even letting this jackass get to her. "Want me to go beat him up?"

"If it were that easy, I would beat him up on my own. A good kick in the balls would do him a world of good."

I snicker. "Why am I here, then?"

"So…he's from Edmonton," she starts.

A frown touches my lips. I'm not quite sure where this is going. I assume this guy is an Oilers fan, but I won't be playing there until next year. "I still don't see where I fit into this."

"The only time during the interview today that he actually seemed interested in me was when we were discussing Edmonton.

And you," she adds grudgingly. "He thinks you're exactly what they need to win the Cup."

I think I agree with him. The team's record is decent, but I plan on making it even better. I'm a damn good hockey player, not only due to talent, but because I work my ass off. I've worked for this my entire life.

"Anyway..." Brenna trails off. She takes a hasty sip of her coffee. "Why'd you bring me here, Jensen? I've got class soon, too."

"Because, like I said, the first time he paid any positive attention to me was when I told him I knew you."

I grin in delight. "Dropped my name, eh?"

"Shut up. It made me sick doing it."

Laughter spills out. This chick is really something. I'm so used to girls throwing themselves at me that it's almost refreshing when one does the opposite.

"I did more than drop a name," she confesses.

My forehead wrinkles. "Okay. What'd you tell him?"

She mumbles something under her breath.

I lean forward. "What's that?"

"I told him you were my boyfriend," she grinds out. Her jaw is so tight I'm surprised it doesn't snap in two.

I stare at her for a second. When I realize she's dead serious, I'm hit with another wave of laughter. "You fucking didn't."

"I did. And you promised not to gloat."

"Sorry. Promise broken." I can't stop chuckling. "This is too fucking good. That was so much more than a name drop. It was like...like human centipede level of kiss-ass." I wipe tears from the corner of my eye.

Brenna glares daggers at me. "First of all, *gross*. And second, I'm sorry, but unlike you I actually need to get a job when I graduate. I don't have the luxury of a multimillion-dollar contract with a profes-sional hockey franchise. Journalism is my dream, so if kissing that jerk's ass is what I need to do to get this internship, then I will."

I force myself to stop laughing. It's difficult. "Okay, so you told him I'm your boyfriend." Oh man, I love this. I love it hard. I can practically picture the expression on her face when she told him. The agony. "That doesn't explain why we're sitting here right now."

"Needless to say, he came in his pants at the idea of having easy access to you." She sighs. "He's hosting a dinner party on Friday and he wants us to go."

"Us?" I'm grinning so hard. "We're an *us* now?"

"Trust me, that's the last thing I want, but I told him we'd be there. And now, as humiliating as it is, I'm asking you to do me a solid and go with me." She looks and sounds like she'd rather roll around in a dark pit full of razor blades.

I grin even harder. I think my face might break.

"Don't do this to me," she says miserably. "I'm aware of how ridiculous this is, but I need your help. You already pretended to be my boyfriend once, remember? You had no problem putting your hands all over me at the concert, but I guess that was okay because it was *your* idea to put on the charade?"

She has a point.

"Well, I need you to do it again, okay?" There's a splash of bitterness in her tone. "It's one night—I'll even pay you if you want."

"Hey, I'm no gigolo."

"Fine, then do it for free. Be a good Samaritan."

I ponder for a moment. "Nah."

"Come on, Connelly." I don't think I've ever seen Brenna so flustered. "Don't make me beg."

A bolt of lust streaks straight to my groin. "That sounds so fucking appealing."

Her mouth tightens. "It's not happening."

"Mmmm, you on your knees…begging…" My cock twitches.

It's official. I'm hot for this girl. I've slept with my share of women, but I can't remember the last time I lusted this hard over someone. I can feel my eyes glazing over as I envision the scene I just described. Brenna on her knees, unzipping my pants. Gripping my cock. Peering up at me with big eyes. Pleading for it.

"I'm not begging," she says firmly. "I'm asking. If you're saying no, then fine, I'll get up and leave."

I snap myself out of my lust trance. "I'm not saying no."

"Great. Then come with me on Friday."

I chuckle. "Oh, I'm not saying yes, either."

If looks could kill, I'd be on the floor surrounded by a chalk outline right about now. "Then what are you saying?" she demands.

"I'm saying—quid pro quo. I don't know if you learned this in school, but nothing comes for free." I wink. "I scratch your back, you scratch mine."

"I am not scratching any part of your body."

"All I mean is, if I help you out, I want something in return."

"Like what?" She starts fidgeting with the end of her braid, clearly unhappy.

I'd kind of like for her to undo the braid altogether. I want to see her dark hair loose around her shoulders. Actually, nah. I want to see it fanning over my bare chest as she crawls her way down my body and—

"Like what?" she repeats when I take too long to reply.

Once again, I force myself to concentrate. "So, you want a date on Friday night—"

"A fake date."

"A fake date," I amend. "Well, in return, I want a real one."

"A real what?"

"A real date. You get a fake date, I get a real one."

"Are you joking?" Her mouth falls open. "You want to go out with me?"

I examine her incredulous expression. "I know, right? It caught me by surprise, too." I offer a shrug. "But it happened and now here we are. I think you're hot, and I know you think *I'm* hot—"

"I think *you* think you're hot," she interjects with a snort.

"I don't think that. I know that. And I've seen the way you check me out, so..." I hold up my hands in a careless motion, before gesturing from me to her. "I think there's something here—"

"There is nothing here. Nothing."

"Okay. Cool. I'll just be on my way." I lift my ass off the chair.

"Connelly," Brenna growls. "Sit back down." She briefly closes her eyes. "You're saying you'll come to the dinner party with me, and all I have to do is go out with you for real."

"Yeah, but don't make it out like you're meeting up with a serial killer. At least *pretend* to sound excited about going out with me."

"Okay!" She claps her hands. "I get to go on a date with you! Hurray!"

"Much better," I tell her, and I don't think I've stopped smiling since I learned the reason she'd summoned me. "So. Is that a yes?"

She sighs. Loudly.

13
BRENNA

TUESDAY BRINGS ANOTHER STORM. EVEN THE METEOROLOGIST AT the local cable station seems fed up with the weather. When I watched the morning news earlier, he was glaring at the camera the entire time he read the forecast, as if he holds his viewers accountable for the buckets upon buckets of rain that have been dumped over New England this past month.

Luckily, I'm spared the walk home from campus because Summer and I have class around the same time. Mine lets out an hour before hers, so I work on an assignment in the lobby of the Art and Design building. Comfy couches litter the big space, which is surprisingly empty. It's just a girl with a laptop on a couch near the windows, and me with my laptop on another couch across the room, giving me some semblance of privacy while I wait for Summer.

My assignment is for my least favorite course: Broadcast News Writing. Since I can't major in All Things Sports, my classes involve all areas of journalism. This particular class requires writing copy for television news as opposed to print news, and my prof decided it would be fun to assign me a political topic. Which means coming up with copy about our president's latest shenanigans, while worrying whether my professor supports this current administration, or condemns it. He's never revealed his political leanings, and I'm sure, if questioned, he'd give some spiel about how journalists always remain objective. But come on, let's be real. At the end of the day, we all have our biases. Period.

I write about five hundred words before taking a break. I scroll through my phone, checking my messages, but there's nothing new. Jake's name taunts me from the list, because we exchanged numbers at the coffee shop yesterday so we wouldn't have to communicate via Insta.

A groan gets stuck in my throat. What, oh *what*, compelled me to tell Ed Mulder that Jake was my boyfriend? *Why* did I do that? I regretted the lie about a nanosecond after it slipped out, but it was too late to take it back. Mulder was so overjoyed, you'd think I'd offered to blow him. Though, really, he'd probably be more excited to receive a BJ from Jake. God knows he has a massive hard-on for the guy.

And speaking of Jake, what, oh *what*, compelled *him* to ask me out? I'm still baffled, not to mention leery of his intentions. The night of the concert proved that the two of us have some chemistry, but that doesn't mean we have to act on it. He plays for *Harvard*, for Pete's sake. That's inexcusable.

A message pops up as I'm scrolling, eliciting a rush of unhappiness. It's from Eric. *Again.*

ERIC: Please, B. I don't know why you're ignoring me.

Technically, I'm not ignoring him. I responded to his previous message on Sunday night when I got home from Malone's. I told him the next few weeks will be super busy thanks to final exams and life in general, and that I won't be around at all. Clearly he didn't like my answer.

Another text comes in: Call me

Crap. I know Eric. If I don't call, he won't stop texting. And when I don't text, he'll start calling. And calling. And calling.

Fighting a burst of aggravation, I dial his number.

"B, hey!" His relief is palpable, even over the line. "I'm glad you called."

He's on something. I can tell from the way he speaks, the breathy tone he uses when there's toxic shit coursing through his blood. I'm glad I can't see his eyes right now. That was always the worst part for me, seeing his eyes when he's high. It was like looking at a completely different person. The Eric Royce I was madly in love with was replaced by a pathetic stranger. And being there for him was—*is*—exhausting.

Maybe it makes me a terrible person to think that, but I don't care anymore. He's not my responsibility. I didn't sign up to be his mom. That's a job for his *mom*.

But Mrs. Royce is, and has always been, an absentee parent. She's a corporate lawyer, and Eric's father was a stay-at-home dad before he died. And after he died, Mrs. Royce didn't cut back on her work hours to spend time with her son. She just kept chugging along without paying a lick of attention to him.

The only effort she made after it became apparent he had a substance-abuse problem was to try to ship him off to Vermont. But Eric refused to go. According to him, he's not an addict. He simply likes to party "here and there."

"You don't sound good," I tell him. "You're wheezing."

"Ah. I have a bit of a cold."

Is that what we're calling it these days? "You should try to get some rest, then." I hear what sounds like a gust of wind. "Are you outside right now?"

"I'm leaving a Dunkin' Donuts. This rain…it's crazy, right?"

I stifle a curse. "You didn't ask me to call you to talk about the rain. What do you need, Eric? What's going on?"

"I just…" An agonized note enters his voice. "I'm, ah, strapped for cash right now, B. My rent's due next week and everything in my account is gonna go to cover that, and, you know, that doesn't leave me much for groceries and, ah, basic shit…"

By "basic shit" I assume he means meth, and anger brews in the pit of my stomach. "You live with your mother," I remind him. "I'm sure she'll let you off the hook for this month's rent."

"She doesn't give a fuck," he mutters. "She said she'll kick me out if I don't pay rent."

"Well, luckily you have enough money to cover the rent," I remind him. "As for groceries, I'm sure your mom isn't going to let you starve."

"Please, I just need like fifty bucks, a hundred tops. Come on, B."

He isn't asking for an obscene amount, but I don't care. He's not getting a dime from me ever again, especially when I know it's all going to drugs. Besides, it's not like I'm rolling in money. I don't pay tuition, but I still have expenses. Rent, food, "basic shit" that *isn't* crystal meth. I have some saved up from waitressing jobs, but I'm not using it to fund Eric's self-destruction.

"I'm sorry, you know I'd help if I could, but I'm broke," I lie.

"No, you're not," he argues. "I *know* you have some cash lying around, B. Please. After everything we've been through, you can't just forget about me. We're in this together, remember?"

"No, we're not," I say sharply. "We broke up years ago, Eric. We're *not* together anymore."

Voices echo from a nearby corridor, floating into the lobby. I pray that Summer's class has finished.

"I'm sorry." I soften my tone. "I can't help you. You need to talk to your mom."

"Fuck my mom," he snaps.

I bite the inside of my cheek. "I have to go now. I'm about to walk into class," I lie. "But…we'll talk soon, okay? I'll call you once things settle down on my end."

I disconnect before he can argue.

When Summer appears, I paste on a smile and hope she doesn't notice I'm quieter than usual on the ride home. She doesn't. Summer can carry a conversation all by herself, and today I'm grateful for that.

I think I need to cut Eric out of my life for good. It's not the first time I've thought that, but I'm hoping this time it'll be the last. I can't keep doing this anymore.

The rain has eased up by the time Summer drops me off at home. "Thanks for the ride, crazy girl." I smack a grateful kiss on her cheek.

"I love you," she calls as I dart out of the car.

Friends who say "I love you" every time you part ways are important. Those are the ones you need in your life.

Summer peels out of the driveway, and I round the side of the house toward my private entrance. A short flight of stairs takes me down to my little entryway, and—

Plop.

My boots sink into an ocean.

Okay, not an ocean. But there's at least a foot and a half of water lapping at the base of the steps.

Sickness swirls in my stomach. Holy shit. The basement flooded. My fucking apartment *flooded*.

A surge of panic spurs me forward. I slosh through the ocean in my leather boots and assess the damage, horrified by what I find.

The basement has wall-to-wall carpeting—ruined. The legs of the coffee table are underwater—ruined. The bottom half of the couch I bought at a secondhand store is soaked—ruined. My futon—ruined.

I bite my lip in dismay. Luckily my laptop was with me today. And the majority of my clothes are untouched. Most of them are hanging in the closet, well above the ocean, and my shoe rack is one of those tall ones, so only the soles of the shoes on the last shelf are wet. My bottom dresser drawer is full of water, but I only keep PJs and loungewear down there, so it's not the end of the world. All the important stuff is in the top drawers.

But the carpets…

The furniture…

This is not good.

I wade back to the entry where I hung my purse. I find my phone and call my landlord, Wendy, who I'm praying is at home. Neither her nor Mark's cars were in the driveway, but Wendy usually parks in the garage, so there's a chance she's upstairs.

"Brenna, hey. I just heard you come in. It's really raining out there, huh?"

She's home. Thank God. "It's really raining in here, too," I answer bleakly. "I don't know how to break it to you, but there's been a flood."

"*What?*" she exclaims.

"Yup. I think you'd better put on some rain boots, preferably ones that go up to your knees, and come downstairs."

———

Two hours later, we're facing a nightmare scenario. The basement is fucked.

At Wendy's SOS, her husband Mark rushed home from work early, and, after turning off the electricity to avoid, well, dying, the three of us conducted a thorough assessment with flashlights from upstairs. Mark assured me that insurance would cover the furniture I lost. Lost being the operative word, because none of it can be salvaged. There was too much water damage, so everything needs to be thrown out. All I could do was pack up the items that survived the Great Flood.

According to Mark, the house doesn't have a sump pump installed because Hastings isn't an area where flooding is at all common. My landlords will need to bring in a professional to pump the water; there's far too much of it to be removed by a wet vac or mop. Mark estimated they would need at least a week to pump and thoroughly clean the basement, maybe even two weeks. Apparently without the proper cleanup, there's danger of mold growth.

Which means I need to make alternate arrangements until the process is complete.

AKA, I'm moving back in with my father.

It's not ideal, but it's the best option I've got. Despite Summer's insistence that I stay at her place, I refuse to live in the same house as Mike Hollis. No way can I deal with Hollis's personality and him constantly hitting on me for an extended period of time. A home is supposed to be a safe, sacred place.

The dorms are out, too. My friend Audrey isn't allowed to have anyone stay with her for more than a night or two—her resident advisor is a stickler about that kind of stuff. And while Elisa's RA is more lenient, she lives in a cramped single, and I'd have to crash in a sleeping bag on her floor. Possibly for two weeks.

Screw that. At Dad's house, I have my own bedroom, a lock on the door, and a private bath. I can suffer through Dad's bullshit as long as that trifecta is met.

He picks me up from Mark and Wendy's, and ten minutes later we trudge through the front door of his old Victorian. Dad carts my suitcase and duffel into the house, while I shoulder my backpack and laptop case.

"I'll take these upstairs," he says brusquely, disappearing up the narrow staircase. A moment later, I hear his footsteps creaking on the floor above my head.

As I unzip my boots and hang up my coat, I silently curse the weather. It's been the bane of my existence for more than a month now, but it's officially crossed the line. I'm declaring war on the climate.

I go upstairs and approach my room as my father is exiting it. It jars me how close his head comes to the top of the doorframe. Dad is tall and broad-shouldered, and I heard that the hockey groupies at Briar salivate over him as much as his players. And to that I say *ew*. Just because Dad's handsome doesn't mean I want to think about him in a sexual context.

"You okay?" he asks gruffly.

"Yeah, I'm fine. Just irritated."

"I don't blame you."

"I swear, the last few days have been a nightmare. Starting from the interview on Friday and ending with tonight's flood."

"What about the follow-up interview yesterday? How did that go?"

Abysmally. At least until I pretended Jake Connelly was my boyfriend. But I keep that part to myself and say, "It was all right, but I'm not holding my breath. The interviewer was a total misogynist."

Dad arches one dark eyebrow. "Is that so?"

"Trust me, if I get hired, it'd be a miracle." I shove a strand of hair off my forehead. "Anyway, I'm wet and my feet are frozen from wading around in the basement all afternoon. Do you mind if I take a hot shower?"

"Go ahead. I'll leave you to it."

I crank the shower in the hall bathroom, strip out of my damp clothes, and step into the glass stall. The warm water seeps into my bones and brings a shiver of pleasure. I make it even hotter, and it almost triggers an orgasm. I'm so tired of being cold and wet.

As I soap up, I think back to my arrangement with Jake. Was it a mistake? Probably. It's a lot of effort to go to for an unpaid internship, but if I want to gain experience by working at a major sports network *and* be able to do it during the school year, I only have two options: ESPN and HockeyNet. And the former is even more competitive.

I dunk my head under the spray and stand there for as long as I can justify. When I can imagine my father lecturing me about running up his hot water bill, I turn off the shower.

I cocoon myself in my terrycloth robe, wrap my hair in a turban, and cross the hall to my room.

Because Dad bought this house after I'd already moved out, this bedroom doesn't really feel like home to me. The furniture is plain, and there's a noticeable lack of personal items and decorations. Even my bedspread is impersonal—solid white, with white pillows and white sheets. Like a hospital. Or a mental institution. At our old house in Westlynn, I had one of those four-post beds and a colorful quilt, and on the wall over the headboard there'd been a glitter-painted wooden sign that said PEACHES. My dad had it custom made for my tenth birthday.

I wonder what ever happened to that sign. A bittersweet taste fills my mouth. I don't remember the exact moment that Dad stopped calling me "Peaches." Probably around the time I got together with Eric. And it wasn't just mine and Dad's relationship that suffered. What started out as admiration for a talented hockey player turned into a deep hatred that exists to this day. Dad never forgave Eric for what happened between us, and he doesn't feel an ounce of sympathy that Eric has been spiraling ever since. *A real man admits when he has a problem*, Dad always says.

I unzip my suitcase and pull out some warm socks, panties, leggings, and an oversized sweater. I've just finished dressing when Dad knocks on the door.

"You decent?"

"Yup, come in."

He opens the door and leans against the frame. "You want anything special for dinner tonight?"

"Oh, don't worry," I tell him, amused. "You don't have to cook."

"Wasn't gonna. I thought we'd order a pizza."

I snicker. "You know I've seen those meal plans you force the boys to follow, right? And meanwhile you're over here ordering pizzas?"

"You're home," he says with a shrug. "It's cause for celebration."

Is it? Our interactions are so strained and awkward that it feels like two strangers talking to each other. There's no warmth between us anymore. No hostility, either, but he's definitely not the same man who used to call me Peaches.

"Okay, then. Pizza sounds great," I say.

A short silence falls. He seems to be examining me, searching my gaze for...something.

For some reason, I feel it's imperative to say, "I'm an adult now."

Except saying *I'm an adult now* pretty much ensures that the person claiming adulthood is viewed as the complete opposite.

Dad's mouth quirks wryly. "Well aware of that."

"I mean, just because I'm staying here for a week or so doesn't mean you can give me the 'you live under my roof, you follow my rules' shtick. I won't follow a curfew."

"And I won't have you lumbering in here drunk at four in the morning."

I roll my eyes. "That's not really a habit of mine. But I might come home a little tipsy around midnight after hanging out with my friends. And I don't need you to lecture me about it."

Dad drags his hand over his close-cropped hair. He's sported this no-nonsense military buzz cut as far back as I can remember. Dad doesn't like to waste time on frivolous things. Like hair.

"You do your thing, I do mine," I finish. "Deal?"

"As long as your thing doesn't harm yourself or others, then I won't have a reason to interfere."

My throat grows tight. I hate that when he looks at me, he still sees that self-destructive girl with the poor decision-making process. But I'm not her anymore. I haven't been her for a long time.

Dad turns away. "Let me know when you're getting hungry and I'll place the pizza order."

He firmly closes the door behind him.

Welcome home, I think.

14
BRENNA

"OMIGOD, BEE, YOU WOULD'VE *DIED!*" IT'S FRIDAY NIGHT AND I'M on the phone with Summer, who's filling me in on the crazy shit that apparently went down yesterday, courtesy of one Rupi Miller.

"She seriously showed up at the house and dragged Hollis on a date?" The balls on that girl. I love it.

"Yes! She was wearing the cutest black dress with a white lace collar and really sweet heels, and he's sitting on the couch in sweatpants, playing video games with Fitz. She took one look at him and screamed, 'Upstairs! Now!' You should have seen his face."

I'm in public, so I can't hoot the way I want to. But I'm hooting inside, because I can *totally* picture Hollis's expression. "I bet he thought he was about to get laid."

"I don't know what he thought. She's been texting him all week about their 'big date,' but he thought it was some sort of joke. He didn't actually believe there'd be a date until she showed up at our door to pick him up." Summer starts laughing hysterically. "So she took him upstairs and went to his closet and *picked out an outfit for him—*"

A cackle slips out. I can't help it, and I don't care if everyone at the train station hears it. This is priceless.

"—and now they've been gone for about an hour and I don't know whether to file a missing-person report or see how this plays out."

"See how it plays out," I say immediately. "Please don't come between Rupi and her man. I beg of you. Hollis needs to feel what it's like to be harassed."

"I think they might be a match made in heaven."

"Here's hoping."

Headlights catch my attention. I've been outside the train station for the past ten minutes, waiting for a blue Honda Civic to arrive, and I think it's finally here. I squint as the car approaches the curb. "Sorry, babes, I gotta go. My car's here."

"I cannot *believe* you're going on a date and I know nothing about this guy."

"There's nothing to know. It's just a Tinder guy. Probably won't amount to anything other than a hookup." Yes, I'm a liar. So sue me. And yes, of course I feel bad lying to my friends, but there's no way I'm telling Summer the truth about tonight. It's bad enough that *I* know what I'm doing tonight.

I offer a hasty goodbye and hang up just as the passenger door of the Civic pops open. Hmmm. Jake is sitting up front with the driver. I peer at the driver's seat and spot a cute girl with turquoise drop earrings and big hair. Why doesn't that surprise me?

"Hey," he calls as he hops out of the car.

For a second I lose my voice. He's wearing his Harvard jacket, a sin I reluctantly forgive because the rest of him is so damn appealing. His dark hair is swept back from his face, emphasizing chiseled cheekbones and a jawline that makes me drool. He's completely clean-shaven tonight. Last weekend he had some scruff. Now he looks young and smooth and…fine, he looks incredible.

Unfortunately, Jake Connelly is a very attractive man.

I walk over to him. "Hey." Then I slide through the back door he holds open for me, and greet the driver as I settle in the backseat.

Jake gets in beside me, we buckle up, and then we're on our way. According to the email that Ed Mulder's secretary sent me, Mulder's address is in Beacon Hill. He must haul in quite the salary at HockeyNet.

"You look weird," Jake murmurs.

"Weird how?" And that is not what you're supposed to say to your fake girlfriend. My nerves are already on edge.

"You're wearing lip gloss. And it's *pink.*"

"So?"

"So I don't like it," he growls.

"You don't? Oh no! Let me run home and choose a makeup palette that's more to your liking!"

From the front seat, the driver snorts.

Jake's dark-green eyes flicker with amusement. "Fine, disregard my opinion. But I dig the red lips. The pink ones aren't doing it for me."

They're not doing it for me, either, but I won't give him the satisfaction of admitting it. I purposely toned down my appearance for tonight. Some sad, sick part of me is hoping to impress Ed Mulder.

As we head toward Beacon Hill, I scroll through the sports news on my phone. I frown deeply at one headline. "Have you been following this Kowski thing?" I ask Jake. "I swear, the refs have a conspiracy against him."

"You think?"

"He's the most fouled player in the league. And the amount of missed calls on him is astronomical. Something's going on there." I scan the rest of the article, but the author doesn't add any new insights. Basically, the referees keep missing calls and Sean Kowski keeps paying for it.

Our driver turns off Cambridge Street and slows down in front of a row of tall brownstones. Man, what I wouldn't give to live in one of those townhouses. They're old and oozing with charm, most of them still retaining their original historical features. With its mature trees and gas streetlights, Beacon Hill is one of the most scenic neighborhoods in the city. And it's impossibly quiet considering it's splat in the middle of Boston. Coming here is like stepping back in time, and I love it.

"Here we are," the driver says.

Jake leans forward and touches her shoulder. "Thanks, Annie. Enjoy the rest of your night."

"You, too, Jake."

I'm trying not to roll my eyes as we exit the car. I guess they're best friends now. For some reason, the way Jake seems to get along with everyone rubs me the wrong way. It's hard to think of him as THE ENEMY when faced with evidence that he might be a decent guy.

"Your face is a bit green," Jake remarks as we climb the front stoop. "I thought you had balls of steel."

"I do," I mutter, but he's right. I'm beyond nervous. I chalk it up to the two very terrible encounters I've already had with Mulder. "I don't know. I just feel sick that I have to try to impress this jackass."

"No one's forcing you to," he points out.

"I want this internship. That leaves me no choice but to impress him."

I ring the doorbell, and two seconds later the door swings open to reveal a woman clad in black pants, a black shirt, and white apron. I doubt it's Mulder's wife, because I see another woman in an identical outfit hurrying toward a doorway I assume is the kitchen.

"Please come in," she says. "You're the last guests to arrive. Mr. and Mrs. Mulder are entertaining the others in the sitting room."

Oh brother, they're one of those couples? I suppose we'll all congregate in the sitting room before being ushered into a dining room and the men shall retire to the study while the women do the dishes. Seems like a Mulder move, for sure.

"May I take your coat?" the woman prompts.

Jake slips out of his and hands it over. "Thank you," he tells her.

I unbutton my pea coat and slide it off my shoulders. I hear a sharp intake of breath, and glance over to find Jake's admiring gaze on me. "You clean up nice, Jensen," he murmurs.

"Thanks." I couldn't very well wear my usual all-black attire, so

I chose a tight gray sweater, black leggings, and cute brown suede ankle boots. My makeup is subtle and I feel naked without my lipstick, AKA, my armor. But I wanted to look classy tonight.

I don't know what to expect as we approach the sitting room. Will it be an older crowd? Younger? And how many people?

To my relief, there aren't many. The dinner party consists of Mulder and a pale-skinned woman at his side who I assume is his wife. Then there's an older couple in their forties, and a younger couple in their twenties. The younger guy seems familiar, but it isn't until Jake whispers in my ear that I realize who it is.

"Holy shit, that's Theo Nilsson."

Nilsson is a defenseman on the Oilers, whose humble nature and Nordic good looks have made him popular with fans and foes alike. Unfortunately, he's out for the rest of the season with a leg injury.

"I heard he's originally from Boston, but I didn't realize he was in town," Jake murmurs. "This is awesome."

When Mulder notices us lurking in the doorway, his face lights up. "Jake Connelly!"

I swallow my displeasure. And what am I, chopped liver?

"So glad you could make it!" Mulder exclaims. "Come in, come in. Let me introduce you to everyone." He gestures for us to come closer.

Introductions are quickly made. The pale woman is Ed's wife, Lindsay. Her eyebrows are so blond they're almost white, and her hair is arranged in a severe twist at the nape of her neck. She greets us with a wan smile. Next there's Nilsson, who goes by "Nils," and his wife Lena, who has a heavy Swedish accent but speaks perfect English. The older couple rounding out the group is Mulder's brother David and sister-in-law Karen.

"It's an honor to meet you," Jake tells Nils, sounding a wee bit star struck. "I've been following your season. I hated seeing you go out like that."

"That game was so hard to watch," I say sympathetically. Hockey injuries are par for the course, but it's not very common for someone to break their leg on the ice. "It looks like you're doing better, though."

The blond man nods. "Cast came off a couple weeks ago. Now I'm starting the physio, and dear Lord, it is brutal."

"I can imagine," I say.

Nils glances at Jake. "I was watching the draft when you went in the first round. We're excited to have you on board next year."

"I'm excited to be there."

For the next few minutes, Jake and Nils discuss the Oilers organization. The Mulder brothers are quick to join in, and it isn't long before the men slowly ease away from the women toward the wet bar near the grand piano.

Seriously?

The women are relegated to two loveseats near the stately fireplace. Frustration burns my throat as I watch the men talk hockey, while halfheartedly listening to Karen chat about the new yoga studio she recently discovered in Back Bay.

"Oh, the Lotus!" Lena Nilsson gushes. "That's where I've been going now that we're back in the city. The instructors are wonderful."

"How long are you in town for?" I ask Lena.

"Until Theo has to report for training camp. I wish we could stay forever. I'm never excited about going back to Edmonton." Lena's bottom lip sticks out. "It's a very cold place."

The ladies keep chatting, and I have absolutely nothing to contribute to the conversation. I stare longingly at Jake, who's involved in an animated discussion with Nils. He must sense my gaze on him, because suddenly he glances over. I see understanding dawn in his eyes. Then he says something to Nils before waving to me. "Babe, come here and tell them your conspiracy theory about Kowski and the refs."

"Excuse me." I gratefully hop to my feet and hope that Lindsay and the others aren't offended by my obvious eagerness to escape their company.

Ed Mulder doesn't look thrilled by my arrival, but Nils greets me warmly. "Conspiracy, eh? To be honest, I'm starting to wonder the same thing."

"There's no other explanation," I answer. "Did you see the clip from yesterday? The ref was clearly watching that play and decided not to call a foul. And honestly, every time they discount an infraction, it's such a disservice to Kowski. He's fast, but he can't showcase his speed because he's constantly being knocked around without any repercussion to the guys doing the knocking."

"I agree," Nils says, shaking his head incredulously. "It's downright bizarre. The ref—was it McEwen? I think it was Vic McEwen—he had a perfect line of sight to Kowski and the Kings winger who cross-checked him."

Mulder sounds annoyed as he joins in. "Kowski initiated contact."

"It was typical puck protection on his end," I counter. "Meanwhile, the resulting check could have resulted in a serious head injury."

"But it didn't," Mulder says, rolling his eyes at me. "Besides, injuries come with the job, right, Nils?"

I stifle my annoyance.

Nils responds with a shrug. "For the most part, yes. But I agree with Brenna about Kowski. There's a difference between normal contact and the kind of contact that can give you brain damage." He gives Jake a wry smile. "Still want to come play with us next season knowing a ref might allow you to get murdered?"

"Absolutely." No hesitation from Jake, though he follows it up with a rare display of humility. "I just hope I don't disappoint you guys."

"You're going to kill it," I say firmly, because I truly believe he will. "I bet you you'll be the youngest player ever to win the Art

Ross." That's the trophy for the most points in a season, previously won by legends like Gretzky and Crosby.

"Babe. That's a lot of pressure," Jake grumbles. "I'd be happy if I got an assist or two." Then he smirks, displaying the familiar Connelly confidence. "Or a Stanley Cup."

Nils raises his glass. "I'll drink to that."

"You guys are definitely due," I tell them. "The Oilers haven't won a cup since, what, the 1989 season? Not since the Gretzky era."

Nils nods in confirmation. "You know your hockey."

"We went to the finals in '06," Jake points out. He pauses. "Lost, though."

And what followed was an eleven-year playoffs drought, which is embarrassing when you consider that more than half the teams in the league make it to the playoffs. I don't mention that particular statistic, however. I wouldn't dream of it, not in front of an Oilers superfan, an Oilers active-roster player, and a soon-to-be Oilers rookie.

Speaking of the superfan, I feel Mulder's gaze on me, and I turn to find him wearing a shit-eating grin. My first thought is that he's impressed.

But I should know better by now.

"Sorry, it's just funny sometimes." Chuckling, he swirls the ice cubes in his glass. "You know, hearing hockey stats and breakdowns coming from a woman. It's cute."

It's *cute*?

A red mist washes over my vision. Attitudes like that are the reason why women still face massive roadblocks when trying to break into sports journalism. It's a historically sexist profession, and even now there really aren't that many established female sports journalists. It's not for lack of talent—it's because of men like this, who think vaginas don't belong in sports.

"Stats knowledge is one of the many talents Brenna brings to the table," Jake says roughly.

Ed Mulder completely misconstrues that. I know Jake wasn't trying to be sleazy, considering he went out of his way to include me in the hockey talk. But Mulder's brain operates on a different level.

"I bet she does," he drawls. He leers at my chest for several fist-inducing seconds before winking and clapping Jake on the shoulder.

Jake stiffens.

I grit my teeth, pressing my balled fists to my sides. This man is such a pig. I want nothing more than to smack him across the face and tell him to shove his internship up his ass.

Jake sees my face and gives a slight shake of the head. I force myself to relax. He's right. I wouldn't be doing myself any favors by causing a scene.

From the doorway, Mulder's wife consults with the caterer before turning to address the group. "Dinner is served!"

15
JAKE

LAST SUMMER I TAGGED ALONG WITH BROOKS AND HIS PARENTS to Italy for a couple weeks. The Weston family owns a villa in Positano, one of the wealthier regions on the Amalfi Coast. The coast was stunning, but Brooks and I explored other areas as well, including Naples and Pompeii and the infamous Mount Vesuvius. I imagine living anywhere near a volcano would be insanely stressful. I'd constantly be shooting wary glances at it, wondering when it was going to erupt—and knowing it *can* erupt. Knowing it has the power to wipe away an entire civilization, because it happened to Pompeii.

Tonight Brenna is that volcano.

The amount of times that steam has practically rolled out of her ears is almost comical. I'd laugh at her barely checked rage if it didn't match my own.

Theo Nilsson is a cool dude, but the Mulder brothers? Not so much. Ed, in particular, is the supreme jackass that Brenna claimed he was. He cuts his wife down at every chance. He's rude to the catering staff. And worst of all, he's dismissive of Brenna and every word she says.

On the bright side, dinner is fantastic. I love to eat, so I'm all about this menu: fried scallops, stuffed cod cakes, roasted cauliflower. Jesus. And the pan-roasted white fish that serves as our entrée is to die for. Though if it were up to Brenna, Ed Mulder would be choking on his fish and dropping dead at the table.

"How long have you and Jake been together?" Lena Nilsson asks Brenna.

My fake girlfriend manages to find a smile for Nils's wife. "Not long at all. Just a few months."

"We started dating at the start of winter semester," I supply.

"And how does her father feel about that?" Mulder says with a chuckle.

Her father. Rather than pose the question to Brenna herself, he asks *me*, and I notice Brenna's fingers tighten around her fork. She looks like she wants to take that fork and stab Mulder in the eye with it.

Instead, she answers for me. "My father doesn't know."

His eyebrows sweep upward. "Why's that?"

"We're keeping the relationship under wraps for now. Our hockey teams have been competing against each other all year, and now we'll be facing off in the conference championship." Brenna reaches for her crystal water glass. "We decided it was best not to make waves at the moment."

I look around the table with a grin. "So I'm sure it goes without saying, but on the off chance you run into Coach Chad Jensen, don't mention you saw me with his daughter."

Lena smiles broadly. "That's so romantic! Forbidden love."

Brenna tenses at the L-word. I wink at my soon-to-be-teammate's wife and say, "The best kind."

"Lindsay, these centerpieces are gorgeous," Karen Mulder remarks, changing the subject. "Did you make them yourself?"

Mulder's silent, elegant wife nods demurely. I get the feeling she doesn't talk much. I also get the feeling that's the way Mulder prefers it.

"They're beautiful," Brenna agrees, eyeing the three stained-glass bowls that contain an array of fresh flowers and sprigs of baby's breath.

"It's flowers," Mulder cracks. "Hardly deserving of this fanfare."

His brother Dave guffaws.

"Ed," Lindsay says tightly, and it's the first time she's conveyed any negative emotion toward her husband. Any emotion at all, frankly.

"What?" He polishes off the rest of his white wine. "It's a center-piece, sweetheart. Who cares? It amazes me the crap that you deem important."

Brenna puts her fork down. I see her nostrils flare, her lips part, and I slide my hand under the table to cup her thigh.

Her mouth closes. She turns toward me, but I can't decipher her expression. Meanwhile, her thigh is warm and firm beneath my palm. I can't help myself. I give it a slight caress.

Brenna bites her lower lip.

I hide a smile. Then I stroke her thigh again. I wish I could stroke other parts of her, too. That tight sweater looks so good on her, and my fingers are itching to play with her tits.

Fuck me. I'm desperately hoping this night ends with a hookup. That's why I asked for a real date, because I'm wildly attracted to her and want nothing more than to sleep with her. The last few times I've seen her, my body has responded on a primal level.

And I'm not even hurting for sex, for chrissake. I fooled around with a chick from Boston College last week. We met at a party, hit it off, and she offered me a ride home and proceeded to suck me off in her car. Afterward, we found ourselves in the backseat, and judging by the stars in her eyes when I finally lifted my head from between her legs, I think she was pretty satisfied.

I thought I was satisfied, too. But I've been horny as hell ever since Brenna showed up at the Dime in her sexy halter top and grinded all over my teammate. And then the indecent dress she wore to Danny's metal show? Christ. I'm aching for this girl.

For the rest of the dinner, we mostly discuss hockey. Brenna wasn't kidding—Ed Mulder is obsessed with the Oilers and knows everything about them. Over dessert, he goes on and on about the most recent draft, grilling Nils about the latest picks and what Nils thinks of all the new talent.

Although I feel bad about it, I start paying more attention to Mulder than Brenna.

Her accusatory gaze bores into my cheek as Mulder, Nils, and I dissect the incoming rookie class. But I pretend not to notice her displeasure, because, hell, this is my career, too. I'm literally having dinner with my future teammate. Of course I'm going to give him priority.

Brenna's volcanic anger is beginning to feel almost stifling, while the Oilers details that Nils is spilling are energizing and interesting as hell. Maybe it makes me an ass, but my attention is becoming increasingly focused on the good stuff about my future, rather than the bad shit about Brenna and Mulder.

The girls I dated in high school constantly accused me of being selfish and obsessed with hockey, but what's wrong with that? I've worked my entire life to become a professional hockey player. I haven't led women on or made them any promises. I'm always clear from the get-go that hockey is my main focus.

So when Mulder suggests we retire to his den for after-dinner drinks, I'm faced with a decision. I can tell that Brenna doesn't like the segregation of the sexes, and I don't blame her. This isn't the olden days.

But Theo Nilsson is gesturing for me to come along, and this is a man I'll be skating with in the fall, and at the end of the day, I'm a selfish prick.

So I follow him.

"You're pissed," I say.

"Whatever do you mean, Jake? Why on *earth* would I be pissed?"

The sarcasm is strong with this one, my friends.

And I completely deserve it. I spent more than an hour in Mulder's man-cave tonight. Now it's ten o'clock and we're outside waiting for our car, and Brenna refuses to even look at me.

"Oh, I know!" she continues, scorn dripping from her tone. "You mean because I was banished to the sitting room with the other women, where we clutched our pearls and fainted a whole bunch just so we could wake each other up with smelling salts?"

"That is super fucked up. Is that what you think they did back in the day?"

"They may as well have!" Her cheeks are flushed with anger. "Do you realize what a slap in the face that was? Watching you waltz off to talk about sports with *the man who's interviewing me for a position in sports?*"

Remorse ripples inside me. "I know." I let out a breath. "I knew it was a dick move when I did it."

"And yet you did it anyway." Her eyes blaze. "Because you're a dick."

"Hey, one dick move doesn't make me a dick," I protest. "And look, you have to admit, self-interest was your sole motivation tonight, too. You wanted to talk to Mulder about the internship and prove that you were fit for the job. Well, I wanted to prove that I was fit for my job."

"Self-interest was never your motivation, though. You didn't even know Theo Nilsson was going to be there tonight."

"Yeah, it's called adapting. Nils was there, and I decided to take advantage. You would've done the same thing."

"You were supposed to be my hype man, Connelly. And instead you hyped yourself up the whole time. This was such a waste of time," she grumbles. "I should've asked somebody else to come with me. I should've brought McCarthy."

"First off, you wouldn't have even been invited if you hadn't name-dropped me," I point out. "So there'd have been no need to ask *anybody*. And secondly, I'm pretty sure the McCarthy train has left the station. Last I heard, he hooked up with some girl after the semifinals and has seen her every day since."

Brenna glowers at me.

"What?" I say with a shrug. "Don't shoot the messenger."

"You think I care that McCarthy is seeing someone else?" She gives me an incredulous look. "I was over that guy the second he let *you* decide what he could do with his dick. What I care about is the fact that you didn't have my back in there."

"Only at the end," I argue. "The rest of the time, I was totally hyping you up. You know I was."

She doesn't answer. And then our car arrives and she stomps toward it. Originally I set the drop-off location as the train station for Brenna, but now I lean into the front seat and tap the driver's shoulder. "Hey, we're actually going somewhere else first. Could you drop us at O'Malley's on Boylston?"

Brenna swivels her head. "No. We're going to the station."

The man's gaze shifts back and forth between us.

"Come on," I murmur to Brenna. "You know you need a drink." I don't think she consumed a single drop of alcohol tonight. The other women were all sipping on rosé. "A real drink," I coax.

"Fine. O'Malley's," she mutters to the driver.

A short while later, we're sitting across from each other in a cramped booth. The pub is stuffed to the gills with the Friday-night crowd, but we lucked out and showed up at the same time another couple was leaving. Neither of us says a word as we wait for the waitress to come and take our order. It's so loud in here that the curly-haired redhead has to shout just to say hello.

Brenna examines the menu, then lifts her head. "What did you guys drink in Mulder's study?" she says tersely.

"Cognac," I admit.

"Rémy Martin?"

"Hennessy, neat."

"We'll take two of those, please," she tells the waitress.

"Coming right up," the redhead chirps.

Once the server's gone, I gaze at Brenna with genuine regret. "I'm sorry I went to the man-cave without you. I really do feel bad for that."

"Sure," she says.

Her tone is lacking in sarcasm, so I think she's being sincere. Only I'm not clear on what she's being sincere about. "Is that you accepting the apology or just acknowledging it?" I demand.

"It's whatever you want it to be, Jakey."

Thank God. The Jensen I've come to appreciate is back in full form, complete with the tiny smirk curving her lips. I missed seeing it tonight.

"Mulder was a douchebag," I say frankly. "Do you honestly want to work for someone like him?"

"I guarantee you that every network in the world employs a douchebag or two. And I wouldn't be working directly under him. I'd report to one of the lower-level producers and probably wouldn't have much contact with Mulder. I hope." Her expression becomes bittersweet. "They gave me a tour of the station on Monday and I got to see the *Hockey Corner* set. It was so cool."

"Kip and Trevor? I love those guys! Imagine how sick it would be to guest on their show?"

"Hey, a guest spot might very well be in your future, Mr. Hockey Star."

"What about you? Would you want to be on camera or behind it?" I wink. "I recommend on camera. Think of all the boners you'd inspire in the male demographic."

"Gee, the idea of all those hockey fans jerking off to me is so thrilling! Every little girl's dream."

I'm gratified to see that she's starting to relax. Her shoulders are finally loosening after being stiffer than boards all evening. When the waitress returns with two tumblers of cognac, I raise my glass to Brenna's.

"Cheers," I prompt.

After a beat of hesitation, she taps my glass with hers. "Cheers," she echoes.

We drink, eyeing each other over the rims of our respective glasses.

"I'm curious," I say.

She takes another sip. "About what?"

"Is your father the reason you want this internship so bad? Did he push you into it? Or maybe you're hoping to impress him?"

Brenna rolls her eyes. "No, no, and no. Obviously my dad is the reason I started watching hockey, but he couldn't make me love it. The game itself was responsible for that."

"What was it like growing up with him? He seems like such a hard-ass."

"He is."

She doesn't elaborate, which triggers a rush of wariness.

When she notices my face, she says, "Relax, my childhood was normal. Dad wasn't abusive or anything like that. We're just not as close as we used to be. And yeah, he can be a total ass sometimes. His way or the highway, you know? I guess it's a coach thing."

I think of my own coach and the expression he gets any time someone mentions Chad Jensen. "Coach Pedersen hates your dad."

"The feeling is mutual. They have history, though."

"History," I echo, shaking my head at the concept. "History is such bullshit. I don't get why people can't let things go. Why can't they leave the past in the past? It's over—what do we gain from stewing about it?"

"That's true." A pensive glimmer crosses her gaze. "I try not to think about the past, ever."

"Didn't you just tell me that your past wasn't dark and twisted?"

"No, I told you my childhood was normal. I never said there was nothing dark and twisted in my past."

Because *that's* not intriguing. "Let me guess. You're not going to tell me about it."

"Good guess."

We sip our cognac. I watch her lips, the way the bottom one clings to the rim of her glass before she sets it down. Her tongue peeks out to lick at the drop of moisture left on that lip. I'm obsessed with her lips.

"What are you thinking about right now?" Brenna asks.

"You don't want to know."

"Try me."

"I'm thinking about your lips."

The lips in question curve slowly. "What about them?"

"I'm wondering what they taste like."

"Probably like cognac."

I put down my glass and slide out of the booth.

"Where are you—" She halts when I squeeze my big frame in beside her. "I'm not in the mood, Connelly."

"Not in the mood for what?" We're sitting so close that our thighs are touching. I stretch one arm along the top of the booth, rest my other forearm on the table, and angle my body towards hers. "Come on, don't you want to find out?"

"Find out what?"

"If there's sparks."

"Sparks are overrated."

"I disagree." I lick my bottom lip, and her gaze tracks the movement of my tongue.

Brenna sighs. "You're very sexy."

I grin. "I know."

"You're very cocky."

"I know that, too."

She sweeps her hair over one shoulder. I don't know if she's intentionally trying to draw my attention to her neck, but that's where it goes. I want to bury my face against that long, sleek column and breathe her in.

"You're very sexy." I echo her previous remark, my voice coming out hoarse.

She smirks. "I know."

"And cocky."

"That, too."

"Guess that makes us two peas in a pod?"

"Maybe. And that's probably why we'd never work."

I tip my head. "Work...what do you mean, work?"

"As a couple."

My answering laugh is low, seductive. "Who says I want us to be a couple? Right now I want to see if there's chemistry."

Brenna leans in closer, her warm breath tickling my jaw. She places one hand on my knee and strokes me with her thumb before gliding her hand very slowly toward my crotch. There's no possible way she can miss the bulge in my pants. She doesn't cup or squeeze it. But one fingernail scrapes along the edge of the hard ridge, and I groan out loud.

"Of course we have chemistry," she says, her perfect mouth inches from my face. "We both know we have chemistry. There's never been a single doubt as to whether or not we have chemistry." She flicks up an eyebrow. "So why don't you cut this bullshit about needing to find out, and just tell me what you really want."

"Fine," I answer, because I'm not one to back down from a challenge. "I want to kiss you."

16
BRENNA

Nothing good can come from kissing Jake. But my defenses are weak at the moment. Ed Mulder chipped away at my armor all night, once again proving that every interaction with that man is a complete waste of time. Thanks to him, my nerves are raw, and my stomach is full of cognac.

And Jake is seriously attractive. His chiseled face could stop traffic. His broad, athletic body could cause a ten-car pileup. Basically, if you're in a car and spot Jake Connelly? You're in grave danger.

I eye his lips. They're not pouty, but the bottom one is a tad fuller than the top. I can't deny that when those lips brushed mine at the concert last weekend, I wanted more. I wanted a real kiss. And I still want it now. I want to taste him. To hear the sound he makes when my tongue slips into his mouth.

Anticipation quickens my pulse. "One kiss," I concede.

"You won't be satisfied with just one."

The arrogant gleam in his eyes is such a turn-on for me. I like guys like this. Direct, assertive, and self-assured. Alpha, but not the kind of alpha that orders you around and gets too overbearing.

Jake possesses an easy confidence, a surety about who he is and what he wants. I guess that's why I was so quick to forgive him for his behavior at the dinner party. Not only do I have a slight (okay, fine, more than *slight*) fondness for cocky asses, but I appreciate a man who goes after what he wants. That's the difference between Jake and someone like Mike Hollis. Hollis is confident, but at the end of the day he's not the guy who'd slide into my side of the booth and tell me he's going to kiss me. Hollis would wait for me to kiss him.

And *why* am I thinking about Hollis right now?

I trail my fingers up Jake's thigh and inch them toward his chest. His muscles are so defined I can feel the tantalizing ridges even with him wearing a shirt. I stroke him over his dark-blue button-down, a quick tease that brings heat to his eyes. When my fingers reach his collarbone, his Adam's apple twitches as he gulps.

I smile faintly. "Everything all right?"

"Good. I'm good." He clears his throat.

My hand reaches its destination—his insanely beautiful face. I rub his bottom lip with the pad of my thumb. His gaze grows impossibly hotter. Before I can blink, long fingers tangle in my hair and there's a big hand cupping the back of my neck.

Jake brings my head forward and slants his lips over mine, and it's the kind of kiss that's been missing from my life for so long. One that starts off as a slow burn, a soft meeting of lips and the feather-light flick of the tongue. It's like he's laying the groundwork for something fierce. He's building a fire, each teasing kiss serving as the kindling, until finally he unleashes a groan, drives the kiss deeper, and the fire engulfs us. His mouth is hot and hungry, but he doesn't try to lick my face off or swallow me whole. It's a controlled kiss, firm but greedy, thick with passion and the perfect amount of tongue.

I moan. I can't help it. He chuckles against my lips before pulling back. "You're a good kisser," he rasps.

"Not so bad yourself." And then we're devouring each other's mouths again, making out hardcore in this booth, and I don't even flinch when I register the sound of catcalls over the music. Let everyone around us watch. Give them popcorn for all I care.

That girl in the bathroom last week, the one who praised Jake's tongue, was right on the money. His tongue is incredible. Feels like heaven in my mouth. And his big, warm hand is now squeezing my thigh. I want to climb into his lap and maul him, but we're at a bar, and we're fully clothed. The fact that we're in public is the only thing saving me from making a really stupid decision.

I pull away, breathing heavily. Jake's gorgeous eyes peer back at me. A deep, dark green, like the jungle after a heavy rainfall. I can see why women go a little nutty for him.

I gulp down a hasty swig of cognac, then jerk when he takes the tumbler from my hand. Callused fingertips rub over my knuckles. I shiver.

"That was mine," I accuse as he finishes my drink.

"We'll order another round."

"Probably not a good idea." My voice sounds gravelly, so I clear my throat. Twice. "I should go."

Jake nods. "Okay. Let me grab the check."

I gesture to our empty glasses. "By the way, this counts as our date."

He lets out a low, sexy laugh. "Dream on. This ain't the date. This is still me being your fake boyfriend."

"Oh really? Was that a fake make-out?"

"This isn't the real date," he says sternly. "But we should probably schedule that. When are you free?"

"Never."

"How about tomorrow?"

Back-to-back nights? Is he nuts? I don't even do that with the people I date for real. "Wow. You're dying to see me again, huh?"

"Yes," he admits, and my heart betrays me by skipping a beat. "So. Tomorrow?"

I cave like a house of cards. "Fine. But I'm not coming back to Boston. In one week I've spent enough time in this city to last me a lifetime."

"I'll pick somewhere closer to Hastings," he assures me. "I'll have Brooks's car—should I come get you?"

"Absolutely not." There's no way I'm letting Jake show up on my father's doorstep to pick me up for a date. "Unless you're in the mood to get murdered."

He chuckles knowingly. "I hoped you'd say no, but I'm a gentleman so I had to ask. I'll pay your cab fare, though."

"I don't need your charity," I mock.

"You just like being difficult, don't ya?"

"Yup." I rummage in my purse for my wallet.

"Want to make out some more before we go?" Jake's tone is boyishly hopeful.

"Nope."

His gaze turns devilish. "How about a blowjob?"

"Aw, I appreciate the offer, but I don't have a penis."

Jake's laughter heats my blood. It's deep and husky and I want to record it so I can hear it whenever I want. Which is beyond creepy and insanely unsettling. I'm starting to enjoy this guy's company, and that worries me. A lot.

"You got in late last night." My father's disapproval greets me when I walk into the kitchen the next morning. "Out partying, I suppose?"

I stick my head in the fridge and roll my eyes at a tub of margarine, because I can't do it to his face. "I got home around midnight, Dad. On a Friday night. And I had to catch an eleven o'clock train in order for me to get back here for midnight. So really, I was done 'partying'—" I turn so he can see the air quotes. "—at eleven. On a Friday night."

"You're too old to be giving me sass."

"And I'm too old to be reprimanded about my social life. We talked about this. You said you wouldn't lecture."

"No, you talked about it. And I didn't say a damn thing." He's not afraid to openly roll his eyes. He brushes by me in his plaid pants, wool socks, and pullover sweater with the Briar hockey logo on it.

He stops at the coffee maker, the fancy one Aunt Sheryl got him for Christmas last year. I'm surprised that he's using it. Dad doesn't care if a product has all the bells and whistles, unless it's state-of-the-art hockey equipment. Otherwise he doesn't give a shit.

"Want a cup?" he offers.

"No, thanks." I hop onto one of the stools at the kitchen counter. The legs are uneven, so it wobbles for a beat before finding its equilibrium. I open a mini yogurt and scarf it down, while Dad stands near the sink, waiting for his coffee to brew.

"You didn't have to take the train," he says gruffly. "You could've borrowed the Jeep."

"Seriously? I'm allowed to drive the precious Jeep again? I thought I was banned after the mailbox incident."

"You were. But that was, what? Two years ago? One would hope that you've smartened up since then and learned how to drive properly."

"One would hope." I swallow another spoonful of yogurt. "I don't mind taking the train. It gives me time to get my course readings done and read all the game highlights. So this weekend is the charity game, right?"

Dad nods, but he doesn't look thrilled about it. This year the Division I Hockey Committee decided that every team would participate in a charity exhibition the weekend before the conference finals, rather than immediately playing the final game after the semifinal round. The exhibitions are hosted by various cancer societies throughout the country, and all proceeds from ticket sales and concessions go to these charities. It's obviously a great cause, but I know Dad and his players are anxious for the finals.

"And what about the finals? Are you guys ready?"

He gives another nod. Somehow he manages to cram so much confidence into one nod. "We will be."

"The Crimson'll be tough to beat."

"Yes. They will be." That's my dad, a gifted conversationalist.

I scrape the last bit of yogurt out of the plastic container. "They're good this year," I remark. "They're very, very good."

Not just at playing hockey, either. Jake Connelly, for example, is highly skilled in other areas. Like kissing. And turning me on. And—

And I need to derail this train of thought, pronto. Because now my body is tingling, and I'm not allowed to be tingling in such close proximity to my father.

"You know, you're allowed to say a nice thing or two about Harvard," I tell him. "Just because you hate the coach doesn't mean the players are terrible."

"Some of them are good," he acknowledges. "And some of them are good but dirty."

"Like Brooks Weston."

He nods again. "Kid's a goon, and Pedersen encourages it." There's venom in his voice when he says Pedersen's name.

"What kind of player was he?" I ask curiously. "Pedersen, that is."

Dad's features grow taut, tension rippling from his broad frame. "What do you mean?"

"I mean, you played with him at Yale. You were on the same team for at least a couple seasons, right?"

"Right." Now his tone is guarded.

"So what kind of player was he?" I repeat. "A power forward? An enforcer? Did he play dirty?"

"Dirty as mud. I never respected his gameplay."

"And now you don't respect his coaching."

"Nope." Dad takes a long sip of his coffee, watching me over the rim. "Are you saying you do?"

I think it over. "Yes and no. I mean, there's dirty gameplay, and then there's rough gameplay. A lot of coaches encourage their players to play rough," I point out.

"Doesn't make it right. It promotes violence."

I have to laugh. "Hockey is one of the most violent sports there is! We've got guys skating around on ice with sharp blades on their feet, holding big sticks. They get slammed into the boards, they're hit over and over again, they take pucks to the face..."

"Exactly. The sport is already violent enough," Dad agrees. "So why make it even more so? Play clean and play honorably." His jaw tightens. "Daryl Pedersen doesn't know the meaning of clean or honor."

He makes a valid point. And I suppose I can't ascertain one way or the other about Pedersen's level of dirtiness. I've only seen a couple of Harvard games this season, which makes it difficult to accurately gauge how dirty those boys play.

I know how dirty Jake kisses. Does that count?

"What do you have planned for today?" Dad asks, changing the subject.

"I need to finish up an article for my News Writing class, but I'll probably do that later. I'm heading over to Summer's house now."

"On Saturday morning?"

"Yeah, she wants me to help her clean out her closet."

"I don't understand women," Dad says.

"We are pretty fucking weird. I'll give you that."

"I've heard things about that girl Summer," he adds, his trademark frown marring his face.

I frown back. "She's a good friend of mine."

"Her brother said she was nuts."

"Well, yeah. I can't deny that. She's strange and melodramatic and hilarious. But you shouldn't believe everything Dean says, anyway."

"He said she burned down her school."

I grin at him. "Considering Brown University is still standing, I think we can assume Dean exaggerated." I slide off the stool. "I need to get dressed. I'll see you later."

An hour later, I'm lying on Summer's bed scrolling through my phone. Needless to say, watching her try on every outfit in her closet and then model it for me got real old, real fast.

"Bee!" she complains. "Pay attention."

I put the phone down and move into a sitting position. "No," I announce. "Because this is insanity. You just tried on four different cashmere sweaters in the same shade of white. They were identical. And they all looked brand new!"

She starts to give me a whole speech about Prada versus Gucci versus Chanel until I hold up my hand to stop her, because I swear to God if she goes on about Chanel, I'm going to lose it. She's obsessed with that fashion house and, unchecked, could talk about it for hours.

"I get it, they're designer sweaters. But the whole point of spring cleaning is to get rid of stuff—and you haven't thrown out a single thing." I jab my finger at the meager pile of clothing at the foot of the bed. It's the donation pile, and it consists of two T-shirts, a pair of jeans, and one cardigan.

"I have a hard time letting go of things," she huffs, whipping her blonde hair over her shoulder.

"Don't you have a walk-in closet at your place in Greenwich? And another one in Manhattan?"

"Yes. So?"

"So nobody needs that many closets, Summer! I get by with a handful of outfits that I rotate."

"You only wear black," she retorts. "Of course it's easy to throw an outfit together when all you wear is black. You don't give a shit about fashion—you put on a black shirt and black pants and black boots and red lipstick and you're done. Well, black isn't my color. It makes me look too BDSM. I need color, Brenna! My life is colorful. I'm a colorful person—"

"You're a crazy person," I counter.

"I am not crazy."

"Yes, you are," her boyfriend confirms as he waltzes into the room. Fitz's full-sleeve tattoos ripple as he wraps his arms around Summer from behind, bending his head to plant a sweet kiss on her cheek.

"I hate you two," I grumble. "You're so disgustingly happy. Go be happy somewhere else."

"Sorry, Bee, but we're not going to hide our love from the world," Summer says, and begins peppering kisses all over Fitz's cheek, making loud smooch noises that make me want to vomit.

Well, not quite, but I pretend to gag because she is being ridiculous.

"What are you guys up to?" Fitz glances at me. "I didn't even realize you were here."

"You were sleeping when Bee got here," Summer says. "We're cleaning out my closet. I'm donating a bunch of stuff."

He looks at the full closet and then the tiny pile on the bed. "Cool. Did you just get started?"

I snort. "We've been at it for more than an hour! In one hour she's decided to give away a T-shirt."

"It's more than a T-shirt," Summer protests.

Our voices lure Hollis in from the hall. He wanders into Summer's room and flops down near the foot of her bed. He's in sweatpants and a tank top, and when his bare feet knock over the meager donation pile, he doesn't even notice.

"Sweet. Are you trying on clothes for us? When do we get to lingerie? Fitz, tell your girlfriend I require a lingerie fashion show as a reward for the emotional distress she's caused me."

"What are you babbling about now?" I ask him.

I'm at the head of the bed, so he has to crane his neck to meet my eyes. "Summer told me what you assholes did to me."

I give him a blank look.

"My stalker?" he prompts. "I know you encouraged it."

"She's not stalking you," Summer argues.

"Are you serious?" Hollis gapes at her. "She's called me *every single day* since we went out for dinner."

"You went out on Thursday," Summer reminds him. "That was literally two days ago. Which means she's called you twice. Chill the eff out."

"Twice? I fucking wish! She calls *at least* three times a day."

"Yeah, and you pick up *every* time," Summer shoots back, "and talk to her for an hour, sometimes more."

"*I* talk?" He rakes both hands through his hair. "*She* talks! That chick doesn't shut up."

"I assume we're talking about Rupi?" I hedge, fighting laughter.

"Of course we're talking about Rupi!" he roars. "She's kind of bananas, you realize that, right? Are you sure she didn't come from one of those woo-woo self-discovery spa retreat places in Bali?"

"Bali?" I echo.

"She said that's where her mom is from. She's some movie star in Bali."

"A *Bollywood* star." Summer giggles. "That means India, not Bali."

"Oh." He thinks it over, then shakes his head. "Nope, that doesn't make it better. She's still nuts."

"How did the dinner go?" I ask him.

He twists around to glare at me.

I blink politely. "Not well?"

His face is cloudy. "She talked the entire time, and she wouldn't even let me kiss her good night."

"Wait, you're saying you *wanted* to kiss her good night?" Fitz speaks up. He's leaning on the edge of Summer's desk. His girlfriend, meanwhile, is back inside her closet, flipping through hangers.

"That's exactly what I'm saying, *Colin*," Hollis says haughtily. "Just because she's weird doesn't mean I don't want to make out with her."

"Classy," I tell him. "You're a real romantic at heart."

He waggles his eyebrows. "Hey, the Hollis store is still open. Pop in whenever you want, Jensen."

"Pass. Anyway, so no kiss, huh?"

"Nope!" He looks outraged. "She doesn't kiss on the first date. She's making me wait! Until date *three*."

Fitz doubles over in laughter. "Hold on a sec," he wheezes. "You're going out with her again?"

I snicker. "Two more times?"

"I don't think I have a choice," Hollis moans. "Apparently I'm taking her to a movie on Tuesday."

Fitz nods. "Nice. It's half-price on Tuesdays. You should go see the new Marvel movie."

"I don't want to see the new Marvel movie, you jackass. I don't want to go out with this girl. She's too young and too annoying and—" He startles, then sticks his hand in the pocket of his sweatpants. He produces his phone and blanches at the screen. "Oh my God, it's her."

"You saved her in your phone?" I demand.

"*She* did. She grabbed my phone in the middle of dinner and created a contact for herself. She saved it as Rupi with the heart-eyes emoji. She's in my phone with heart-eyes, for fuck's sake."

I roll onto my side and quake with silent laughter.

At the desk, Fitz is shaking his head in amusement. "You know you can change that, right?"

Hollis is too busy answering the call. He barely gets out a "hello" before excited chatter pours out of his phone.

Fitz and I exchange a grin. I have no idea what Rupi's saying, but she's talking a mile a minute, and the horrified expression on Hollis's face is priceless. This is the most entertainment I've had in years.

"But I don't like romantic comedies," he whines.

The tinny chattering continues.

"No, I don't. I don't want to see a movie. If you're so determined to hang out, then let's go somewhere and bang."

Shrieking ensues.

I curl over in hysterics.

"Holy shit, fine! We'll go see your stupid movie, but you better make out with me, Rupi, and don't give me any bullshit about not kissing on the second date, because if you were any other chick we'd already be banging."

The rest of the world no longer exists to Mike Hollis. He climbs off the bed and wanders out of Summer's room. His flustered voice drifts in from the hall. "I am not a sex maniac! I haven't had sex since I met you."

I glance at Fitz. "Is that true?"

"I think so. But let's be real—it's not like he was a hookup king before that. He talks a big game, but he's actually a lot pickier than he lets on. I don't believe he gets laid half as often as he claims."

"Oh, he definitely doesn't," comes Summer's muffled response from the closet. "That boy has no game whatsoever."

"He's a hockey player," I point out. "Hockey players don't need much game off the ice. The groupies are always happy to see them."

"What do you guys think about this dress?" Summer reappears wearing a white strapless number with fringe on the hem.

"It's nice," her boyfriend says.

"Bee?"

"Way too innocent. I'd never wear it."

"Of course you wouldn't wear it—it's not black. Tell me whether or not *I* look good in it."

"You look good in everything. It's disgusting and I hate you, and seriously, you can get rid of half that closet and still look like a supermodel in whatever's left."

She beams. "You're right, this is a great dress. I'll keep it."

I exchange another amused glance with Fitz. It still boggles my mind that these two are a couple. Yet somehow the fashion major and the nerdy gamer make it work.

"What are you guys doing tonight?" I ask. "I imagine my dad will be working the team pretty hard this week, so this might be your last chance to unwind, right?"

"For real," Fitz says. "And I don't know, we'll probably just..." He shrugs sheepishly.

Translation: they're going to spend the whole night in bed.

"How about you?" he asks.

"Probably staying home," I lie.

"Really? No repeat with the Tinder date?" Summer rejoins the conversation. She drops two faded sweatshirts in the donate pile.

"What Tinder date?" Fitz demands.

"Bee had a date last night. Which she didn't even tell me about."

"There's nothing to tell. We didn't click, and I'm not seeing him again." It's disturbing how naturally lying comes to me.

Summer offers an apologetic smile. "We'd invite you to hang out with us tonight, but we're going to be very busy having sex."

Fitz sighs heavily. "Babe."

"What?"

He just shakes his head.

"Don't worry about it," I say, grinning at them. "I have a ton of homework to do, anyway."

"Sounds exciting," Summer teases.

She doesn't know the half of it.

17
BRENNA

JAKE TEXTS ME THE LOCATION OF OUR DATE WHILE I'M EATING dinner with my father. We're having vegetable stir-fry that I cooked, and it's been a mostly silent meal, seeing as how we don't have much to say to each other these days.

When he notices my phone light up, a deep groove appears in his forehead. "No phones at the dinner table."

"I'm not even checking it," I protest. "I can't control it from going off."

"Sure you can. It's called the power button."

I glance pointedly at the phone near his right hand. He's already received four emails since we sat down. "You can turn yours off, too."

We stare at each other. Dad makes a grouchy sound, twirls some noodles around his fork, and shoves them in his mouth.

I don't open Jake's message until I'm upstairs in my room. My jaw drops when I learn where we're going tonight.

ME: Bowling????
JAKE: What do you have against bowling?
ME: Nothing. But I suck at it, so if you're hoping for any sort of competition, you won't get it from me.
JAKE: No competition necessary. Let's just have fun. You cool with it?

ME: Sure, what the hell.
JAKE: Meet around 8?
ME: Sounds good.

That gives me an hour and a half to get ready, but I've already decided I won't go to great lengths to look good for Jake. The only reason I'm going out with him tonight is because he came to the dinner party with me.

Once I'm showered and dressed, I pull up Google Maps and load the address of the bowling alley. It's a twenty-five-minute drive, which makes it much closer to Hastings than Cambridge.

A while later, I go downstairs and linger in the living room doorway. Dad's on the couch, fast-forwarding through the Harvard-Princeton game from last weekend. Jake is a streak of lightning across the screen, and I wonder if my father would appreciate the irony that I'm about to go meet Jake in person.

"Hey," I say to get his attention. "I wanted to see if I could borrow the Jeep. I'm meeting a friend tonight."

"All these mysterious friends," he mutters, his eyes remaining glued to the screen. "Do any of these friends have names?"

"They sure do." But I don't offer them.

Dad snorts. "The keys are in the front hall. Try to be back at a reasonable time."

I want to say something snarky, but he's lending me his car, so I refrain. "Don't wait up," I say instead.

Jake is already there when I pull into the nearly empty parking lot in front of Bowl-Me-Up. The name of the bowling alley is perplexing to me. Maybe it's supposed to be a play on "Beam me up"? But a dated sci-fi reference doesn't quite convey bowling, so I'm not sure what they were really going for.

I park the Jeep next to the shiny Mercedes that Jake is leaning against. Along with our cars, the lot contains a sedan, a pickup truck, and five or six motorcycles parked near the front doors. It's basically a ghost lot. "Nice wheels," I remark as I jump out of the Jeep. "Did you buy that with your signing bonus?"

"Nope. I haven't spent a dime of it, actually," Jake admits. "This is Brooks's car."

"Why does he need a car in the city?"

"Because he's a millionaire, and millionaires own cars. Jeez, Hottie."

I have to laugh. "Makes perfect sense to me." I gaze up at the massive sign above our heads. Next to the words Bowl-Me-Up is a huge neon-pink bowling ball that keeps flickering. "You come here often?" I ask dryly.

"Every weekend during the off-season. This place is dear to my heart."

That catches me by surprise. "Really?"

"No. Of course not. I picked it because it's roughly halfway between our houses." He snorts. "So gullible."

"Yeah, that's on me," I say with a sigh. "I should've known better than to believe you have a heart." I lock the Jeep and tuck the keys in my purse.

As we walk toward the entrance, I notice Jake slowing his long gait to match my much shorter one. "I totally have a heart," he argues. "Here, feel."

Next thing I know, he's grabbing my hand and placing it inside his unzipped coat. Man, oh man, his pecs are delicious. And I can feel his pulse fluttering beneath my fingers.

"Your heart's beating fast, Connelly. You worried I'm going to kick your butt in there?"

"Not in the slightest. You already told me you sucked."

Damn. He's right. I chide myself for telegraphing my suckiness in advance.

Inside, we encounter another ghost town. The bowling alley consists of ten lanes, and only two of them are in use. At the main counter stands a gray-haired gentleman with leathery skin that hints at too many years in the sun. He greets us with a smile that crinkles the corners of his mouth.

"Evening, folks! How 'bout some shoes?" His voice is so raspy, it sounds like he smokes two packs of cigarettes a day.

We get our bowling shoes, and the old man with the gray ponytail tells us we can take any available lane. We choose the one that's farthest away from the other patrons—an older couple, and a group of scary-looking bikers who've been taunting and catcalling each other since Jake and I walked in. One of them, an overweight guy with a bushy beard, just bowled a strike and he thrusts his arms up in a victory pose.

"That's what I'm talkin' about, motherfucker!" he shouts.

The man behind the counter winces. "Don't mind those fellas. They're harmless, but someone needs to wash their mouths out with soap."

"It's all right," I tell him. "My dad coaches hockey players. I've heard worse."

We head over to our lane and sit down in the seating area to switch shoes. My boots take longer to remove because of all the zippers, so Jake's done before I am. "I'll grab some drinks," he offers. "Any preference? Beer? Soda?"

"Beer's good. Thanks." I'm okay to have a beer or two. I'll nurse them throughout the night.

"Cool," he says before sauntering off.

I stare at his retreating back and admire his tight backside. God. I can't believe I'm on a date with Jake Connelly. What is life?

Sighing, I slip into the really dorky bowling shoes, and then walk up to the screen that instructs me to enter our names. On the Player One line, I type *Brenna*.

For Player Two, I type *Little Jakey*.

I lock it in, and I'm still grinning to myself when Jake comes back carrying two bottles of Bud Light.

I grimace. "Bud Light?"

"All they had," he says ruefully. "This ain't exactly a classy joint."

"We'll make do," I assure him. "Thank you." I accept the bottle he hands me and take a quick sip. Ick. This is my least favorite beer brand.

"Let me enter our names in the—" Jake stops, noticing the overhead screen. He sighs. "Really? What are you, a five-year-old?"

"No, but it sounds like you are, Little Jakey."

"I'll show you who's little," he growls.

"What are you gonna do, whip your dick out right here in front of the Sons of Anarchy and that nice old man?"

Jake pretends to think it over. "You're right. I'll save that move for later." He holds out his bottle. "Cheers."

"Cheers."

For the second night in a row, we clink our drinks together. This is all sorts of wrong, and not only because he plays for Harvard. I don't usually date. I haven't had a serious boyfriend since Eric, and I haven't wanted one. And for argument's sake, even if I did want a boyfriend, Jake is the last candidate I should consider for that position. He's moving to Edmonton in a few months. What kind of relationship could we even have?

I look around the not-so-lively bowling alley, taking in the sounds and sights. Pins smashing together, the loud chatter of the bikers, the bright lights, the shiny wood surface of the long lanes.

What am I doing here?

"Brenna."

A hot shiver rolls through me at the sound of my name on Jake's lips. Which further solidifies my conviction that I shouldn't be here. I hate how much he affects me.

"You're overthinking," he says bluntly.

I lick my suddenly dry lips. "How do you know that?"

"You always get the same look on your face when you're analyzing something." He shrugs. "You're questioning why you're here."

"Aren't you?"

"No. I told you, we've got chemistry and I want to see where it goes."

I blow out a breath. "It won't go anywhere, Connelly, so get that idea out of your head. The only reason I'm here is because you bullied me into a date."

"Keep telling yourself that, babe."

Do I feel a little bit tingly when he calls me babe? Yes.

Do I like the sensation? Not at all.

I take a desperate gulp of my beer and then set the bottle down on the ledge. "All right. Let's do this thing."

18
JAKE

BRENNA IS A TERRIBLE BOWLER, BUT SHE'S DAMN FUN TO WATCH. She saunters up to the foul line in those abysmal shoes, her hips swaying and her ass looking phenomenal in those tight, black jeans. I'm an ass man, and I can't take my gaze off her backside.

Despite the fact that she sucks at bowling, she gives every frame one hundred and ten percent. Concentration creases her features as she swings her arm back, rotates her wrist, and releases the bright pink ball. Her timing is off and her follow-through is nonexistent, but for the first time in six frames, the ball moves in a straight line.

Brenna cheers happily as her ball careens toward the jackpot. At the last second it veers, knocking over four pins instead of giving her the strike.

"So close!" she wails.

Then she turns around and she's never looked more beautiful to me. Her cheeks are like two red apples, her eyes are sparkling, and she performs a cute little dance as she shimmies off the shiny floor.

"I'm getting better!" she exclaims.

"Nowhere to go but up," I agree, and then I get up and bowl a strike.

"I hate you," she announces when my score appears on the screen.

I'm beating her in the ass-kicking of the century, but I don't think she truly cares. To be honest, I'm not paying much attention to the score. Usually I'm competitive as fuck, but tonight I'm just happy to hang out with Brenna. It's been ages since I've been on a real date. Last night's dinner party doesn't count, because neither of us had much fun. And the cognac at the bar afterward doesn't count either, because we did more kissing than talking.

Tonight allows me to see Brenna in a way I haven't seen before. Bowling isn't the most romantic of activities, but it can give you insight into a person's nature. Are they competitive? Petty? Are they a sore loser, or, worse, a sore winner? And with girls specifically, a bowling date can reveal whether a chick is high-maintenance. I know women who would turn their noses up at the alley's sticky floors or crappy beer. But not Brenna.

After I win the first game, it's Brenna who suggests another one. "Ha!" I gloat. "You like bowling."

"I do." She heaves an overdramatic sigh. "I'm really into this."

I study her to see if she's fucking with me. But there isn't an ounce of fuckery on her face.

"I'm serious. This is awesome." She shakes her head in amazement. "I think I actually like bowling."

Her visible shock makes me double over in laughter. Once I've recovered, I move closer, my tone going serious. "I guess we'll have to do this again sometime…" And then I wait.

She doesn't answer. Instead, she approaches the touchscreen and says, "All right, I'll let Little Jakey go first this time."

But when my name flashes on the screen, it simply reads: Jake.

I swallow my satisfaction. I think I'm growing on her.

She's definitely growing on me.

"So are we allowed to talk hockey?" I ask as I walk over to the ball return. I've fallen in love with a neon-green ball I've been calling the Strikemaker.

"What about it?" she asks suspiciously.

"Well, we're playing each other soon. It's a big game."

"It's a big game," she agrees.

"Which raises the question—who will you be rooting for when you're sitting in those stands? Your school or your new boyfriend?" I flash a cheeky smile over my shoulder.

It's her turn to double over in laughter. "You're not my boyfriend."

"That's not what you told Mulder..."

"Mulder is a prick, and I don't feel bad lying to him. Now turn around and bowl, Jakey. I want to check out your ass."

My grin nearly breaks my face in half, and I'm grateful she can't see it. For her benefit, I make a big production out of my turn, flexing my arms, stretching forward in a way that makes my ass stick out. I hear a choked noise from behind me. When I turn my head, there's heat sizzling in Brenna's dark eyes.

"You're such a tease," she accuses.

"I'm just bowling," I say innocently.

"Uh-huh, sure you are." She slides off the chair. "Man, is it hot in here?"

The next thing I know, she's pulling her black long-sleeve shirt over her head, leaving her in a thin black camisole that clings to her perfect tits. I glimpse the lacy cups of her bra peeking out from the neckline, and my mouth goes completely dry. I return to the seating area and grab my beer. We're both on our second beer, but there won't be a third. I told the concessions kid to cut us off after two.

I gulp down the cold liquid as Brenna saunters to get a ball, her gait more seductive than ever. She tosses her long, glossy hair over one shoulder, spins around, and actually licks her lips.

Lord help me.

Her first throw knocks over seven pins.

"That's your best yet!" Standing at the edge of the lane, I offer words of encouragement. "Go for the spare, Hottie. You've got this."

"Really?" she says dubiously. "I haven't bowled a single spare yet."

"So? Doesn't mean it won't happen."

It doesn't happen. Her second ball rolls into the gutter.

"You jinxed me," she complains, trying to brush past me.

I hook an arm around her slender waist before she can escape. I want to tug her body against mine and kiss the hell out of her, but I settle for a chaste peck on the cheek.

"Did you just kiss my cheek?" she asks in amusement.

"Yeah. Got a problem with that?" I rest my hands above her ass, fighting the urge to move them lower. "Your ass looks amazing in these jeans, by the way."

"I know. That's why I wore them."

I chuckle. My palms dip half an inch lower, but then I think, screw it. My back is to the other patrons, and nobody can see what my hands are doing, anyway. So I give her a nice, firm squeeze.

She makes a husky sound. "Dammit, Connelly, we're in public."

"So?"

"So you can't go around squeezing my butt."

"Why not?"

Brenna pauses. Several seconds tick by before she shrugs. "You know, I can't think of a good enough reason."

"Exactly." Grinning, I squeeze those juicy ass cheeks again, then give them a light smack before going to take my next turn.

I don't throw a strike this time. One stubborn pin insists on staying upright, but I knock it over on the second throw. Once again I'm crushing Brenna, and once again she doesn't care. She makes definite progress, though, her second score nearly doubling her score from the first game. After the final numbers flicker on the screen, we sit on the bench and unwind for a bit.

I rest my hand on her thigh, absently stroking. She doesn't push me away, but she does give me a contemplative look. "You're a very handsy guy."

"Is that a problem?"

"No, it's just unexpected. I didn't think you'd be this affectionate."

"Well, I am." I shrug. "With chicks I like."

"And how often do those come along? I thought we established you don't do girlfriends, only hookups."

"That doesn't mean I don't like the girls I hook up with." I trace teasing circles on her knee. "Seems to me you don't do boyfriends, either. Or if you do, it's not public knowledge."

"You been asking around about me, Jakey?"

"Yes," I say bluntly. "And from what I hear, you haven't dated anyone since you transferred to Briar."

"I haven't," she confirms.

"Where did you go before Briar?"

"Community college in New Hampshire."

"Did you date anyone there?"

"Not really. My college track record is mostly a string of meaningless hookups, at least until McCarthy."

Jealousy pricks my chest. I don't like that she doesn't view McCarthy as meaningless. "So McCarthy wasn't a hookup?" I ask carefully.

"A hookup is usually a one-time deal. Josh was more of a…" She mulls it over.

"Fuck buddy?" I fill in.

"Minus the fucking."

Wait, what?

I set my beer on the table. Brenna officially has my undivided attention. "You didn't have sex?" Surprise wrinkles my forehead. I just assumed they'd slept together.

"Nope."

"But you fooled around."

"Yup."

"But no sex."

She looks amused. "What part of this don't you understand?"

"I don't know…I guess it's kind of weird to me." I pause. "No, not kind of. It's very weird to me."

"Why is that weird?" She sounds a tad defensive.

I gesture toward her. "I mean, look at you. You're smoking hot. Are you saying he didn't try to…?"

"I never said he didn't try. But…" She trails off again.

"But what? Are you a virgin?"

"No. I'm just picky about who I let inside me."

Damned if that doesn't make my dick hard. She's not allowed to say things like "inside me," because now I'm picturing being inside her, and I'm horny as hell.

"We did other stuff," she says. "There's always other stuff."

"Is there?" My throat is full of gravel.

"What, no one's ever told you that you can come without having sex?"

"Nah. I didn't know that." I blink with the utmost innocence. "Can you show me?"

Brenna punches my shoulder. Light and teasing. "You wish."

"I do wish. I don't want to alarm you, but please direct your attention to my crotch."

Despite her amusement, she does what I ask. Instantly, her gaze sizzles. "Oh my. Thinking about McCarthy gets you hard?"

"Like stone." I pull her onto my lap, eliciting a squeak of surprise.

But she recovers quickly, and soon she's rubbing that sweet ass all over me as she tries to get comfortable. "Tell your boner to stop stabbing my butt," she grumbles.

"Hey, you're the reason I even have a boner." I tug her head down so I can whisper in her ear. "You're evil, talking about all the ways you can make a guy come without putting him inside you."

Damn, she smells so good. I breathe in the scent of her shampoo, sweet with a mere trace of spice. Which is funny, because Brenna is the exact opposite—spicy, with a hint of sweetness. I like the spice, though. I like it a lot.

"What about you?" I ask her.

"What about me?"

"What did you get out of the McCarthy arrangement?"

She arches a brow. "You really want to know what your teammate did to me?"

"No. Yes. I don't know. Maybe in the broad sense," I finally decide.

"Nah. I'll leave it up to your imagination."

And my imagination is running wild, except I'm not picturing Josh McCarthy in bed with her. I'm picturing myself.

"That thing is going to poke right through your pants," she teases, and I feel a distinct sense of loss when she slides off my lap. "Anyway, what now? Want to play one more game before we take off?" She checks her phone "It's ten. How long is this place open until?"

"I think eleven."

"Should we close it down?"

"Might as well."

Bowling with a stiffy isn't the easiest task, but I manage. I beat her for a third time, and we return our shoes and pay for our lane.

Outside, Brenna bypasses her Jeep and walks to the Mercedes instead. "Unlock it," she orders.

My pulse quickens. I unlock the car.

Rather than open either of the front doors, she settles in the backseat. "Get in here," she says impishly.

I'm not one to keep a lady waiting. I dive into the car, and my mouth is on hers before she can say another word. She tastes like beer and mint, and her body is soft and warm against mine. She crawls into my lap, her tongue hungrily exploring my mouth. I run my hands down the bumps of her spine before digging my fingers into her waist. I want to be *in* her. Desperately. But apparently that isn't something she allows so readily.

"You're not gonna let me fuck you tonight, are you?"

"No." It's a playful whisper. "You have to earn that."

I groan against her lips. "How do I earn it?"

She merely smiles and kisses me again, sliding her hands underneath my shirt to stroke my bare chest. Christ, I love having her hands on me. And I need my hands on *her*. I pull her long-sleeve shirt off and tug her camisole up to her collarbone. The bra beneath it is paper-thin. She doesn't need the padding, though. Her breasts are full, perky, fucking perfect. I tweak her nipples through the lacy material and enjoy the sweet moan I'm rewarded with.

"I've been dying to do this," I growl, yanking the bra down to expose her tits. Goddamn gorgeous. I pull one beaded nipple into my mouth, suck hard, and almost get a contact high. Her skin tastes so good, and her nipple feels like heaven beneath my tongue. I'm painfully aroused as I lick the distended bud.

She moans again. At first I think it's from pleasure, until I register the note of misery.

"What's wrong?" I say immediately.

"I can't believe I'm letting a Harvard player touch my boobs."

I relax. Laughing softly, I flick my tongue against her other nipple. "Hey, it's not like this is your first time with a Harvard player."

"You're the *captain* of the team," she says gloomily. "This is such a bad idea. We're playing you next week, dammit. My friends would be furious if they saw me right now."

"Let's not talk about hockey. And who gives a shit what your friends think." I suck her nipple between my lips.

"I do. I care what my friends think."

"Then you should stop."

My mouth conquers hers in a blistering kiss that robs me of sanity. I flip her over, and now I'm on top of her, grinding my lower body against her. The backseat doesn't offer room to maneuver, but I don't need much. With my lips pressed tight to hers, I undo the button of her jeans and pull them down along with her panties, low enough that I can access the warm paradise between her legs.

She whimpers when I drag the pad of my thumb over her swollen clit. "That feels good."

"Yeah?" I say thickly.

"Oh yeah."

I keep rubbing, teasing, exploring. I skim my fingertips down to her opening and find her impossibly wet. Jesus. I want to be inside her more than I want my next breath. I practically weep at the knowledge that I can't be in there tonight. I dip my fingers in all that sweet moisture and then use it to rub slow circles over her clit.

Her hips start rocking. I prop up on one elbow, watching her expression go hazier and hazier as I play with her pussy. "I like having you like this," I whisper. "On your back. Legs spread." I kiss her again, and she sucks hard on my tongue, summoning a low groan from me.

"This is such a bad idea," she whispers back.

"Then tell me to stop."

"No."

"No what?"

Brenna pushes her pussy into my hand. "Don't stop."

I chuckle against her shoulder before dipping my head so I can suck and lick her nipples again.

She lets out a breathy moan. "Don't *ever* stop."

I smile. I distinctly remember her telling me not so long ago that she would never, ever hook up with me. And now here we are, fooling around in the backseat of a car, her pussy mine to discover. My finger slides inside her and—

"Oh my fucking God," I choke out. My head pops up from her tits. "You're so tight." I wonder if it's because she hardly ever fucks, or maybe I'm making assumptions about that. Just because she didn't sleep with McCarthy doesn't mean she hasn't recently slept with someone else. She said she was picky, not celibate.

I find myself praying to a higher power that I make the cut. Maybe not tonight, but tomorrow, next week, a year from now. I'll take whatever I can get. That's how badly I want her.

I add a second finger and she clamps even tighter around me. There's hardly any room for two fingers. *Two*, for chrissake. While my thumb tends to her clit, I push my fingers in and out in a lazy rhythm. Brenna's eyelids go heavy, her breathing labored. I aimlessly rub the rock in my pants against her thigh as I finger her.

"I want you to kiss me." She yanks my head down, her fingers running through my hair as her tongue finds mine.

The kiss is urgent, sloppy. She's practically riding my fingers, making the sexiest noises I've ever heard. I come up for air. "Are you going to come for me?"

Her mumbled response is unintelligible.

I chuckle. My hand keeps working her. My fingers are soaked. I push them deeper inside her, then withdraw and curl them right near her opening, stroking hard.

"Oh my *God*," she squeezes out.

Her orgasm ripples around my fingers, and I feel it travel up her slender body in a wave of shivers. She releases a sigh, from her lips to mine. I swallow the breathy sound with a kiss, and ease the pressure on her clit, slow the thrust of my fingers, letting her come down from the high.

Her eyelids finally flutter open and she smiles at me.

"Good?" I murmur.

"So good," she murmurs back. She sighs again and curls toward me, burrowing her cheek in my neck.

"Holy shit, you like to snuggle after sex," I accuse.

"I do not." The denial is muffled against my chest.

"You totally do."

She nips at my throat. "Don't tell anyone."

"Why? Afraid it's going to ruin your reputation?"

"Yes. I'm a bad girl, Jakey. I don't do things like snuggle."

"Why not? Snuggling is awesome." I thread my fingers through her silky hair. Downstairs, I'm still throbbing and it's not something that either of us can really ignore.

Brenna lifts her head, a devilish glint in her eyes. "You and this boner, dude."

She slips a hand between our bodies and places it directly over my package. I can't help but thrust into her hand.

"What should we do about this…" She waits expectantly.

"Anything," I grunt. "You can do anything you want to me."

"Anything, huh?"

"Anything." My voice sounds strangled to my ears. "But please, do *something*."

One finger teasingly glides up and down my zipper before toying with the little metal tab. I damn near stop breathing. My heartbeat is out of control. I feel like I just played a five-minute shift. In penalty-kill mode.

As my pulse drums in my ears, my body pleads for release. I want Brenna Jensen sucking on my cock, jacking it, kissing it. I don't care *what* she does. I just need her hand or her mouth or her tongue on me.

I will up some patience, but my muscles remain rigid, tense with anticipation as I wait for her to make a move.

Right when she's about to undo my pants, a phone rings.

Brenna swears under her breath. "I should check that."

"No," I mumble.

She sits up. "How often do people call instead of text these days?"

I have to relent. "Not very."

"Exactly. Phone calls usually mean it's important." She grabs her purse from the floor mat and rummages through it. The moment she has her phone in hand, her demeanor changes. All traces of desire are gone.

"Everything okay?" I ask gruffly.

She stares at the screen for another second before clicking the phone off. "It's nothing." And yet now she's shimmying into her panties and jeans, and I know without a doubt that Little Jakey won't be getting any attention tonight.

"It's later than I thought," she says awkwardly. "I should head home."

"Okay."

She hesitates. "You don't mind?"

"Of course not." Did she expect me to admonish her? Accuse

her of leaving me with blue balls? Because that implies that she owes me something, which she doesn't. I'm not entitled to a damn thing from this girl, or any girl. I want Brenna to blow me because she *wants* to blow me. But clearly she's no longer in the mood. The mysterious caller ruined that for us.

"I really did have a good time," she confesses as I walk her to the driver's side of the Jeep.

"So did I." I meet her eyes. "Should we do it again?"

"I don't know."

"Yes, you do." I grasp her chin, keeping our gazes locked. I repeat the question. "Should we do it again?"

After a long beat, Brenna nods.

19
BRENNA

By Wednesday, I haven't heard so much as a peep from anyone at HockeyNet. Granted, Ed Mulder didn't say when the internship slots would be filled. I suppose it could take weeks, but I'm impatient for news.

Even though I know I didn't impress him, a part of me is still clinging to hope that I have a shot. And fine, maybe hope is for fools. But I guess that makes me a fool.

Dad's still at the arena when I get home after a long day on campus. The Briar boys had weight training this morning, and ice time this afternoon, so I don't expect my father until six or seven.

I make dinner. Nothing fancy, just spaghetti and a Caesar salad. I eat my share in front of the TV, watching highlights on HockeyNet. Which is super irritating, because whoever put this clips package together didn't include some of the best parts of last night's Bruins game. I could do a way better job compiling a good reel. I hope I get the chance.

There I go, being foolish again.

My phone buzzes on the coffee table, revealing a text.

JAKE: Can I call you?

Oh boy. The little spark of excitement that tickles my belly is alarming. We spoke on the phone last night, too, mostly about said Bruins game, since we were watching it at the same time.

I won't deny that our bowling date was a lot more fun than I expected. The orgasm was equally unexpected. I didn't plan on fooling around with Jake. I thought I had more willpower than that, but the guy is irresistible. Even now, days later, I'm still thinking about it. His fingers inside me, his hot mouth glued to mine... Connelly is very good at what he does. I'd wanted nothing more than to make him feel good, too, until that phone call from Eric.

Each time I think I've made myself clear, that I've set firm boundaries with him, Eric reveals another level of persistence. And I don't feel right being a bitch to him, ordering him to leave me alone, because our history holds me hostage.

History is bullshit.

Jake's words, the thoughts he'd expressed at O'Malley's, float through my head. History is bullshit. And trust me, I would love to put the past behind me. Unfortunately, that's easier said than done.

At least this time Eric wasn't making demands of me—he followed the call up with a text, apologizing for asking for money. But that doesn't matter. It killed the mood as effectively as rain snuffing out a candle.

On the other hand, I'd been seconds away from having Jake's dick in my mouth, so maybe Eric did me a favor. Saved me from blowing THE ENEMY.

But if I'm being honest, it's been a while since I thought of Jake in that context.

Once I finish my dinner, I reach for my phone. "Your crush on me is getting out of control, Jakey," I say after he picks up.

His deep laughter tickles my ear. "Don't flatter yourself, Hottie."

"You just called me *Hottie*—that is literally you flattering me."

"True." Another chuckle. "What are you doing right now?"

"Had an early dinner, and now I'm watching HockeyNet highlights."

"Still no word from Mulder?"

"Nope."

"What about Agent Scully?"

I snicker. "You're hilarious. Did you have class today?"

I'm still amazed by the knowledge that he's majoring in psychology—I found that out last night during our very long phone call. Before that, I'd assumed he was a communications or broadcasting major, like most other athletes.

"No, Wednesday is my day off. I usually use it to catch up on reading, clean the house, that kind of stuff. Any big plans tonight?"

"Not sure. I might grab a drink with Summer, do a girls' night. You?"

"Grabbing some drinks, too. The boys and I are hitting the Dime tonight." He pauses. "I'd invite you to join us, but you'd say no...right?"

"Duh. I can't be spotted out in public with Harvard players. It's bad enough that one gave me an orgasm last weekend."

"I think you might be exaggerating this rivalry," Jake says, humor in his voice. "Do your Briar boys hate us that much?"

"Oh, they absolutely hate you. Brooks, in particular. They don't like his style of play."

"They don't like it because it works."

"Really? So you're telling me you're perfectly cool with all his trash-talking? With all the penalties he draws and provokes? With how rough he is?"

"It's part of the game," Jake replies. "Even I do that shit. To a lesser extent than Brooks, sure, but I trash-talk and provoke with the best of them. And don't kid yourself, babe—your boys do it, too. I've heard the filth that comes out of their mouths on the ice. That Hollis guy says shit about my mother all the time."

"Is he any good at talking shit? Because he's terrible with pick-up lines."

"How would you know that?" I can almost hear Jake's scowl.

"That boy's been hitting on me since the day we met." I don't mention my drunken hookup with Hollis, because it's completely insignificant. "Anyway, heckling is different than playing dirty," I point out.

"Brooks never crosses the line."

"Sure he does. He draws the line wherever he wants and then decides whether or not to cross it."

"How is that exclusive to Brooks? Everyone has their own lines, right? And we all decide which ones we're not willing to cross."

"Fair enough." Curiosity bites at my tongue. "What's your uncrossable line? What is the one thing Jake Connelly absolutely refuses to do?"

His response is swift. "Sleep with a friend's mom. I'm never doing that." He stops. "Well, again."

I burst out laughing. "You slept with a friend's mother? When? How?"

"It was one hundred percent a Stifler's mom situation," he says sheepishly. "I was a senior in high school, and one of my teammates threw a huge kegger at his place. I got wasted, stumbled upstairs in search of a bathroom, and wound up in his mom's bedroom by mistake."

I'm hit with a wave of uncontrollable giggles. "Was she wearing a negligee? Smoking one of those long cigarettes like Audrey Hepburn?"

"No, she was actually wearing a tracksuit. It was bubble-gum pink, and I think it said Juicy on the butt."

"Oh my God, you fucked the mom from *Mean Girls*."

"No idea who that is."

I laugh harder, wiping tears from my eyes. "I can't believe you fell prey to a cougar."

"What's wrong with that? She was hot, the sex was hot. Good times."

He's completely unfazed by my mockery, and that's one of the things I'm grudgingly starting to like about him. He possesses a steely confidence that I genuinely admire. Nothing rattles this man.

He's so sure of himself, of his masculinity, his skill. Jake Connelly doesn't have an insecure bone in his body.

"Wait, if it was so hot, then why would you never do it again?" I demand.

"Because it cost me one of my best friends," he says glumly, and I realize that he *is* capable of being rattled. "What about you? What's your most embarrassing hookup story?"

"Hmmm. I don't know." I think it over, but even if my brain had conjured up a crazy Stifler's mom-esque scenario, I wouldn't be able to reveal it because a car door slams from outside. "Ugh. My dad's home," I tell Jake.

"I still can't believe you're living at home again. Has there been any news about your apartment?"

"My landlords pumped all the water out, and now they're bringing in a cleaning crew. Hopefully it won't be much longer." I hear the key turn in the lock. "I gotta go now. We'll talk later."

Later? a little voice taunts.

Oh boy, this is bad. Getting to know Jake shouldn't be an item on my agenda.

"Wait," he says roughly. "When's our next fake date?"

I have to smile. "*Fake* date?"

"Yeah. When do we need to pull the wool over Mulder's eyes again?"

"Um, most likely never? It's not like we've been invited to do anything else." I wrinkle my nose. "Why do you even want to?"

"Because isn't that the arrangement? A real date for a fake one? And I want a real one."

My heart skips a beat. "You just want to have sex with me."

"Yes. Badly."

At least he's honest. "Well, I think the fake-date ship has sailed, I'm afraid."

His voice thickens. Husky and endearing. "What about the real-date ship?"

My teeth dig into my bottom lip. Then I take a breath. "I think that one might still be in the harbor."

"Good. Let's try to do something this weekend? Maybe after the charity games?"

Dad's footsteps near the living room. "We'll figure it out. I have to go now."

I hang up as my father enters the room. "Hi," he greets me. His absent-minded gaze flicks to the television.

"Hey. There's dinner in the microwave. You just need to nuke it."

"Perfect. Thanks. I'm starving." He turns on his heel and marches into the kitchen.

"How was practice?" I call out.

"Davenport was throwing an attitude," he answers from the other room, and there's no mistaking his displeasure. "I don't know what's going on with that kid."

"Maybe it's girl trouble. I heard he's going through the puck bunnies like hotcakes."

Dad appears in the doorway, running a hand over his buzz cut. "Women," he mutters. "Always the root of this shit."

"Actually, I meant that Hunter was being the obnoxious one and using the bunnies to deal with his own issues. But, cool, blame everything on us, the evil demon women." I roll my eyes. "I hope you didn't say this kind of stuff to Mom."

"No," he says gruffly. "Your mother wasn't a demon. She had her issues. But we all do." He gives me a pointed look, but then the microwave beeps and he turns to get his dinner.

I'm glad that he leaves the room. I'm so tired of seeing his harsh judgment. He's never going to let me forget my mistakes.

I wonder how other people cope with the knowledge that their parents are ashamed of them. The weight of my father's shame has been pressing down on my shoulders for years, and I've yet to find a way to deal with it.

The girls' night that Summer and I anticipated doesn't pan out. We walk into Malone's to find Hollis, Nate, and Hunter at the bar. When they spot us, Nate suggests grabbing a booth, and it's impossible to say no in the face of Nate's dimples. So we pile into a booth near the pool tables, where Hollis announces we're doing shots.

"After today's practice, we all need it," he says darkly.

I give a wave to Jesse Wilkes and his girlfriend, Katie, who are shooting pool at one of the far tables. Katie waves back enthusiastically.

"That was brutal," Nate agrees.

I shift my gaze back. "Yeah, my dad said there was some tension today." I fix a knowing look at Hunter.

"Aw, is Coach trashing me behind my back?" he mocks.

"I'm pretty sure whatever he said to me, he also said right to your face. I know my father, and he doesn't mince words."

"Oh, Coach reamed him out good today," Nate confirms, his eyes twinkling.

"What'd you do to deserve it?" I ask Hunter.

He shrugs. "I was ten minutes late."

"I think he was more pissed that you had a chick in the locker room," Hollis argues.

My jaw drops. "You brought a girl into the locker room? Don't tell me he caught you two hooking up?"

Hunter shakes his head irritably. "Dude, it was so harmless. I crashed at her place last night and she dropped me off at the arena, wanted a quick tour of the facility. Which is what made me late for practice."

"What chick is this?" Hollis asks. "The one from Jesse's party? Or Pierre's cousin who's visiting from Montreal?"

"Wow, look at you, Hot Stuff," I crack. "It's a veritable girl parade in the life of Hunter."

He grins at me. "Who doesn't love a good parade?"

"I love parades," Hollis agrees. "When I was a kid we lived in San Francisco, and the Pride parade there was so—" He stops when his phone lights up. He whips it to his ear. "You can't call me every five minutes, Rupi. That's not how life works."

When her high-pitched voice ripples out of the phone, I bury my face against my forearm and start to laugh. Beside me, Summer is giggling.

"What do you want to do, put a GPS in my phone? I'm with the guys, okay?" He pauses. "Brenna and Summer are here, too." He pauses again. "If you're so fucking concerned, come and hang out with us. I *invited* you."

He did? He's inviting her places now?

"Then get a fake ID!" he growls. "You know what? I don't care if you're mad. There. I said it. I don't care. You're always mad about something and it's driving me insane."

And yet oddly enough, I don't hear a trace of genuine hostility in his tone. It almost seems like he's into this toxic tornado we inadvertently—okay, deliberately—placed in his path.

"Fine…" He halts every few seconds to listen. "Fine… Fine… Fine… Nope, I will not. Nope, I'm not gonna apologize. You can come here if you want. I'm not coming to see you. Bye Felicia."

He hangs up.

My eyebrows shoot up. "Did you hang up on her?"

Hollis ignores me. His brawny shoulders hunch over as he frantically types on his phone.

"Texting her?" Nate guesses dryly.

"Apologizing for saying 'Bye Felicia,'" Hollis mumbles, except the phone rings in his hands and he picks it up again. "I told you, I can't talk right now. I'm sorry I said 'Bye Felicia,' but seriously. *Bye Felicia.*"

He hangs up and instantly starts texting again, I assume to apologize for the second "Bye Felicia."

Nate glances around the booth. "This is my new favorite thing in the world. Is it just me?"

Summer is still tittering like crazy. "It's a train wreck and I love it." She tosses her blonde hair over her shoulder before sliding out of the booth. "I'm going to change up the music. Actually, I'll order our drinks while I'm up. What are you in the mood for?" she asks me. "Tequila? Fireball?"

"Vodka," I decide.

Nate makes a gagging noise. "Girls and their vodka."

"Oh, I'm sorry, do you require something yummy and fruity for your delicate palate?" I ask in a polite tone.

Hunter snickers.

"Vodka shots for the booth," I tell Summer.

As she bounces off, I don't miss the way Hunter's eyes linger on her ass. Summer can rock a pair of skinny jeans like nobody's business.

"Still have a thing for her, huh?" I say, nudging his arm.

"No." He sounds completely truthful.

"Really?" I frown. "So why are you being such a dick to her?"

"I'm not being a dick to her. I'm just living my life, Brenna."

"By boning a different girl every night?"

"So what?" He rests his muscular arms on the tabletop and clasps his long fingers together. I like his hands. He might be acting like a jackass lately, but he does have good hands. "I'm in college. If I want to sleep around, then I'm allowed to sleep around."

"Of course. But did you know there's such a thing as sleeping around and also not being a dick to your friends?"

"I'm not being a dick," he repeats. "But I'm also not going to pretend that Fitz didn't make a complete fool out of me. I asked him if there was something going on with them, and he flat out said no. And then he let me ask her out on a date, all the while knowing she was into him. And then *on* the date, she left in the middle of dinner and went home to have sex with him." Hunter chuckles softly. "But somehow *I'm* the asshole?"

"He's got you there," Nate says.

Yes, I can't deny Hunter has a point. But I'm Summer's friend, and I know she didn't intentionally set out to hurt him.

Hunter's hand curls over my shoulder. "Move over. I gotta get out of here."

"Don't leave on my account."

He rolls his eyes. "I'm hitting the head."

After he disappears in the crowd, Nate scoots into Hunter's spot and slings his arm over my shoulders. "So what do you think about the finals? Any tips on how to stop Connelly?"

I falter. Why would I have tips about how to stop Jake? I study Nate's expression. Does he know I went out with Jake this weekend? Did somebody see us?

"Why are you asking me?" I mutter.

"Because you know your hockey?" he prompts. "Because you're currently living with Coach and I'm sure he's making you watch hours and hours of game tape?"

Oh. Talk about paranoid. "Yeah, he is," I admit.

"So give me some ammo we can use against Harvard."

"Well. I don't know if anyone told you this, but...Jake Connelly is really fast."

Nate snorts and tweaks a strand of my hair. "Gee, I was completely in the dark about that. Someone told me his nickname was Lightning, but I assumed it's because he's into storms."

A laugh flies out. "I heard he's an avid storm chaser." My voice turns serious. "In all honesty, Connelly is sort of unstoppable. He's the best college player in the country."

"Thanks," Nate grumbles.

"Look me in the eye and tell me you think you're better than him."

After a beat, Nate scowls at me. "Fine. He's the best college player in the country."

"All you can do is try and slow him down. As for Brooks Weston, just don't fall into his trap."

"Easier said than done." Hollis rejoins the conversation. "When you're hopped up on adrenaline and that asshole is taunting you in the face-off? You want nothing more than to clock him one."

"It's true," Nate agrees. "He's such a prick."

"Who's a prick?" Summer asks, returning to the booth.

"Brooks Weston," I reply. "You know, your best friend."

"He's not my best friend. We just went to high school together."

Hollis lobs an accusation at her. "You partied with him a couple times this year."

"So?"

"See this, folks?" Hollis points his index finger at Summer. "This is the face of disloyalty."

"Who is he talking to?" I murmur to Nate. "Are we the 'folks'?"

"I think so?"

"Oh my gosh," Summer exclaims when Hollis starts texting again. "That girl has you completely whipped. You know you don't have to keep texting back, right?"

"Oh really." His blue eyes gleam in challenge. "Do you want that hurricane blowing into our house and yelling at me all night?"

"What do I care? She wouldn't be yelling at me."

"Oh *reeaallly*," he repeats, dragging out each syllable this time. He waves his iPhone around. "All it takes is one text from me saying you said something nasty about her, and she'll be blowing up *your* phone."

Summer pales. "Don't you dare."

"That's what I thought."

Our waiter brings over the vodka shots, but we don't drink until Hunter comes back. He flops down beside me and reaches for his glass. We all raise our shot glasses, even Hollis, though his gaze keeps darting to his phone. Whipped, all right.

"Here's to crushing Harvard in the finals," Nate toasts.

The vodka burns a fiery path down my throat on its way to my belly. Whew. I forgot how potent vodka is for me. For some reason, it's the liquor that hits me the hardest.

"Ugh, that tastes like ass," Hollis whines. "I hate vodka. And I hate this *song*. Is that what you picked?" he asks Summer, as Taylor Swift's "Shake It Off" starts playing in the bar.

"What's wrong with T-Swift?" she protests. "We love T-Swift."

"No, we don't love T-Swift," he reminds her. "We love *Titanic*. We love the Kardashians. We love *Solange*. But we sure as hell don't love T-Swift—"

He's interrupted by the arrival of Jesse and Katie. Jesse's in his hockey jacket, and Katie is wearing a spring coat, so I assume they're coming over to say good night. Instead, Jesse addresses Nate in an outraged tone. "Come outside. Right now."

I'm instantly on guard. You don't usually hear the younger guys barking orders at their team captain.

"Everything okay?" Summer asks in concern.

"No. Come see this." Without another word, Wilkes spins around and stomps toward the door.

I glance at Katie. "What's going on?"

She simply sighs and says, "You don't mess with a boy's car."

Uh-oh.

When our group steps outside, Jesse is already ten yards away, his black-and-silver jacket flapping in the evening breeze. Even if I didn't have him as a point of reference, I'd still be able to pick out his car.

It's the one that looks like a fluffy, white marshmallow square.

"Oh boy," Summer murmurs.

Jesse's car used to be a black Honda Pilot. Now it's completely white, thanks to the shaving cream. Or maybe it's whipped cream? When we reach the car, I dip my pinkie into the white substance and bring it up to my nose. Smells sweet. I pop the finger in my mouth and confirm that we're dealing with whipped cream.

"Those Harvard fuckers did this," Jesse announces, his features creased with anger. "And we can't let them get away with it. I'm driving out there."

"Absolutely not," Nate commands.

The sophomore's eyes flash. "Why not? They can't mess with my property!"

"It's a stupid prank, Wilkes. If you drive out to Cambridge and throw a tantrum, or worse, if you retaliate with a dumb prank of your own, then we're stooping to their level. And we're better than that. We're grown men."

Jesse's face is tomato-red. He doesn't resemble a grown man right now. He's a nineteen-year-old-kid whose car was vandalized. I get it. It sucks. But Nate is right. Retaliation is never the answer.

"How do you know it was Harvard?" I can't help but ask.

Jesse thrusts a piece of lined paper into my hand. "This was sticking out of the windshield wipers."

Summer peers over my shoulder as I unfold the note. I suppress a sigh, because the message couldn't be any clearer.

Can't wait to cream you in the finals!

20
BRENNA

PING PING PING.

I ignore the rain beating against my bedroom window. I don't remember when it started, but it was sometime after I got home from Malone's. I've been focused on my assignment since then, but now the noise is starting to annoy me. On the bright side, the rain will wash away the whipped cream on Jesse Wilkes's car and maybe he'll quit crying over it.

Ping ping.

Then my phone buzzes.

JAKE: Please tell me I'm not throwing rocks at Chad Jensen's bedroom window.

I fly up into a sitting position. What the hell is he talking about?

I immediately call him. "Are you standing outside my window?" I demand.

"Okay, so you *can* hear me," he grumbles. "And you're just ignoring me."

"No, I kept hearing pinging noises on the window but I thought it was the rain."

"Why would the rain *ping*? Rain makes more of a pitter patter sound."

"Take your pitter patter and shove it up your butt, Jake."

His husky laughter tickles my ear. "Are you going to let me in or what?"

"You couldn't ring the doorbell like a normal person?"

"Cool, you want me to ring the doorbell?" he says mockingly. "Sure, I'll go do that—"

"Oh shut up. My dad is in the living room watching TV."

"Well aware of that. I saw him through the window. Hence the rocks."

I scan my brain, wondering how I can let him in. You can't access the stairs without passing the living room. And even if he did manage, this Victorian is old and squeaky, and the fourth and fifth stair treads creak like a haunted house. It's our alarm system.

"Um, yeah…I think the only way you're getting in is if you climb the drainpipe up to my window."

"Are you serious? You're really making me Romeo and Juliet this? Can't I come in the back door?" He chortles. "That's what she said."

"Your maturity levels astound me. And no, you can't. The living room looks onto the back door. Dad'll see you."

"Here's a great idea," Jake says cheerfully, "you could come outside."

"Then he'll ask where I'm going. Besides, it's raining. I don't want to go out there."

"It's raining! I don't want to *be* out here!" A loud, aggravated sigh reverberates through the line. "You are so fucking difficult. One second."

He hangs up. For a moment I wonder if he's calling it and going home. I hope not, because I don't want to be with a man who gives up so easily.

A grin touches my lips when I hear the creak of metal. It's followed by a rustling noise that grows louder and louder, until finally a sharp knock shakes the windowpane, and a blurry fist appears in the rain-streaked glass. As I approach the window, a finger pops out of the fist like a Jack-in-the-Box. Jake is giving me the finger.

Fighting laughter, I quickly open the window. The screen ripped years ago, so I have a perfect view of Jake's wet face. A streak of dirt mars his sexy cheek.

"I can't believe you made me do that," he accuses.

"I didn't make you do anything. You're the one who showed up without warning me. You wanted to see me that bad, huh?" I feel guilty all of a sudden. Not because he scaled a drainpipe for me, but because of the ripples of happiness the sight of him evokes.

I just spent several hours with a group of Briar hockey players, listening to them indict Harvard for the juvenile bullshit with Jesse Wilkes's car. Meanwhile, I sat there, harboring secrets. Knowing I've been in contact with Jake, that I've gone out with him, kissed him...

It feels like a betrayal of my friends, but at the same time, we're not in middle school anymore. I'm not going to stop seeing somebody because my friends might throw a hissy fit.

"Come in," I order. "If anyone drives by and sees half your body hanging out the window they'll call the police."

Jake climbs over the ledge, his boots gracefully landing on the pine floor. "Let me get rid of these so I don't get mud all over your floor." He unlaces his boots and tucks them directly beneath the window. Then he shrugs out of his jacket and shakes his wet head like a dog that just had a swim.

A cascade of moisture splashes my face. "Thanks," I say sarcastically.

"You're welcome."

The next thing I know, his hands are on my waist. No, scratch that—his cold, wet hands are sliding underneath my tank top.

"You're so warm." He sighs happily, then rubs his damp hair against my neck.

"You are so obnoxious," I inform him as I try to squirm out of his grip. "I really hate you right now."

"No, you don't." But he does release me and conducts a quick examination of my very plain bedroom. "This is not what I expected."

"I was already living on my own when Dad bought this house. Neither of us bothered to give my room a personal touch. Now, are you going to tell me why you showed up out of the blue? Actually, wait. First I'd like to know what the hell was up with that stunt you pulled at Malone's tonight. That was incredibly immature." I texted him about it when I got home from the bar, but he hadn't provided an explanation. Or a response, come to think of it.

"Hey," he says defensively, "don't lump me in with my idiot teammates. I investigated after you texted. Turns out the Whipped Cream Bandits are two of my sophomores—Heath and Jonah. They were in the Hastings area tonight, off their faces. They claim it was just a joke."

"Dumb joke. I could've come up with something way more diabolical." I give him a stern look. "You should keep a better eye on your guys. Jesse Wilkes wanted to drive out to Cambridge tonight and exact his revenge. Me and Nate talked him out of it, but that boneheaded stunt nearly started a prank war."

Jake's expression becomes pained. "Thanks for doing that. Last thing I needed was a brigade of angry Briar boys storming the Dime. Don't worry, I'll have a talk with them tomorrow." He walks toward the bed and falls onto it, making himself comfortable.

I admire the long, lean body stretched out on my mattress. He's wearing cargo pants and a black sweatshirt. The latter doesn't stay on for long—he peels the shirt off and tosses it on the floor, then settles back down. The T-shirt he's left with is so thin it looks like it's been washed a thousand times. There's a hole near the hem, and the logo is almost completely faded away. I can barely make out the words *Gloucester Lions*.

"Is that your high school team?" I ask, while trying not to focus on how the thin material clings to the most impressive chest I've ever seen. And I'm constantly surrounded by ripped dudes, so that says a lot.

Connelly's body is amazing. Period.

The crooked grin he gives me sends a shiver up my spine. "Yup, we were the Lions." He picks up my closed laptop and puts it on the nightstand, then pats the empty space. "Come here."

"No."

"Why not?"

"Because if I go there, we're going to fool around, and my dad might hear." I immediately feel like a total loser for saying those words. It's like I'm fifteen years old again, sneaking Eric into my room.

But I snuck him in often, I remind myself. And in all that time, we didn't get caught, not even once.

The reminder of my previous stealth is what propels me to join Jake on the bed. I settle beside him in a cross-legged position. He takes my hand, his thumb rubbing the inside of my palm in lazy circles.

"Why are you here?" I find myself blurting. "You didn't come all this way to talk about the whipped-cream incident, did you?" A thought suddenly strikes me. "How did you know where I live?"

"I came because I wanted to see you," he says simply. "And how did I know where you live...I'm gonna take the Fifth on that one."

"Oh my God. Please don't tell me you hacked into my school records or my phone or something."

"Nothing that nefarious."

"Then how?"

He shrugs sheepishly.

"Connelly."

"Fine. Freshman year we played Briar and got our asses kicked. Your dad was an asshole to Pedersen after the game, and, well, we loved our coach and wanted to avenge him, so..."

"So, what?" I demand.

"So we drove back to Hastings later that night and toilet-papered your house," he mumbles.

I gasp. "That was *you*? I remember that! Dad was livid."

"That was us. In my defense, I was eighteen and kind of a moron."

"Not much has changed," I offer sweetly.

He laces his fingers through mine and squeezes. Hard.

"Ouch," I complain.

"That didn't hurt."

"Yes it did."

"No it didn't." He pauses. "Did it?"

"No," I admit.

"Brat." Jake brings my hand to his lips and kisses my knuckles.

I gaze down at him, trying to make sense of this guy. He constantly shows me new sides of himself. It's unnerving. "I can't believe how touchy you are."

"Touchy as in testy, or touchy as in I like to touch you?"

"The latter. I honestly didn't expect you to be so cuddly." I purse my lips. "I don't think I like it."

"We already talked about this, babe. You love it."

"Stop telling me what I love. I don't like that."

"Sure you do."

I groan in exasperation. But I can't deny that his silly humor amuses me. I trace the Gloucester Lions logo with the tip of my finger. "Did you play any other sports in high school?"

"No. Only hockey. What about you?"

"I played volleyball, but I never really took it seriously. And I certainly wasn't good enough to land a scholarship and play on a college team. I didn't even get into college."

Jake looks startled. "For real?"

"My grades weren't the best." A flush rises in my cheeks. "I did two years of community college until I was able to transfer to Briar."

"So you really were a bad girl," he muses.

"Yes," I admit.

"I like bad girls." He captures a chunk of my hair and threads it around his finger. "Did you grow up around here?"

I shake my head. "I grew up in Westlynn. It's a small town in New Hampshire. And I went to school there even after Dad got his job at Briar. My friends were there. My cousins."

My boyfriend. I leave that part out. Bringing up Eric is never a good idea. I already know for a fact it kills the mood.

"I didn't have the best judgment in high school," I admit. "And Dad never let me forget it. It's one of the reasons I moved out as soon as I could." A million more questions flash in Jake's eyes, so I change the subject before he can ask any of them. "Gloucester is a fishing town, isn't it?"

"Yup."

"Does your family own a boat?"

"My granddad does." Jake carelessly plays with my hair. It seems a part of him always needs to be in motion, whether it's toying with the ends of my hair, or stroking my knee with his knuckles. "My dad works in construction, but Pops worked on a boat his entire life. I work with him in the summers, actually."

"Really? Doing what?"

"Clam diving."

"Come on, Jake. Gross."

"I'm serious!" He grins. "I dive for clams in the summer. Pops and I are a two-man dive operation. Clamming is a lucrative business, actually. I make enough money in one summer to pay my expenses for the whole year."

My lips twitch wildly as I attempt not to laugh. "You're a clam diver."

"Yup." He drags his tongue over his bottom lip in a lewd manner. "Turns you on, doesn't it?"

"I don't know what it does to me, but I'm pretty sure turned on is not what I'm feeling right now."

"Mmm-hmmm. Sure."

"Do you get along with your granddad?"

"Oh yeah, he's a tough old fucker. Love that guy."

"And your dad?"

"Also a tough fucker. We get along, for the most part." Jake's hand snakes underneath my shirt again. "Anyway, how about we don't talk about our parents anymore?"

His fingers are no longer cold. Now they're warm and dry and feel like heaven skimming over my bare skin.

"Wanna make out?" He lifts a brow.

"Maybe." My heart beats faster as I dip my head to kiss him. The moment we make contact, ribbons of heat uncurl inside me.

To me, a kiss is the most intimate act there is. More intimate than oral sex and penetration. Sure, it's the simple act of mouths touching, tongues dancing. But a kiss, at its very core, is an emotional experience. Or at least it is for me. Anyone can give me an orgasm, but not everyone can touch my soul. One kiss can make me fall in love with someone. I know it, because it happened once before. And that's why kissing scares me sometimes.

"I fucking love kissing you," Jake whispers, and I wonder if he somehow read my mind.

His lips are hot against mine as he gently nudges me backward. I part my legs and he nestles his powerful body in the cradle of my thighs, kissing me over and over and over again.

Arousal builds in my belly. Throbs in my clit. I tear my mouth away and meet his lust-glazed eyes. "I didn't get to play last time," I tell him. "You got to have all the fun."

His answering smile is smug. "You're the only one who came. I'm pretty sure that means *you* had all the fun."

"But I didn't get to torture you." I rise on one elbow and give his chest a firm shove, forcing him onto his back. Once he's at my mercy, I inch up the hem of his T-shirt to expose the hard ridges of his abdomen.

My heart races as I stare down at him. His muscles are perfectly defined, and he's got that drool-worthy man "V" that disappears into his waistband. I bring my lips to the center of his chest, and a shudder rolls through his broad frame. He tastes like citrusy soap and a hint of salt. It's delicious. I lick my way up his chest, pulling his shirt up as I go, revealing more and more skin. I reach a nipple and give it a soft bite.

Jake groans.

"Quiet," I whisper before flicking my tongue over the flat brown disc.

"Sorry. I forgot."

I tease his other nipple, then kiss my way to the strong column of his throat. The material of his shirt is bunched up there, but I don't remove the shirt because I'm still entirely aware that my dad is downstairs watching TV. I nuzzle his neck, my fingers stroking the stubble dotting his jaw.

He makes a husky sound of approval. I brush my lips over his, but the contact is fleeting. I'm busy admiring his gorgeous face.

Jake's eyes flutter open. A dark, bottomless green. "You're not kissing me anymore," he mumbles. "Why aren't you kissing me anymore?"

"Because I want to do something else. But I need you to remember to be quiet. Are you going to be quiet for me?"

His tongue darts out to moisten his top lip, then quickly swipes over the bottom one. "I'll try."

I undo his zipper.

Gaze burning with desire, he lifts his ass so I can ease his pants and boxers down. His thighs are rock-hard, and they don't have much hair, only a light dusting. The perfect amount.

My mouth waters when his dick springs up. Oh, I like *this*.

I curl my fingers around his thick girth. He's big and hard in my hand, the velvety heat of him bringing a rush of moisture between my legs. I squeeze my thighs together, squirming to control the ache.

It's been a while since I actually *ached* to have someone inside me. I give him a slow, teasing stroke, and we both choke out a curse. I want nothing more than to rip off my clothes, sink down on this hard penis, and ride him until we're both coming.

But that can wait. I lick my lips, and then lower my head to engulf him with my mouth.

21
JAKE

Holy shit.

This blowjob is...

Brenna is...

Her mouth is...

Yeah, my brain stopped functioning a while ago.

My fingers are tangled in Brenna's dark hair as her tongue glides along my shaft. She squeezes the base of my cock with her hand as she runs her tongue over the tip, tasting me, teasing me. I swallow a groan but can't prevent a hoarse breath from slipping out.

She gazes up at me with big brown eyes.

"I'm being quiet," I choke out. "Promise."

She smiles and resumes her ministrations. She sucks on my tip, and I watch her lips, mesmerized, as they gobble me up. Her head dips down again, and suddenly my cock is nearly poking the back of her throat. I barely have time to register the incredible sensation when she eases off, her head swiftly moving back up, her hand working in perfect unison with her wicked mouth.

I can't believe Brenna Jensen is blowing me.

Life is full of unexpected surprises. A few months ago, this girl was provoking me at a house party, swearing she'd never fall into bed with a Harvard man. And now here we are. In her bed, with her mouth on my cock and my fist in her hair.

Her lips are…

The suction is…

Dammit, my brain shorted out again.

Pleasure zips up my spine. I love seeing her delicate throat work when she swallows me on every downstroke. Her perfect ass is jutting in the air, and my hands are itching to cup it, squeeze it.

I tighten my fist in her long hair and tug her head up. "Twist around so I can lick you at the same time," I rasp.

Pure arousal darkens her gaze. "That's such a good idea," she whispers.

She moves in a blur, wiggling out of her flannel pants and straddling my face. When my tongue comes out for a taste, she makes a strangled noise. A loud one.

"Quiet," I taunt, before giving her clit a long, languid lick.

She retaliates by stuffing half my dick in her mouth, and it's my turn to make noise again. "Oh my God," I groan against her pussy. "We're never going to get through this."

Her soft laughter tickles my shaft, creating a vibration effect that travels through my body. My hips involuntarily jerk upward, pushing me to the back of her throat.

She yelps in surprise, and I quickly withdraw. "Sorry," I murmur. "That wasn't on purpose."

"It's okay, you just startled me."

I return my attention to her sexy body, reaching up to squeeze her ass cheeks. This is fucking amazing. Her sweet flavor on my tongue, her mouth on my dick. It's so, so good. I move my tongue slowly over her clit, hoping to tease her, to draw out her pleasure, but it isn't long before she's whimpering impatiently and grinding down on my face.

Greedy little thing. I chuckle at her eagerness, until she starts jacking me against her tongue, and the laughter dies. Red-hot pleasure buzzes up my spine. My balls tingle in warning, and I wrench my mouth from her pussy and mutter, "I don't want to come until you do."

"Then get me there," she dares.

Challenge accepted. I wrap my lips around her clit and suck.

She squirms in delight. "Oh, that's good. Do that again."

With my tongue tending to her clit, I bring my index finger into the mix and push it inside her. She's so wet and so tight and I am so close to erupting in her mouth. It takes all the willpower in the world to hold off.

"Come on, babe," I whisper. "Don't make me come alone."

She moans quietly and rocks her hips.

"That's it," I coax.

Her lips tighten around the head of my cock. She mumbles something against it, I think signaling her orgasm, because suddenly I feel her inner muscles contracting around my finger, her clit throbbing beneath my tongue.

I explode without warning, but my mouth is occupied and I hope she doesn't get pissed that I don't ask for permission. The orgasm surges to the surface and fills her mouth. The pleasure's so intense I almost black out.

I feel moisture pool on my abs. Brenna sits up and says, "Sorry, Jakey, I don't swallow. Let me get a tissue."

And now I'm sputtering with laughter because only this girl could do what she just did to my body and then crack me up.

She grabs a wad of tissues from the box on the nightstand and cleans me up. "That was fun," she informs me.

I fully agree. "Give me like ten minutes and then we can do it all over again—"

"Brenna?"

We both freeze.

"Who are you talking to?" a brusque voice demands. "Who's in there?"

"Nobody," she calls, cautioning me with her eyes to keep quiet.

Right, like I was about to open my mouth. That's Chad Jensen on the other side of the door. He'd probably skin me alive if he found me in here.

"I heard his voice, Brenna, and don't tell me it was the TV because there's no TV in there."

"I'm watching something on my laptop," she lies.

"Bullshit. I know when you're lying. How about you introduce me to your friend?"

I don't miss the flare of panic on her face. "No, Dad, how about I don't."

There's a tense pause. "Can we have a word, please?"

Brenna's jaw is locked shut. It looks like she's grinding her teeth as she tries to unhinge it. "One second," she tells the door. Then she's hurriedly putting on her pants, while gesturing for me to do the same. "I'll be right back," she mouths.

Maybe coming here was a bad idea, after all. As Brenna steps out into the hall, I pull up my boxers and cargo pants, tug the zipper closed, and say a prayer that I'm not about to get murdered.

Brenna's voice is muffled, but her father's isn't. Coach Jensen is a commanding, terrifying figure. And yet I still find myself creeping toward the door.

"…talked about this." Brenna sounds annoyed.

"You can't lock your door with some stranger in there. If you're going to have guests over, then you should be prepared to introduce them to your father."

"You're being ridiculous. I'm not introducing you to every single person in my life. It's just a friend."

"Then there's no reason for you to hide him, is there?"

"Dad, please drop it, okay?"

"I'm not going through this with you again." Coach Jensen is clearly starting to get upset. Not angry, but genuinely *upset*. Which triggers my uneasiness. "I can't deal with all the secrets and sneaking around again. You know what happened the last time we weren't upfront with each other."

"There's nothing to be upfront about," she replies in frustration. "It's just some guy."

I flinch. Just some guy?

I mean, she's right. It isn't like we've been dating for years. I don't have an engagement ring in my pocket. And I understand why she can't tell her father that she's hooking up with the hockey player who's going to demolish his team next week. But I'm more than just *some guy*.

Aren't I?

It's not an easy pill for Coach Jensen to swallow, either. "So it's some casual Craigslist thing?" he roars.

"Dad! Ew! First of all, nobody my age uses Craigslist! It's a breeding ground for pedophiles and deviants."

I choke down a burst of laughter.

"And second of all, my personal life is none of your business."

"When you live in my house, it becomes my business."

It's starting to get intense, so I edge away from the door.

"Please, Dad. Just…go to sleep," she says wearily. "My friend is leaving, anyway. I have to finish writing my article for tomorrow."

"Fine." Her father doesn't sound at all appeased. "Tell your friend to use the front door this time. I don't want him breaking that drainpipe out there, or the lattice, or whatever the hell he used to get up here."

Busted.

Heavy footsteps thud in the hallway, while softer ones approach the door. When Brenna reappears, the flush has left her cheeks. Her eyes are devoid of desire. Of any emotion, actually. "You need to go."

"I figured." I'm already putting on my jacket.

"I'm sorry about that. He's…it's…difficult." She won't meet my gaze, and I can tell by the way she's wringing her hands together that she's nervous.

Or maybe it's embarrassment making her fidget. I didn't think Brenna Jensen was capable of feeling embarrassed, though. Or defeated. She's usually so tenacious, but for the first time since we met, it seems like all the fight has gone out of her.

"Has he always been so strict?" I ask.

"Yes, but it's not all on him. I kind of gave him cause to assume the worst when it comes to me."

The cryptic remark sparks my curiosity. I want to push for details, but her guarded demeanor isn't a promising indication that I'd receive any answers.

"Jake," she starts. "I don't know when or if we'll get to see each other again."

I frown. "Why's that?"

"Because..." Her gaze finally shifts from her feet to my face. "It's too complicated. I don't know when my apartment will be ready, and as long as I'm living here I can't have you sneaking in and out. And I can guarantee my father won't approve of this."

"Why, because I play for Harvard? He'll get over it."

"It's not even that. He's not going to approve of anyone after—" She stops, shakes her head, and starts again. "It doesn't even matter anymore. You helped me out with Mulder, and I stuck to my end of the bargain."

"Bargain?" I echo darkly.

"You wanted a real date. You got one. We hooked up a couple times, gave each other some orgasms. So let's call it a successful fling and move on. What's the point of keeping it up, anyway? It won't go anywhere."

I want to argue, but at the same time I know she's right. I'm leaving town in the summer. And right now I need to focus on this game against Briar, and then, if all goes well, the first round of the national tournament. And if *that* pans out? We're looking at the Frozen Four.

Brenna is a distraction. And the irony of that does not escape me. A few weeks ago I was lecturing McCarthy about this same issue. No, I was lecturing *all* my guys about their vices, ordering them to shelve everything until the season was over.

And yet here I am, getting tangled up with Chad Jensen's

daughter. When she texted me earlier about that ridiculous whipped-cream bullshit? Instead of staying at the Dime with my teammates or tracking down Heath and Jonah to reprimand them, all I could think about was how I hadn't kissed Brenna in *days*. And what did I do? I borrowed Brooks's car and drove all the way to Hastings like a lovesick loser.

Maybe she's right. Maybe we do need to cool it.

But I don't want to, dammit. So I voice the sentiment. "I want to keep seeing you."

"That's great, Jake. But I just told you, I'm done."

Frustration rises in my chest. "I don't think you mean it."

"How about you don't tell me what I mean or don't mean?"

Sighing, she walks over to the window ledge and picks up my boots. "It's time for you to go."

"Are you sure your father isn't going to pop out of the shadows?" I ask warily.

"He won't. He might be a jerk sometimes, but he won't cause a scene in front of a stranger."

A stranger. Once again I feel a prick of hurt, which is irritating. I'm Jake Connelly, for chrissake. My feelings don't get hurt, and I only give a damn about one thing: hockey. I shouldn't care what Brenna thinks of me.

We creep out of her bedroom. Light spills out from under a door at the end of the hall. I assume Coach Jensen's room. Luckily, the door remains closed. On the way downstairs, my socked foot connects with a step that creaks so loudly it's like the entire house is groaning in displeasure. *I hear ya, house. I'm not too happy right now, either.*

In the front hall, I slip into my Timberlands and lace them up. "You really don't want to see each other anymore?" My voice is slightly hoarse, and not because I have to whisper.

"I…" She drags one hand through her tousled hair. "I can't deal with this right now. Just go, Jake. Please."

So I go.

22
JAKE

Hazel comes with me to Gloucester on Saturday morning to visit my folks. On the train ride up, she does most of the talking. I try hard to pay attention, because we haven't hung out in a while, but my mind is elsewhere. It's back in Hastings, at Brenna's house, replaying that entire night.

I don't understand the weird tension between Brenna and her father. She admitted to being a bad girl, but I can't help but wonder—what on earth did she do to earn his complete distrust? Did she murder the family pet?

She's been ignoring me for three days, and my ego has officially taken a dive. Four unanswered messages? This has never happened to me before. Meanwhile, we have one week until the conference finals, and my head is all over the place. I'm not worried about the exhibition tonight and tomorrow for the Boston Cancer Society, because it's not about a win or a loss; it's about helping a good cause. But I definitely need to get my shit together before next week.

"Oh, and you know who's getting married," Hazel is saying.

"Hmmm?"

"Are you even paying attention to me?" she demands.

I drag the back of my hand over my face. I had such a shit sleep last night. "Yeah," I say absently. "You said you're getting married—wait, what? You're getting married?"

"No, not me. I'm not getting married, you dumbass." She rolls her eyes and shoves a strand of dirty-blonde hair behind her ear.

Her hair is down, I suddenly realize. She usually braids it or has it in a ponytail. "Your hair's down," I blurt out.

A faint blush reddens her cheeks. "Yep. It's been down for the last forty minutes."

"Sorry."

"What's going on with you? Why are you such a space cadet today?"

"I'm thinking about the game this weekend." Her skeptical expression tells me she doesn't buy that, so I don't give her the chance to follow up. "So who's getting married?"

"Tina Carlen. She was a year behind us in school."

"Petey's sister?"

"Yep."

"Wait, how old is she?"

"Twenty."

"And she's getting married? Did you get an invite to the wedding?"

"Yep. You probably did, too. You never check your email."

My jaw falls open. "They sent *e-vites* for their wedding?"

"Millennials, am I right?"

I snicker.

The train rolls into the station ten minutes later, and then we're on our way to my parents' house. "Mom's going to be thrilled to see you," I tell Hazel as we approach the front stoop.

"Did you tell her I was coming?"

"No. I thought it would be a fun surprise."

I'm not wrong. Mom is overjoyed when she spots Hazel in the entryway. "Hazel!" she exclaims, throwing her arms around my child-hood friend. "I didn't know you were coming! What a great surprise!"

Hazel hugs her back. "It's so good to see you, Mrs. C."

"Hang up your coat and come see what we've done with the family room! We completely redecorated." She grabs Hazel's hand and ushers her away. A moment later, they're in the family room, where Hazel is pretending to like all the changes. I know it's an act, because Hazel's always been a tomboy. My mom's flowered wallpaper and frilly curtains are way too feminine for her liking.

"Jake." My father appears in the kitchen doorway, his dark hair messy as usual. "Sorry I wasn't here last weekend, but I'm sure glad to see you today."

"Good to see you, too." We exchange the manliest of greetings: a combination of side hug, shoulder slap, and handshake.

I follow him into the kitchen. "Coffee?" Dad says.

"Yes, please."

He pours me a cup, then goes to the fridge and starts pulling out ingredients. "I'm on breakfast duty today. What do you think about omelets?"

"Sounds great. Need any help?"

"You can chop up this stuff." He gestures to the array of vegetables on the counter.

I find a cutting board, grab a knife, and start chopping. On the other side of the kitchen island, Dad cracks eggs into a ceramic bowl.

"So I was watching a segment on HockeyNet last night," he says as he whisks the eggs. "Top ten most promising rookies for the upcoming season. You were number two."

"Who was number one?" I demand. Because fuck that. Not to toot my own horn, but the last player out of college who came even close to my stats is Garrett Graham, and he's killing it in Boston.

"Wayne Dodd," Dad says.

I relax. Acceptable. Dodd is a goalie for one of the Big Ten schools. He's an excellent player, but the goalie position requires a whole other set of skills. I might be number two, but technically I'm number one in the forward position. I can live with that.

"Dodd has a mean glove," I say. "I saw one of their televised games, and he looked terrifying."

Dad narrows his eyes. "Think you might face him in the Frozen Four?"

"Good chance. Once all the conference finals are decided, we'll find out who'll be moving forward." And that should be my primary focus—getting my team to the national tournament. The pressure is insane. Sixteen teams will be whittled down to four in the course of a weekend. From four it'll become two, and then one. We need to be that one.

Dad changes the subject. "Are you looking at places in Edmonton yet? Checking out the online listings?"

"I haven't had time to do much browsing," I admit. "I've been concentrating on preparing for the Briar game."

"Yeah, you're right, good call." He takes the cutting board from me and uses the knife to scrape the diced mushrooms and green peppers into the omelet bubbling in the pan. "So...you brought Hazel home with you today..."

"Is that suddenly an issue?" I chuckle, because Hazel's been over to our house hundreds if not thousands of times.

"No, of course not." He looks over his broad shoulder and grins sheepishly. "That was my cool, macho way of asking if you two are finally together."

My folks are incorrigible when it comes to this. "No, we're not together."

"Why not? Along with making your mother very, very happy, dating Hazel would be good for you. Keep you grounded when you move to Edmonton."

I sit down at the counter. "We're just friends, Dad."

"I know, but maybe—"

"Something smells amazing," Hazel declares, and I'm grateful for the interruption.

My mother comes up behind me and ruffles my hair, then kisses the top of my head. "You didn't hug me hello," she scolds.

"Yeah, because you were so eager to show Hazel the family room."

Hazel slides onto the stool beside me, and the mood in the kitchen gets substantially lighter. But inside, I'm once again dwelling on the fact that I haven't spoken to Brenna in three days.

It isn't until we're heading back to Cambridge that Hazel finally calls me on it. "Okay, what the heck is going on with you, Connelly? You've been distracted and grumpy all morning. Even your mom noticed."

"Nothing's going on," I lie.

She searches my face. "Are you nervous about playing us this weekend?"

"Not at all. We're gonna kick your ass."

She sticks out her tongue. "I'm so torn about who to root for."

"No, you're not. Obviously you're rooting for your best friend."

Hazel rests her head on my shoulder as the train speeds forward. "You're acting weird, whether you want to admit it or not. And you've sounded distant the last few times we've talked," she admits. "Are you pissed at me or something?"

"Of course not. I just have a lot on my mind."

There's a long beat of hesitation. "Girl trouble?"

"Nah."

Her head pops up, and suddenly there's a pair of highly suspicious eyes fixed on me. "It's actually girl trouble, isn't it? Are you seeing somebody?"

"No."

"Are you lying?"

"Yes."

Hazel laughs, but it sounds a bit weak. I can't decode her expression, but I think it might be conveying a hint of disapproval.

"What, I'm not allowed to see anyone?" I say casually.

"It's not that. It's…you don't do girlfriends, remember?"

"Yeah, and this is one of the reasons." My tone turns bleak. "Being ignored sucks."

"You're being ignored?" she exclaims. "You, the mighty Jake Connelly, are the victim of *ghosting*?"

"Sort of? It's not exactly ghosting, because she didn't disappear without a word. She ended it to my face, but it was kind of a vague breakup."

"Breakup?" Hazel echoes in surprise. "How long have you been seeing each other?"

"Honestly, not long. A few weeks."

She starts toying with her thumb ring. Hazel wears a lot of chunky jewelry, mostly rings and bracelets, and the one she's playing with now was my Christmas present to her. The silver band winks in the overhead light as she spins it around her thumb.

"And you're this attached after a few weeks?" she finally says.

"Well, she's been on my radar for longer than that. But we only recently started going out."

"Have you been on a date? Like, an actual date?"

"Yes."

She spins the ring some more. "Was it good?"

"Really good," I confess. "I don't know, we were really hitting it off and she just bailed."

"Then she's a moron."

"Nah, she's not. She's cool, actually. I think you would like her."

"What's her name?"

"Bre—" I stop abruptly.

"Breh?" A groove appears in Hazel's forehead. "What kind of name is that?"

I hesitate before deciding to be honest. Hazel's not part of the hockey scene, anyway, so I can't see her putting two and two together about Brenna.

"Her name is Brenna," I reveal.

"That's a pretty name." Hazel tips her head. "Is she pretty?"

"Gorgeous."

"I guess she has to be, right? I mean, you can't be a scrub and capture the heart of the elusive Jake Connelly."

I shrug. "She hasn't captured my heart and I'm not elusive."

"Dude, every girl in high school wanted to be with you, and not a single one was able to lock you down. You are unquestionably elusive. Like an eel." She starts toying with her thumb ring again. "Tell me about this Brenna."

"Nah, let's not do this."

"Why not? We're not allowed to talk about relationships?"

"We never have before."

"So?"

"Fine. You go first," I challenge.

"No problem. Let's talk about my relationship." Hazel smirks at me. "I don't have one. Your turn."

I can't help but laugh. She got me there. "I dunno, what do you want me to say? Her name is Brenna. She's amazing. We're broken up. Or maybe on a break. That's really all there is to know."

"Does she go to Harvard?"

"No."

"Does she go to college?"

"Yes."

Hazel sighs dramatically. "Are you going to tell me where she goes?"

I think it over. "Do you promise to keep it between us?"

"Of course." The crease in her forehead deepens.

"She's at Briar."

Something indecipherable flickers in Hazel's eyes. Her jaw tenses, briefly, before relaxing. She twists her ring again. "All right. She's at Briar. And?"

"And her father coaches Briar's hockey team."

Despite her total disinterest in all things hockey, even Hazel comprehends the foolishness of this move. "Are you serious?"

I nod. "Brenna Jensen. She's Chad Jensen's daughter." I let out a sharp breath. "She's gotten in my head."

"What do you mean?"

"I mean I can't stop thinking about her. And I know it's a bad idea to get involved with her, especially since we're playing you next weekend. But…" I shift awkwardly. "I like her."

"You like her," my friend repeats.

"Yes."

"And you've been preoccupied and cranky because she's ignoring you."

"Yes."

Hazel falls silent.

"What?" I demand. I always know when there's something heavy on her mind. "What are you thinking right now?"

"It's just…did it ever occur to you that this might be part of her plan?"

"What plan?"

"Do you really not see it?" Hazel stares at me as if I'm the biggest chump in the world. "Everyone knew the conference finals would likely come down to Harvard and Briar, and a few weeks before this hugely important game, the daughter of the Briar coach is suddenly interested in you, and, I quote, 'getting in your head.' And now you're so distracted, I bet you're not giving your usual hundred and ten percent in practice because all you're doing is obsessing over this girl. Do you get my drift, Jake?"

I do, and it's funny, because that first night at the diner, I accused Brenna of doing exactly what Hazel is suggesting. Brenna had denied it, and I believed her then and still believe it now. I no longer have a cynical viewpoint about Brenna Jensen. "Brenna's not like that," I say simply. "Yes, she roots for her team and supports her dad, but she's not trying to sabotage me."

"How do you know that?"

"Because I do."

"Would you bet your life on it?" Hazel says in challenge.

"I don't need to bet my life on it," I answer in a dry tone. "But yes, I'm confident that this isn't some dastardly plot on her end."

"If you say so."

But the *omg you're such an idiot* look on Hazel's face tells me she doesn't buy it.

23
JAKE

"Do I have a bubble butt?"

I scroll through my messages, but there's nothing from Brenna. It's been five days. Five days of complete radio silence. That is un-fucking-acceptable.

"Yo! Are you listening to me?"

I lift my head to glance at Brooks. We're in the media room at the arena, waiting for everyone else to arrive for the team meeting. We're scheduled to watch game tape this morning, which'll be fun. Watching Brenna's friends skate around on a huge screen.

Shit. Hazel's right—I am thinking about this nonstop, and that's not good.

"You're not going to answer the question?" Brooks demands.

"No, because I don't understand what you're asking me." I set my phone down and lean back in my padded chair, crossing my arms behind my head.

"It's not that hard, Connelly. Do I have a bubble butt or what?"

I stare at him. "What the hell's a bubble butt?"

"Exactly what it sounds like." He rakes a frustrated hand through his blond hair.

"Okay, so like a fat ass?"

"No, not a fat ass. For fuck's sake. It's like two perfectly round globes, and they're usually super tight. You know, like two bubbles, but on your butt. A bubble butt." He sounds exasperated. "What part of this don't you understand?"

I'm genuinely bemused. "Why are you asking?"

He flops down in a chair. "Because last night I was banging Kayla—"

"Oh, I know," I say dryly. "I heard every second of it."

"—and we were up against the wall, you know, with her legs wrapped around me. I was holding her ass and pushing her down on my cock—"

"Dude. I legit don't want to hear this."

"There's a point, I swear," he insists.

Our teammates start filing into the room. Coby, McCarthy, Dmitry. Heath and his fellow Whipped Cream Bandit, Jonah. A few seniors.

Brooks is unfazed by the audience. "So we were doing it standing up and she's clawing at my shoulders. And my closet door was open so she could see the mirror, you know, the full-length one on the inside of the door?" Outrage colors his tone. "And suddenly she starts giggling, and I was like, what the hell are you laughing at, and she said it's because she just noticed I have a bubble butt!"

"What is happening right now?" Adam the freshman says miserably. The poor kid still hasn't adapted to us yet. You'd think after almost an entire season he'd be used to the lunacy.

Brooks spins around in his chair. We have a sweet setup here in the video room. Padded chairs that actually swivel, a huge screen that takes up nearly an entire wall. Plus a ton of cool tech that Coach likes to utilize when he's freezing frames or highlighting certain plays.

"What's a bubble butt?" Heath asks.

"It's when your ass looks like two globes," Coby supplies.

"See! *He* knows what I'm talking about!" Brooks points to Coby, nodding in approval. "Do I have that?" he asks the room.

"Dude, I hate to disappoint you," I say, "but I haven't spent much time staring at your ass. I also haven't spent much time examining other dudes' asses, and since I don't know what a bubble butt looks like, I can't tell you if you have one. So for the love of Jesus, can we talk about something else?"

Apparently not, as Brooks is already marching toward one of the laptops on Coach's desk. He clicks the track pad a few times, and a web browser appears on the big screen behind him. "Okay, so…" He types the words "bubble butt" in the image search.

Two seconds later, rows and rows of thumbnails appear on the screen, all featuring some very sexy female behinds.

"Ugh, sorry, no, I don't want to look at *girls*." Brooks alters the search to say "man bubble butt."

The first image that pops up is one of a fully clothed grown man in an actual bubble.

"The fuck's that dude doing in a bubble?" Coby guffaws.

"Maybe he's got that bubble disease," someone offers. "You know, where you need to be shut away from the rest of the world."

"The bubble isn't the disease," Dmitry says with a snicker. "The bubble is the solution to the disease."

"Why is it so hard to find pictures of male asses?" Brooks growls. "All right, boys. Brace yourself."

"Weston," I caution. "Whatever you're about to do, please don't."

Unfortunately, there's no stopping Brooks when he goes on a tangent, especially when it's related to his appearance. The man is vain as fuck.

When a porn site appears on the screen, I'm quick to issue another warning. "You better get out of there before Coach comes in."

He glances at the clock mounted over the door. "We have ten minutes, and he's never early. Coach is an on-the-dot kinda guy."

That's true, but that doesn't mean I want to be looking at porn on university property.

Brooks clicks the search bar and keys in "bubble butt," and we're not surfing porn anymore. We're surfing *gay* porn. Awesome.

"There!" Brooks says triumphantly. "This is what she says it looks like!" He clicks on a thumbnail labeled: *bubble butt gets pounded*.

Coby groans. "Bro, I don't want to see this shit."

But Brooks pauses the scene before the sex gets underway. In fact, there's still only one dude in the frame, a tall Nordic blond who decides to take all his clothes off in a jiu-jitsu studio because that's what real people do.

Brooks zooms in on the guy's behind. And okay, I'm not going to lie—his butt cheeks *do* resemble two bubbles. The rest of his body is lean and ripped, so those tight globes really do attract the eye.

"It's the first thing I notice when I look at him," Coby admits. "My eyes go right to the ass."

"Mine too," I say. "That's weird, right?"

"Is this me?" Brooks demands. "Because if it is, I'm *pissed*. Look at it. It's completely disproportional to the rest of his body."

"Dude, we just told you, we don't pay attention to your butt," I say irritably. "We can't compare."

"Fine, here."

He turns around and drops trou.

At the same time Coach Pedersen enters the room.

Coach stumbles to a stop. His gaze travels from the naked man on the screen to Weston's bare ass. Then he scowls at the rest of us. "What the hell is wrong with you idiots?"

"It's not what it looks like," Brooks tries to reassure him.

"Really? Because it looks like you're trying to compare your ass to the one up there, and the answer to that is, yes, they're identical. Now zip up your goddamn pants, turn that garbage off, and take a seat, Weston."

My teammate appears genuinely devastated as he pulls up his pants. "I have a bubble butt, you guys. I feel like my whole life has been a lie."

Our goalie Johansson snickers. "Plastic surgery's always an option."

"Enough," Coach snaps. "We don't have time for this shit. We're facing off against Jensen and his crew in five days. It'll be televised on all the New England stations, and I'm hearing rumors about HockeyNet, too. So tell me, do you want to make fools of yourselves or do you want to win?"

"We want to win," everyone mumbles.

"Do you want to jerk off to Weston's ass or do you want to win?"

We raise our voices. "We want to win!"

"Good. Then shut the hell up and pay attention."

After the meeting, Pedersen stops me before I can follow the rest of my teammates out the door. "Connelly, stay behind."

I shove my hands in my pockets as I walk over. "What's up, Coach?"

"Have a seat." Based on his harsh expression, I'm obviously not in store for a pep talk. Once I'm seated, he stands in front of me, arms crossed over his bulky chest. "What's going on with you, Jake?"

"What do you mean?"

"I mean, what's going on with you? You were off at morning skate today. Two seconds slower than usual. Granted, that's still faster than an average player, but it's slow for you."

"I was distracted," I admit.

"And this afternoon? Normally when you show up early, I walk in and you're already leading the meeting, going over tape. Instead I walk in and Weston is shaking his ass in front of everyone and you're watching gay porn."

"We weren't watching gay porn," I assure him. "We were just..." I trail off.

Because he's right. I'm always deeply focused on the game. It's a single-minded dedication that's been with me since I was old enough to skate. I lead team meetings. I show up early, offer extra help to guys who need it. I sacrifice my own time, my own sleep, and my own schoolwork to ensure that every weapon on our team is locked, loaded, and in working order.

For the past five days, my head hasn't been in it. And maybe five days doesn't sound like a long time in the grand scheme of things, but it is when you only have five more to prepare for arguably the most important game of the season. Not the second most important, because that's operating on the assumption that the Frozen Four is a given, and it isn't. We need to beat Briar in order to move forward; therefore, this is *the* most important game, and the only thing that should matter at the moment.

"You're right," I tell him. "I haven't been as focused as I should be."

"What's going on? School? Do we need to set you up with a tutor?"

"No, I'm good with all that. A couple final papers left to write, but I'm not having any trouble. They're not due till May, anyway."

"So what is it? Shit at home?"

"No." I readjust myself in my chair. Uncharacteristic embarrassment heats the back of my neck. "I feel like a moron saying this, but it's a girl."

Coach rumbles in displeasure. "You want my advice?"

"Please."

"Forget her."

A laugh pops out. Well. That's not helpful. "That's one solution," I say carefully, because Coach Pedersen doesn't appreciate being challenged.

"Trust me, kid, it's the *only* solution. Women are goddamn headaches. Even the nice ones," he says, shaking his head. "It's like they all take a master class in manipulation, learning how to play with your emotions. They either turn us into slaves, or fools."

His volatile reaction catches me off-guard. I hear a lot of bitterness in his tone, and I wonder who broke his heart. As far as

I know, Pedersen's never been married. He doesn't have kids, and if he has a girlfriend then he never talks about her. A few of the guys have posited the theory that he might be gay, but I don't think he is. There was a team event at a Boston hotel last year, and I saw Coach leave the party with a hot redhead in a skintight dress. That doesn't mean he isn't gay, but, hell, who knows?

From the sound of it, though, he has absolutely no interest in relationships.

"At the end of the day, these women want something from you, kid. They *always* want something. They take and take and take, and they don't give anything back. Nobody gives a shit about anybody else, so you might as well look out for yourself, right?"

That's what I usually do. It's what I've done my whole life. I'm not sure why the approach isn't working for me lately. My stomach's been twisted up in knots ever since Brenna ended things.

"You know what I like most about you, Jake?"

"What's that?" I ask warily.

"You're selfish."

I find myself bristling. He's presenting it as a compliment, and it's not even a new revelation for me—I *know* I'm selfish. Yet for some reason, being called selfish by my coach raises my hackles.

"You don't let anything come in the way of your goals," he continues. "Your own needs come first, and that's how it should be. That's the reason you're destined to be a superstar." Coach shakes his head again. "This girl that's causing you all this grief? Forget about her. Focus on winning, focus on this sweet new job you'll have come August. One misstep on the ice can end a career. Loss of focus leads to dangerous outcomes, and not only the risk of injury. A bad game reflects poorly on you, and you'd better believe that your new bosses are watching every single game and studying your film afterward."

He's right.

"So get your head in the game. Forget this girl. There'll be others. When you're up in Edmonton I guarantee you'll find a lot of cute bunnies to keep you warm." He leans forward and claps a hand over my shoulder. "We good?"

I nod slowly. "We're good. Don't worry. I'll get my head on straight."

"That's what I like to hear."

And yet the first thing I do when I step out the main doors of the Bright-Landry Hockey Center is contact Brenna again.

Coach's speech got to me, but not in the way I'm sure he'd hoped. I don't want to be the man who gets hurt by one woman and goes on to despise the entire sex. I don't want to be bitter and angry.

I can't force Brenna to go out with me again, but at least I can let her know that she's still on my mind.

ME: Hey, Hottie. Me again. Feel free to keep avoiding me, but just know that I'm here if you change your mind.

24
BRENNA

It's Tuesday morning and a skinny blonde is giving me the stink eye.

My friend Audrey is supposed to be meeting me at the Coffee Hut, but she's five minutes late. Maybe the skinny blonde at the counter is pissed that I'm taking up a two-person table for myself? But that's bullshit. She's alone, too. Why should she get the two-person table? This is America. *First-come first-served, girlfriend.*

Still, I send an SOS to Audrey, because the coffee shop is packed, and I can't nurse the same cup of coffee for much longer without the barista coming by to tell me they need the table.

ME: Where are you? Peeps are trying to steal our table.
AUDREY: Still waiting to talk to the prof.

Ugh, really? She's still at the lecture hall? The journalism building is a ten-minute walk from the Coffee Hut. Her next message confirms my fears.

AUDREY: I'll be at least 15. Do you mind waiting or should we meet this afternoon?
ME: I won't have time this afternoon :(Class starts at 1, ends around 5. We can do dinner maybe?

AUDREY: Can't :(

Grrr. Despite sharing a major, Audrey and I haven't hung out in a while. We don't interact much during classes, since most of the time we're assigned a story on the spot and then ordered to go forth and write it. I've barely seen my friend Elisa this month, either. I guess it's that time of year. Final papers and exams, the hockey season at its peak, and before we know it, it'll be May and the semester will be over.

ME: OK, I'll wait. I miss your face.
AUDREY: Aw love you, boo. See you soon.

"Brenna Jensen?"

I lift my head to see the stink-eye girl from the counter. She's two feet away now, and her expression hasn't gotten any brighter. It matches the overcast sky beyond the window.

"Who's asking?" I ask warily.

"I'm Hazel. Hazel Simonson."

I give her a blank look. "Okay. Do we know each other?"

A groove digs into her forehead, but I'm not quite sure what that signifies. "Jake never mentioned me?"

My hand tightens around my coffee cup. "You know Jake?"

"Yes. Very well, actually."

I attempt to keep my expression neutral. Swear to God, if this girl tries telling me that he's her boyfriend…

No. I'd call bullshit if she did. I don't think Jake is a dishonest person. He said he doesn't do girlfriends, and I don't believe he's got a side piece stashed somewhere.

"Can I join you?" Hazel says coolly.

"I'm actually meeting somebody—"

She sits down, anyway. "I'll keep you company until they get here." Hazel clasps her hands on the tabletop. "There's a couple things we need to discuss."

I lean back in the chair, keeping my body language relaxed. Hers is confrontational, and I always meet aggression with indifference. It's a tactic that tends to ruffle the aggressor's feathers. "Look. Hazel. No offense, but I don't know you. You're claiming to know Jake, but he hasn't once brought up your name to me."

Her light-brown eyes flash briefly.

"So forgive me if I don't trust the strange girl who sits down without invitation and glares at me like I strangled her cat." I cross my legs, loosely resting a hand on my right knee.

"I do know Jake," Hazel says curtly. "We grew up in Gloucester together. Went to school together. I know his parents... Lily and Rory?" she prompts.

I can't challenge her on that. Jake never mentioned his parents' first names to me.

"We all had breakfast together on Saturday. At their place." A trace of smugness creeps into her expression. "Jake and I took the train up."

An unwelcome feeling pulls at my stomach.

"I know him better than anyone," she finishes. And it's no longer a *trace*—she's smug as fuck.

"Is that so?" I drawl.

"Yes. I know he has a good head on his shoulders, and I also know he's way smarter than he looks. He doesn't usually get played like this."

The lioness act is starting to grate. "He's getting played?"

"Don't play dumb." She laces her fingers together in a tight grip. "I know exactly who you are. I cyber-stalked you after he told me you were dating."

I manage to swallow my surprise before it reaches my eyes. Jake told this chick that we were dating?

Hazel smirks. "Like I said, Jake and I are old friends. We don't keep secrets from each other."

That sensation in my gut intensifies. It starts churning in a hot eddy of…I think it might be jealousy. But there's a hefty dose of anger in there, too, because who the hell is this girl?

I meet her haughty eyes. "That's great that you two are so tight. Although if that's truly the case, then you would know that he and I aren't seeing each other anymore."

Saying it out loud triggers a wave of regret. I won't deny that I miss him. It hasn't even been a full week since I asked him to leave my house, but it feels like forever. He's constantly been on my mind, which has been made worse by his daily texts. The one he sent yesterday about being around if I change my mind…I almost caved and called him.

At the last second, I regained my senses. Reminded myself why it's better that it's over. I don't want a boyfriend, and especially not one who's moving to another country in a few short months. And fine, maybe a part of me is still embarrassed by what happened in my bedroom. I could barely meet Jake's eyes afterward. He got a front-row seat to my father lecturing me in the hallway as if I was a disobedient child.

It was so humiliating.

"Yes, I do know that," Hazel says, interrupting my thoughts. "He told me that you ended it. And say what you will about Jake, but he's not a cynical person—"

"What does cynicism have to do with this?" I interject.

"Everything. Because I *am* a cynical person, and I know what you're up to."

"Okay." I'm beginning to grow tired of this entire exchange.

"Coach Jensen's daughter hooks up with the Harvard hockey captain during the playoffs. She puts him under her spell, gets under his skin, and drops him right before the biggest game of the season. And now he's so upset he can barely focus on hockey—the only thing that's ever mattered to him, by the way—because this girl ghosted him."

A new emotion joins the cocktail brewing in my gut. Guilt. "He's upset?"

"Yeah. Congratulations. You got what you wanted."

"That's not what I wanted at all."

"Right. I'm sure." She scrapes her chair back but doesn't stand yet. "Stay away from him. Jake and I watch out for each other, we have since we were kids, and I'm not going to let some puck bunny sabotage his season or distract him from his goals."

"You're not going to *let* me, huh? I'm sorry to break it to you, but, to quote my cousin Leigh's four-year-old daughter—you're not the boss of me." I chuckle. "And I'm the farthest thing from a puck bunny."

"Right," she drawls again.

"Oh, and FYI, I'm not sabotaging a damn thing, but that's the last thing I'm saying on this subject. I'm not going to explain myself to you or discuss my relationship with Jake, because it's none of your business."

She stiffly gets to her feet. "Whatever. You ended it. Keep it that way and we won't have a problem."

I smile, all teeth and no warmth. "Are you done?"

"For now. Enjoy the rest of your day." She marches to the door, and I watch as Jake's (alleged) best friend in the whole wide world saunters out of the Coffee Hut.

On one hand, I do appreciate it when claws come out in defense of someone you care about. But I don't appreciate the accusation that I'm sabotaging Jake's season, or that being with him was some nefarious scheme on my part.

I didn't intend on hooking up with him. Ed Mulder and his stupid obsession with Edmonton was the only reason Jake and I went out. And things turned physical because that's what happens when two people have chemistry. Chemistry is hard to find and even harder to fight.

Ha. I'd like to see *Hazel* try to resist Jake. If he fixed that seductive green-eyed gaze on her and—

Something occurs to me. Was this encounter more than just a friend defending her friend? Does she have a thing for him?

On further thought, I realize that wouldn't surprise me in the least.

When my phone rings, I half expect it to be Jake, and my pulse speeds up. When the words *HockeyNet* flash on the screen, my heart beats even faster. *Finally.*

I take a breath, trying to steady my nerves. "Hello?"

"May I speak to Brenna Jensen, please?" inquires a brisk female voice.

"Speaking."

"Brenna, hi. This is Rochelle from Ed Mulder's office. Mr. Mulder was hoping you'd be able to come in tomorrow to discuss the internship position."

"Oh. Um." I quickly run through tomorrow's schedule. My first class isn't until one o'clock again. It'll be close, but I could make it. "Yes, but only if it's first thing in the morning. I have a seminar at one."

"I'm afraid he's all booked up in the morning." I hear typing on the other line. "How about later afternoon? Does five thirty work for you?"

"I can make it work," I say instantly, because I'm not about to be difficult.

"Perfect. We'll see you tomorrow."

She disconnects.

Excitement flutters inside me. In the back of my mind, a little voice cautions me not to get ahead of myself. This doesn't mean I got the job.

But...how am I *not* supposed to be hopeful? He wouldn't make me drive all the way to Boston just to turn me down.

Nobody is that big of an asshole, right?

"We decided to go with somebody else."

Oh. Apparently Ed Mulder *is* that big of an asshole.

From my perch on his visitor's chair, I swallow my resentment and muster up a calm tone. "For all three slots?" There were three internships up for grabs.

"Yes. We've got some good guys coming in. Don't get me wrong, your academics are on par, but two of them are athletes, and all three simply brought something unique to the table."

Penises.

They brought penises to the table.

There is no doubt in my mind of that. But I force myself to remain courteous. "I see. All right. Well, thank you for your consideration." *Thank you for making me drive all the fucking way here.*

He could have easily sent an email like a regular old jackass, but noooo, he had to prove that he's a supreme jackass.

I start to get up, but Mulder chuckles and holds up a hand. "Wait. That's not the only reason I asked you to come in."

My butt sinks back on the chair. Despite myself, a teeny flicker of hope tickles my throat. Maybe he's offering me a different position. Maybe a paid one, or—

"I wanted to invite you and Jake to the Bruins game this Sunday." He beams at me, as if expecting me to clap my hands together in glee. "The network has a private box at TD Garden. Oh, my brother and sister-in-law will be there, too. Lindsay and Karen really enjoyed meeting you the other night. You ladies can catch up while us boys enjoy the game."

Is murder illegal in Massachusetts?

It's illegal in all fifty states, I remind myself.

Maybe I could get a good lawyer who could spin it as self-defense? Summer's dad is a defense attorney. I'm sure he'd be able to keep me off Death Row.

The fury bubbling inside me is so close to spilling over. This asshole made me drive all the way to Boston so he could reject my internship application and invite me to talk about knitting and interior design with his wife and sister-in-law while he and my fake boyfriend get to watch my favorite hockey team.

It's probably a good thing I don't own a gun.

"I appreciate the invitation. I'll have to ask Jake," I say tightly, hoping the sheer rage isn't showing on my face. "I'll let you know."

"Perfect. Hope you guys can make it. My wife can't stop gushing about what a great couple you two make." He winks. "Don't worry, it's still our little secret."

I fake a smile. "Thank you."

"Let me walk you out."

"No bother!" My cheery expression is in grave danger of collapsing. "I know the way out. Enjoy the rest of your day, Mr. Mulder."

"Ed."

"Ed."

The fake smile disappears the moment I exit the office. My movements are stiff as I grab my coat from the row of hooks near the door. "It was nice meeting you," I tell Rochelle.

"Yes. Best of luck to you," she says sympathetically.

I step out into the corridor, but I don't leave the building right away. I want to walk by the studio one last time, give it one last longing look. When I reach the cavernous space, there's a news show in progress. I creep in, keeping a discreet distance, and watch as two analysts recap last night's Ottawa Senators game and the game-winning goal by Brody Lacroix. One of them says, "Geoff spoke to Brody after the game. Here's what the rookie had to say."

From the corner of my eye, I catch a flurry of activity in the control booth. The director signals to someone, and a video of the interview suddenly comes on the screen between the two hosts. Geoff Magnolia's annoying face appears. He's the one who does most of the locker room interviews after games, and players view him as "one of the bros."

Most of the time, Magnolia is too busy exchanging wisecracks with the players to ask about the actual game. With this Senators game, however, he's attempting to be a real journalist while chatting with star player Brody Lacroix. They discuss Lacroix's success in the third period, as well as his overall success during the season so far. At three different times, Magnolia says that Lacroix's parents must be very proud of their son, and all three times, Lacroix gives an uncomfortable half-smile before finally mumbling some lame answer and turning away.

I shake my head. "Moron," I mutter at the same time that a low female voice growls, "Idiot."

I spin around to find Georgia Barnes, my idol, standing a few feet away. She eyes me, looking intrigued.

"And it's time for a commercial," one of the hosts tells the audience. "After the break, we'll catch up with Herbie Handler down in Nashville and hear his predictions for tonight's Predators matchup against the Flyers."

"And we're out," a cameraman barks.

As if a switch has been flipped, the set comes to life. Bodies rush by, the chatter of voices echoing in the studio. "Someone fix that light!" one of the hosts complains. "It's burning my goddamn retinas."

A lowly assistant sprints over to deal with the lights. Georgia Barnes glances at me again, then walks off the set.

I hesitate for a beat. Then I hurry after her, awkwardly calling out her name.

She stops in the brightly lit corridor, turning to face me. She's wearing a black pinstripe skirt, a white silk top, and black flats. Despite the elegant attire, I know that she has a fiery streak in her.

"I'm sorry to bother you," I tell her. "But I wanted to let you know what a huge fan I am. I think you're one of the sharpest, most intelligent journalists in the country."

Georgia responds with a warm smile. "Thank you. I appreciate that." Her shrewd gaze sweeps over me. "Do you work here?"

I shake my head. "In fact, I was just informed that I didn't get the internship I applied for."

"I see." She nods ruefully. "It's a competitive program, from what I hear." A dry note enters her voice. "Although you should probably be prepared—this entire industry is competitive. Even more so for women."

"So I hear."

She studies my face again. "Why did you call Geoff Magnolia a moron?"

A rush of heat suffuses my cheeks, and I hope to hell I'm not blushing. "Uh, right. Yes. I'm sorry I said that—"

"Don't be sorry. But tell me why you did."

I offer an awkward shrug. "Because of the questions he was asking. Someone needs to tell that man to perform at least a modicum of research before his interviews. He asked about Lacroix's parents three times."

"So what?" Georgia says. Her tone is light, but I sense she's testing me.

"So the kid's mom died of cancer less than a month ago, and he looked like he was about to burst into tears. Magnolia should've known about that."

"Yes. He should have. But as we've established, Geoff Magnolia is a moron." She lowers her voice conspiratorially. "I'll tell you a secret—what's your name?"

"Brenna."

"I'll tell you a secret, Brenna. Magnolia is the rule, not the exception. If you ever find yourself working here someday, be prepared to deal with morons on a daily basis. Or worse, sexist blowhards who will spend every minute of every day telling you that you don't belong here because you have a vagina."

I smile halfheartedly. "I think I experienced that today."

Her features soften. "Sorry to hear that. All I can say is, don't let one rejection, one door-slam, stop you from trying again. Continue applying to networks, cable stations, anywhere that's hiring." She winks. "Not everybody wants to keep us out, and a change is coming. Albeit slowly, but I promise you it's coming."

I feel a bit awestruck as Georgia squeezes my arm before sauntering off. I have faith that she's right, that a change *is* coming. But I wish it would hurry up. It took decades for female reporters to be allowed to interview athletes in the locker room. It required a *Sports Illustrated* reporter to file a lawsuit before a court finally ruled that banning female journalists from locker room interviews violated the 14th Amendment.

And yet changing laws does nothing to change social attitudes. ESPN has made strides by hiring more female columnists, analysts. But it pisses me off that women in sports continue to face hostility and sexist behaviors when they're simply trying to do their jobs, just like their male counterparts.

"Brenna, hey!" Mischa, the stage manager I met last week, bumps into me near the elevator bank. "You're back."

"I'm back," I say wryly.

"Good news, I assume?"

"Sadly, no. Mr. Mulder asked me to come so he could tell me to my face that I didn't get the job."

"Oh. I'm sorry. That sucks." He shakes his head, visibly disappointed. "I would've enjoyed having you around."

"Yeah, well, I'm sure the new interns will be great."

"Maybe. But I have a feeling Mulder is missing out by letting you go."

"Feel free to tell him that." When the elevator doors slide open, I reach out to touch his arm. "It was nice to meet you, Mischa."

"Nice meeting you too, Brenna."

My smile fades once I'm alone in the elevator. Tears prick my eyes, but I order myself not to cry. I'm not allowed to cry. It was just an internship. I'm sure I can find a local TV or radio station to gopher at this summer, and in the fall I can reapply at HockeyNet, or maybe I'll find an even better work placement. This isn't the end of the world.

But dammit, I really, really wanted this internship.

My fingers tremble as I pull my phone out of my purse. I should order a car to take me to the train station. Instead, I think about Jake's text from yesterday, the one urging me to call him.

I bite my lip.

Calling him is probably a terrible idea.

But I do it, anyway.

"Wow, you're talking to me again," Jake says when we meet up twenty minutes later. "What did I do to deserve this honor?"

My spirits are so low I can't even conjure up a sarcastic remark. "I didn't get the internship," I say flatly. "Mulder chose three guys with penises instead of me."

"As opposed to guys without penises?" He smiles, but his humor doesn't linger. "I'm sorry, Hottie. That sucks." He reaches out as if to touch me, but then thinks better of it and drops his arm to his side.

We're on the front steps of the Bright-Landry Hockey Center, which feels like absolute blasphemy. Luckily, none of his teammates are around. When I called him, he admitted that practice ended hours ago and he'd stayed behind to watch game tape on his own. That's dedication. And while I admire it, that also means I have to meet him here instead of his condo. The condo would have been highly preferable.

To add insult to injury, the sky decides to mimic my mood, taking this exact moment as opportunity to dump a mountain of rain on us. It's been cloudy and chilly all day, but suddenly the sky is black and it's pouring buckets, soaking our hair in seconds.

"Come inside," Jake urges, grabbing my hand.

We rush into the building, where I cringe at the sight of the championship pennants and all the framed crimson jerseys. "What if someone sees us?" I hiss as I shove my damp hair away from my forehead.

"Then they see us. Who cares? We're just talking, right?"

"I feel exposed. We're too out in the open," I grumble.

He rolls his eyes. "Fine. Let's go to the media room. It's private and I'm the only one in there."

I follow him down the hall, my gaze eating up his long stride. It's been less than a week since I last saw him, and somehow I forgot how tall he is, how attractive. He didn't hug or kiss me hello. I didn't hug or kiss him hello, either. Now I kinda wish I had.

In a state-of-the-art media room that rivals the one we have at Briar, I unzip my leather jacket and drape it over the back of a nearby chair. Then I plop into one of the plush chairs and stick out my chin glumly. "I really wanted that internship."

"I know you did." Jake settles in the chair next to mine, stretching those impossibly long legs out in front him. "But maybe it's a blessing in disguise. Even if he hadn't been your direct supervisor, you still would've had to interact with Mulder. And that guy is the worst."

"True." I suddenly notice the image on the big screen. It's Hunter Davenport's lean body crouching during a faceoff. "Spying, are we?" I crack.

"It's not spying, it's due diligence. And don't tell me your boys aren't doing the exact same thing right now."

"Well, I didn't come here to reveal Briar secrets, so don't ask me anything about my boys."

He glances over, his chiseled face serious. "Then why are you here?"

"What do you mean?"

"I mean, your cousin lives in the city. And I assume you have other friends here, too."

"So?"

"So why was I the first person you called after you got the bad news?"

I flick my gaze to his. "You don't know that you're the first person I called. Maybe nobody else picked up."

"Did you call anybody else?" Jake asks politely.

"No," I admit, which forces me to look inward, because why *did* I call him? We went on a couple of dates, talked on the phone a few times, fooled around a time or two. There is no reason why Jake should have been my go-to comfort person today. I have a good support system—Summer, Audrey, Elisa, to name a few. Why didn't I reach out to any of them?

"Why me?" he pushes.

I let out a frazzled breath. "I don't know."

"Yes, you do." He chuckles softly. "You like me."

"I don't like you."

"Yes, you do. That's why you kicked me out last week."

"No, I kicked you out because my father was standing outside the door while we were sixty-nine-ing."

Jake makes a growly sound. "You just had to bring that up."

"What, my father?"

"No, what we were doing." His eyes gleam seductively. "Now I'm hard."

"I feel like you're always hard," I grumble back.

"Come here and test that theory." He pats his lap, while enticingly waggling his eyebrows.

I can't stop a laugh. "What theory? You already admitted to being hard."

He crosses his ankles together, staring down at his Converse sneakers for a few seconds. "Okay. So you're saying you threw me out because your father almost caught us."

"Yup."

That's not entirely true. I kicked him out because I refused to show him any more vulnerability. In the span of an hour or two, I allowed him to see how badly I wanted him, how wildly he turned me on. I allowed him to overhear a mortifying exchange with my father, in which I was admonished like a child and accused of being a train wreck.

I don't want anybody else, let alone a guy, to ever view me the way my father does.

I feel Jake's gaze on me. "What?" I mutter.

"I don't believe what you're saying." His tone roughens. "What are you so afraid will happen if we keep seeing each other?"

"I'm not afraid. I simply don't see the point when it can't go anywhere."

"Do you only spend time with guys you think it'll go somewhere with?"

"No."

He looks thoughtful. "C'mere."

Before I can blink, he's tugging me off my chair. I wind up in his lap, and the bulge in his jeans is impossible to miss or ignore. I sigh in resignation, adjusting my position so that I'm straddling him. His quickly growing erection is pressed directly against my core, and it feels so good I can't help but rock against it.

Jake makes a husky sound. He slides one big hand to the base of my spine, while the other moves upward to tangle in my hair.

Against my better judgment, I lower my head. My tongue prods the seam of his lips, and he parts them to grant me access. I whimper when my tongue touches his. He tastes like mint gum and his lips are so soft and warm. I lock my hands around his neck, losing myself in the heat of him.

"Kissing you makes me so hard," he murmurs.

"You were hard before I kissed you."

"Yeah, because I was thinking about kissing you."

I laugh, and it comes out a bit breathless. "You're—" A crash of thunder drowns out my voice. The overhead lights flicker for a second.

Jake's dark eyebrows fly up. "Shit, that was nuts."

I stroke the wispy hairs at his nape. "Aw, Jakey. Are you scared?"

"Terrified," he whispers.

Our lips meet at the same time the lights flicker again. This time they go out.

Darkness engulfs us. But instead of jumping up in a panic, we kiss harder. Jake's hands travel beneath my black sweater. He pulls the thin material up to reveal my bra, but he doesn't unclasp it, just pushes it down to reveal my boobs. Wet heat surrounds my nipple. He draws it deep in his mouth, and I shiver uncontrollably.

He squeezes my breasts while continuing to lave my nipple, licking and suckling until it grows impossibly harder in his mouth. I moan, louder than I should considering our surroundings.

Jake responds by capturing my other nipple and teasing it senseless. Then he gives an upward thrust, rubbing our lower bodies together. God. This guy. I'm so hot for him, it's insane.

The room is still dark, but just when I'm starting to get used to it, the fluorescent lights flash back on.

Jake lifts his head, his gaze burning as he gets a nice eyeful of my chest. "So fucking beautiful."

Groaning, he cups both my breasts before burying his face between them.

And that's when Coach Pedersen walks into the room.

25
JAKE

"For fuck's sake, Connelly!"

At the incredulous exclamation, my head flies up and I swiftly shove Brenna's sweater down to cover her bare tits. She dives off my lap and into the neighboring chair. But it's too late. Pedersen's not an idiot. He saw us, and he knows exactly what we were doing.

"Coach, hey." I clear my throat. "We were…" I decide against lying. I'm not an idiot, either. "I'm sorry," I say simply. "This isn't the place."

"No shit," he snaps. "I'd expect this kind of behavior from Weston or Chilton, but not you, Connelly. You don't usually screw around on the job."

Coach doesn't even acknowledge Brenna. He stalks to the front of the room and grabs one of the laptops. From the corner of my eye I see Brenna smoothing out the front of her sweater. She wiggles discreetly, and I realize she's trying to put her bra cups back in place.

"I'm having a meeting with the assistants and forgot this," he says tightly. "And here I thought you were being a conscientious player, studying film on your own time. But boys will be boys, won't they?" There's a sharp edge to his every word.

Brenna warily tracks his movements as he tucks the laptop under his arm and stalks to the door. "Get your guest out of here, Connelly. This is no place for girlfriends."

"I'm not his girlfriend," Brenna blurts out, and I know it was completely involuntarily because she briefly closes her eyes, as if mentally scolding herself for speaking.

Pedersen finally spares her a look. A long, intent one. During his scrutiny, his frown gets deeper and deeper until his eyebrows are practically touching. "You're Chad Jensen's kid."

Shit.

Brenna blinks. For once, she doesn't have a smartass comment locked and loaded.

I want to lie and tell him he's mistaken, but he clearly recognizes her. He places the computer on a desk near the door and slowly approaches. His cynical gaze takes in Brenna's rumpled sweater, her disheveled hair.

"We met at a banquet a couple years ago," he tells her. "Yale alumni dinner. You were still in high school at that point. Chad brought you."

"Oh." She visibly swallows. "Yes. I remember that."

"Brianna, is it?"

"Brenna."

"Right." His beefy shoulders lift in a shrug. "Even if we hadn't met, I'd know you from anywhere. You're the spitting image of your mother."

Brenna does a terrible job of hiding her shock. Or maybe she's not trying to hide it. She openly gawks at my coach. "You knew my mother?"

"We went to college together." His tone is completely wooden, and his expression lacks any and all emotion. Which isn't out of the ordinary. Pedersen's emotional repertoire is limited. His go-to ones are anger and disapproval.

He continues to stare at her. "You really do look like her." Then he shakes his head, turning to address me. "You didn't tell me you were seeing Jensen's daughter."

Brenna answers for me. "He's not. This is just...it was nothing. So, please, don't say anything to my father, okay?"

Pedersen arches a brow at me as if to ask what I think.

I shrug. "She's right. It was a one-time thing."

"The only reason I'm here right now is because it's pouring outside and Jake didn't want me waiting in the rain for my Uber. Speaking of which," she says with false brightness. She holds up her phone. "My car is here. I just got an alert."

The back of her phone case is facing Coach, while the screen faces me. Which means I can clearly see that there's no alert.

"I should get going," she says hastily. "Thanks for letting me wait out the storm, Connelly. Nice to see you again, Mr. Pedersen."

"Nice to see you, too."

"I'll walk you out," I offer.

Pedersen glances at me. "You might as well take off, too. There's already been one power outage. I don't want you sitting here in the dark if the storm knocks out the power again." With that, he stalks off.

I release the breath I hadn't realized I was holding. "Shit," I say.

"Shit," Brenna echoes. "You think he'll tell my dad?"

"Doubtful. They're not best buds."

"Exactly. What if he snitches out of spite?"

"That's not really Coach's style. He prefers to let out all his aggression on the ice."

We reach the lobby to discover that the apocalypse is in full swing beyond the huge front windows. The sky is nearly black. Gusts of wind smash tree branches against each other, and one branch has already crashed onto the hood of someone's car. Thankfully it's not Weston's Mercedes, which I borrowed again. I might as well start calling it my own, considering how infrequently Brooks drives it.

My gaze shifts from the windows to Brenna, who's zipping up her leather jacket. "I think you should come back to my place," I suggest seriously.

"Of course you do."

"I'm not kidding, Hottie. That storm looks deadly, and you know the roads are going to be terrible. Bad weather turns drivers into maniacs." My voice grows firm. "Wait it out at my place. Please."

Brenna finally relents. "Okay."

———————

By nine o'clock, the storm hasn't let up. Power at the condo went out around six, so we lit a bunch of candles and ate cold leftover pizza for dinner. Brooks digs up some board games and the three of us settle in the living room to play one. Brenna and Brooks have been bickering all evening, ragging on each other as if they've been best friends for years.

When I first walked into the apartment with Brenna at my side, Weston's jaw scraped the floor. But the thing about Weston is, he doesn't care what school she attends, who her father is, or what team she roots for. To him, a hot girl is a hot girl, and he's immediately on board. At least until we get a moment alone. When Brenna disappears into the hall bathroom, Brooks unfolds the Scrabble board and asks, "Does McCarthy know about this?"

"About what?"

"About you and the bombshell in our bathroom."

"No," I grudgingly admit.

"Think maybe you should tell him?"

"I probably should, eh?"

Brooks snickers. "Um. Yeah. You told the poor kid to dump 'er and now you guys are together? Harsh, bro."

"We're not together, and neither were they," I point out.

"He liked her, though."

"He's with that Katherine chick now." McCarthy is still seeing the girl he met after the semifinals. Which tells me he probably didn't care about Brenna as much as he cared about hooking up with someone.

"It's still bro code," Brooks argues. "I know the team captain card trumps all, but you should do the right thing and let him know."

"Do the right thing? Since when do you have a conscience?" I ask in amusement.

"I've always had a conscience." He hops off the couch. "I'm grabbing a beer. You want one?"

"Nah."

"Jensen!" he shouts. "Beer?"

Brenna emerges from the corridor. "Sure. Thanks." She joins me on the sectional and reaches for her letter tray. "All right, let's do this thing."

A few minutes later, the game gets underway. Brooks gathers a few decorative pillows that his mother purchased for us, and sprawls on the floor. He rearranges the wooden squares on his tray. "Yo, lemme go first. I have the best word ever."

Brenna grins. "Let's see it, Wordsmith."

He lays down the word *bang*.

"*That's* the best word ever?" she mocks. "Bang?"

"Yes, because banging is my favorite hobby."

"Uh-huh, well, in terms of actual points, that word earned you…" She checks the letter values. "Plus the double-word score… Fourteen points."

Brooks is quick to protest. "That's great for the first turn."

"If you think fourteen points is great, then you've never played Scrabble with my dad."

He laughs. "Coach Jensen is a Scrabble fiend?"

"Oh, he's nuts about it. He's the kind of player who puts down those two-or three-letter words on a triple-word score, and the next thing I know he's beating me by two hundred points."

"That's no fun," Brooks replies. "I play for the words, not the points. Connelly, it's your turn."

Extending vertically from his "B," I add the word *butt*.

"As in, 'bubble,'" I explain innocently.

My roommate flips me the bird. "Oh fuck off."

Brenna grins at us. "What am I missing?"

"He has a bubble butt," I tell her.

"I have a bubble butt," he says glumly.

"Oh. Cool?" Brenna's amused gaze lowers to her tiles. She rearranges a few of them as she tries to come up with a word.

"Do you want to see it?" Brooks offers.

"Not really—"

"Nah, let me show you. Just be honest and tell me what you think of it."

Brenna glances at me. "Is this for real?"

"Afraid so. His girlfriend pointed out his bubble butt and now he has a complex about it."

"She's not my girlfriend," Weston objects.

I rephrase. "Fuck buddy?"

"I'll accept it." He hops to his feet. "Okay, Jensen. Look at this."

My idiot roommate shoves his sweatpants down to his ankles, presenting his bare ass to my...girlfriend? Fuck buddy? I honestly can't fill in that blank.

I see Brenna's lips quivering in the candlelight, as if she's trying so hard not to laugh.

"Well?" he demands. "Thoughts."

Her gaze focuses on his backside. "You've got a nice butt, Weston," she concedes. "I wouldn't worry about it."

He hauls up his sweats. "Seriously?"

"Seriously. It's a great ass."

A grin stretches his face. "Say that again."

"No."

That grin shifts to me. "Your girl likes my ass. She's into me."

"Nope," Brenna says cheerfully. "I don't know where you got 'I'm into you' from that, but I can assure you I am not." She uses one of the "T's" to put down the word *trolley*.

"Good one," I say.

"Thanks, Jakey."

Brooks flops back onto his pillow mound. "Jakey? Is that what we're calling you now?" He sounds delighted. "I like it. I'm using it all the time."

"Sure thing, Brooksy."

"I take it back. I do not like it."

"That's what I thought."

As the game continues, it's more competitive than I expect, especially with Brooks in the mix. Our scores are so close it's impossible to predict the victor. And while I'm having a good time, I'm not giving one hundred percent of my attention to Scrabble. I keep sneaking peeks at Brenna. It's hard not to. The girl is a smoke show. And I love hearing her laugh. Every time she does, the musical tone makes my heart beat faster.

When Brooks goes to use the john, I move closer to Brenna and slide my hand beneath her sweater.

I'm rewarded with another laugh. "We're in the middle of a Scrabble game and you decide to stick your hand up my shirt?"

"Yup. Can I leave it here until he gets back?" With a wicked grin, I squeeze her left tit.

"You're so weird."

"Nah."

She snorts. "You can't always say 'nah' to whatever other people say about you."

"Why not?"

"Because...well...I guess I don't know why not." She pauses suddenly, one ear cocked toward the window. "Hey. The thunder stopped."

"Power's still not back," I point out.

"No, really? I thought the candlelight was just setting the ambience for our threesome."

"We're having a threesome?!" Brooks exclaims as he bounces back into the room. He looks like an elated little kid. "For real,

Connelly? You didn't want to have a threesome with Kayla but you'll do it with your girl and—oh dear God, why am I complaining? Shut the fuck up, Brooks," he scolds himself.

"Kayla?" Brenna echoes.

"His girlfriend."

"Not my girlfriend."

"You were going to have a threesome with them?" Brenna narrows her eyes.

"Not at all." I glance at my roommate. "And make sure Kayla knows that, because I don't need her ambushing me naked in the kitchen anymore."

"Oh no, a naked girl in the kitchen! We need to install an alarm system! Someone get us a guard dog!" He gives an exaggerated eye roll. "Anyway. Are we doing this?"

I let him down not so gently. "We're not having a threesome, now or ever. This new ass-flashing craze of yours is bad enough."

Brenna's gaze strays toward the windows again. "I should probably go soon."

"Wait until the power's back," I say gruffly. I don't like the idea of her being out on the roads. Several traffic lights had been out on our drive home, and I spotted more than one fender-bender.

"What time is it?" she asks. "If I'm going to leave, it needs to be sooner rather than later."

I lean forward to check her phone. "It's almost ten. Maybe you should—" The screen suddenly illuminates with an incoming call, and since I'm looking right at it, I can't miss the name of the caller.

"Eric's calling," I tell her, my tone harsher than I intend.

My peripheral vision catches Brooks grinning at me. Yeah. He knows exactly how I feel about this.

"You'd better get that," I prompt.

Her expression is suspiciously stricken. She snatches the phone and hits the Ignore button.

"Who's Eric?" Brooks attempts to sound casual but fails. I'm glad he asked before I did, though, and the wink he gives me reveals it was intentional. I nod back, appreciating the solid.

"Nobody," she says tightly.

Well, that tells me nothing. Is she seeing somebody else? Does she have a roster of guys she hooks up with, a bench full of McCarthys?

The hot jealousy burning my gut is not a pleasant sensation. I'm a competitive guy, but I've never competed for the affections of a woman before. Because no woman has ever chosen another man over me. That sounds pretentious and I don't care. The idea of Brenna seeing other dudes is not okay with me.

Which creates another first: I've never been the one to initiate the are-we-exclusive conversation. How does one even bring that up?

When her phone buzzes with a voice-mail alert, I feel even testier. "Are you going to check that?"

"No need. I know what he wants."

The unwelcome jealousy burns hotter. "Is that so?"

"Yup. Whose turn is it now?"

"Mine," Brooks offers. But as he sorts the tiles on his tray, Brenna's phone rings for a second time.

And then, after she ignores it, a third time.

"Just answer it," I mutter.

With a heavy breath, she reaches for the phone again. "Eric, hey. I told you I don't have time for—" Her sentence comes to an abrupt halt. When she speaks again, concern has softened her voice. "What do you mean you don't know where you are?"

Brooks and I exchange a wary look.

"Slow down, slow down. You're not making any sense. Where are you?" There's a long silence. "Okay, stay put," she finally says, and I swear her voice cracks a little. She blinks rapidly, as if fighting tears. "I'll be right there."

26
JAKE

"THANK YOU SO MUCH FOR DOING THIS."

Brenna's voice is barely audible, and she's sitting directly beside me. The rain is nothing more than drizzle now, the brunt of the storm having finally blown past us, but beyond the windshield, several streetlights still aren't functioning. I'm behind the wheel of the Mercedes, because Brooks had too much to drink. He's in the backseat, though, after insisting on tagging along.

"I mean it," she stresses. "You guys didn't have to come. You could've just let me borrow the car."

I glance over darkly. "Really, and let you drive in a storm—"

"It's not storming anymore," she protests.

"—in a storm," I repeat, "to track down your ex-boyfriend?"

At least that's what I understood of her objective, when, in a panic, she begged to borrow Brooks's car. Apparently she dated this Eric dude in high school and now he's in trouble.

"What kind of trouble is he in, anyway?" I demand.

"I'm not sure."

I give her a sharp look.

She seems to be grinding her molars. To dust, from the looks of it. "Drugs," she finally mutters.

"What kind of drugs?" I'm not purposely trying to interrogate her, but I do need to know exactly what we're walking into.

Rather than respond, she gazes down at her phone to examine the map. Two fingers pinch the screen to zoom in. "Okay, so he said he can see a street sign—Forest something," she says absently. "He *thinks* it's Forest Lane."

"That narrows it down," I say sarcastically. "There are probably dozens of Forest Lanes or Streets or Avenues around here."

She scans the map. "Four," she corrects. "One is about ten minutes away, the others are upstate. I think it's probably this one near Nashua. That's closest to Westlynn."

I blow out a breath. "So we're driving to New Hampshire?"

"Is that okay?"

I don't answer. But I do click on the turn signal and get in the right lane to be ready for the I-93 ramp. "Who is this guy, Brenna?" I grumble. "He sounds sketchy."

"Super sketchy," Weston agrees from the backseat.

"I told you, we dated in high school."

"And this requires you to drop everything and rescue his ass?"

Bitter? Who's bitter?

"Eric and I went through a lot together. And yes, his life has gone off the rails, but—"

"Off the rails how?" Before she can even answer, I pull over abruptly, flicking on the emergency signal. I draw a loud honk from the motorist who was behind us, but everyone else goes around.

"What are you doing?" she demands.

"I'm not driving another inch until you give us more details. And not only because this feels like a wild goose chase. We need to know what we're walking into. We're playing the most important game of the season this weekend, and if you're taking us to some crack den—"

"He's not in a crack den." She rubs her face with both hands, clearly upset. "All right. Let me call him again."

Seconds later, Sketchy Eric is back on the line.

"Hey, it's me," Brenna says gently. "We're in the car." She pauses. "Just a couple friends, don't worry about it. We're in the car and we're on our way to come get you, but you need to be more specific about where you are. You said Forest Lane—what else is around you?" She listens for a few beats. "The houses, what do they look like? Okay. Row houses. How did you get there? Do you remember?" A pause. "All right. You were with your friend. Got it, he drove. And he left you there. What did you do there?" Another pause, this one thick with tension. "Okay, you smoked."

I meet Brooks's uneasy eyes in the rearview mirror. I hope to God we're talking about marijuana. Cigarettes would be ideal, but I doubt a pack of Marlboros is responsible for this insanity.

"My map shows a few streets with the word Forest in them. Are you near the coast at all? Did you go toward Marblehead? No? Are you sure?" Brenna suddenly brightens. "Oh, okay, I know where that is. No, I remember Ricky. I can't recall a Forest Lane, but I definitely remember the neighborhood. Okay. I'll call you when we're getting close. Bye."

She hangs up and says, "Nashua. He's near our old 'hood, just like I thought."

We're facing a forty-minute drive, then. Longer if we encounter more pitch-black intersections on the way.

"I'm gonna crash," Brooks says. "Wake me when we get there."

We drive in silence for a good ten minutes before I finally can't take it anymore. "You're really not going to tell me about this guy?" I growl at Brenna. "You're gonna let me walk blindly into whatever fucked-up situation your ex is in?"

"I can't tell you what the situation is, Jake." She sounds tired. "I haven't seen him in a long time. He called recently and asked for money, but I told him no."

"And yet now we're going to rescue him."

"Yes, we are," she shoots back. "You didn't hear his voice, okay? He sounded so messed up. What would you do if someone you used to care about called you up in a panic and said he doesn't know where he is, that he's cold and he's wet and lying in some gutter? Would you leave them there? Because I can't do that."

"Why? Because you dated in high school? Who is this guy? Eric—Eric who?" My frustration only keeps growing. "Who is he to *you*?"

"His name's Eric Royce."

I wrinkle my forehead, vague recognition floating through my mind. The name is familiar to me. Why do I know that name?

"He was a number one draft pick out of high school," Brenna continues. "Drafted by Chicago."

That's it. "Oh shit," I say. "What ever happened to that guy?"

She pointedly holds up her phone. "He's high on meth in some gutter, Jake. *That's* what happened to him."

"Meth?" Brooks straightens up, his nap forgotten. "We're going to meet a meth head?"

"I don't know," she says unhappily. "Last I heard, meth was his drug of choice, but for all I know he could be high on oxy, or drunk off his ass. I honestly *don't know*." She rakes both hands through her hair. "You can drop me off and I'll deal with it alone. You guys don't have to be there. Stop two blocks away or something, I'll walk the rest of the way and then grab an Uber home."

I stare at her in disbelief. "I am not abandoning you in a fucking meth neighborhood, Brenna."

"It's not a meth neighborhood. It's one town over from where I grew up, and I grew up in a safe, normal town, okay? And yes, every town has the occasional druggie, and in this case that druggie is Ricky Harmon, but I'm just assuming we're dealing with crystal meth. I don't actually know for sure, and you freaking out on me isn't going to miraculously produce any answers."

A tense silence hangs between us. In the rearview mirror, I see Brooks's expression soften. He reaches out and squeezes her shoulder. "It's all good, Jensen. We got your back, 'kay?"

She bites her lip and gives him a grateful look.

I change lanes to pass a truck that's traveling half the speed limit even though it's not raining anymore. "So you went out with Eric Royce," I say roughly.

Her head jerks in a nod.

I remember playing against Royce a few times in high school. He was damn good. "He never went to the NHL," I muse.

"No." Sadness hangs in her voice. "His life turned to shit after graduation."

"Why, though?"

"The short version? He had some emotional issues, and he liked to party. And when he partied, he partied hard." She hesitates. "Plus, I broke up with him not long after the draft. He didn't take it well at all."

"Jeez," Brooks pipes up. "You dumped the guy and sent him spiraling into a pit of drugs and despair? Brutal."

She bites her lip again.

"Brooks," I chide. To her, I try to offer reassurance. "I'm sure his spiral wasn't your fault."

"No, it was. Or at least partially my fault. The breakup destroyed him. He was already prone to drinking and drugs, but after we broke up, he took it to the next level. Drinking every night, skipping school to go smoke joints with Ricky Harmon and a few guys who graduated the year before and were doing nothing with their lives. And then one weekend he fucked off to this EDM festival and got so high he forgot to show up for a crucial game. The missed practices were bad enough, but when he didn't suit up for that game, his coach kicked him off the team."

Speaking of coaches. "Did your dad know you were seeing Eric?"

"Yeah. It was a whole big mess." She drops her head in her hands and lets out a weary groan. "Eric and I started dating when I was fifteen. Dad was okay with it at first, mostly because he had no choice but to be okay with it. He knew he couldn't stop me from seeing Eric. I was too stubborn."

"Was?" I crack.

She ignores the jab. "Anyway, after he missed that game, it was the beginning of the end for him. Chicago found out he was kicked off the team. And Eric hadn't signed a contract yet. They were still in the negotiation phase."

I nod in understanding. A lot of guys don't realize that just because a team drafts you it doesn't mean you're immediately on that team. It simply means that franchise has exclusive rights to you for a year, during which you're negotiating your contract.

"They didn't want to sign him anymore," she says sadly. "Word got around that he was a party boy, and then nobody else wanted to sign him, either. So he started partying even harder and running with a new crowd, and now here we are."

Here we are. Ten thirty at night, driving to another state, searching for Brenna's ex-boyfriend who may or may not have smoked meth tonight.

Awesome.

From the corner of my eye I notice Brenna wringing her hands together. I hate seeing this badass girl so shaken. And although I'm still not comfortable with this situation, I reach across the center console and grip her hand.

She glances over gratefully. "Thank you for helping me."

"No problem," I murmur, then pray that I'm telling the truth and there isn't going to *be* a problem.

Thanks to the bad weather and late hour, the roads are blessedly empty, and we make it to the Nashua area faster than anticipated. As I get off the highway, Brenna calls Eric again.

"Hey, it's me. GPS says we're two minutes from Forest Lane. We're going to turn onto it, but you need to give me a landmark or something we can use to find you."

"This is Forest Lane," I tell her, making the turn. Luckily the entire area has power, so the streetlamps are in working order.

"I'm seeing row houses," she says into the phone. "Are you sitting on a curb? Sidewalk?" She curses. "In the bushes? Jesus Christ, Eric."

I suddenly feel incredibly sorry for her. The disgust she's trying to keep out of her tone is twisting her beautiful features, and I can't imagine how shitty that would be, feeling so repelled by someone you were once intimate with.

"A garden with what?" she asks. "A huge spinny thing? A metal spinny thing…Eric, I don't know what—"

"There," Weston says, his face glued to the window. "On the right. I think he's talking about the mini-windmill in that garden over there."

I pull up at the curb. Brenna swings the door open before I've even come to a complete stop. "Wait," I say sharply, but she's already gone.

Shit.

I jump out of the car. Brenna is making a beeline for a tall hedge that separates two front yards. I catch up to her just as she drops to her knees.

Peering over her shoulder, I spot a hunched-over figure hugging his knees. The T-shirt he's wearing is soaked through and plastered to his chest. Chin-length hair, dark strands either wet or greasy, frame a gaunt face. When the guy gazes up at us, his pupils are so dilated it looks like he doesn't have any irises. Just two black circles glowing in his eyes.

He starts talking the moment he recognizes Brenna. "You're here, oh thank God, you're here," he babbles. "I knew you would come, I knew you would, because we were together and you were there for me and I was good to you, right? I was good to you?"

"Yeah." She's utterly emotionless. "You were great. Come on, Eric, up you go." She tries to help him to his feet, but he doesn't budge.

I step forward.

Eric's eyes widen in fear. "Who's this?" he demands. "Did you call the cops on me, Bren? I thought—"

"I didn't call the cops," she assures him. "This is my friend, okay? He drove because I don't have a car, and he's agreed to take you home. Now let us help you up."

I think he's about to comply, but then his gaze focuses on someone behind me. Brooks's timing couldn't be worse.

"Who's that!" Eric shouts in a panic. His eyes, with those enormous pupils, dart wildly between me and Brooks. "They're here to take me away, aren't they? I'm not going to that fucking rehab, Brenna! I don't need it!"

"The only place we're taking you is home," she says calmly, but the sheer frustration clouding her face reveals that calm is the last thing she's feeling.

"Promise!"

"I promise." She leans in to move a hunk of wet hair off his forehead. Her fingers are shaking as she does it. I no longer feel any jealousy toward this guy. Only pity. "We're going to take you home, okay? But you need to let my friends help you up, because I can't do it by myself."

Without a word, I extend a hand toward Brenna's ex.

After a moment of hesitation, he accepts it.

I haul him to his feet. Once he's vertical, I discover he's around my height, six-two, or maybe a bit taller. I suspect he used to be a lot bulkier. Now he's skinny. Not twig-skinny, but certainly not built like the hockey player he once was.

Brooks is startled as he examines Eric. He flicks a look in my direction, and I see the same pity I'm feeling reflected back at me. My teammate shrugs out of his windbreaker and steps closer to drape it over Eric's shoulders.

"Here, man, you need to warm up," Brooks murmurs, and the three of us guide the shivering guy toward the car.

"Westlynn is a ten-minute drive from here," Brenna tells me when we reach the Mercedes.

This time Brooks gets in the passenger side, and Brenna sits in the backseat with Eric, who spends the entire car ride incessantly thanking us for coming to pick him up. From what I can glean, he went to visit his friend three days ago.

Three days ago.

The revelation makes me think of all those shows and documentaries about drug users. Crystal meth, in particular, is a nasty drug to be addicted to, because apparently the high doesn't last long at all. Which leads users to take more and more, going on binges in order to maintain the high. And that's what Eric Royce had been doing, bingeing for seventy-two hours straight. But now he's crashing. He left his friend's house to walk home, became completely disoriented, and wound up in a stranger's bushes.

This was a number one draft pick.

I can't even wrap my head around that. One minute someone is on top of the world. The next, they're hitting rock bottom. It's terrifying how fast and how far people can fall.

"I knew you'd come," Eric is mumbling. "And now you're here, and maybe you can give me fifty bucks and—"

My eyebrows shoot up.

"Well, that took a turn," Brooks mutters to me.

"No." Her sharp tone invites no argument. "I'm not giving you money. I drove almost an hour to—no, not just me. I dragged my friends out in the rain to come find you, to *help* you, and now you're hitting me up for money? So you can buy more drugs, which are the reason you're in this situation to begin with? What is *wrong* with you?"

He starts to whine. "After everything we've been through—"

"Exactly!" she thunders, and both Brooks and I flinch at her vehemence. "After everything we've been through, I don't owe you a thing. I don't owe you a goddamn thing, Eric."

"But I still love you," he whispers.

"Hoo boy," Weston says under his breath.

I swallow a sigh. I've never met a more pathetic person, and I force myself to remember that this man clearly has addiction issues. But from the sounds of it, he's the one refusing to go to rehab. Refusing to save himself.

Either way, I'm more than a little relieved when we arrive at his house. "Let me talk to his mom before we take him in," Brenna says. "I need to warn Louisa."

She hops out and hurries toward the two-story home. It has a white wraparound porch, big bay windows, and a welcoming red door. It's hard to picture a meth addict living there.

I wait for Brenna to reach the porch, then twist around in my seat to address Eric. "Listen, I don't know what your history with Brenna is," I say in a low voice. "But this is the last time you're going to be calling her."

Confusion fills his eyes. "But I have to call her. She's my friend and—"

"She's not your friend, pal." My jaw goes so tight I can barely get a word out. "You just risked her life, made her drive in a storm to rescue you from some bender, and then thanked her by asking for drug money. You are *not* her friend."

I think a sliver of guilt manages to penetrate the high, because his lips start trembling. "She's my friend," he says again, but it doesn't hold as much conviction as before.

Brenna returns to the car, accompanied by a dark-haired woman in a flannel robe and rain boots. She looks like she was dragged out of bed.

The woman throws open the back door. "Eric, honey, come here. Get in the house."

He manages to slide out of the backseat on his own. Once he staggers to his feet, his mother latches on to his arm. "Come on, honey, let's go inside." She glances toward the driver's seat. "Thank you so much for bringing him home."

As she guides him away, a dismayed Brenna peers at Brooks's open window. "Your coat," she reminds him.

"Let him keep it. I'll buy another." A response that reveals just how badly he wants to disentangle himself from this entire situation.

I don't blame him.

When Brenna is buckled up in the backseat, I twist around and prompt, "Hastings?"

She slowly shakes her head, and I'm startled when I glimpse unshed tears clinging to her long eyelashes. "Can I spend the night at your place?"

27
BRENNA

"I'M SO EMBARRASSED." I FLOP DOWN IN THE CENTER OF JAKE'S BED, wearing one of his T-shirts, a pair of his thick socks, and nothing else. My cheeks are still burning from the humiliation of scouring the streets of New Hampshire for my druggie ex-boyfriend—and dragging two other people along for the ride.

Jake closes the door. "You don't need to be embarrassed. We all have our shit."

"Really? So you have a meth-addicted ex-girlfriend lurking in the shadows who might require rescuing at any moment? Sweet! We have so much in common!"

His lips quirk up. "Fine. Maybe my shit isn't quite as exciting as yours." He runs a hand through his hair, which is still damp from the shower.

We both showered—separately—the second we got back to Jake's apartment. After being out in the cold April rain with Eric and then driving home in wet clothes, we desperately needed warming up. A part of me is still floored that Jake and Brooks did this for me tonight. It's definitely going above and beyond.

I can't get Eric's face out of my mind. His enlarged pupils, the rapid-fire jabbering. It's horrifying to know that he smoked meth for three days straight, got lost in a quiet residential neighborhood, and passed out in the bushes. Afraid. Alone. Thank God his mother continues to pay for his cell phone so that he has the means to communicate and call for help.

I just wish he hadn't called *me*.

"I can't believe that's the same Eric Royce who almost played for Chicago," Jake says, and there's a flash of pity in his eyes.

"I know."

He joins me on the bed. "Are you okay?"

"I'm fine. This isn't the first time I've had to deal with him." I have to amend that. "Not to this extent, though. Usually he wants money. Last year I made the mistake of giving him some, so now he thinks it's okay to keep asking."

"You dated for how long?"

"About a year and a half."

"And you broke up with him."

I nod.

"Why?"

"Because it was too much." I swallow the lump in my throat. "It got too intense, and we weren't good for each other anymore. Plus, my dad hated him by that point."

"Doesn't your dad hate everyone?"

"Pretty much." I smile faintly. "But he especially hates Eric."

"I'm not sure I fault him for that."

"Me neither, but you weren't there. We went through some stuff and it hit Eric hard. He was immature and didn't know how to properly deal with his emotions. He made a lot of mistakes." I shrug. "Dad doesn't allow for mistakes."

My voice cracks and I hope Jake doesn't notice. Because that's the problem—there's no such thing as forgiveness with my father. He hasn't forgiven me for my relationship with Eric and all the trouble it caused. I don't think he ever will.

Once again I feel my cheeks heat up. "See, I told you that you didn't want to get involved with me. I'm way too fucked up."

"You're not fucked up," Jake says. "If anything, you seem to have your shit together, a good head on your shoulders. Especially compared to your ex."

"Well, one of us needed to be the grown-up in that equation." Bitterness coats my tongue. I gulp it down. "I was carrying the entire relationship by the end of it. Eric fell apart and couldn't be there for me when I needed him and yet I was expected to be there for him, always. It was exhausting."

"I can imagine."

I rub my weary eyes. My relationship with Eric taught me so many tough lessons, the most important one being that you can't rely on anyone but yourself. He wasn't equipped to handle my emotions, and I don't know if that's exclusive to Eric, or boyfriends in general. What I do know is that I'll never be so careless with my heart again.

"If he ever calls again, I don't want you to pick up," Jake says roughly.

"Really. So if he's lying in some ditch and needs my help, I should just let him die?"

"Maybe."

I stare at him in shock.

"I don't mean to be callous, but sometimes people need to hit rock bottom in order for things to change. You can't always rescue them," Jake says somberly. "They need to crawl out of that hole and rescue themselves."

"I suppose so." I sigh. "But you don't have to worry about this happening again. My days of rescuing Eric are over."

"Good." He crawls to the head of the bed and lifts the corner of the comforter. "Come here. It's been a long day. Let's get some sleep."

"Our first sleepover, Jakey. Isn't this exciting." My sarcasm lacks its usual bite. He's right. I'm tired. And I just want to erase the memory of Eric Royce from my head. I was as devastated as Eric was when everything fell apart. I almost died for that guy. But enough is enough. He's a ghost from my past, and it's time to forget about him.

I slide under the covers and snuggle up next to Jake. He's lying on his back, and my head is on his bare chest. He smells fresh and clean from the shower, and his skin is so warm. I feel his heart thumping beneath my ear. Steady, soothing beats.

I can't believe he did this for me tonight. I could've gone to find Eric on my own, but Jake wouldn't let me. He had my back, and the thought causes my throat to close up a bit, because I can't remember the last time someone was truly there for me.

"Can I ask you something?" he murmurs in the darkness.

"Of course."

"Can I kiss you or are you too tired for that?"

"God no, please kiss me."

He rolls on his side, one arm stretched out with his cheek pressed against it. He inches closer until our lips are touching, and then we kiss, and a wave of pure emotion spills over me.

I'm not sure if it's the adrenaline wearing off, or if I'm feeling overly needy given tonight's events. But the emotional connection we made tonight is merging with the deep physical ache I feel for him whenever we're together. I don't know how long we lie there making out, but soon kissing is not enough. My breasts feel heavy and my core is throbbing. I push him onto his back again and climb on top of him, grinding against him in a desperate attempt to ease the ache.

He squeezes my ass and groans against my mouth, and suddenly his thick erection pokes out of his boxers.

"Oh, hello there," I greet it.

Jake grins up at me. "Sorry, that was unintentional, I swear."

Unintentional or not, it's a welcome sight. I stroke the hot, hard length of him, shivering when I remember how it felt filling my mouth, the wave of satisfaction that hit me when I brought him to climax. I want to feel that satisfaction again.

No. I want more than that.

"I want you inside me," I tell him.

"Yeah?" he says thickly.

"Yeah." I take a slow breath. Now that I've made the decision, my pulse kicks into high gear, thudding in my ears. Sex isn't something I give freely. "Do you have condoms?"

"Top drawer."

I lazily stroke him before reaching for the nightstand. I grab the box of condoms from the drawer, pull out a strip, and rip one off. Before I can open it, Jake sits up and removes my shirt, his big hands cupping my breasts. Then I'm the one on my back, crushed by his muscular body, completely at his mercy.

"Get in me already." I kiss him back impatiently, my hips rising of their own volition, seeking relief.

"Let me get you ready first." His lips travel down my body, leaving shivers in their wake.

His callused fingertips abrade my skin as he lightly strokes my inner thighs before parting my legs. When his mouth touches my clit, pleasure dances through my body.

Jake rubs the tip of one finger over my opening. "Fuck," he groans. "You're *so* ready."

I am. Kissing him is such a turn-on. "See? Now get up here."

"No." I feel him smiling against my flesh. His tongue comes out for another taste, and he goes down on me for several excruciating minutes, until my head lolls to the side and my hands clutch the sheets.

The telltale tingling in my clit warns of impending orgasm. I fight it, desperate to save the orgasm for when he's inside me, because I haven't had sex in so very long. And what if I can't come again tonight?

"Jake," I beg. "Please." I snatch the condom and thrust it at him.

Chuckling, he suits up and kneels between my legs. The light from the bedside lamp is dim, but I don't need much more than that to admire his chest. I trace his muscles with my fingers, loving the way they quiver at my touch.

The gleam of desire burns his gaze as he lifts my ass and angles his hips. I find myself holding my breath as I wait for him to slide inside. And when he finally does, it's the sweetest, most exquisite feeling in the whole world. He stretches me, fills me up completely.

When the full length of him is buried in me, he bites out a low, tortured curse.

"Are you okay?" I ask immediately.

Jake's chest rises as he sucks in a deep breath. "Why are you so tight? Are you sure you're not a virgin?"

I chuckle. "I told you, I just don't do this often."

"Why not?" he asks, then shakes his head as if to scold himself. "Uh, yeah, we can talk about that later. Right now I'm about three seconds from exploding."

"Don't you dare. We haven't even started!"

He's breathing harder. "I'll do my best." His features are strained, though. He moves ever so slightly. Groans again. Then he slowly curls his body over mine so we're in the missionary position.

He kisses me, a slow, teasing seduction of my mouth. Meanwhile, his hips are moving so excruciatingly slowly that it isn't long before I'm squirming with impatience. "Are you doing this on purpose?"

"No," he growls. "I told you, I'm way too close. If I start pounding into you, I'm going to lose it."

"Where's your stamina?" I taunt.

"It's inside your tight pussy, babe."

Laughter sputters out of my chest. "So you're saying I just need to get plowed more often so that it doesn't feel as good for you?"

"Only if you're being plowed by me. Or a vibrator. Anything else is against the law."

"What law?"

"My law," he mutters. He thrusts deep and we both make a strangled noise.

His chest is covered with a sheen of sweat. He hasn't increased his pace at all, and it's driving me crazy. I wrap my arms around his broad shoulders and stroke his back. His mouth latches onto the side of my throat as his hips move lazily. It's almost unbearable. I want him to go faster, but I also never want this to end. I reach between us and lightly rub my clit.

That's when he stops moving altogether.

"Are you kidding me?" I wail. "You're going to lie here inside me without moving?"

"Only for a bit. Just while you get yourself close." He watches my face as I stroke myself. "You're goddamn beautiful."

I swallow. Heat swims in his green eyes as they bore into me. It's insanely intimate and yet I can't break the eye contact. I rub harder and we both hear my breathing quicken.

"That's it," he encourages. "Fuck yeah, that's it."

I moan, trying to rock my hips.

He splays a big hand over my belly to still me. "Not yet."

So I keep stroking with his cock lodged inside me. I feel so full. Our gazes are still locked. He's so sexy I can't look away. He licks his lips, and that's what sends me flying over the edge.

"I'm coming," I choke out, and suddenly he gives me what I've been begging for this entire time—deep, fast strokes, and holy hell the orgasm is like an explosion of pleasure.

The rest of the world disappears. It's me and Jake. Body and soul. He's plunging into me so hard. And when he comes, he honest-to-God bites my neck, a husky, blissed-out groan vibrating against my skin, and that one beautiful moment makes this entire night worthwhile.

28
BRENNA

"Where have you been?"

I jump like a spooked horse when Dad suddenly appears behind me. I was at the kitchen counter waiting for my coffee to brew, and I hadn't even heard him come in.

I turn to find him frowning at me. I frown back. "I texted you last night that I was staying with a friend in Boston."

"And when I asked what friend, you didn't text back."

"Because you didn't need to know more. You knew I was safe."

"Is that a joke? Just because you stayed with a friend doesn't mean you were safe. Who was this friend? Was it the boy who was here last week?"

I sigh. "You promised you weren't going to do this anymore."

"And you promised you weren't going to be reckless."

"How am I being reckless? Yes, sometimes I drink with my friends or go dancing. Sometimes I party—with *your* players, by the way."

"As if that makes it better?" Anger flashes in his eyes. "The last time you went out with a hockey player, you almost destroyed your life."

I experience a jolt of guilt. Dad would go apocalyptic if he knew I was helping Eric last night. Turning my back to him, I open the cupboard and grab a mug. "That was a long time ago, Dad. Five years, to be exact."

"And yet you're still sneaking around and staying out all night."

"Dad." I spin around. "Look at me." I wave my hands up and down my body. "I'm in one piece. I'm alive. I'm not even hungover, because I didn't drink last night. I stayed in Boston because of the storm and the power outages. I didn't feel comfortable being out on the roads." I slam the mug down in the middle of the counter. "I did the responsible thing and I'm getting shit for it. Do you to realize how ridiculous that is?"

"Really? So you were acting *responsibly* when you drove to Westlynn in the aforementioned storm and power outages to rescue Eric Royce from a crackhouse?"

I freeze. How the hell does he know about that?

As guilt climbs up my throat, I inhale slowly and remind myself that I have nothing to feel guilty about. I'm not obligated to tell my father every detail of my life.

He waits for me to say something. When I don't, he spits out an expletive. "Louisa Royce called me last night. She didn't have your cell phone number, and she wanted to thank you again for getting her son home safe. And here you are telling me you're not doing anything reckless. Why are you seeing him again, Brenna? He's trouble."

"I'm not seeing him. He was in trouble and I went to help him."

"Why? He doesn't deserve your help. He doesn't deserve shit." The raw hatred in his voice is terrifying. Dad isn't a Care Bear. He's never going to shower you with kisses and compassion. But he's also not coldhearted.

"Dad. Come on. Eric's not an evil person. He's just in a bad place."

"And it's not your duty to rescue him from that place." He drags both hands over his scalp. His gaze is a little wild. "Do you know how worried I was after I got off the phone with his mother? Not knowing if you were all right?"

"You knew I was all right. I told you I was staying with a friend."

"What friend?" he demands again.

"It doesn't matter. But you know it wasn't Eric, because Louisa wouldn't have called to speak to me if I'd spent the night there. So please, just relax."

"You want me to relax," he mutters. "We have a crucial matchup this weekend, and instead of preparing for it, I'm worrying about whether or not my daughter is placing herself in danger."

"I'm not placing myself in danger." My throat tightens in frustration. I want to stomp my foot like a little kid, because I don't understand him. Dad has two modes: he's either ignoring me and completely disinterested in my life, or he's screaming at me for shit that didn't even happen.

I'm trembling as I pour my coffee. "I'm only going to tell you this once," I say, and my voice is as shaky as my hands. "I am *not* involved with Eric again, and I never will be. He still calls me sometimes, usually to hit me up for money."

I turn to face my father. His expression is harder than stone.

"I gave him money, one time," I admit. "And then I realized it would become a habit, so I never did it again. He doesn't phone that much anymore, maybe a couple times a year. Last night when he called me up, crying and scared because he didn't know where he was…forgive me if it makes me a reckless fool that I didn't want somebody I used to love to die in the fucking street."

"Brenna," Dad starts gruffly.

"What?"

"Just…" He blows out a ragged breath. "Tell me who you're staying with next time you're out all night. Don't make me worry like that again."

Then he leaves the kitchen.

JAKE: You ok?

ME: Yes and no. Dad's gone back to ignoring me, so I assume he's gotten over it. Heading to Summer's now for girls night.

JAKE: Fuck ya. Film it for me.

ME: What do you think happens at girls night?

JAKE: Naked stuff, obviously. Pillow fights. Kissing practice. Actually, wait, forget that. We're in college. You're teaching each other how to eat pussy.

ME: Yes that's exactly what we do. You're such a pervert.

JAKE: Yup. Anyway, I'll call you later.

ME: You don't have to do that.

JAKE: I know I don't have to. I want to.

I bite my lip to stop from smiling at my phone. But I can't stop the warm, fuzzy sensation in my belly. Last night started out so awful, and ended up so…not awful.

I still can't believe I slept with Jake. Figuratively and literally. I had sex with him and then I fell asleep wrapped up in his strong arms. I'm in trouble. I think I really like this guy, and I don't know who I can talk to about it. Summer would tell Fitz in a heartbeat, and Audrey and Elisa suck at keeping secrets.

As I'm approaching Summer's house, my landlord Wendy sends an update about the basement.

WENDY: Basement's still not ready. Maybe another week, possibly less. We found mold growth in the utility room, and we're working to contain it. For now, I need you to send me a complete inventory of what you lost in the flood. We're filing the insurance claim this week.

ME: I'll send it later. And please tell the mold guys to hurry up! I can't live with my dad anymore.

WENDY: LOL the idea of living with my parents again makes me want to die.

ME: Exactly. Hurry!

WENDY: We'll do our best :)

I put my phone away and enter the house without knocking. The high-pitched giggles in the living room tell me that the girls are already here. I find Summer on the couch with Audrey. Summer's friend Daphne is curled up in the armchair, and rounding out the group is a face I haven't seen since the morning at the diner. Rupi Miller. AKA, Hollis's stalker-slash-girlfriend.

"Brenna!" Rupi says happily. She's on the floor lounging on an oversized pillow and wearing a similar outfit to what she had on at the diner. A light-blue, A-line dress with a lacy collar, black tights, and two sparkly barrettes in her raven hair. She looks cute and prim, and the blue shade of her dress goes amazing with her skin tone.

"Come sit with me," she urges. "Also, you look gorgeous! Guys, how gorgeous does she look? I can't believe your skin—it's so luminous. What do you use for it? On mine I use a homemade mask that my mom told me about. That's how I get my pinkish hue. It's—"

"I'm going to grab a drink," I interrupt.

Rupi is still chattering as I leave the room. I don't even know who she's talking to anymore. Maybe herself?

Summer trails after me into the kitchen. "Holy moly, Bee, that girl can *talk*. And I thought I was a blabbermouth."

"You are and so is she. Two blabbermouths can exist in the same realm, babes. It's not like *Highlander*."

"What's *Highlander*? I haven't seen it. Is that the one where the woman travels back in time?"

"No, that's *Outlander*. Which, by the way, we absolutely need to watch because the leading man is smoking hot."

"Oooh! All right. Let's do it after the semester ends."

"Done."

As I pour myself a glass of water, Summer raises her eyebrows. "It's girls' night," she reminds me. "We're drinking margaritas."

"I'm hydrating first. I've barely had anything to drink today. I was holed up in my room working on my final paper for Comm Theory."

When we wander back into the living room, Rupi is still gushing about her homemade face mask. "It's just chickpea flour and yogurt, and I *swear* it is the *best* exfoliant ever. You'll be glowing after."

Audrey and Daphne are hanging on her every word. "I'm officially intrigued," Daphne says. "I'm always on the hunt for a good exfoliator. My skin is garbage lately."

"We should do it now," Audrey suggests. "Do you have chickpea flour and yogurt?"

Summer dons a blank look. "I have no idea."

"Let's go check." Rupi races toward the kitchen with Audrey and Daphne hot on her heels.

I watch them go. "Did they just become best friends?"

"I think they did."

"Are she and Hollis actually a thing?" I ask as I steal Daphne's spot. I settle in the armchair and curl my legs under me.

"I have no idea. It's the strangest relationship I've ever seen." Summer lowers her voice. "She's either screaming at him or he's screaming at her. Otherwise, they're making out."

I bite my lip to keep from laughing. "If you think about it, that's exactly the kind of relationship I would expect Hollis to be in."

"Me too. But it's so weird."

"Exactly, like him."

Summer smirks. "Says the person who made out with him."

"So? You've never made out with a weirdo before?"

"You made out with Mike?" Rupi appears in the doorway, jaw agape.

Uh-oh.

For a second, I debate lying to the girl, until I realize how ridiculous that is. Who cares if I kissed Hollis? Besides, it's not like he cheated on her with me. "I did," I confirm. "But you don't need to—"

"Ha!" she interrupts, her brown eyes twinkling. "I totally knew! Mike tells me everything."

He does?

"And don't worry, I'm not mad at you," Rupi assures me.

"I wouldn't have cared if you were."

"Ha, you're so funny." She giggles, then asks Summer a yogurt-related question before darting into the kitchen.

"I wasn't joking," I tell Summer. "I wouldn't have given a shit if she was mad."

She snorts. "I know."

My phone vibrates, and I commit a girls' night faux pas by checking it.

> **JAKE:** How's it goin' over there? Have you had a girl-on-girl orgasm yet?
>
> **ME:** Not yet. So bummed.
>
> **JAKE:** Not as bummed as I am.

Detective Di Laurentis is instantly on the case. "Who are you texting with?"

"Nobody."

"Don't say nobody. You literally just texted *somebody*." Her green eyes light up. "Are you still secretly dating that Harvard guy?"

I almost blurt out *how did you know* before I realize she's referring to McCarthy, not Jake.

"We were never dating," I answer with a shrug. "We just hooked up a few times." I hurry on when I see her opening her mouth. "That was Nate, okay? Relax."

"Ugh. Say hi to him." She looks disappointed that she hadn't stumbled upon a major scoop.

If she only knew.

The other girls come back. Rupi is holding a plastic bowl full of a beige-colored mixture. She quickly teaches everyone how to put it on. "Are you wearing any makeup?" she asks me.

"No."

Daphne glares at me. "Are you messing with us? You're really not wearing makeup? Not even concealer?"

"Nope."

"How does your skin look so good?"

"Genetics?" I offer.

"I hate you," Daphne says frankly.

Under Rupi's sharp eye, we all start slathering the weird yogurt concoction on our faces. "How long do we leave it on for?" Summer asks.

"Until it dries. No longer than ten minutes, though." Rupi flops down on her pillow throne near my feet.

From the armchair, I grin down at her. "So what's the deal with you and Hollis? Are you together now?"

"Of course we are." She stares at me like I'm from a different planet. "We were together after our first date."

"Does he know that?" Summer asks in amusement.

"Of course he does."

I truly can't figure out if this girl is delusional or—

Actually, there's no "or." I think she might be delusional, period.

"It's been ages. We're pretty much an old married couple now." The freshman beams at me. "That's why I don't care about you guys hooking up. You weren't serious about him, anyway."

I needle her just because. "Maybe I was…"

"No." Her confidence is astounding. "He's not your type."

"What makes you say that?"

"Because he's a puppy dog."

"Who's a puppy dog?" asks a male voice, and then the puppy dog himself bounds into the room. He yelps when he notices our faces. "Why the fuck are your faces covered with glue?"

"Of all the things you could've picked, why *glue*?" Summer asks in exasperation. "Why the hell would it be glue?"

"I don't know." He scans the seating situation, as if he actually has a choice about where to sit.

Rupi pats the pillow next to her.

I swallow my laughter.

Hollis lowers his big body onto the floor. Puppy dog, indeed. He's wearing basketball shorts and a blue T-shirt that brings out the blue of his eyes. The shirt also hugs his impressive muscles, a sight that's always a bit jarring for me. Mike Hollis is like an obnoxious kid in a hot guy's body.

He slings an arm around Rupi's tiny shoulders. "Yo," he says.

I hide a smile. I swear, he's so into her.

"See, you're a puppy dog," she informs him. "So silly and lovable."

"I'm not silly and lovable," he argues.

"Yes, you are."

"No, I'm not. You can't compare me to a puppy. You gotta pick something good. Like a stallion."

"You can't be a stallion unless you're super hung," I crack.

Audrey snorts.

Rupi glances at me in horror. "Brenna! You can't make disparaging comments about a boy's penis. It's damaging to the ego. Just because Mike doesn't have a stallion penis doesn't mean—"

"Why are you talking about my dong?" Hollis interrupts. "Which you haven't even seen, by the way."

"I've touched it," she says smugly, before patting his knee. "I was just telling everyone that our anniversary is coming up."

Confusion washes over his face. "We have an anniversary?"

"Yes. Our one-month anniversary."

"It hasn't been a month."

"Well, it's been almost a month—"

"Two weeks!"

"Twenty days! That's almost *three* weeks." Rupi studies his face. "When is our anniversary, Mike?"

"What?"

I lean back in my chair and enjoy the show.

"When was our first date?" she pushes.

"Why would I know that?"

"Because you were there!" Rupi flies up to her feet and plants both hands on her hips. "You didn't write down the date? What's wrong with you?"

"What's wrong with *me*? What's wrong with *you*? Who writes down the date of a date?"

"It was our *first* date. Are you telling me it wasn't worth remembering?"

Hollis stands too. At six-one, he towers over five-foot Rupi. And yet any bystander can see who really wields the power.

"You showed up here and dragged me to dinner," he reminds her. "I didn't even know who the fuck you were."

"I really wish you wouldn't curse at me."

"Well, if wishes were horses we'd all be equestrians."

"Ha!" Summer lets out a high-pitched laugh.

Daphne looks utterly fascinated. "What on earth does that mean?"

"That's not a real saying," I inform him.

"It's a real saying," Hollis growls. "My father uses it all the time."

Summer grins broadly. "Oh my gosh, Mike, your father is as incomprehensible as you are."

I glance over at her. "Where do you think he learned it from?"

Rupi doesn't appreciate the digression. She takes an angry step toward him, and now the two of them are in each other's faces. Hers is covered with that gunk, and his is bright red from frustration.

"I can't believe you don't care about our anniversary." Rupi spins on her heel. "I need to reflect on this," she declares over her shoulder. A moment later, we hear her stomping up the stairs.

Hollis turns to me and Summer. "Why did you do this to me?" he asks miserably.

"We like her," Summer announces.

"Of course you do. Of course you fucking do." He stalks out, too. There's a beat of silence.

"Do you think we can wash our faces now?" Daphne asks, grinning.

"Probably?" Audrey answers.

We pile into the hall bathroom where we take turns ridding ourselves of the mask. After I pat my face dry, I can't deny that my skin feels insanely smooth.

"Rupi said you have to apply moisturizer immediately," Daphne instructs.

"Lemme grab something." As Summer disappears, the rest of us admire ourselves in the mirror.

"Oh my gosh, I really do have a pinkish hue," Daphne raves.

"My skin feels amazing," Audrey gushes. "We should package and sell this stuff."

"We can call it Face Glue," I suggest.

Daphne snickers.

Summer returns with moisturizer, and our skin routine is back in business. Even though they're all the way upstairs, we can hear Rupi and Hollis yelling at each other. I really wish they'd come downstairs and do it in front of us. It's *such* good entertainment.

Instead, we're provided with entertainment in the form of Hunter arriving home. He looks sexier than usual. Maybe because his dark hair is rumpled and there's a seductive gleam in his eyes.

He's exuding so much swagger, I have to ask, "Got laid?"

"A gentleman doesn't kiss and tell." He winks before heading for the kitchen.

"Could you grab the yellow pitcher from the fridge, please and thank you?" Summer calls after him. "We need refills!"

"Sure thing, Blondie."

"Huh." I look at Summer. "You two seem better."

"We are," she confirms. "I think it's all the sex he's having. The endorphins are making him warm and fuzzy."

Hunter reappears and sets the plastic margarita pitcher on the coffee table.

"So who was the lucky lady tonight?" I tease.

"No one you know. Some girl at a bar in Boston."

"Classy," Audrey says.

He rolls his eyes. "We didn't fuck in the bar."

"Does bar girl have a name?" Summer asks as she tops off everyone's glasses.

"Violet." He shrugs. "Not to be a dick, but don't bother remembering her name. She kicked me out like two minutes after the sex."

I can't help but laugh. "Cruel woman."

"Nah. Made my life easier," he admits. "I didn't want more than one night, anyway."

"Classy," Audrey repeats.

Now he chuckles. "Right. I'm a horrible person for wanting a one-night stand, but she's not a horrible person for wanting the same thing. Makes perfect sense to me."

I change the subject, reaching for my margarita. "You ready for the game this weekend?" I ask him.

"Ready as we're ever going to be. They'll be tough to beat, though." The intensity in his voice is promising. At least his head is in the game, and not on all the girls he's hooking up with. "If we can find a way to contain Jake Connelly, stop him from wrecking us, then we've got a good shot."

Ha. If they find a way to not be wrecked by Jake, I'd love to know it. God knows I haven't found the solution.

29
JAKE

EVERY PLAYER PREPARES DIFFERENTLY FOR A GAME. SOME GUYS are obsessive about their superstitions, like Dmitry, who got a paper cut once and went on to shut out the opposing team, so now he gives himself a paper cut before every game. Or Chilton, who needs his mom to say, "Break your leg, Coby!"—those exact words, because in high school it won his team a state championship.

Me, I just need my trusty beaded bracelet and some silence. I need to sit quietly and get my head ready, because hockey is as mental as it is physical. It requires laser focus, the ability to react mentally to any situation, any obstacle. And there's no room for self-doubt on the ice. I have to trust my brain, my instincts, my muscle memory, to create opportunities and bring on a desired outcome.

This entire season, I haven't given any pep talks. The guys don't expect it of me. They know that when I'm hunched over on the bench, not looking at them, not saying a word, it's because I'm mentally preparing.

Everyone stands to attention when Coach strides into the locker room. He sweeps his gaze over the uniformed bodies crowding the space. "Men," he greets us.

We tap our sticks on the floor in a hockey salute. We need to get out there for our warmup skate, but Coach has a few words to say first.

"This game is the single most important game you play this season. We beat Briar, we go to the national tourney. We beat Briar, we're one step closer to bringing home a national title." He rumbles on for another full minute, pumping us up, telling us we need to win, growling that the title belongs to us, that we need to bring it home. "What are we gonna do?" he shouts.

"Bring it home!"

"Can't hear you."

"*Bring it home!*"

Coach nods in approval. Then he throws me a curveball. "Connelly, say a few words."

My head jerks up in surprise. "Coach?"

"You're the captain, Jake. Say something to your team. This could be the last game of the season. Hell, your last game at Harvard."

Fuck, I don't like that he's messing with my ritual. But I can't object, because unlike nearly every other athlete in the world, Coach doesn't believe in luck or superstition. He believes in skill and hard work. I suppose I admire that philosophy, but…respect the rituals, dammit.

I clear my throat. "Briar's good," I start. "They're really good."

"Great speech!" Brooks breaks out in hearty applause. "Standing ovation!"

Coby snickers loudly.

"Can it, Bubble Butt. I wasn't done." I clear my throat. "Briar's good, but we're better."

My teammates wait for me to go on.

I shrug. "I was done that time."

Laughter rings out all around me, until Coach claps his hands to silence everyone. "All right. Let's get out there."

I'm about to shut my locker when the phone I left on the shelf lights up. I crane my neck to take a peek, and a satisfied smile tugs at my lips. It's a message from Brenna, wishing me good luck. There's also one from Hazel, offering the same sentiment, but I'd expect it from *Hazel*. From Brenna, it's unprecedented.

"Coach, my dad's calling," I lie as I catch Pedersen's attention. "Probably wants to wish us luck. I'll just be a minute, okay?"

He gives me a suspicious look before muttering, "One minute."

As he and my teammates lumber toward the tunnel, I call Brenna. But I don't get the greeting I expect.

"Why are you calling me?" She sounds outraged. "You should be on the ice warming up."

I chuckle. "I'd think you'd be happy to hear that I'm not out there."

"Wait, is everything okay? You're still playing, aren't you?" Concern echoes over the line.

"Yes, I'm still playing. But I saw your text and I wanted to make sure you're not in danger."

"Why would I be in danger?"

"Because you said good luck. I assumed someone was holding a gun to your head."

"Oh, don't be a brat."

"So you were seriously wishing me good luck?"

"Yup."

"Did you mean it?"

"Nope."

"Who's the brat now?" I hesitate. "Look…whatever happens tonight, I don't want to stop seeing you." Then I hold my breath and wait, because I genuinely don't know what she'll say.

I know what I want her to say. I want her to say that she hasn't been able to get me off her mind since we slept together, because I haven't gotten her off *my* mind since we slept together. The sex was unreal. So goddamn amazing. And that was our first time. If it's that good when we don't even know each other's turn-ons yet? When we don't know exactly how to get each other off? Means it's only going to get better. That blows my mind.

"I want to keep seeing you," I press when she still hasn't answered. "Do you want to keep seeing me?"

There's another delay. Then she sighs. "Yes. I do. Now get out there so we can kick your ass."

A smile cracks my face in half. "You wish, babe."

I shut the locker and turn around, flinching when I spot Coach in the doorway.

Shit.

"Babe, eh?" Coach mocks. "You call your father 'babe'?"

I release a weary breath. "I'm sorry I lied."

"Connelly." He grabs my shoulder when I reach him. Even with my padding on, I can feel the steel in his grip. "That girl... whether or not you're serious about her...you have to remember, she's Jensen's daughter. You need to consider the possibility that she's playing mind games with you."

Hazel said the same thing. But I think they're both being paranoid. Brenna doesn't play games. "I'll take that into consideration." I force a smile. "Don't worry, it won't affect my performance on the ice. We got this."

We don't got this.

From the second the puck drops, the game is a complete cluster-fuck. It's speed and aggression. It's two teams that aren't competing for a win, but competing to fucking kill each other. The hits are brutal, and I suspect the refs are letting a lot of calls go because of the high intensity of the game. It's hockey the way it's meant to be played. With absolute abandon.

The fans are losing their minds. I've never heard the arena this *alive*. Screams, cheers, and boos crash together in a symphony that fuels the adrenaline coursing through my veins. Despite all that, Briar is outplaying us. They're fast, particularly Davenport. And Nate Rhodes? I don't know what he's been putting in his Wheaties, but holy shit. He gets the first goal of the game, a bullet that Johansson has absolutely no chance of stopping. Even I'm impressed by it, but one look at the fury reddening Coach's eyes and I know I can't let that slide.

"You gonna let them do that to you?" Coach roars at us. "You gonna let them do that to you *in our house?*"

"No sir!"

The adrenaline kick sends me diving over the wall with Brooks and Coby. It's our power line, and there's a reason we call it that. Brooks is the Incredible Hulk when he's on the ice. He delivers body checks that are bone jarring. Coby has a mean elbow and can battle against the boards better than anybody. I win the faceoff, but rather than pass, I deke out Fitzgerald and skate forward. I wait for the others to cross the blue line before sending a pass back to Coby, close to center.

He skates around the net, stops for a second, then flies out. He shoots and misses. Davenport almost gets his stick on the rebound, but I give him a shove and it's my stick that connects with the puck. I shoot and miss. The puck bounces toward Brooks, who shoots and misses. A deafening roar goes through the stands.

Jesus fucking Christ. Three fucking shots, denied, denied, denied, and since when did Corsen get this fucking good? I'm growling in frustration when Coach calls to change it up, and off the ice we go.

Breathing hard, I sit on the bench next to Brooks. "What the hell is going on here?"

"I don't know," he mutters. "Corsen's not usually that fast with the glove."

"Just gotta keep hammering him, tire him out."

Brooks gives a grim nod.

Coach appears behind us, clamping a hand around Weston's shoulder. "Get us a power play," he orders.

I tense up, because any time Coach encourages Brooks to draw a penalty, there's real potential for tempers to fly. Our line returns to the game, and Brooks is immediately out for blood. In the faceoff, he starts taunting Davenport, who's crouched to the right of Nate Rhodes. Mike Hollis is at Rhodes's left.

I'm too focused on the puck to register what Brooks says, but whatever it is, it summons a feral growl from Davenport. "Go fuck yourself," the sophomore spits out.

"Enough," the ref shouts.

Once again I win the face-off. I snap the puck to Brooks, who muscles his way into Briar's zone. He snaps it back to me, but I don't have a shot. The D-men are protecting Corsen and the net like the fucking Kingsguard in *Game of Thrones*. I need an opening. I need—

The whistle blows. I didn't see what happened, but I turn to find Hollis shouting something at Weston.

It's a high-sticking call, and Hollis is hauled into the penalty box. Brooks and I exchange a look. He did his job. Now it's time to do mine.

Our line stays out for the penalty kill, but we don't need much time. Briar is a man down, and although they manage to ice it right off the face-off the moment we get the puck back? Stick a fork in them cuz they're done. I deke out Davenport and release a shot that even Corsen and his new glove skills can't stop. The lamp lights and relief ripples through me.

The score is tied.

"Good job," Coach says when I swing over the wall.

I pop out my mouth guard, a piece of equipment that isn't mandatory, but I value my teeth, thank you very much. My breathing is labored, chest sucking in and out, as I watch my teammates speed by. That was exhausting. My shift lasted more than three minutes, which is unheard of.

"Get your shit together," I hear Heath growling to Jonah.

I glance down the bench, frowning deeply. "We got a problem?" I call to the younger guys.

"Nah, it's all good," Heath says.

I'm not convinced. Jonah's angry gaze is glued to the action in front of us, but I can't quite pinpoint where his anger stems from. Maybe he took a dirty hit and is pissed at the player who got away with it.

Dmitry's line manages to hold Briar off. When McCarthy flops down beside me, I pound his shoulder with my glove. "Good hustle," I bark.

"Thanks." He blushes at the compliment, and I know he's trying hard not to grin. I don't throw out praise haphazardly, so my teammates know that when I praise them, I really mean it.

His obvious happiness brings a rush of guilt to my throat. Brooks got in my head the other night about "doing the right thing" with McCarthy. I'd already made the decision to tell him that I'm seeing Brenna, but I'm waiting until after the game. I didn't want to take the chance that the news might distract him from the finals.

Coach changes up the lines again. Now it's me and Brooks, and Coby's been swapped out for Jonah, a right-winger who's excellent at taking advantage of rebounds. There's almost an immediate offsides call. At the whistle, I skate over and get in position.

The face-off is a disaster from the word *go*. The bullshit starts, but this time it's not courtesy of Weston. It's from Jonah.

"Davenport," he barks.

The Briar player spares him a glance before focusing on the ref.

"I'm talking to you, asshole. Stop pretending you can't hear me."

"Not pretending anything," Davenport snaps back. "I just don't give a shit about what you're saying."

The puck drops. I secure it, but Jonah is still distracted from the exchange and he misses the pass I flick his way. Davenport intercepts and takes off on a breakaway. We chase after him, but it's Johansson who saves us from that potentially costly mistake. He stops the shot and passes the puck off to Brooks.

"Unacceptable," I hiss at Jonah as I skate by. That kind of screw-up isn't typical of Jonah Hemley. "Keep your head in the game."

I don't think he hears me. Or maybe he doesn't care. When he and Davenport are tangled up against the boards during our next shift, Jonah starts up again. "Thursday night," he's growling. "Where were you?"

"Fuck. Off." Davenport elbows Jonah hard and wins the battle for the puck.

I hit Davenport with a crosscheck and steal the puck, but once again Jonah is too caught up in whatever the hell this is. He doesn't drive forward like he's supposed to, and we're offsides again. The whistle blows.

I don't know what's happening, and I don't fucking like it.

The next face-off is to the left of our net. As we line up, Jonah's interrogation resumes. "Thursday night, asshole," he spits out. "You were at the Brew Factory."

"So what?" Davenport sounds annoyed.

"So you're not denying it!"

"Why would I deny it? I was at the bar. Now shut the hell up."

"The redhead you left with—you remember her?" Jonah demands.

My stomach drops, and I pray that the puck drops, too—*now*—because I've figured out where this is going, and it needs to be squashed. *Now.*

"Who? Violet? What do you care who I stick my dick in?"

"*That was my girlfriend!*"

As Jonah heaves himself forward, he knocks over the referee, who goes sprawling on the ice in a tangle of limbs.

Fuck. Fuck fuck fuck!

"Hemley!" I thunder, but Jonah's not listening.

He tackles Hunter Davenport, and his fists start flying. When Jonah's gloves come off, anger sizzles up my spine, because dammit, this is cause for ejection. I try to haul him off our opponent, but he's strong. He screams at Davenport for sleeping with Vi, while whistles blast all around us.

Davenport sounds genuinely confused. "She didn't tell me she had a boyfriend! Jesus! Get off me!" He's not even fighting back.

"I don't believe you!" Jonah's fist slams down. The whistles keep blowing.

Blood pours from the corner of Davenport's mouth. He still has his gloves on, and he hasn't thrown a single punch. If anyone gets kicked out of this game, it'll be my guy and not Davenport.

I once against attempt to calm Jonah. Nate Rhodes, my rival captain, skates over and tries to give me a hand. Together, we succeed in yanking Jonah to his feet. He's still beyond pissed. "He fucked my girlfriend!" Jonah shouts.

Another whistle blows. It's chaos. Davenport manages to get up, but my teammate escapes the hold I have on him and lunges at the Briar player again, slamming him into the boards. Once again they fall to the ice.

Only this time, it's accompanied by a loud grunt of pain.

I pull Jonah up again, but the agonized sound hadn't come from him.

Davenport's helmet comes off. He drops his gloves and cradles one wrist, pressing it against his chest. And he's swearing up a blue streak, the pain in his eyes unmistakable. "You broke my wrist," he snarls. "What the hell is wrong with you?"

"You fucking deserve it," Jonah spits out, and suddenly there's a blur of motion and Nate Rhodes lunges and drives his fist into Jonah's jaw.

Other players spill onto the ice, and chaos becomes catastrophe. The whistles keep blowing and blowing as the refs try to regain control. But the control train left the station a long time ago.

30
BRENNA

THE SECOND THE BUZZER GOES OFF TO SIGNAL THE END OF THE first period, I jump out of my seat. So does Summer, but I rest my hand on her shoulder. "They're not going to let you in."

"How do you know?" she demands.

"Because I know my father. Hell, he might not even let *me* in. But if anyone has the chance, it will be me. I promise I'll text you the second I know something."

"Okay." Summer looks shell-shocked, and the expression isn't unique to her. Everyone around us is still beyond stunned.

Nobody knows what the hell happened down there, except that the game turned into some sort of bloodsport. Hunter left before the period ended, cradling his arm. So did Nate and one Harvard player whose name and jersey number I didn't catch.

For the rest of the first period, we were missing two of our best players, but we somehow managed to hold Harvard off until the buzzer. There are two periods left and I have no idea what's going on. Neither the referees nor the announcers up in the media booth revealed why those players left. In college hockey, fighting is not allowed. It can get you ejected. Except, Hunter didn't start the fight, nor did he fight back. And I have no clue why Nate got involved. He's usually more levelheaded than that.

I hurry out of the rink in search of answers. Other people are also leaving, so I elbow my way through the crowd as I walk toward the locker rooms. Dad always gives me a pass, just in case. It doesn't guarantee entrance into the actual locker room, but it means I can access any off-limits areas. I flash my pass to a security guard and turn down another corridor.

Another guard stands near the visiting team's locker room. "Hey," I greet him, holding up my lanyard. "I'm Coach Jensen's daughter and the team manager." The second part is a lie, but I'm hoping it aids my case.

It does. The man quickly steps aside.

I open the door in time to hear my father's voice. It sounds deadly as fuck. "What the *hell* did you have to go and do that for, Rhodes?"

I don't hear Nate's mumbled response.

I slowly creep toward where the players are gathered. Nobody notices me. Why would they? I'm hidden in a sea of big bodies that all tower over me.

"Well, Davenport's out. He's getting x-rays, but the team doc says she doesn't need the scans to tell her the wrist is broken."

My stomach drops. Dad doesn't sound at all happy, and I don't blame him. Hunter is out of the game.

"And Rhodes, you've been ejected for your part in the scrum."

Holy shit. Nate's out, too? They're our best players!

"On their side, we have Jonah Hemley getting ejected. Which is no big loss to them." Dad sneers. "The kid was filling in for Coby Chilton, who might've pulled a hammy. Except he didn't pull a damn hammy, and now the power line is back in business."

My God. This is a travesty. Panic weakens my muscles, because... we might actually lose now.

My father doesn't vocalize my fear, but I know he's thinking it, too. And he sounds enraged as he addresses his players. "What the hell went on down there?"

There's a long, fearful silence. Fitz is the one who finds the balls to speak up. "From what I gathered, Hunter slept with Hemley's girlfriend. Unknowingly," Fitz adds.

"Is this a fucking joke? And if you're going to screw one of their girlfriends, it couldn't have been *Connelly's*?" Dad growls. "At least then we wouldn't have to worry about him."

Even though I'm upset for my team, I have to swallow a wave of laughter—because I don't think Dad would be endorsing anyone having sex with Connelly's girlfriend if he knew it was *me*.

Not that I'm Jake's girlfriend, but I am the girl in his life, and—no, I can't think about this right now. We're in crisis mode.

"Jesus, Rhodes. What were you thinking!" Dad is clearly livid at his captain.

I'm not too thrilled with him, either. What happened to being the better man? Nate was so adamant about taking the high road after the whipped-cream incident, ordering Wilkes not to retaliate. And now he goes and loses his cool on the ice? Retaliating against Hemley for the attack on Hunter? It's completely unlike him.

Nate's tone tells me that he's as angry and disgusted with himself as my father is. "I snapped," he says shamefully. "That asshole broke Hunter's wrist, Coach. And then he had the balls to say Hunter *deserved* it. It was the most sickening thing I'd heard, and...I snapped," he repeats. "I'm sorry, Coach."

"I hear you, kid. But an apology ain't gonna put you back in this game."

AKA, we're utterly screwed.

I edge backward and leave the locker room. "Doesn't sound good in there," the security man says sympathetically.

"It's not."

I hurry back to our seats, where I file a report with Summer and the others. "Looks like Hunter is out, and so is Nate."

Summer gasps.

So does Rupi, who as usual is dressed like a walking J. Crew ad.

Or a super-prissy American Girl doll. I wonder how many girlie, collared dresses she actually owns. Thousands, probably.

"This is a disaster!" Summer moans.

"Yup," I say morosely, and we're not wrong.

When the second period gets underway, you can see the difference in Briar's game almost immediately. It's like watching an Olympic sprinter crush the first heat of the 100-meter dash, only to come out for the next heat to find that there are spikes on the track. Without Nate, the captain of the team, and Hunter, our best forward, we're struggling right out of the gate. Fitz and Hollis can't carry the entire team. Our younger players aren't fully developed yet, and the best ones, Matt Anderson and Jesse Wilkes, are physically incapable of keeping up with Connelly.

My eyes track Jake as he scores early in the second. It's a beautiful shot, a work of art. Now Harvard is leading 2–1. And two minutes before the end of the period, Weston gives Harvard a power play by drawing a penalty from Fitz, who rarely visits the box.

Summer drops her face in her manicured hands. "Omigod, this is awful." She finally glances up, seeking out her boyfriend. "His head looks like it's about to explode."

Sure enough, Fitz is stewing and simmering in the penalty box. Red-faced and clenching his jaw so tight, the muscles there are actually quivering.

Harvard takes advantage of the penalty Weston the asshole provoked. And just because I played Scrabble with the guy and he helped me out with Eric doesn't make him any less of the enemy right now. Right now I loathe him. Maybe a couple days from now we can play Scrabble again, but right now I want him erased from the face of the planet.

Unfortunately, Briar is shorthanded, and Weston is the one who ends up scoring the power-play goal. Then Fitz is back and we're able to breathe easy again.

Weston tries the same thing on Hollis during his next shift, but

Hollis doesn't fall for it, bless his puppy-dog heart. Instead, the refs catch Weston's dirty hit and he takes a two-minute minor, and we're all on our feet screaming ourselves hoarse when Briar scores.

3–2 now.

The second period is over. "You can do it," I whisper to the boys as they disappear in the chute toward the locker rooms. Hopefully my dad gives them a *Miracle*-worthy speech and we can come back, tie it up early in the third, and then score again and win the damn game.

"We still have a chance, right?" Summer's eyes glimmer with hope.

"Of course we do. We got this," I say firmly.

We're on our feet again when the third period starts. It's scoreless for almost six minutes, until, in the middle of a shoving battle in Harvard's zone, Jesse Wilkes gets a shot off that careens right between Johansson's legs. It's a total fluke, but I'll take it. The Briar fans go insane as the scoreboard switches to 3–3.

I can't believe everyone is still maintaining the same level of speed that kicked off the game. They must be exhausted after two grueling periods. But both teams are still playing like the entire season is on the line. Because it is.

I'm mesmerized as I watch Jake do what he does best. He's impossibly fast and I can't help imagining him in Edmonton next year. He's going to have a hell of a season if he plays even half as well as he's playing tonight.

"He's so good," Summer says grudgingly, as Jake literally dekes out three of our boys to charge the net.

He takes a shot. Luckily he misses, and I'm ashamed to say I experience a spark of disappointment when Corsen thwarts Jake's attempt.

Oh God. Where do my loyalties lie? I want Briar to win. I truly do. And I *hate* what that Harvard player did to Hunter and Nate.

But I also want Jake to succeed. He's magnificent.

We're still tied, and the clock is winding down. The possibility of overtime worries me. I don't know if we have enough juice left to hold them off. Especially Corsen. He's good in the net, but he's not the best.

Johansson, on the other hand, I'd definitely rank in the top three of college goalies. He stops every shot like a pro. He didn't enter the NHL draft when he became eligible, but I hope he tries to sign with someone after college. He's too good not to.

"Come on, guys!" Summer screams. "Let's do this!" Her shouted encouragement is drowned out by the shouts of everyone around us.

My ears are going to be ringing hardcore after this game, but it's worth it. There's nothing better than live hockey. The excitement in the air is contagious. Addictive. I want to be able to do this for a living, not as a player, but a participant. I want to cheer for these athletes, talk to them while they're still hopped up on whatever it is that makes them come alive on the ice. Adrenaline, talent, pride. I want to be part of that, in whatever capacity I can.

Three minutes left, and the score remains 3–3.

Jake's line is back. Brooks is up to his usual tricks, except no one's falling for them anymore. I think it's pissing him off, judging by the hard set of his shoulders. Good. He deserves it. It won't be dirty tricks that win Harvard this game. It'll have to be skill. Unfortunately, they're drowning in skilled players.

There's exactly two minutes and forty-six seconds left when Jake gets a breakaway. My heart is torn, sinking when he gets the puck, and yet soaring when he nears our net. He winds up his arm to take a shot, and it's another work of art. A gorgeous bullet. When the announcers shout, "GOALLLLLL!" my heart is somehow caught in both a tailspin and a steep climb. I'm surprised I don't vomit from the nauseating sensation.

Harvard is in the lead now, and we've only got two and a half minutes to try to tie it up again. The Briar fans in the arena are screaming. The clock keeps ticking.

Two minutes left.

A minute and a half.

Briar scrambles. Fitz gets a shot on net, and a collective groan rocks half the stands when Johansson stops it. The goalie holds on, and the whistle blows.

I cup my mouth with both hands. "Come on, boys!" I shout as they line up for the faceoff. They have one minute and fifteen seconds to make something happen.

But Coach Pedersen is no fool. He puts his best guys on the ice for the last minute, treating it like a penalty kill. It's the A-Team: Will Bray and Dmitry Petrov on defense; Connelly, Weston, and Chilton filling the forward slots. And they're so fucking solid. The puck remains in their possession the entire time. Harvard is on the attack and Corsen is like a ninja, fending off shot after shot after shot. And although it helps us, this is *not* what we need to be doing. We shouldn't be stopping bullets, we should be unleashing our own.

Ten seconds to go. Disappointment forms in my belly. I peer toward the Briar bench, seeking out my dad. His face is completely expressionless, but his jaw holds a lot of tension. He knows what's about to happen.

BUZZZZZ!

The third period is over.

Briar loses.

Harvard wins.

"I can't believe this." Summer tucks a strand of golden hair behind her ear as she and I stand in one corner of the lobby. "I feel so bad for Fitzy."

"Me too. And for the rest of the guys."

"Well, of course. Them, too." She rests her head against my shoulder, her glum gaze fixed on the entry to the corridor. We're waiting for the players to come out, and we're not the only ones. Fans and puck bunnies alike loiter in the cavernous space, ready to offer support and comfort to both the winners and the losers. At least most of the Briar guys will get laid without much effort tonight.

Since it's an away game, my father and the guys have to ride the bus back to campus. Some Harvard players trickle out first, and the girlfriends and groupies swarm like bees. Jake and Brooks appear, both looking undeniably fine in their dark suits. I love whoever came up with the after-game dress code. Their suit jackets stretch across impossibly broad shoulders, and my heart does a little flip when I notice Jake's hair is still damp from the shower. Which plants in my head the image of a naked Jake in the shower. Which is delicious.

Weston's face lights up when he spots Summer. "Di Laurentis!" He saunters over and opens his arms for a hug.

She glowers at him. "Don't you dare. No hugs tonight."

"Come on, don't be a sore loser." He widens his arms.

After a moment, she gives him a quick hug.

Jake winks at me from over Weston's shoulder and Summer's head.

My lips curve slightly. "Good game, Connelly."

I see him fighting a smile. "Thanks, Jensen."

Summer steps out of Weston's embrace. "So," she tells him. "Looks like your penalty provoking didn't work too well in the second and third."

"Yeah, the refs got meaner after the Jonah thing."

"The Jonah thing?" she echoes, poking Brooks in the center of his chest. "It was more than a 'thing'! He broke Hunter's wrist!"

"It was an accident," Brooks protests.

As they argue, a familiar face catches my eye. It's the girl from the Coffee Hut—Jake's friend. Hazel, was it? She's moving through the crowd, scanning faces until her gaze suddenly collides with mine. Then she notices Jake standing two feet away from me, and a frown mars her face.

I tense in anticipation of her approach, but for some reason she stays rooted in place. Interesting. Didn't she proclaim herself Jake's closest friend and confidante?

I arch a brow in her direction. Her frown deepens.

As I break the eye contact, my peripheral vision snags on another familiar figure. I turn to see my father emerging from the corridor. Unfortunately, his arrival is perfectly timed with that of Daryl Pedersen.

Uh-oh.

The two coaches exchange a few words as they fall into step with each other. Dad is stone-faced, as per usual. He nods at something Pedersen says. I can easily guess their exchange—the usual *good game, thanks*, some fake camaraderie. But as they get closer, I distinctly hear Pedersen say, "Nice try."

I'm not sure what he means, and I guess Dad is also stumped, because rather than walk away, he stops. "What do you mean by that?"

"You know exactly what I mean. Solid effort with the tricks." Pedersen chuckles. When he notices me standing near Jake, his eyebrows flick up, and a little smirk forms on his lips.

A sick feeling swirls in my stomach.

Since my father doesn't think rationally when it comes to the Harvard coach, he digs his feet in, his stance aggressive. "What tricks?" he asks coldly.

"I'm just saying, your plan to distract my star player didn't work." From the corner of my eye, I see Jake frown.

"I didn't expect that of you, though." Pedersen shrugs. "Not the Chad I know, that's for sure."

Jake steps closer to me, and it feels almost like a protective gesture. My father doesn't notice, however. He's too busy glowering at Pedersen. The interaction has drawn a small audience, mostly comprised of Briar players.

"I don't know what you're talking about," my father says irritably.

"I'm sure you don't." Pedersen laughs again. "But it's nice knowing you're not above pimping out your own daughter."

Oh my God.

Silence descends, like dead air in a live newscast. My pulse races, and I'm pretty sure my blood pressure has dropped, because I'm feeling light-headed.

Dad glances at me for a second, before directing a glacial stare at his nemesis. "As usual, Daryl, you're talking out of your ass."

The other man cocks a brow. "To be honest, it was extremely satisfying being proven right. I've always suspected you're not the honorable, rule-abiding martyr you present yourself as. The *pillar* of honesty and integrity, right?" Pedersen rolls his eyes. "Always thought it was an act. And while I'm glad to know the level you'll stoop to, for chrissake, Chad. Your daughter setting up a honey trap for Connelly? I get that you hate me, but come on, that move was beneath you."

Pedersen stalks off, leaving my father and the rest of our audience to absorb the impact of his accusation. Several seconds of silence pass.

Summer is the first to address the issue. "Bee?" she says uncertainly. "Is that true?"

And suddenly all eyes are on me and Jake.

31

BRENNA

Twenty-four hours after the shit show that was the conference finals, I'm still dealing with the fallout.

My anger over Daryl Pedersen's actions hasn't abated in the slightest. That spiteful dickhead didn't need to drop that bomb and certainly not in public. After he did that, the Harvard players followed him, my dad ushered the Briar boys onto the bus, and I drove home with Summer, who was visibly hurt that I'd kept her in the dark about me and Jake Connelly.

But at least she's still talking to me. My father hasn't said one word to me since last night. I genuinely don't know if he's pissed or simply indifferent. I'm definitely not confused about how Nate and the others feel, however.

The guys are outraged. Hollis called me a traitor last night. Nate, still sore about being ejected from the finals, was livid that I would even *dare* to be with a Harvard guy after the bullshit Jonah Hemley pulled during the game. And when I got home from Cambridge, Hunter bitterly texted me: Wrist's broken in 2 places. Thank your boyfriend for me.

They're being babies. I'm well aware of this. But these babies are still my friends, and they dealt with a brutal loss yesterday. A loss that might not have occurred if Jake's teammate hadn't instigated Hunter's and Nate's ejections.

Doesn't matter that Jake himself wasn't responsible. He's the Harvard captain, he's the enemy, and I'm an asshole for "choosing him over us"—Hollis's words, not mine.

"I still can't believe you don't trust me."

Summer's unhappy voice echoes in my ear. I'm lying on my bed staring up at the ceiling, trying to ignore my rumbling stomach. I'd hoped Summer's phone call would distract me from the hunger, but no such luck. Sooner or later I'll have to drag myself downstairs to find something to eat. Which means having to face my father, who's been holed up in the living room all evening.

"I do trust you," I assure her.

"Do you really?" she says doubtfully.

"Of course. But like I said in the car last night, I didn't want to risk it. You're the girl who tells her boyfriend everything, and that's fine, at least most of the time. But tensions were already running high between us and Harvard, especially after that dumb prank on Jesse's car. I just didn't want to take the chance that you might tell Fitz, at least not before the finals. But the game's over now, and Harvard's moving on. There's no reason to hide it anymore."

"I guess that makes sense," she says, albeit grudgingly. After a few beats, she changes the subject to Hunter. "I can't believe that jerk broke Hunter's wrist."

"I know."

"And all because Hunter's been banging everything in a skirt lately. If he hadn't slept with that girl, we might've won the game."

"He didn't know she had a boyfriend," I point out.

"I know. But still. Why are men so stupid?"

"I honestly don't know."

There's another pause. "So is Jake Connelly your boyfriend?"

"No." I can't stop a grin, because I've been waiting for this cross-examination since last night. I think Summer was too hurt over being left out of the loop to properly question me about Jake. Now that her feelings aren't stinging anymore, Detective Di Laurentis is back on the case.

"Have you slept with him?"

"Yes."

"How was it?"

"It was good."

"Just good?"

"It was very good," I amend.

"Just very good—"

"I'm not doing this anymore, you brat," I interrupt.

"Sorry." The interrogation resumes. "So you slept with him. And you've been sneaking around with him for years—"

"It has not been years," I grumble.

"But since my fashion show?" she presses.

"Yeah, around then."

"Do you like him? Wait, why am I even asking. I know you do." Her voice is growing more and more excited by the second. "I think this is great, by the way. I mean, he's insanely attractive—I could stare at him for hours and hours."

I try not to laugh. "Glad you approve?"

Her tone becomes serious. "I do, you know. Approve."

"You're the only one."

"They'll get over it."

We chat for a couple more minutes. After we hang up, my stomach grumbles again, and I decide it's time to bite the bullet and go downstairs. I can't avoid my father forever. Plus, I'm famished.

I know he hears me descending the stairs because of the horrible creaking, but he doesn't turn around as I reach the doorway. He's watching HockeyNet, and since yesterday's game aired on the network, they're not only showing highlights of it, but Kip Haskins and Trevor Trent are actually discussing the game on their show.

Or rather, arguing about it.

"There's fighting in the pros," Kip is grumbling. "I don't see why the NCAA is so severe about it."

"Because these are kids," Trevor points out.

"Are you kidding me? Some of these guys are older than actual NHL players!" Kip argues. "Toronto has an eighteen-year-old on their active roster. Minnesota is starting two nineteen-year-olds. Those boys are thrust into a high-stakes violent environment and *they're* able to handle it. And what, you're telling me twenty-one and twenty-two-year-old college men are too *delicate* to throw a few punches and—"

Dad pauses the DVR when he notices me.

"Hey," I say.

He grunts. I don't know if that means *hello* or *get out of my face.*

"Can we talk?"

Another grunt.

Swallowing a sigh, I enter the room and sit on the other end of the couch. Dad watches me warily but doesn't say a word. He's clearly waiting for me to start, so I do.

"I'm sorry I didn't tell you I was seeing Jake Connelly." I shrug awkwardly. "If it helps, I didn't tell anyone."

His jaw ticks. "Daryl Pedersen seemed to know."

"He saw us together at Harvard once."

Anger sharpens Dad's features. "You've been around Pedersen?"

"Yes. I mean, no. Just one time, one conversation."

My father goes silent for a long, tense moment. I can't read his expression anymore, and I have no idea what's going through his mind.

"I want you to stay away from that man," he finally mutters.

"Dad—"

"I mean it, Brenna!" He raises his voice, and now his expression is easy to decode—bitter, cold, and disapproving. But what else is new? "Daryl Pedersen is a selfish prick. He was a dirty player, now he's a dirty coach, and he has no honor, on or off the ice. Stay away from him."

I shake my head in exasperation. "Dad. I don't care about your stupid feud with Coach Pedersen, okay? I. Don't. Care. It has nothing to do with me, and if you're worried I'm hanging out with him in my spare time, I can assure you I'm not. Why would I? As for Jake—"

"Stay away from him, too," Dad growls.

"Come on." I exhale slowly. "Jake's a good guy. What's wrong with me seeing him?"

"I'm not doing this with you again." He locks his gaze to mine. "I will *not* watch this happen again. We already did it with Eric—"

"Jake is not Eric. And our relationship is nothing like my relationship with Eric was. I was *fifteen* when we started dating. And I was sixteen when—"

"We're not going through it again!" he booms. "Do you hear me?"

"I hear you. But you're not hearing *me*." I rake my fingers through my hair, agitation rising inside me. "Jake is nothing like Eric. He's smart, he's disciplined, he doesn't party. I swear, this guy is a generational talent, Dad. People will be talking about his career for decades to come. And he's a good guy. He was with me the night I went to help Eric—"

"So that's the friend you spent the night with?" Dad's lips tighten. "And I suppose he's the one you keep going to Boston to see? Is this why the HockeyNet internship fell through? Because your mind's been so wrapped up in this guy that you didn't properly prepare for your interviews?" He laughs humorlessly. "And you're telling me this is nothing like it was with Eric?"

My jaw drops. "Is that a joke? I absolutely prepared for those interviews. I didn't get the job because the man in charge thinks my sports knowledge is *cute*." Anger heats my throat. "And yes, I stayed at Jake's place that night, and I'm not apologizing for that."

"Fine, then maybe you should go and spend a few more nights there," Dad snaps back.

A second ticks by. Two. Three.

"Are you kicking me out?" I ask in amazement.

"No." He shakes his head. "Actually, yes. If you're determined to revert back to this bullshit high school behavior, where you stay out all night and throw your life away for another hockey player—"

"I'm not throwing my life away. Not only are you overreacting, but you're being ridiculously irrational right now."

"Irrational? You have no idea what it's like to almost lose your child," he spits out. "You have no idea, Brenna. And forgive me if I'm not feeling optimistic about this relationship with Connelly. You have a track record of making terrible decisions."

I feel like I've been struck. My heart beats double time as I try to collect my thoughts. As I try to put into words why his accusations are such a slap in the face.

"Despite what you think, I've actually been making solid decisions," I say bitterly. "I turned a miserable high school transcript around by going to community college, where I excelled. So much so that I was able to get into an Ivy League university, without you pulling strings, without anyone else's help. How's that for terrible decisions? But no, you refuse to acknowledge that I've grown up or matured. You want to keep thinking of me as the selfish teenager who lost her head over a guy? Then fine, keeping doing that." I stand up on stiff legs. "I'll get my stuff and leave."

32

JAKE

"THANK YOU FOR LETTING ME STAY HERE." GRATITUDE SHINES IN Brenna's eyes as she drops her bag on the floor near my bed.

"No problem." I wrap my arms around her from behind and kiss the side of her neck. "I cleared out a drawer for you. I wasn't sure how long you're staying."

"You're giving me a *drawer*?"

I release her, my arms awkwardly falling to my sides. I've never actually spent more than one night with a girl, so I'm not entirely sure of the etiquette. Was the drawer too much?

But Brenna's surprise is quickly replaced with approval. "Aw Jakey, you're the bestest." She winks at me.

Drawer for the win.

I clasp my hands on her waist and lean down to kiss her. She kisses me back, but it's only a peck. Then she kneels to unzip her black carry-on. "So what kind of destruction did Pedersen's bombshell cause on your end? Any of your boys mad at you?"

"Not really. I mean, McCarthy wasn't thrilled when he found out I've been seeing you. He's full-on dating that Katherine girl now, but he still called me a douche." I let out a rueful breath. "I was a bossy prick when I ended your hookup. And then to get together with you right afterward? I don't blame him for being pissed."

"No, you were right to do it. He was starting to really like me, and I knew there was no chance of it ever going anywhere. You called him a puppy once, remember? I can't be with a puppy."

"That's right. You need the stallion."

Brenna snorts. "What is it with you guys thinking you're either a puppy or a stallion? How is this the metric by which we're measuring masculinity?"

"It's not. It's the metric by which we're measuring my dick." I cup my package and wiggle my tongue at her.

"Ugh. You're the worst." Grinning, she opens her assigned drawer and starts placing items of clothing into it, arranged in neat piles.

"You're already unpacking?"

"Yeah. You gave me a drawer. Why would I leave my stuff in my suitcase?"

"Oh Christ, you're the person who goes on vacation and immediately puts all their shit away."

"Yes, Jake. Because then it's easier to find," she says primly. "Who wants to dig through a huge pile of clothes every time you're getting dressed?"

"I don't think we can be together," I inform her.

"Tough, because I'm staying for a few days." And just like that, her grin fades and her mood turns somber. "I can't believe my dad asked me to leave."

"That's brutal," I agree.

"Summer said I could stay at her place, but talk about uncomfortable. None of those jerks are speaking to me at the moment. Well, Fitz is, but he's not one for drama. The others, not so much."

"Don't you think they're kind of overreacting?" I say tentatively.

"Oh, they're definitely overreacting. At least with my dad I can understand why he overreacts all the time. Considering everything I put him through during high school."

As usual, her vagueness piques my curiosity. But I force myself not to press for details. She'll tell me when she's ready. I hope.

"I bet your parents are so chill, right?" Brenna says enviously.

"Yeah, they're awesome," I confirm. "Except for their constant nagging about how I don't have a girlfriend. They'd probably throw a party if they knew I gave you a drawer."

She laughs, then closes said drawer and turns to me. "Done. What do you feel like doing?"

"Want to watch a movie?" I suggest. "I can make some popcorn."

"Oooh, I like that idea. Let me put on comfy clothes and I'll meet you out there."

I give her ass a playful smack on my way out the door. In the kitchen, I experience a wave of déjà vu when I find Kayla at the sink, pouring a glass of water. This time she's wearing clothes. And instead of filling with hunger, her eyes cloud over when they land on me.

"Hey," I grunt.

"Hey."

I open the cupboard and grab a packet of microwave popcorn.

"Movie night?" She sounds a tad testy.

"Yep. You and Brooks can join if you want. I'll make another bowl." It's a bogus offer—I ask only because I'm confident she'll say no.

No way Kayla is going to willingly spend time with Brenna. The moment my girl walked through the front door, Kayla had reacted like a territorial cat. The claws came out, and she might as well have hissed. What made the entire encounter awesome was Brenna's complete disinterest in the chick.

"So… Jake Connelly's got a girl spending the night." Even testier now.

"Yeah."

"Must be serious."

I don't answer. Turning my back to her, I stick the popcorn in the microwave and punch in the time.

"Or is it not serious?" she prods.

Again I refrain from answering, because guess what—it's none of her fucking business. But then Brenna speaks up from the doorway.

"Oh, it's *very* serious." She saunters over, and even in a pair of plaid pants and a T-shirt, she's so sexy that my body instantly responds to her. Or at least it does before I notice the Briar hockey logo on her chest.

"That's blasphemy," I say, pointing at her shirt.

"No, that's blasphemy," she replies, pointing at *my* shirt.

I glance down and remember I'm wearing a gray tee with the Crimson logo over the left breast.

Near the counter, Kayla makes a disparaging sound.

Which spurs Brenna to twist around and beam at her. "Aren't we *so* cute?" she gushes. "We're like Romeo and Juliet!"

For a second, the blonde looks like she's going to hiss for real. Instead, she flashes a mocking smile. "Uh-huh, you two are the *cutest.*"

"Aw, thank you, Kaylee."

"*Kayla,*" she snaps before stomping out.

Brenna starts to laugh.

"You're such a bitch," I tell her.

"Yup. That girl wants you, though."

"Who doesn't?"

"You might be right about that. I swear, I can't go anywhere without bumping into someone who's into you. The chick in the bathroom, Bubble Butt's girlfriend, your friend Hazel."

"Hazel?" I frown at her. "Why would you say that? You don't even know Hazel."

"Oh, you mean she didn't tell you she ambushed me on campus?"

What?

"I'm sorry—what?" I vocalize my shock. Hazel hadn't mentioned that at all. Granted, we haven't spoken much this week, but if she actually had confronted Brenna, you'd think that would be something she deemed important enough to share with me.

"She tracked me down at the Coffee Hut," Brenna explains. "She basically gave me the whole what-are-your-intentions-with-Jake speech and the I'm-gonna-kick-your-ass-if-you're-playing-him threat."

I chuckle. "Yeah…she's kinda protective of me. We grew up together."

Brenna gives a faint smile. "She's a lot more than protective."

"Nah."

"Remember that thing we were saying about men being dumb?"

I scowl at her. "When were we ever saying that?"

"Oh, right. That was me and Summer. Forget what I just said, Jakey." She blinks, the poster child of innocence. "Men aren't stupid at all."

Neither of us pays much attention to the movie. We snuggle up under a blanket and spend the next hour teasing the hell out of each other. Brenna's hand constantly brushes my dick. At one point she starts giving me an over-the-pants hand job…before reaching for the popcorn again and leaving me with the biggest case of blue balls.

I return the favor by stroking her nipples through her shirt until they're harder than icicles and straining into my palm. When she tries to push her tits into my hands, I take the popcorn bowl and start munching.

About halfway through the movie, Brenna presses Stop and sets the remote control on the table.

I look over in mock outrage. "I was really into that."

"Oh really? Tell me what that movie was about, Jake."

I dig into my memory bank and come up empty. "Aliens?" I guess.

"Incorrect." Snickering, she practically drags me to the bedroom, where she plants her hands on her hips and says, "Lie down."

Because I'm not the stupid man she thinks I am, I lie down.

And before I know it, I'm naked and at her mercy. She's kissing me everywhere, her soft lips gliding over my chest, warm tongue grazing my abdomen on her teasing journey south. She licks my oblique muscles, her breath tickling my skin, and then she abruptly sits up and removes all her clothes. Now we're both naked, with my erection poking up between us like a huge spike.

She moans happily. "You are so effing sexy."

"Right back at you."

It's my turn to give a happy moan, because her mouth lowers and suddenly she's sucking my dick. I lazily thread the fingers of both hands through her hair, guiding her along the length of me. "Feels nice," I murmur.

"Just nice?"

"*Very* nice."

"Just very nice?"

"Jesus Christ, babe."

Her laughter heats the tip of my cock. "I'm kidding. Sorry. Summer pulled that on me earlier and I told her she was a brat."

"Mmm-hmmm, and then you decided to do the same thing to me?"

"Yup."

"And men are the stupid ones?"

"Are you calling me stupid when I'm giving you a blowjob? Because to that I say, I rest my case."

Dammit. She's right. Men *are* dumb.

"Forgive me," I beg.

Grinning, she resumes the task of torturing me. When her tongue scrapes the underside of my cock, pleasure sears into my balls, drawing them up tight. She cups my sac, squeezes it, and my hips arch off the bed. "Oh fuck. That feels so good."

She jacks me faster, her tongue swirling around my tip at every upstroke while her other hand continues to tease my balls. They start tingling, my heart beats faster, and I fist one hand in Brenna's hair to stop her.

"No," I croak. "I don't want to come this way. I want to be inside you."

"I want that, too."

She grabs a condom from the nightstand and rolls it on me. I pinch the tip to make sure we're good, then beckon at her with my cock.

"Have a seat," I say graciously.

"Oh my God, Jake. That was so lame."

"Really? So this isn't enticing you at all?" I wave my dick again.

"It's enticing," she relents, but although she straddles me, she doesn't guide me inside her yet.

My erection rests heavy against my stomach. Brenna places both palms on my chest and bends down, her breasts swaying seductively as she brings her perfect lips to mine. We kiss, and it draws a husky groan from my throat. She swallows the sound, and then her tongue touches mine and it's like an electric current running from the tip of my tongue to the tip of my cock. Fuuuuck. This girl turns me on something fierce.

"You like being teased," she remarks. "I find that interesting."

"Why's that?"

"Most guys don't have the patience for it." Her mouth travels to the side of my jaw. She rubs her cheek over my stubble, before kissing her way down to my neck. "Other guys would have flipped me over by now and started drilling into me from behind."

"How about we don't talk about other guys? How about we talk about *this* guy?" I tug her head back to my lips, and this time it's my tongue filling *her* mouth and her moaning against *my* lips. "But yes," I whisper, "I like foreplay. I like dragging it out."

"You like begging?" Her voice is throaty.

"Who's begging?"

"Not yet, but you will be." She goes back to kissing and sucking on my neck like it's candy, all the while rubbing her naked body all over me. My dick remains trapped between us, weeping inside the condom, because it needs somewhere to go so damn bad and—

"*Please,*" I plead, and she gives an evil laugh, because she succeeded in making me beg.

She lifts up, grabs the base of my erection, and impales herself on it. And holy hell, it's like a hot fist clenched around me.

Pleasure darkens Brenna's eyes. She sweeps her long hair over one shoulder, and it cascades down, veiling her nipple. I reach through the dark strands and tweak the rigid bud before muttering, "Ride me."

She does. But it's just the slight rocking of her hips.

Again, she's teasing me. And again, I'm loving it. I gaze up at her breasts, groaning when she cups them with her hands. Christ, that's sexy. I stroke her hips, caress her thighs, rub her clit with my thumb. I can't stop touching her. Luckily, she's not complaining. Each time a fingertip makes contact with her flesh, she moans or whimpers or releases a contented breath.

"I like you, Jake," she murmurs.

"I like you, too."

Her pace quickens, and my eyes close. I more than like her. I think I'm falling for her. But I'm not going to say it out loud, and especially not during sex. From what I've heard, chicks don't take a sex I-love-you seriously. They think it's induced by semen.

But semen has nothing to do with the warm sensation ballooning in my chest. It's a feeling I've never experienced before, and that's how I know it's real. It's not lust—trust me, I know lust. This is something entirely new.

I am definitely falling for this girl.

As she rides me, a flush rises on the tops of her breasts. "These are so pretty," I mutter, squeezing them gently.

She leans forward. "Put your mouth on them."

So I do, nuzzling the swell of one soft tit before capturing a nipple between my lips. Her pussy clenches around me, and she starts moving faster.

"Getting close?"

She nods wordlessly. Her breathing quickens. She's no longer riding me so much as grinding furiously against me. I have to grip her hips to steady her, because she's trembling so wildly.

"That's a good girl. Give it to me."

She comes apart, collapsing on my chest and struggling for breath. And as she's climaxing I dig my fingers into her waist and thrust upward, pounding into her until I come too.

Within seconds of our respective orgasms, Brenna lifts her hips, grips the base of the condom so nothing spills out, and pulls me out of her. Then she turns on her side, snuggling up beside me. I hold her close to me and we fall asleep like that.

33
BRENNA

I LOVE JAKE'S APARTMENT. IT'S BIG, ROOMY, AND ALWAYS NICE AND toasty, not frostbite cold like my basement in Hastings. I know I can't stay forever, but for now I'm enjoying being here. Being with *him*.

It sucks that some of my friends still aren't speaking to me, but to be honest, I'm starting not to care. Jonah Hemley didn't purposely set out to break Hunter's wrist. I do believe it was an accident. And yes, it wasn't Hunter's fault—he had no idea that he'd slept with Jonah's girlfriend. Violet, or whatever her name is, was the one pretending to be single while cheating on her boyfriend. But at the same time, she *was* Jonah's girlfriend, and the kid was upset. Sure, he handled the situation poorly, but not maliciously.

Speaking of upset, my friends are undoubtedly feeling the sting tonight. The Division I Men's Ice Hockey Committee made its selections—and Briar won't be one of the sixteen teams playing in the national tournament. Harvard has their auto-bid because they won the conference tournament. And from our conference, Princeton and Cornell received at-large bids from the committee over Briar.

Right now, the talking heads on TV are picking apart the conference finals. I'd been scrolling through my phone while Jake watched the segment, but my head jerks up when Kip Haskins mentions a familiar name.

"Are they talking about Nate? Turn it up."

Jake hits a button on the remote control. The volume gets louder.

"Briar University should've won that game," Kip is telling his cohost.

I turn to Jake with a huge grin. "Hear that, Jakey? Even the talking heads agree."

"Uh-huh, well, you *didn't* win the game, now did you?"

"Hush, baby, I'm trying to watch."

He snorts.

On the screen, Kip is raising very good points. "Their two best players were ejected. How in good conscience can you call that a fair matchup? That's like the '83-'84 season Oilers playing in the Stanley Cup finals without Wayne Gretzky and Paul Coffey."

"Oh fuck off," Jake scoffs. "There's no way he's comparing Hunter Davenport and Nate Rhodes to Gretzky and Coffey!"

"They are really good," I point out.

Jake is agape. "Gretzky-level good?"

"Well, no," I relent. "But nobody is."

"I am," he says smugly.

I roll my eyes, because I don't want to encourage his grandiose delusions, but deep down I suspect he might be right. Aside from Garrett Graham, there haven't been many players out of college lately with Gretzky potential. Jake is definitely an anomaly.

"Playing with the big boys is a lot different than college," I warn him.

"Oh really, played on a lot of NHL teams, have ya?"

"Absolutely. I did a few seasons with New York—Islanders *and* Rangers. Two seasons with the Maple Leafs—"

"Oh shut up." He pulls me into his lap and starts kissing my neck.

"I'm not done watching," I protest. The announcers are still arguing, but now it's even more hilarious, because Trevor Trent is basically saying the same thing as Kip Haskins. They're now both

in complete agreement that the Briar-Harvard game was unequiv-
ocally lopsided.

"See!" I say victoriously. "Even they know the truth! You can't say
you won that game."

"Of course I can say we won the game." He's exasperated.
"Because *we won the game*! Hello? Auto-bid?"

"Yes, but… Okay, I'm not going to argue about this," I grumble.
"Just know that if Hunter and Nate were skating that night, the
outcome could've been a lot different."

"That is true," Jake agrees.

"I heard it was about a girl," Trevor is saying, and the two
HockeyNet hosts chuckle at each other, until Kip dons a thoughtful
look.

"But that raises a good question," Kip muses. "If you're so
immature that you're swinging your fists over a girl during the most
crucial game of your season—do you not deserve to get ejected?"

"Hunter didn't get ejected!" I yell at the screen.

Trevor backs me up. "Davenport wasn't ejected. He was injured.
The instigator was Jonah Hemley."

"And what's Rhodes's excuse?" Kip shoots back. "He's the team
captain. What's he doing throwing himself in the middle of a brawl?"

"Damn right!" Jake chimes in. "Rhodes made his own bed."

"You know these hockey players—they're hot-blooded," Trevor
counters. "They operate on aggression and passion."

Jake hoots. "You hear that, Hottie? I'm aggressive and passionate."

"I am *so* turned on right now."

"Good. Get on your knees and suck me off. See how aggressive
and passionate I am?"

I punch him in the arm. "That is so unappealing to me."

"Fine, then spread your legs so I could eat you out."

"I'll think about that one."

He grins at me. "Keep me posted."

The lighthearted mood dies when the hosts bring up the topic of my father. "Jensen had a great season," Trevor says. "Shame they didn't get a berth, but hopefully next year will garner a different result. I really do believe he's the best coach in D1 hockey right now."

Sadness coats my throat. I wonder if I should text my dad. He must be so disappointed that Briar's season ended this way.

"I should text my dad," I say out loud. "You know, offer my condolences."

Jake's tone goes soft. "I'm sure he'd appreciate that."

Would he? I have no idea, but I still send him a short message saying they played a good season and next year will be even better. He doesn't immediately respond, but he's not much of a texter. I simply hope he reads it and knows I'm thinking about him.

To my horror, actual tears well up.

"Are you…" Jake doesn't miss my watery eyes. "Are you crying?" he asks with a note of concern.

"No." I rub the side of my finger underneath my eye. "Sending that message made me a bit sad. I hate it when he's mad at me. I mean, he doesn't show much emotion around me anymore, but when he does, it's usually more disapproval than anger."

"Do you realize how messed up that sounds? You hate the anger, but you're totally cool with the disapproval?" Jake asks incredulously.

"Well, no. I'm not *cool* with it. I'm used to it, is all." I let out a sigh. "And I guess I understand it. I told you, I haven't exactly been the perfect daughter."

"Why? Because you ran wild in high school? What teenager doesn't?"

"I did more than run wild. I…" A lump rises in my throat, and it's difficult to talk through it. "Honestly, I think he's ashamed of me."

Jake looks alarmed. "What did you do, babe? Murder a teacher?"

"No." I manage a weak smile.

"Then what?"

Hesitation lodges in my chest. I haven't talked about this with anyone, save for the shrink my father made me see senior year. He'd consulted with the team therapist at Briar, who told him that after what I'd been through, it could be useful for me to talk about it with someone who wasn't him. So I saw a therapist for a few months, and while she helped me come to terms with some of it, she couldn't quite tell me how to fix my relationship with my father. And it's only gotten worse in the ensuing years.

I study Jake's patient expression, his supportive body language. Can I trust him? This story is embarrassing, but it wouldn't be the end of the world if people found out. I just don't like the idea of being judged by someone whose opinion actually matters to me.

But Jake hasn't judged me, not even once, since we met. He doesn't care that I'm a bitch. He doesn't care that I taunt him—he enjoys taunting me right back. He's been fairly open about his own life, but then again, it's easy to be open when you don't have skeletons in your closet.

"Are you sure you want to meet my skeletons?" I ask wryly.

"Oh boy. You totally killed someone, didn't you?"

"No. But I got knocked up when I was sixteen and almost died."

The confession flies out before I can stop it. And once it's out there, hanging in the air between us, I awkwardly stare into Jake's wide eyes and listen to the crickets.

It's a solid five seconds before he responds, whistling softly through his teeth. "Shit. Okay." He nods slowly. "You got pregnant. Was Eric…?"

I nod back. "I lost my virginity to him. But despite what my father thinks, we weren't irresponsible about sex. We were having it regularly for more than a year, and we were very good about using condoms. I wasn't on the pill because I was too embarrassed to ask my dad, so I was super strict about condoms."

"I've noticed that," Jake says. "Now I get why."

"When I missed my period, I was in total denial about it. I thought, okay, maybe it's just stress. It's not abnormal for women to miss a period, and sometimes it has nothing to do with pregnancy. But when I was two months late, I took a test."

I'll never forget how my stomach dropped when I saw the plus sign on that pee stick. The first thing I did was call Eric, who was less than helpful.

"Eric said it was no big deal and we'd get it taken care of. But he was right in the middle of playoffs, so his schedule was chaotic. He promised he'd take me but not until after the playoffs."

Jake frowns deeply. "How long were you expected to wait?"

"A few weeks. But I did some research and found out the procedure is perfectly safe at three months. And before you ask, yes, I wanted to get it done. I didn't want a baby. I was only sixteen. And Eric didn't want a baby, either."

Sadness washes over me as I remember those days. I'd been so terrified. "I couldn't go alone," I explain to Jake. "I was too scared, and way too humiliated to tell my cousins or any of my friends, and especially not my father. I needed Eric to take me, and we had it all planned out. He would have more time after the playoffs, and he'd drive me to Boston and we would get it done there."

Jake runs his hand up my arm in a comforting gesture. "I'm sorry you had to go through that."

"I… I didn't actually get the abortion," I confess. "We had the appointment booked, but we never made it. I started bleeding one morning a few days before it. Well, spotting. I looked it up online, and most of the websites said that spotting during the first trimester was normal. I called Eric, and he went online too and concluded it didn't sound like a big deal."

"Where was he?"

"In Newport with his teammates. They were playing their semifinal round that afternoon. He said he'd check in with me after the game, and he did. I was still spotting but not too heavily." I shake my head irritably. "Eric's team crushed their opponent, so they were going out to celebrate. I asked him to come home, but he said there was no point because it was probably nothing, and he told me not to say anything to my dad."

"So you just sat there at home, bleeding?" Jake says in dismay.

"Yes and no. Like I said, it started off really slow. Eric told me not to worry about it, and even I thought I was probably freaking out for no reason. So I ignored it and hoped the bleeding would go away. I had dinner with my dad, watched a movie in my room. And then a couple hours later, it went from spotting to…not spotting." My throat tightens. "I called Eric again and told him it was getting worse and that I was going to tell my dad I needed to go to the hospital. And he said no way, because he didn't want my dad to find out and kill him."

"Selfish prick."

I feel sick as I relive that terrifying night. "Eric decided to come back and take me to the hospital himself. He said to sit tight, and that he was on his way and would get there as soon as he could. He was two hours away."

"And your father was right downstairs?"

The incredulity in Jake's expression makes me swallow a lump of shame. "I get it, I'm a fucking idiot. I already know that, okay?" Tears leak from the corners of my eyes, and I hurriedly swipe them away.

"No, I'm not calling you an idiot," Jake says instantly, reaching for my hand. "I swear I'm not. I totally understand—you were scared. You were sixteen, and the guy who was supposed to support you chose to keep partying with his friends instead of driving home the second you told him you thought something was wrong." Jake sounds furious on my behalf, and it's actually kind of sweet.

I nod. "And at that point, I wasn't going to risk waiting another two hours for Eric to show up. If he even did show up."

"So you told your father?"

"I never got the chance." My voice cracks. "I'd been bleeding all day long, and now it was nine o'clock at night, and I was feeling so weak and light-headed. When I stood up I was hit by a wave of dizziness and I passed out in the bathroom, and that's how my father found me." Queasiness pulls at my stomach. "Lying in a huge pool of blood. We actually had to tear out the bathroom floor after that, because the bloodstains wouldn't come out."

"Jesus."

"Dad took me to the hospital. I don't remember this part. I only remember everything going black in the bathroom. And then waking up in the hospital, where I was told I had a miscarriage and almost hemorrhaged to death."

Jake's eyebrows shoot up in alarm. "Is that normal?"

"Nope. Apparently I had an incomplete miscarriage, which is when not all the fetal tissue is expelled from the uterus. That's why the bleeding was getting heavier instead of improving."

"Shit. I'm so sorry."

I nod in gratitude. But I don't tell Jake everything else that happened in my hospital room. Like how I had a total breakdown in front of my father, crying hysterically and saying I was sorry, over and over again, while Dad stood there stoically, hardly even looking at me. And the longer I sobbed, the more embarrassing it became. I'd always been so strong and resilient, and suddenly I was wailing like a child in front of him.

He hasn't looked at me the same way since. He wasn't just ashamed that I'd gotten knocked up—I think he was equally ashamed of the way I fell apart. Dad doesn't respect soft people, and that night I was beyond soft.

"Things were never the same with Dad after that. He pulled me out of school for two months because I was so emotional. Depressed, crying all the time. We told everyone I had mono, and Eric was the only person who knew the truth."

"I can't believe you were still with him," Jake says darkly.

"Oh, I wasn't." I give a humorless laugh. "For so many reasons. He officially became public enemy number one to my father. Dad despised him, and he almost beat the shit out of Eric one day, because

Eric kept showing up at our door trying to talk to me. Dad forbade me from ever seeing him again, and I was perfectly cool with that. I couldn't forgive Eric for the way he behaved the night I lost the baby. I was crying and begging him to come home, to take me to the hospital, and he just didn't care." Anger bubbles in my throat. "I could have *died*. But getting loaded with his buddies and smoking weed was more important to him than making sure I was all right."

I lean my head against Jake's shoulder, and he plays with strands of my hair. "Dad became overprotective, but it's funny—he was so busy with his job that he couldn't really enforce all the rules he was trying to make me follow. So most of the time I did whatever I wanted anyway, and he'd lecture me about it afterward. I went back to school, started senior year, and acted out like every other teenage girl who's trying to get her parents' attention. It was the typical adolescent crap, and the more stupid shit I did, the more he noticed. So I'd stay out all night, drink, party, make him worry on purpose."

It's mortifying looking back on it. But we all do dumb things when we're teenagers. It's all those raging hormones.

"Anyway, now it's five years later and Dad still views me as a disappointment, as weak. Even though I cleaned up my act a long time ago." I shrug sadly. "But it is what it is, right?"

"I'm so sorry you had to go through that." Jake presses a kiss to the top of my head. "You're not weak, Brenna. Coach Jensen's blind if he doesn't see that. And calling your daughter a disappointment because she accidentally got pregnant? That's a dick move. You don't deserve that. And you definitely don't deserve what that prick Eric did to you. I can't believe you're still in contact with him, that you actually allow yourself to feel any compassion for the guy."

I sigh. "The breakdown I had after the miscarriage was nothing compared to the one Eric had. Losing me sent him into a tailspin. He blew off the championship game because of me."

"No, because of *him*," Jake corrects. "Don't kid yourself, babe—he would've gotten kicked off the team eventually, even if he had played in the championship. Eric Royce was never going to the NHL. He clearly already had a burgeoning substance-abuse issue. He would've failed a piss test, gotten busted for possession, something. I guarantee it."

"Maybe you're right. But at the time, I felt responsible for him. I didn't want to date him anymore, but I also felt an obligation to take care of him. It's so messed up, I can't even explain it." I lift my head from Jake's shoulder. "Eric was never there for me when I needed him, so why couldn't I say 'boy bye' and let him self-destruct?"

"Because you're a good person."

"I guess." I hesitate. "So are you," I tell him.

"Nah."

A hot lump of emotion fills my throat. "You are," I insist. "Look at everything you've done for me—you helped me rescue my undeserving ex. You gave me a place to stay. You just listened to that whole sordid tale without judging me. Eric was—is—one of the most selfish people I've ever met. But you're not. You're a good guy, Jake."

His big body shifts in discomfort, and it's kind of adorable. You'd think he'd be thrilled to hear someone singing his praises.

I swallow repeatedly, because the lump keeps growing in size. This is so unlike me. I'm not usually this sappy. But despite the tickle of embarrassment in my belly, I still vocalize the words that are tugging at my heart.

"Thank you for being there for me."

34
JAKE

Morning sex is something I don't get to indulge in very often. Which is a damn shame, because I love it. There's nothing better than an orgasm first thing in the morning to set the tone for the rest of the day. But since I never have women stay over, nor do I crash at their places, I'm constantly missing out on one of my favorite activities. Until now.

For the past three days, I've woken up with my morning wood nestled between Brenna's firm ass cheeks, one hand cupping a warm breast, my nose buried in her hair. It's the best feeling in the world. No, scratch that—the best feeling in the world is when Brenna climbs on top of me and seats herself on my dick. We've been sleeping naked since she got here, because whenever we're in my bed, our clothes end up coming off anyway.

"Don't kiss me," she warns, as she has every morning since she got here. She has a strict rule about not kissing with morning breath, which I guess I'm down with. But I'm also too impatient to get up, go to the bathroom, brush my teeth, and *then* fuck her brains out. I'd rather kick off with the fucking.

There's something different about this morning, though. It feels like more than fucking. Feels more intimate.

Maybe it's because of the confession she made last night. Opening herself up to me, allowing me to experience, at least secondhand, the traumatic events she'd gone through. She'd been so vulnerable, and for a moment I'd almost felt inadequate. As if this glimpse into her soul that she was trusting me with was beyond what I was capable of taking on.

I'm seeing the same vulnerability in her eyes right now, and it's making the sex feel—

Nope, it's not our locked gazes heightening the intimacy. It's the fact that my dick is surrounded with warmth and wetness.

I'm not wearing a condom.

"Babe." I groan, stilling her by grabbing her hips. "Condom," I remind her.

She looks stunned that we'd forgotten. And I know it's a big deal for her, because she's typically such a stickler for condoms. After her confession, I understand why.

"I'm on the pill," she says in assurance, and her expression becomes unusually shy. "I get tested twice a year. My last results were all clear…" There's an unspoken question there.

"Mine too," I say huskily.

"So maybe we should…" She visibly swallows. "Keep going?"

My pulse quickens. "You sure you want to bareback it?"

She nods slowly. "Yeah. But maybe you can pull out at the end, if that's okay?"

The fact that she's even allowing me to be inside her this way is a beautiful gift. And my mother always told me to never look a gift horse in the mouth.

"Of course it's okay." I roll us over so that she's lying beneath me, her dark hair fanned out across my pillow. Jesus, she's beautiful.

And because I don't know when or if the bareback gods might bless me again, I drag out the out-of-this-world sensations for as long as I can. I fuck her impossibly slow. My hips move in a lazy rhythm, and so does my tongue as I slide it between her parted lips. We kiss and fuck and fuck and kiss, for what seems like forever.

It almost becomes too much to bear. I bury my face in the

crook of her neck, kissing her there. She squeezes my ass and rocks upward, meeting me thrust for thrust. By the time I finally increase the tempo, we're both moaning with impatience.

"Dammit, Connelly, stop taking your sweet-ass time and *move*."

I choke on my laughter. "Jeez. So bossy," I chide.

"Move," she growls.

I stop completely. "I'm not your sex toy, Jensen. I don't fuck on command."

"You're such a baby. Are you going to get us off or not?"

I love that she says *us* and not *me*. Brenna isn't selfish in bed. She doesn't lie there like a starfish and make me do all the work like some women I've slept with in the past. Brenna is an equal participant, and I love it.

I gaze down at her with mock seriousness. "I'll let your insolence slide. This time," I warn. And then I pound into her until we're both coming.

Afterward, we lie on our backs, naked, and I can tell without even looking at her that her mood has shifted. Tension rolls off of her. "You okay?"

"Yeah. Sorry. I was thinking about my dad."

"We just had sex and you're thinking about your dad. Awesome."

"We just had sex. Period. And now I'm thinking about my dad. Period. Those are two unrelated events," she assures me.

"What's troubling you?"

"I want to go home and talk to him about everything, but I'm worried because I have such bad luck initiating heart-to-hearts with him. He's so hard to talk to." Her sigh heats the air between us. "But I think it's time to have a real conversation about everything I've been feeling. Maybe for once he'll actually listen to me, you know? Maybe I'll finally be able to get through to him and convince him I'm not the same person I was back then."

I trail my fingers over her shoulder. "I have the utmost confidence you'll make him see the light, Hottie."

"That makes one of us, because I'm not confident in the slightest. Like I said, I have terrible luck when it comes to conversations with Chad Jensen."

I purse my lips for a moment. "I have an idea." Then I hop off the mattress and onto my feet.

"Where are you going?" she demands as I duck out of the room.

"Hold tight," I call over my shoulder.

In the front hall, I throw open the closet door and drag out my hockey bag. I unzip it, ignore the rising smell of old socks, and rummage around until I find what I'm seeking. As I saunter back to my room, something nags at the back of my mind, but I can't quite bring the thought to the forefront.

"I'm about to do you a huge solid," I tell Brenna.

"Oh really." She sits up, and my attention is instantly drawn to her bare breasts. They're round and perky, and her nipples are puckered from being exposed.

I have to snap myself out of it before the lust takes over. "I'm going to lend you my good-luck charm," I announce, holding up the tacky pink-and-purple bracelet.

She gasps. "Seriously?"

"Yup."

"But how is *your* good-luck charm going to help me? Aren't all the mojo and good vibes it holds associated with you?"

"That's not how it works, babe."

She seems to be fighting a smile. "Uh-huh, how does it work, then?"

"It's a good-luck charm. It brings luck to whoever is wearing it, not just me. Jeez. Don't you know anything about charms and superstitions?"

"No!" she replies. "I don't." Despite the humor in her tone, her eyes soften. "But I'm willing to give it a shot if you think it will help."

"I don't think, I *know*."

I sit at the edge of the bed, naked as a jaybird. I take her hand

and slip the beaded bracelet onto her delicate wrist. It sits a bit looser on her than it does on me, and when she lifts her arm to admire it, it slides halfway down to her elbow.

"There," I say with a pleased nod. "You're all set."

"Thank you. I'll probably head over there and talk to him while you're at—" Her face suddenly pales.

Mine does too, panic careening up my throat. Shit. *Shit.* I glance at the alarm clock, which confirms my worst fear. It's nine thirty, and I'm an hour late for practice.

Coach doesn't let my tardiness go unpunished. After I've suited up in the empty locker room, I sprint down the tunnel—on skates— and practically hurl myself onto the ice. My teammates are running a shooting drill, but Coach blows his whistle when he spots me. He doesn't even let the guys finish what they're doing. He abandons them mid-drill and skates over to me.

His dark eyes burn like hard, angry coals. "You'd better have a damn good excuse for this, Connelly. We're facing off against Michigan in three goddamn days."

My shameful gaze drops to my skates. He's right. This was a colossal screw-up on my end. The regionals are being held in Worcester this weekend. We're the number-one seed, playing Michigan, the number-four seed. But that doesn't mean we're guaranteed a win. Anything can happen in the national tourney.

"My alarm clock didn't go off," I lie, because the alternative is not an option. *I was having sex with Chad Jensen's daughter who I'm pretty sure I'm in love with.* Coach would have an aneurysm.

"That's what Weston said probably happened," Coach mutters.

I force myself not to send a grateful look in Brooks's direction. He didn't come home last night, otherwise he would've been pounding on my door earlier reminding me about morning skate.

And obviously Brooks knows that Brenna is staying with us, so I'm beyond relieved he kept his mouth shut about it with Coach. I make a mental note to stop calling him Bubble Butt around the house. At least for a few days.

"I'm sorry. It won't happen again. I'll set three alarms tomorrow." Fortitude rings in my voice. The reason I gave for being late is bogus, but that doesn't alter my determination to never let this happen again.

"You'd better." Coach spins around and blasts the whistle a couple times. "McCarthy! You're up!"

Practice is particularly draining, since I'm going out of my way to kick ass. I need to make up for what happened this morning, to absolve myself of this cardinal sin.

I've only been late to practice twice in my entire athletic career—and to put that in perspective, that career began when I was five years old. Both times I was late occurred in high school. The first time, I had the stomach flu, yet I still dragged myself out of bed and drove to the rink. I was thirty minutes late and my coach took one look at me and ordered me to drive right back home. The second time, the coast was hit by an unexpected blizzard and I woke up to a foot and a half of snow outside the door. I spent most of the morning shoveling the driveway and trying to dig our cars out. And even then, I was only forty minutes late.

Today? There was no stomach bug, no blizzard. I was an hour late because of a *girl*.

Don't get me wrong, I'm not blaming Brenna. And despite my complete dissatisfaction with myself, I don't entirely regret what happened this morning. The sex was goddamn spectacular. It was our first time without a condom, and I shiver at the memory. Her tight heat surrounding me...*fuuuck*. So hot and so good.

I'm about to leave the ice when I glimpse a familiar figure waving at me from the stands. Fans are allowed to come and watch us when it's an open practice, like today's.

I execute a sharp turn and skate the opposite direction from the boards. Hazel descends the steps, her blonde braid swinging as she walks. She's wearing a light jacket, and, as usual, her fingers are stacked with rings, including the one I got her for Christmas. She smiles at me through the plexiglass, reaching the little door on the boards at the same time I do.

"Hey. What are you doing here?" I ask.

"I didn't get to properly congratulate you for winning this weekend." Her expression becomes rueful. "You were a bit occupied, what with that little scene between your coach and your girlfriend." The last word—*girlfriend*—has a slight bite.

I stifle a sigh. "Yeah, that was awkward, to say the least."

"Anyway, I owe you a celebratory meal, so I thought I'd surprise you with brunch at that place we both like in Central Square."

"Sounds good." I hope she doesn't notice that I'm not as enthusiastic as I usually am at the idea of eating food. I'm just eager to see Brenna and find out if she spoke to her father yet. "Let me hit the locker room and I'll meet you out front in ten."

———————————

A short while later, Hazel and I are seated across from each other at a small table in the cheesy breakfast place we discovered sometime last year. It's called Egggggs, and although all the dishes have silly names and the way-too-colorful decor is an assault on the eyes, the food is actually excellent. Or eggcellent, as Hazel likes to say.

"Thanks for surprising me," I tell her as I set down my menu. "Please don't tell me you showed up at eight thirty, though."

She blanches. "God, no. The world doesn't exist before nine a.m., remember?"

A waitress comes by to take our orders. And we've been friends for so long that I know exactly what Hazel's going to get before she even says it—two eggs, scrambled. Brown toast. Sausage, because she's the one person in the world who doesn't like bacon. And coffee, two sugars, no milk or cream. And I'm sure she knows my order, too: whatever the biggest breakfast on the menu is, because I'm a total pig.

I wonder what Brenna's breakfast preferences are. She's eaten eggs and fruit for breakfast since she started crashing with me, but I wonder what she'd order at a place like this. Probably makes me a massive loser, but I'm excited to find out. I'm enjoying getting to know her.

Hazel and I catch up as we wait for our food, but it's all very surface level. We talk about our classes and hockey, her mom's new boyfriend, how neither of my parents showed up for the conference finals. That last one still grates. I'm used to them being no-shows, but I had really hoped they might surprise me this time, especially because it was such a big game.

We're about halfway done with our meals when Hazel sets down her fork and demands, "So are you with her now?"

"You mean Brenna?"

"Who else would I mean?"

I chuckle. "Yes. I guess I am. She's actually been staying with me and Brooks since the finals."

My friend is shocked. "You're living together?"

"We're not living together," I answer quickly. "She's just crashing at my place until hers is ready. She got flooded out."

Hazel is quiet for a beat. She picks up her coffee. Takes a long sip. "This is very serious," she finally remarks.

Slight discomfort makes me shift in my seat. "It's not 'very serious.' It's just…" I rely on my trusty motto. "It is what it is."

"Yeah, and what it is, is serious, Jake. I don't think you've ever had a girl spend one night at your place, let alone several nights." She watches me pensively. "Are you in love with her?"

I fidget with my fork, pushing some hash browns around on my plate. My appetite is slowly abandoning me. I don't like talking about this. Or rather, I don't like talking about it with Hazel. For a while now, it's felt as if she's passing judgment on me, disapproving of my actions, and I've never felt that way in all the years we've known each other. Even when I did dumb shit like get wasted at a party and throw up in her bushes, or indulge in a one-night-stand, I didn't feel judged. But I do now.

"It's fine, you don't have to tell me," she says when I remain silent.

"No, it's… It's awkward for me, I guess," I say sheepishly. "I've never really been in love before."

Something akin to pain flashes on her face, and suddenly I'm reminded of Brenna's insinuation that Hazel has feelings for me. There's no way that can be true, though. Wouldn't she have given *some* indication of it in all these years? Before Brenna planted the idea in my head, it hadn't crossed my mind, because Hazel never once acted like she was into me.

"That's a big deal," she says quietly. "Being in love for the first time. This entire thing is monumental whether you want to admit it or not."

"I wouldn't call it monumental."

"You're in a relationship. Relationships are huge."

Christ, I wish she'd stop using words like *huge* and *monumental*. "It's really not the big deal you're making it out to be," I say awkwardly. "We're just going with the flow right now."

My friend snorts. "The mantra of fuckboys everywhere."

"I'm not a fuckboy," I return with a dark scowl.

"Exactly. You're not. Which means this isn't about going with the flow. You're *in* this. You're dedicated to this girl, and that *is* a big deal, because you've never been in a real relationship." She sips her coffee again, watching me over the rim. "You sure you're ready for this?" she asks, her tone light.

My palms are unusually damp as I pick up my own coffee cup. "I can't decide if you're purposely trying to freak me out," I say dryly.

"Why would you be freaked out? I'm simply asking if you're ready."

"Ready for what exactly?" I ask, then release a clumsy laugh and hope she didn't notice how confused I sounded just now.

She's right—I haven't been in a real relationship before. I've fucked a lot of women. I've had some flings that lasted a few weeks or months. But I never developed deep feelings for anybody until Brenna. I never wanted to say the L-word to anybody until Brenna.

"Jake." There's a note of pity in her voice, which gets my back up. "Relationships are work. You realize that, don't you?"

"What, you're implying I'm incapable of working hard for something?" I roll my eyes and point to my chest. "Hello, going to the NHL over here?"

"Which raises another issue," Hazel says. "And tell me, how is that going to affect this relationship? She's a junior. She has another year at Briar. And you're going to be in Edmonton. How exactly is this going to work?"

"People make long-distance relationships work all the time."

"Yes, they do, but those are even harder. Now we're talking about *twice* the work. Twice the effort to try to make the other person feel like they're still a priority for you even though they're in another country. And now we're at our next issue—how can she possibly be a priority when you need to be focusing on the new job?"

An itchy sensation crawls up my spine. Hazel raises some good points.

"Which brings me to my last concern," she announces, as if she's presenting a thesis titled *Why Jake Connelly Will Make a Shitty Boyfriend*. "Hockey is your life. It's all you've ever cared about. You've worked your ass off to get to this point. And I still have reservations about Brenna. Despite what you think, I still think she had an ulterior motive when she got together with you."

"You're wrong," I say simply. At least that's the one thing I'm certain about. Everything else…not so much.

"Fine, maybe I am. But am I wrong about the fact that you spent, what, seventeen years concentrating on hockey and preparing for this moment? You're about to make your professional hockey debut. I *guarantee* that a long-distance relationship will distract you, and it'll frustrate you, and you'll end up spending an inordinate amount of time thinking about this girl and obsessing and assuring her you still love her when she reads articles or sees pictures on the blogs of you and whatever puck bunny throws herself at you that week." Hazel shrugs, cocking a brow at me. "So I repeat, are you ready for this?"

35
BRENNA

I'm just grabbing my coat in the entryway when Jake walks into the apartment. I hadn't even realized he was on his way home, so his sudden appearance startles me. "Jeez!" I exclaim, laughing in relief. "You scared me."

His gaze softens. "Sorry. I didn't mean to."

"How was practice? Is Pedersen royally pissed?" I still feel awful that Jake was late this morning. Obviously it's not entirely my fault—it takes two to tango-bang. But if I'd remembered he had morning skate, I would've made a point to shove him out of bed.

"Yeah, he was none too pleased. Worked me extra hard, but I deserved it." Jake shrugs out of his jacket and hangs it up. Then he rakes both hands through his hair. "I take it you haven't gone to see your dad yet?"

"No. I was actually on my way out now." I texted Dad to let him know I was coming, and his response was *I'll be here*. With my father, that could mean *I'm here and ready to talk*, or *I'm here to yell at you some more*. It's really a crapshoot.

"Do you need to leave right this second or do you have a minute to chat?"

I refrain from furrowing my brow. Chat? And why does he keep running his hand through his hair? Jake's not usually so fidgety. Anxiety flutters in my stomach. "Sure. I've got a minute. What's up?"

He heads into the living room, gesturing for me to follow. I do, but I don't feel great about it. Because now I'm noticing the slump of his shoulders. He's lacking his usual confidence and that worries me.

I allow the concern to surface. "What's going on?" I ask quietly.

"You know I was late for practice today," he starts.

Didn't we just go through this? I study his troubled expression. "Right. You were late, and…?"

"So it was a disservice to my team." His long fingers comb through his hair again. The dark strands are becoming increasingly rumpled. "We're one game away from potentially playing in the Frozen Four. Two games away from potentially winning the whole damn thing." He bites his lip. "I can't afford to be late for practice."

Guilt floods my body again. "I know. I guess what we can take away from this is…no more morning sex?" I offer in a lame attempt at a joke.

Jake doesn't even crack a smile.

Uh-oh.

I lower my butt onto the arm of the couch. He remains standing.

"When the playoffs first started, I told everybody on the team they had to make sacrifices. I told Brooks he couldn't party. Told Potts and Bray they couldn't drink. Enforced a drink limit on the other guys." He gives me a pointed look. "Forced McCarthy to end it with you."

My stomach continues to churn.

"And they all did it without question. They put the team first." He shakes his head, clearly miserable. "I used to put the team first, too. But I've completely lost my head since I met you."

I'm starting to feel sick. I don't need to be clairvoyant to know where this is heading, and I can't fucking believe it.

Last night, I was more vulnerable with him than I've ever been with anybody else. I told him about the pregnancy and the miscarriage, the emotional breakdown, the broken relationship with my father. I sliced myself open and said, *Look, here it is. Here I am.*

For the first time in a long time, I allowed myself to be *soft*.

And this is the result?

My eyes are stinging. I press my lips tightly together. I don't say anything, because I'm scared I might cry, and I refuse to show any weakness.

"I forced everyone to get rid of their distractions. Which makes me a total hypocrite, because I wasn't willing to give up mine."

"And I suppose I'm yours?" I'm surprised—and rather proud—by how steady my voice sounds.

"You are," he says simply. "Since I met you, you're all I think about. I'm fucking smitten."

My poor, confused heart doesn't know how to react. Does it soar because Jake—a guy I admire and respect and who I've been falling hard for—admitted to being smitten with me? Or does it sink because he's acting as if that's a bad thing?

"And that's why I think we need to cool it."

It sinks. My heart greets my stomach and they both begin to ache.

"I can't ask my guys to place all their focus and energy on the team if I'm not willing to do the same. So maybe when you go to your dad's today…" Jake trails off, awkwardly sliding his hands in pockets. "Maybe it would be better if…"

Another harsh dose of reality settles in.

"…if you just stayed there," he finishes.

"You want me to leave?" I say flatly.

"I'm going to be spending every waking hour of the next three days preparing to beat Michigan. That's all I'm allowed to think about, Brenna. You being here is a distraction. We already saw that this morning." His voice sounds tortured. "I need to be there for my team."

What about me? I want to shout. *Why can't you be there for me?*

But I know better. There's no way in hell I'm revealing my internal devastation over this. I revealed myself to him last night, and today he's dumping me.

Lesson learned.

"Hockey needs to come first for me right now."

And that's when I hear it—the tiniest flicker of dishonesty. Is he lying? His expression is so pained and unhappy that it's obvious he's not jumping for joy at the idea of breaking up. But I'm not about to beg anybody to be with me. I'm going to take his reasons at face value. Because I'm an adult and I don't play games. If he's telling me it's over, then it's fucking over.

"It's fine, Jake. I get it."

He falters. "You do?"

"Hockey comes first," I echo with a shrug. "And it should. This is what you've worked for your entire life. I don't expect you to throw it away for a relationship that was going to end anyway."

A slight frown touches his lips. "You really believe that?"

"Yes," I lie. "I told you this once before—this can't go anywhere. You're moving to Edmonton. I have another year of college left. It would be stupid to even try." I rise from the couch. "I'm sure my dad will be fine with me moving back. And if he's not, then I'll stay with Summer. My landlords said the basement will be ready any day now. Who knows, maybe it's ready now and they haven't had a chance to call me yet."

His fingers slide through his hair for the millionth time. "Brenna..." He doesn't continue. His remorse is unmistakable.

"It's all good, Jakey. Let's not drag this out. We had some fun, and now it's time to move on. No biggie, right?"

Pretending I don't care is one of the hardest things I've ever done in my life. And I must be doing a convincing job of it, because Jake nods sadly.

"Anyway, I'm going to go grab all my stuff now, make it easier. It's only one drawer so..." My voice breaks. He gave me a drawer and now he's taking it away. It feels like someone took a rusty blade and stabbed it into my heart a hundred times.

In Jake's bedroom, I quickly empty the contents of the drawer and dump everything in my suitcase. Then I duck into the hall bathroom and sweep up my toiletries. I'm sure I've forgotten something, but if Jake contacts me about it later, I'm going to tell him to throw it out. Even though I'm alone, I force myself not to reveal a sliver of emotion. One slip-up and I'll be crying. And I'm not allowed to shed a single tear inside this apartment.

Rolling my suitcase behind me, I return to the living room. I saunter over to Jake, squeezing his arm. Touching him makes me want to die.

He stiffens for beat, and then he raises his hand and touches my cheek. His thumb brushes lightly over my bottom lip. It comes away with a faint crimson smudge.

"Rocking the red lips this early in the day, eh?" he says roughly.

"It's my trademark." *It's my armor*, I think silently.

Right now that armor is the only thing keeping me from breaking down in tears at his feet.

36
BRENNA

JAKE DUMPED ME.

Those three miserable words run through my mind during the train and bus rides to Hastings. I still haven't cried. I thought I would, but I guess when I buried my emotions during the goodbye with Jake, I did too good of a job. Now I feel nothing. Nothing at all. I'm numb. My eyes are dry and my heart is stone.

Dad's Jeep is in the driveway when I walk up to the front door dragging my carry-on behind me. I hope he doesn't kick me out again. On the bright side, if he does tell me I can't stay, I'll only need to find a place to crash for one night. Wendy called when I was on the train, giving me the news that I can move back in tomorrow morning. She and Mark are even going to IKEA this evening to pick up some basic pieces of furniture. I told them they didn't have to do that, but apparently the insurance claim still hasn't gone through, so they're insisting on at least getting me a bed.

I find Dad in the kitchen unloading the dishwasher. He's turned away from me, and for a moment I'm startled. He's tall and broad, built like a hockey player, and from the back he almost resembles Jake, only Dad's dark hair is shorter. Strength radiates from him, and it reminds me that I need to be strong, too. I always have to be strong in front of my father.

I take a breath. "Hey."

He turns, offering a brisk "hey" in response.

There's a brief silence. Our gazes lock. Suddenly I feel so very tired. I already dealt with one emotional confrontation today, and it's only one p.m. I wonder how many more devastating exchanges are in store for me.

"Can we go sit in the living room?" I suggest.

He nods.

When we're seated on opposite ends of the couch, I inhale slowly, then release my breath in a long, measured puff. "I know you appreciate it when people get right down to the point, so that's what I'm going to do." I clasp both hands in my lap. "I'm sorry."

Dad gives a slight smile. "You'll have to be more specific. There are a few things you could be apologizing for."

I don't smile back, because I resent the jab. "No, actually, there aren't. I'm not going to apologize for dating Jake, or having friends, or partying every now and then. I'm not going to apologize for any of that, because I've been doing it all responsibly." I exhale in a rush. "I'm apologizing for getting pregnant."

There's a sharp intake of breath. "What?"

It's rare to catch my father off-guard, but he looks beyond stunned. I play with the beads on my wrist and—Crap, Jake's bracelet. I'm still wearing it. That means I'll need to find a way to get it back to him before his game on Saturday.

Right now, however, it's fueling me in a strange sort of way. I don't know if it's bringing me luck exactly, but it's definitely giving me courage, which I usually lack around my dad.

"I'm sorry I got pregnant," I repeat. "And I'm sorry I didn't tell you. For what it's worth, it really was an accident. Eric and I were always careful, *always*." I shake my head bitterly. "And then one fluke time a stupid condom breaks, and now my father hates me."

His eyes widen. He opens his mouth to speak, but I cut him off.

"I know I disappointed you, and I also know that I—what's that phrase they use in old-timey movies? I brought shame upon our house?"

Dad barks out a laugh. "Jesus, Brenna—"

I interrupt again. "I know you're ashamed of me. Trust me, I'm ashamed of myself for the way I behaved. I should've told you I was pregnant and I absolutely should've told you I was bleeding that day. Instead, I was so scared of how you would react and I let Eric convince me that it wasn't a big deal. I was a stupid kid, but I'm not stupid anymore. I promise."

My throat closes up, which is probably a good thing because a sob was about to fly out. I blink repeatedly, desperately trying to keep the tears at bay. I know that when they finally come, it's going to be epic waterworks.

"I'm asking you to give me another chance," I tell him.

"Brenna—"

"Please," I beg. "I know I'm always disappointing you, but I want to try to fix that. So please just tell me how"—*to make you love me again*—"to fix this. I can't live with you being ashamed of me anymore, so I need you to tell me how I can make it better and how to—"

My father starts to cry.

Shock slams into me. My mouth is still open, but I'm no longer talking. For a moment I think I'm imagining his tears. I've never seen my father cry, so this is a completely foreign sight to me. But… those are tears, all right.

"Dad?" I say uncertainly.

He drags his knuckles over his face to try to scrub the moisture away. "Is that what you think?" Shame glimmers through his tears, only it's not directed at me. I think he's ashamed of *himself*. "Is that really what I've led you to believe? That I hate you? I'm ashamed of you?"

I bite hard on my bottom lip. If he keeps crying, I'll cry too, and one of us needs to maintain a level head right now. "You're not?"

"Christ, of course not." His voice is beyond hoarse. "And I never once blamed you for getting pregnant, Peaches."

There is absolutely no stopping the tears this time. They flood out and spill down my cheeks, the salty flavor touching my lips.

"I was young once," Dad mutters. "I know the stupid things we do when hormones are involved and I know that accidents happen. I wasn't thrilled it happened, but I didn't blame you for it." He rubs his eyes again.

"You wouldn't even look at me afterward."

"Because every time I looked at you I remembered finding you on the bathroom floor in a puddle of blood." His breathing goes shallow. "Jesus, I've never seen so much blood in my life. And you were white as a ghost. Your lips were blue. I thought you were dead. I walked in and actually thought you were dead." He drops his face in his hands, his broad shoulders trembling.

A part of me wants to move closer and wrap my arms around him, but our relationship has been so strained for so long. Hugging has been missing from it for a long time, and I feel awkward doing it now. So I sit there and watch my father cry, while tears stream down my own cheeks.

"I thought you were dead." He lifts his head, revealing a ravaged expression. "It was like your mother all over again. When I got the phone call about the accident and had to go identify her body in the morgue."

A gasp cuts off my airways. This is the first time I'm hearing of this.

I knew my mother died when her car hit a patch of ice and skidded off the road.

I didn't know my father had to identify her *body*.

"You know how your aunt Sheryl is always saying you look exactly like your mother? Well, you do. You're the spitting image of her." He groans. "And when I found you in the bathroom, you were the spitting image of her corpse."

I'm so nauseous I'm afraid I might vomit. I can't even imagine how he must have felt in that moment.

"I couldn't look at you after because I was scared. I almost lost you, and you're the only thing I have in the world that I give a damn about."

"What about hockey?" I joke weakly.

"Hockey is a game. You're my life."

Hoo-boy. The waterworks start up again. I have a feeling I'm ugly-crying like crazy, but I can't keep my eyes from watering or my nose from running. Dad doesn't pull me in for a hug, either. We're not there yet. This is brand-new territory for us...or rather, it's old ground that needs to be replanted.

"I almost lost you, and I didn't know how to make things better for you," he admits gruffly. "If your mom had been there, she would've known exactly what to do. When you were crying in the hospital, and then all those months that you were at home. I was out of my element. I didn't know how to deal with it, and every time I looked at you, I pictured you bleeding on the floor." He shudders. "I'll never forget that image. I'll remember it until my dying day."

"I'm sorry I scared you," I whisper.

"I'm sorry I made you think I was ashamed." He lets out a ragged breath. "But I won't apologize for the shit that happened afterward. Grounding you, enforcing the curfew. You were out of control."

"I know." I hang my head in regret. "But I turned everything around. I grew up and went to college. I'm not acting out to get your attention anymore. You were right to be overprotective back then, but I'm a different person now. I wish you could see that."

His somber gaze sweeps over me. "I think I'm starting to."

"Good. Because that's the only way we'll ever be able to move forward." I eye him hopefully. "Do you think we can clean-slate this? Forget about the past and get to know each other as adults?"

His head jerks in a quick nod. "I think we could do that." He nods again, slowly this time, as if his brain is working something over. "In fact...I think that's an excellent idea."

37
BRENNA

The following evening I go over to Summer's house, because that's how desperate I am to not think about Jake. I'm willing to walk into the lion's den, be around Hollis and Hunter and maybe even Nate, who all think I betrayed them by sleeping with the enemy. I'm willing to deal with whatever angry words they hurl my way, because it beats obsessing and agonizing over the fact that Jake doesn't want to be with me.

Ironically, I would have been perfectly content hanging out with my dad tonight. After years of avoiding being in the same room as him, I'm finally excited for us to spend time together. But he had a meeting tonight. The dean of Briar is apparently interested in discussing the prospect of extending my father's contract with the university, which he totally deserves. But that meant if I stayed home, I'd be alone. With my own thoughts.

To my surprise, I'm not tarred and feathered the moment I walk through Summer's door. In fact, when I poke my head into the living room, Hollis looks up from the couch and offers a preoccupied, "Hey, Jensen."

"That's it? I expected a lot more yelling."

"Why would I yell?"

I'm dumbfounded. "Are you kidding me? The last time we spoke, you called me a traitor."

THE RISK 343

"Oh. Right." I've never heard him sound so blasé and uninterested. And it takes a second to realize he's not even watching TV. He's staring at a black screen, and his cell phone sits untouched on the coffee table.

"What's going on?" I demand. "Are you okay? Where are Summer and Fitz? Upstairs?"

"No, they went to pick up the pizza. Summer refuses to get it delivered ever since the delivery kid bitched at her for giving him a five-dollar tip."

"Isn't five dollars a decent tip?" If not, then I've been tipping pizza delivery boys wrong for years.

"Not according to Mr. Money Bags over there."

I unzip my jacket and duck into the hall to hang it up before joining Hollis on the couch. His vacant stare is alarming, to say the least. "All right. What's going on with you?"

He shrugs. "Nothing much. Studying for finals. Rupi dumped me, but no biggie."

"Wait, what?" I'm genuinely shocked to hear that. "Seriously? Why did she dump you?"

"Doesn't matter. Who cares, right?" He hops to his feet. "I'm grabbing a beer. You want one?"

"Sure. But this conversation isn't over."

"Nah, it is."

When he comes back and hands me a Bud Light, I'm reminded of my bowling date with Jake and how we had to choke down that watery beer. Also, it doesn't surprise me that it's Hollis's beer of choice. He's totally a Bud Light kind of guy.

"I'm calling bullshit," I say.

"Bullshit on what?"

"Bullshit on the bullshit you're trying to feed me about not caring about Rupi. You do care. You liked her."

"I did not. She's so annoying."

"Really? So why did you keep hanging out with her?"

"Because I was trying to get in her pants, Brenna. Come on. Keep up."

"Uh-huh. So you were just trying to get laid?"

"I was. And now I don't have to work for it anymore. I've got a dozen other chicks lining up to bang me. So, good riddance." His tone holds zero conviction.

"Admit it, Hollis, you like her. You like her shrill voice and her bossiness and her endless chattering."

"I don't," he insists. "She's not even my type."

"She's not," I agree. "She's not a puck bunny with a centerfold body, or one of those plastic girls I see you hitting on at Malone's. She's weird and tiny and has an inexplicable amount of self-confidence." I grin at him. "And you like her. Admit. It."

The tips of his ears turn red. He rakes both hands through his hair, and then glumly sticks out his chin. "She was growing on me," he finally confesses.

"Ha!" I say victoriously. "I knew it. So now give her a call and tell her that."

"No way. She dumped me." He gazes at me in challenge. "If your little Harvard boyfriend dumped *you*, would you go chasing after him?"

Laughter spills out, bordering on hysterical. But I can't stop it. I rest my head on Hollis's shoulder and giggle uncontrollably.

"What's going on right now?" he asks in confusion. "Are you high, Jensen?"

"No. It's just..." I giggle some more. "He *did* dump me."

Hollis straightens up in shock, bumping my head off his shoulder. His blue eyes are wide with amazement. "Are you serious? Was *he* high?"

"He wasn't high, and, yes, I'm serious. He broke it off yesterday. Said he needed to focus on the tournament and his team and I was too much of a distraction, blah blah blah."

"That's horseshit. I always knew Harvard men were dumbasses, but this is a whole new level of dumbassery. Has he seen you? You're the hottest girl on the planet."

Even though the compliment is coming from Mike Hollis, I'm still genuinely flattered. "Thanks, Hollis."

He swings his arm around me. "This just confirmed everything I already knew. Harvard sucks and Connelly sucks harder."

"I second that," drawls Hunter, who enters the living room with a beer in hand. He's drinking a Founders All Day IPA—wait, why didn't I get that option?

I wince when I notice the cast on his left wrist. At least it's not his right one, so he still has use of his dominant hand. And his season is over, so it's not like he'll be missing any games. Nevertheless, the cast triggers a rush of sympathy.

"Hey," I say carefully. "How's the wrist?"

"What? You can't tell?" He raises his arm. "It's broken." But he doesn't sound pissed. Just resigned.

"Can I sign it?" I tease.

"Sorry, but Hollis kind of ruined that for everyone," Hunter answers in a dry tone. He approaches the couch to give me a better view of the cast.

In a black Sharpie, someone drew a dick and balls.

I sigh. "Real mature, Hollis. Also, you used a surprising amount of detail for the balls."

He shrugs. "Well, you know what they say."

I wrinkle my forehead. "No, what do they say?"

Hunter settles in the armchair. "I'm also curious to know."

"For fuck's sake. Seriously? I don't actually have anything to add to that," Hollis grumbles in aggravation. "Most people don't question you when you say, 'You know what they say.'"

I would love to spend one day in Hollis's brain. Just one, though. Any more than that and I'd probably get trapped in the Upside Down. "All right. You've dodged this enough. Why did Rupi end it?"

"Rupi ended it?" Hunter echoes. "Does that mean we don't have to listen to you guys screaming at each other at all hours of the night anymore? Sweet!"

"Be nice, Davenport. He's really bummed about this."

Hunter cocks his head. "For real?"

"No," Hollis says firmly. "Not for real. It doesn't matter to me in the slightest."

"If it doesn't matter, then there's no reason not to tell us why it ended," I counter.

"It was stupid, okay? Doesn't even bear repeating."

"What did you do?" Hunter asks in amusement.

Hollis lets out a heavy breath. "She wanted to give each other nicknames and I wasn't into it."

Um. Okay.

I'm trying very hard not to laugh.

Hunter doesn't try—he bursts out laughing. "What were the nicknames?"

"She didn't actually have any. She wanted us to come up with a list and then—" Hollis is visibly clenching his teeth. "—discuss each one and say how it makes us feel."

Hunter nods solemnly. "Of course. Because that is a thing."

I silence him with my eyes. Hollis is being vulnerable with us right now, and he doesn't deserve to be mocked.

Oh my God. Who am I? *Is* this the Upside Down? Because since when do I pass up the opportunity to mock Mike Hollis?

"Did you not like any of her ideas?" I ask carefully.

He stares at me. "I didn't even let her start brainstorming. Who makes a list of nicknames and sits around voting on them like fucking *American Idol?* I told her it was crazy and that she was crazy and then I suggested that maybe her nickname should be 'crazy' and she lost her shit and stormed out. And then she texted me later to say she can't be with somebody who isn't, and I quote, *all in.*"

"She has a point. It's hard to be in a relationship when both people aren't all in." I shrug. "Also, I don't blame her for bailing. Who wants to be called crazy all the time? It's bound to give someone a complex."

"She already has a complex."

"Hollis," I chide.

He's suitably shame-faced.

"I bet you've called her crazy more times than you've said you liked her. Actually, I bet you've never even said the words, 'I like you.' Have you?" I challenge.

"Yes."

"Hollis."

"Fine. No."

"Be honest—do you want to keep dating this girl?"

After a very long, embarrassed silence, he nods.

"Okay. Then give me your phone."

Despite the misgiving in his eyes, he hands it over. I scroll through his contacts until I find Rupi's name—with the heart-eyes emoji beside it. She picks up on the first ring, which tells me not all hope is lost.

"What do you want, Mike?" She doesn't sound like her usual chirpy self.

"Hey, Rupi. It's Brenna."

"Brenna? Why do you have Mike's phone?"

"I'm putting you on speaker, okay? Hollis is here beside me. Say hello, Hollis."

"Hello," he mutters.

"Anyway, we were having a little chat," I go on, "and Hollis has something he wants to say to you."

"What is it?" she asks warily.

"Hollis?" I prompt.

He doesn't speak.

"Okay, then *I'll* say it. Hollis likes you, Rupi. He pretends he doesn't, but deep down he does. He pretends he doesn't like all the arguing, but deep down he's all about the drama-llama. His favorite show is *Keeping Up with the Kardashians*, for Pete's sake."

Hunter snickers from the armchair and takes a sip of his beer.

"Yeah, but his favorite Kardashian is Khloe," Rupi says darkly. "Everybody knows that Kourtney is the best one."

"Kourtney doesn't even make the top three," Mike grumbles at the phone.

"See! That's why it can't work!"

"Nah," I disagree. "That's why it *will* work. You don't want to be with someone who's exactly like you. You want someone who challenges you, who inspires you to open up when you've been closed off your entire life—" My voice cracks. Oh no. I'm thinking about Jake again, and I notice Hollis shooting me a strange look. I ignore it and keep talking to his stalker. I mean, girlfriend. "Listen, I know he's always calling you crazy, but coming from him, that's actually a compliment."

Hunter snickers again.

"Explain yourself," Rupi orders.

"Have you met him? *He's* crazy. And from the sounds of it, his family's crazy, too."

"Hey!" Hollis protests. "I wish you wouldn't bring my family into this."

"If wishes were horses we'd all be equestrians," I say smugly, and that shuts him right up. "So really, Rupi, when he calls you that, it's because he's recognizing a kindred spirit." I wink at Mike. "He sees his soulmate."

A breathy gasp floats out of the phone. "Is that true, Mike?" He scowls at me, slashing one finger across his throat to signal that he's going to kill me for throwing out the term "soulmate." But after the Kardashian snafu, I had to bring out the big guns.

"Mike?" Rupi says.

"It's true," he mumbles. "I like you, okay? I don't think you're crazy. I think you're awesome."

"Then why don't you want to give each other cute nicknames?" she demands.

"Because it's so—"

I shake my head in warning.

"—important," he finishes, saving himself. "It's a huge step forward in the relationship."

I'm worried that Hunter might die laughing. He presses his face to his forearm to muffle the sounds.

"But fine," Hollis says. "If you want to come up with nicknames, we'll come up with nicknames. My first suggestion is 'kitten.'"

"Kitten!" Hunter howls.

"I don't know if I like that one for me," Rupi says slowly.

"No, it would be for me. I also think—actually, wait, I'm taking you off speakerphone." He taps his phone and brings it to his ear. "I'm going upstairs. Brenna and Hunter don't get a say in the nickname conversation." As he nears the doorway, he suddenly stops. He glances at me over his shoulder and mouths, *Thank you.*

My heart actually melts a little. For *Hollis.* Imagine that.

I smile graciously. Once he's out of the room, I turn to Hunter and say, "My work here is done."

He grins. "Solid job you did there."

I study him. "You seem to be in a pretty good mood, considering, you know…" I nod toward his cast. "And you don't seem pissed at me at all."

"I was never pissed at you."

"You sent me a nasty text about thanking my boyfriend for you," I remind him.

"Yeah, the day after that jackass Hemley broke my wrist. I was still smarting over everything that went down during the game, and you were an easy target."

"Gee, thanks."

He shrugs. "And I was indirectly pissed at Connelly. But… truthfully, he didn't do anything wrong. He tried his best to break up the fight." Another shrug. "That said, I still think if Nate and I were playing that night, we'd be the ones facing Michigan this weekend."

"I think so, too." I release a glum breath. "We were in the lead for most of the first period, until you guys left the game. We had it."

"We had it," he echoes, before taking a hasty sip of his beer. "And then we lost it because of me."

"Bullshit. You didn't get injured on purpose."

"No, but my off-the-ice behavior cost us the game. I spent the last couple months banging my way through campus. And then when that got boring, I started hitting the bars in Boston and picking up strangers, and look what happened." He groans. "Apparently Violet was aiming to get back at Hemley because they got in some fight. She knew who I was when we met."

"Really?" I gasp.

"Oh yeah. And the first thing she did after I left was call him to taunt him about it. So the moment Hemley got on the ice during the finals, he started questioning me, and, well, you know the rest."

Hunter shakes his head in disgust. It's clearly self-directed, though.

"I never used to be like that. I hooked up, sure, but I didn't make it my mission in life to sleep with any chick that crossed my path. I lost my head, became a 'pussy posse of one,' as Hollis likes to call it." He offers a dry grin. "I need to clean up my act, get my shit together. I want to take the team to the Frozen Four next season. Nate's graduating, and I don't know if Coach will be choosing the next captain, or if the guys will vote on it, or what. But I want it to be me."

I whistle. "That's a lofty goal."

"I know. And I plan on working hard to reach it. So…no more fucking around. Literally."

"What does that mean?"

"It means I'm taking a vow of celibacy."

A gust of laughter flies out. "Um. That's never going to happen. I give you one week, tops."

"You think I can't keep it in my pants longer than a week?" He looks mildly insulted.

"You're a twenty-year-old hockey player. No, I don't think you can keep it in your pants longer than a week."

Hunter smirks. "All right, then. Guess I'll just have to prove you wrong."

38

BRENNA

"Holy shit!"

Dad, who's cooking breakfast for us at the stove, turns sharply to look at me. It's Saturday morning, and my phone screen is currently displaying the most shockingly unexpected news since that Toronto player Ryan Wesley announced to the world he was gay.

"Everything okay?" Dad barks.

"Holy shit," I repeat as I reread the message. "Tansy got engaged."

He blinks. "Your cousin, Tansy?"

"Yup."

"Engaged?"

"Yup."

"To who?"

"Lamar, that basketball player she's constantly breaking up with. According to this, he got down on one knee at a nightclub last night and popped the question. He had a ring and everything." I flip the phone around so Dad can see the picture she sent. The diamond on her finger isn't enormous, but it's much bigger than I'd expect from a college student's budget.

Wow. I guess she wasn't kidding when she told me they were talking about getting engaged.

"Oh boy," Dad says. "Sheryl is going to shit a brick."

I snort with laughter, and he responds with a loud chortle. It's only been a few days, and our relationship is already different. It's easier, almost entirely free of tension. Sure, we're not going around hugging each other every other minute, but our conversations flow so much smoother, and we're cracking more jokes. Real ones and not the sarcastic kind veiled with venom.

We're truly starting over.

"Hold on. Let me text her back."

ME: Hey!!! Can't talk right now b/c I'm having breakfast with my dad but OMG!! Congratulations! This is amazing news and I'm so happy for you. You're going to be the most beautiful bride, T!!

Am I more or less bullshitting? I'll be honest—yes. I still don't believe a relationship with their track record is going to last. Lamar proposed at a *club*, for Pete's sake. But Tansy is my cousin and I'll support her no matter what, so while I'm not jumping-up-and-down ecstatic about this engagement, I am happy that *she's* happy. And if by chance I'm wrong and they do end up making it down the aisle, I do believe she'll make a beautiful bride.

She texts back immediately.

TANSY: Thanks, B!! CALL ME THE SECOND YOU'RE FREE!!

I smile at the phone and put it aside as Dad carries two plates to the table. Scrambled eggs, bacon, and cucumber slices. I thank him for breakfast and immediately dig in, talking with my mouth full.

"I can't believe she's engaged. This is going to be such a disaster. She's way too young. Or rather, way too immature. I mean, jeez, *I'm* more equipped to get married right now."

His expression turns wry. "Does that mean I should be expecting you and Connelly to announce your engagement any day now?"

I freeze. Then I pick up my fork and spear it into some eggs. "No. You don't have to worry about that."

"Why's that?"

I chew extra slowly to delay my response. "Because we broke up."

"Why's that?" he says again.

"Because we did." I roll my eyes. "You and I might be semi-cool now, but that doesn't mean we're best friends. I'm not going to reveal all my deep, dark secrets."

"First of all, we're not semi-cool. We're cool. Period. And given that you promised not to scare the shit out of me again, I don't much like hearing this breakup might've been deep and dark." There's genuine concern in his tone.

"It's not," I assure him. "If you must know, Jake dumped me because he wanted to focus on hockey."

Dad frowns.

"It's totally fine. It wasn't going anywhere, anyway. He's moving to Edmonton, remember? Long-distance relationships never work."

"Your mother and I made it work," he says gruffly.

I glance up in surprise. "When were you and Mom in a long-distance relationship?"

"She was a year younger than me," he reminds me. "After I graduated, she still had one more year left at Yale. That was the year that fuckhead made his move and—"

"*Wait* a sec. Back it up like a Tonka truck. What fuckhead?" I suddenly gasp. "Are you talking about Daryl Pedersen?"

"Yes. He was a senior like your mother. Same major, too. Broadcasting." Dad smiles. "Like you, as well. Anyway, he waited until I graduated before making his move on Marie."

I'm horrified. "Did Mom…?"

"Jesus. Of course not. Your mother was a sweet and proper Georgian peach. Loyal to a fault."

"So Coach Pedersen tried to steal Mom away and she shot him down." I'm utterly captivated by this. It's always so jarring to remember your parents lived full, well-rounded lives long before you ever came into the world.

"Daryl played the 'I'm going to take care of your girl when you're gone' card," Dad says with a snort. "We weren't close friends. I didn't like him, but I tolerated him. Had to, because we were teammates. Your mother, well, she had a different opinion. She thought he was sweet, and she accused me of being paranoid for distrusting him. But I played with the fucker for three years, so I knew what kind of man he was. An arrogant prick, not above playing dirty, and damn sneaky—he was a ladies' man, but around your mother he acted like a choirboy."

Dad shoves a forkful of eggs in his mouth, chews, swallows, and then reaches for his coffee. "You know, it's not even that he made a play for your mother that bothers me. He could've been upfront about his intentions. Could've said, 'Hey, I'm attracted to Marie and I'm going to tell her.' Admittedly, I would've laughed in his face, but then I would've said, 'Sure, go ahead.'" My father smirks. "I never had any doubt about your mother's feelings for me."

Must be nice, I want to say. I hadn't doubted Jake's feelings, either, and he turned around and dumped me.

"But he went about it in an underhanded way. You don't have to love all your teammates, but at least respect them. He cozied up to your mother, planned study sessions, platonic outings. And one night they went out with a group of friends, and he walked her home. Escorted her all the way upstairs and then tried to paw her outside her apartment door."

"Please tell me he stopped when she said no."

Dad nods. "He stopped. But not before accusing her of leading him on, using him to help her study, taking his time and affection but then denying him what I guess he believed was his right. Finished off the speech by telling her she needed a real man to satisfy her."

"Gross."

"When I found out, I drove all the way to New Haven from

Burlington—I was a skating coach at the University of Vermont at that point. Took me four hours to get there, but it was worth it to hear the sound of bone crunching when I slammed my fist into Pedersen's jaw."

"Go Dad."

"She was my girl. You don't disrespect a man's girl." Dad shrugs. "He didn't go near her again after that."

"And that was like twenty years ago and you still hate him."

"So?" He pops up a cucumber slice into his mouth.

"So don't you think maybe it's time to bury the hatchet?"

"Can I bury it in his skull?"

I snort. "I was thinking the metaphorical hatchet. Letting bygones be bygones and all that. You got Mom, had a beautiful daughter—" I wink at him. "You're a three-time championship-winning coach. And he's a bitter prick. Why not let it go?"

"Because I don't like the man and that's never gonna change. Sometimes people don't like each other, Peaches. Get used to that, because it's a fact of life. People are going to hate you because you hurt them, either intentionally or inadvertently. People will hate you because they don't like your personality, or the way you talk, or whatever superficial bullshit some idiot can't get past. There'll be people who just hate you on sight for no good reason—those ones are strange." He sips his coffee. "But at the end of the day, that's the way it is. Not everyone is going to like you, and you're not going to like everybody. I don't like that man. I don't need to change that."

"Fair enough." I gaze down at my plate as the thought of Jake once again creeps into my brain.

"I'm sorry about you and Connelly." I guess my sad expression and the reason for it weren't hard to decode.

"Since when? You told me to stay away from him, remember? Compared him to Eric."

"That comparison might have been made in anger," Dad

grumbles. "Connelly has a good head on his shoulders from what I've heard."

"I told you so. He's the one who helped me rescue Eric."

"Speaking of that, have you heard from Eric since then?"

"No, and I have a feeling I won't."

"Good. Is there a way to forward all his calls to you to my phone? So I can give him a piece of my mind?"

"Dad." The murderous glint in his eyes is a tad worrisome. "You're not allowed to give him the Liam Neeson speech. Let's just hope his mom convinced him to go to rehab. Maybe winding up in someone's bushes was the wakeup call he needed."

"Maybe." He doesn't sound convinced.

I'm not, either. It's been five years since high school and Eric still hasn't even acknowledged that he has a problem.

"But I am sorry about Connelly," Dad says, steering the subject back to Jake.

"Me too."

He lifts a brow. "Thought you said it wouldn't go anywhere."

"I did. That's what I told him, anyway. He dumped me and I pretended not to care," I confess. "I didn't want him to see how upset I was. But I *was* upset. He's the first guy I've met in a long time who I could see myself being in a relationship with. He was good for me, and he was good *to* me. Like, when I was nervous about coming home to talk to you, he lent me his—*oh my fucking God!*"

"Language," Dad scolds.

I'm already flying out of my seat. I forgot about Jake's bracelet. I forgot to give it back to him, dammit.

After my talk with Dad the other night, I went upstairs to take a shower and I remember shoving the bracelet in my nightstand. And I spent most of Thursday and Friday at Summer's, because even though my basement is ready, I haven't moved back in yet because I didn't want to be alone. I'm afraid that if I'm alone I'll just be thinking about Jake all the time. I completely pushed him out of my head these past few days. And since *he* wasn't on my mind, neither was his good-luck charm.

He's playing Michigan today. Crap. Why hasn't he called or texted? Hasn't he noticed he doesn't have his bracelet?

"I have Jake's good-luck charm," I blurt out. "He gave it to me before we broke up and I totally forgot to give it back, and he's playing today in Worcester!"

Coaching hockey players for more than two decades, my father has undoubtedly encountered a crapload of superstitions, charms, and rituals. So I'm not surprised when his expression turns grave. "That's not good."

"No, it's not." I gnaw on the inside of my cheek. "What should I do?"

"I'm afraid you don't have a choice." He sets down his cup and scrapes his chair back.

"What are you doing?"

"You don't mess with a man's ritual, Brenna." Dad checks his watch. "What time does the game start?"

I'm already looking it up on my phone. "One thirty," I say a moment later.

Right now it's eleven. It'll take an hour or so to get to Worcester. Relief fills my chest. I can make it there long before the game starts.

Dad confirms my thoughts. "If we leave now, we'll get there with plenty of time to spare."

"We?"

"You think I'm really going to let you drive the Jeep in a panic? Christ. I shudder just thinking about the mailbox destruction you'd be leaving in your wake." My father snorts. "I'm driving."

Jake's not answering his phone or responding to my texts. It occurs to me that maybe he blocked my number, but that would be a total dick move. He's the one who broke up with *me*. He has no reason to block my number. Unless he thought I'd be one of those girls who called him five hundred times begging for a second chance? If so, then I guess he didn't know me at all.

The alternative is that he's too focused on his game-day rituals and isn't checking his phone.

There's a light drizzle outside, lazily sliding down the Jeep's windshield. In the passenger seat, I wonder if there's another way to get in touch with Jake. I don't have Brooks's number, and I deleted McCarthy's. I suppose I could do some online investigating and track down their social media accounts, but that requires a level of panic I'm not feeling right now.

There's lots of time, and when we get there, I'll be bound to run into a Harvard player or someone who could send a message to a Harvard player. Hopefully, I can simply give the bracelet to someone who'll pass it on to Jake, without me ever having to see him. I'm not sure what I would say if I saw him. Plus, he's already accused me of being a distraction. Seeing me right before a crucial game might mess with his head.

When we pull into the arena, Dad bypasses the parking lot and drives directly to the entrance. "Get out here," he orders. "I'll park the car and meet you inside. Keep your phone on."

A thought suddenly occurs to me. "Oh no," I say in dismay. "We don't have tickets."

"Sure we do. I called Steve Llewellyn when you were getting dressed. Told him I needed a favor. There'll be two tickets waiting for us at the box office under your name. Standing room only, though. It was too last minute for anything better."

Llewellyn is the head coach of Michigan. I guess it helps to have a father with connections. "You're the best."

I hop out of the car and dart toward the entrance. As I pick up the tickets, I call Jake again. He doesn't answer.

Although the game doesn't start for nearly an hour and a half, tons of people are already streaming inside the arena and filling up the stands. I glimpse a sea of Harvard fans, along with the gold and blue Michigan colors. I scan the Crimson portion of the crowd for anyone who looks familiar. Nada. Then I search for any signs that might tell me where the locker rooms are. I spot one and take off in that direction.

I'm approaching the corridor when I finally encounter a face I recognize.

It's Jake's friend Hazel.

Lovely. "Hey," I greet her. "I'm looking for Jake."

After a cool appraisal, a flicker of displeasure flares in her eyes. "What are you doing here?"

"I just told you—I'm looking for Jake." I fidget with one of the beads on his bracelet. I wore it on my wrist for safekeeping. "Is the Harvard bus here yet?"

"No."

"Do you know when they're showing up? Have you spoken to him at all today?"

"No." She frowns slightly. "He's not answering his phone. I'm here with his parents—"

My stomach twists. Nope. Not jealous. I am *not* jealous.

"—and none of us can get in touch with him. Maybe his phone's dead. Sometimes when he goes into hockey mode, he forgets to do basic things, like charge his tech."

I hate this girl. I don't know if she does it intentionally, these I-know-him-better-than-you-do jabs. Maybe I'm just feeling insecure, though. Or maybe she doesn't even realize she's doing it. Maybe she knows him so well that it comes out instinctively.

Either way, it's a good thing Jake isn't here yet. Now I won't have to see him, and he won't see me. He wants to focus on hockey? Congrats, he can focus on hockey.

"When he gets here can you give him this?" I clumsily slide the bracelet off my wrist. Removing it brings a pang of sorrow. It's like saying goodbye to the last piece of Jake that I have left.

Hazel's gaze darkens with suspicion. "Where did you get that?"

I set my jaw. I don't appreciate the not-so-veiled accusation. "If you think I stole it, relax. Jake loaned it to me the other day. I was nervous about something and he said it would bring me good luck." I have to smile, because something good did come out of it. Dad and I got our fresh start, after all. "Anyway, I forgot to return it, and I drove all the way here, so…" I thrust out my hand. "Could you please give this to him when he gets here?"

"Jake let you borrow his good-luck charm." Her tone has a dull note to it.

"Yes." I'm starting to get annoyed. And I'm still holding my arm out like a moron. "Look, I get that you don't like me—for no good reason, by the way. You don't even know me. But I care about Jake, same as you. This—" I wave the bracelet at her. "—is important to him. He'll hate me forever if this bracelet isn't on his wrist when the puck drops. So can you please just take it already?"

After a moment of hesitation, Hazel accepts the bracelet. She slips it around her wrist and says, "I'll make sure he gets it."

39
JAKE

I'm alone in the locker room, me versus my thoughts. Voices echo beyond the door, laughter and chatter and the general hum of activity, but I'm good at blocking all of it out. My ritual of silence doesn't require actual silence. I just need to quiet my brain. Meditate on what needs to be done.

Coach gave me permission to make my own way to Worcester today. It's unheard of, but I think my less-than-stellar performance at practice these last three days genuinely shook him up. He's worried I might lose us this game. And he's right to worry. My concentration is shot. Breaking up with Brenna wrecked me.

I made a mistake.

I made a mistake, and I knew it the moment she left my apartment. Ending it was the stupidest thing I've ever done. I acted out of fear, not logic, and it backfired on me, because now my head is even further away from where it's supposed to be.

It's ironic. All that bullshit I spewed about needing to rid myself of distractions—which was a total lie to begin with—resulted in creating an even bigger disruption in my brain. Brenna wasn't a distraction, but this breakup sure as hell is.

So Coach gave me a pass and I drove to Worcester on my own. I found a diner and fueled up with a big, greasy breakfast. At some point I realized I forgot my phone at home, but I don't need it.

Nothing is allowed to exist today beyond this one game. We win this, we progress to the Frozen Four. It's enough pressure to make a weaker man choke, but I'm not that man. I might've been weak about my relationship with Brenna, but I'm not weak about hockey. Never have been, never will be.

Loud footsteps thud out in the hall. For a second I think the rest of the team has arrived early, until I hear evidence of a scuffle. More footsteps, a thump, and an outraged male shout.

"I told you, you can't go in there!"

"We just need a minute," someone insists. "Seriously, what the hell do you think we're gonna do in there? Murder the guy?"

I don't recognize the second voice. I assume the first one is security.

"Sorry, not happening, kid. I can't let you in there."

"Come on, Hollis," urges a third voice. "We'll track him down later."

Hollis? As in Mike Hollis?

I jump up from the bench and sprint to the door. "Wait," I say, flinging it open. "It's cool. I know them."

The security guard's hawk-like gaze sweeps over me. "Nobody else is supposed to be in here."

"We'll keep it quick," I assure him. "Two minutes, tops."

He steps aside.

A few seconds later, I'm in the locker room with the last two people I expected to see today. Mike Hollis has his arms crossed tight to his broad chest. Colin Fitzgerald is more relaxed, with his arms at his sides. He's wearing a V-neck sweater with the sleeves rolled up, and there's ink peeking out from under his collar and his cuffs. Dude's totally tatted up, I realize.

"How did you know I was here?" I ask the Briar players.

"The goon told us," Hollis says.

"The goon?"

"Weston," Fitzgerald supplies, grinning. "My girlfriend Summer texted him."

"Ah."

"Are we done with the small talk?" Hollis asks politely.

I fight a laugh. I wonder if they're going for a good cop, bad cop approach. "Sure, I guess we're done." I make a gracious gesture toward him. "Why are you here?"

"Because we wanted to beat some sense into you."

"Please don't *we* this," Fitzgerald objects. "I just drove you here."

Hollis glares at his teammate. "You're saying you don't give a shit that he broke Jensen's heart?"

I suck in a breath. I broke her heart? Did she tell them that? Hollis spins toward me again. "You are *such* a dumbass, Connelly. You made the biggest mistake of your dumbass life when you broke up with Brenna."

"I know."

"First of all, she's gorgeous. It's almost disgusting how gorgeous she is. She's smart and witty and hilarious and—wait, what do you mean, 'you know'?"

Shrugging, I lower myself onto the bench. They remain standing, and I suddenly feel like I'm a kid being scolded by my two dads.

"I mean I know," I say unhappily. "It was a huge mistake. One I'm going to rectify the second we beat Michigan."

"If you knew it was a mistake, then why didn't you *rectify* it days ago?" Hollis demands.

"Because I have a game to play."

Because I'm fucking terrified of facing her.

There's no way I'm admitting that to these two boneheads, but it's the truth, the *real* truth.

I suppose I could take the easy way out and blame Hazel for my actions. She was the one who induced my panic by hammering me with all those questions, asking if I was ready, warning how hard it was going to be, how impossible long-distance relationships are. Every point she'd raised created more and more pressure inside my chest until I couldn't breathe. The walls started closing in on me, and I felt like I was suffocating.

I know she wasn't doing it on purpose. Those were all things I should've already been thinking about, issues I should've been anticipating.

But I wasn't, because I was still living my Solo Jake life. In that life, I get to be selfish. I get to blow off dates for hockey. I get to concentrate on kicking ass in the NHL. I get to have one priority: myself.

Relationship Jake is required to be there for someone other than himself. Or rather, to be there for someone *along* with himself. The realization scared the shit out of me. I've never had to be there for anybody else. What if I'm bad at it? What if I let Brenna down in some way? I can't promise to be there for her every second of the day, and the way Hazel was going on about it, it was like I wouldn't have a single second to myself ever again.

I'm really not blaming Hazel. But the anxiety attack that began at the diner followed me all the way home. When I saw Brenna, the panic spilled over.

I found myself grasping for the first excuse that came to mind, the tried-and-true reason I used to give girls who demanded more of my time: hockey. I told her I needed to be there for my team, because in that moment I was terrified of the responsibility of being there for *her*.

It only took an hour, maybe two, before my anxiety passed and I was able to clearly process my thoughts. I *am* capable of being there for Brenna. Haven't I already done that for more than a month now? I was there for her with the Ed Mulder charade, rescuing her ex-boyfriend, advising her about her issues with Coach Jensen. She was staying at my house, and other than one late practice—which makes a total of three in the past *seventeen* years—I was perfectly capable of balancing hockey and a girlfriend.

I don't expect next season to be a breeze. I'll be traveling a lot, I'll be exhausted from working my butt off, and I won't get to see Brenna half as much as I'd like to. But it's only one year. We can survive that. Then she'll graduate, and maybe consider moving to Edmonton, if I'm still playing there.

Annnd I'm getting way ahead of myself right now. First I need to convince her to take me back, and then we can worry about her moving to another country for me.

"Are you gonna talk to her after the game?" Hollis asks expectantly. "Or do we need to bring out a shotgun and—"

"Relax, you don't have to make me talk to her at gunpoint," I say with a chuckle.

"What?" His expression is puzzled. "I was going to say we'd clock you in the back of the head with the shotgun, knock some sense into you."

I turn to Fitzgerald, who shrugs and says, "His brain operates on a level us mortals can't comprehend."

Hollis looks pleased. "Dude, that's the nicest thing you've ever said to me."

———

The unexpected visit from the Briar guys is nothing compared to the shock I receive when I leave the locker room to find a vending machine and instead find my parents standing in the corridor. For a moment I think I'm hallucinating, until my mom blurts out my name.

"Jake!" Relief floods her face. "You're here? Rory, he's already here."

"I can see that," Dad says dryly.

I shake my head in confusion, then glance over at Hazel, who's next to my mother. She offers a slight smile, as if to say, *Look what the cat dragged in, right?*

"Yeah. I'm here. I showed up early."

"Why weren't you answering your phone?" Mom asks.

"I forgot it at home." I stare at my parents. "Why are you guys here?"

"We came to support you," Mom replies.

Dad claps me on the shoulder. "This is a big game for you. And if I'm being honest, your mother and I felt bad about not making more of an effort to attend your games. Now that you'll be in the pros, your parents will be expected to make an appearance, right?"

"I don't think anybody cares if some random rookie's parents are in the box or not, Dad."

"Random rookie?" he echoes. "No way!"

"You're going to be a superstar," Mom reminds me, a big smile on her face. "And we're so very proud of you."

My eyes suddenly feel hot. Damn it, I can't tear up right now. Got a game to concentrate on.

"Thank you," I say, and, yeah, my voice is a bit hoarse. I clear my throat. "I know you guys don't care about hockey much, but I appreciate that you came today."

"We might not be hockey fanatics, but we're Jake fanatics," Mom declares.

Hazel snorts. "That was so lame, Mrs. C."

"We should take our seats," Dad says. "It's really filling up in there."

"Good luck, sweetie," Mom says.

I find myself enveloped in a warm bear hug, followed by a less dramatic but equally warm side hug from my dad.

"I'll join you in a minute," Hazel tells them. "I want to talk to Jake first."

Once they're gone, I raise a brow at my friend. "I can't believe they came. Did you know about this?"

She nods. "Your mom called me to get them tickets. They wanted to surprise you."

I slide my hands in my pockets and glance at the door behind me. The team will be arriving soon. "I should head back in and do my mental prep."

"Cool." Hazel seems to hesitate.

"You okay?"

"I'm fine." But her face is a bit pale, and when she smiles it doesn't quite reach her eyes. "Have a good game, Jake."

40
JAKE

Returning to the locker room, I immediately feel centered. Strong. Motivated. Now that I know my parents will be in the stands cheering me on, I'm even more determined to play well.

I'm going to beat Michigan today, and afterwards I'm going to win Brenna back. I don't care if I have to throw myself at her feet and beg. I'm getting my woman back.

Although the team's uniforms and gear were brought here ahead of time, I always have my own equipment bag with me. It's where I keep my spare hockey tape and other random gear, and I usually toss my bracelet in there. I pull the zipper open and rummage around in search of the familiar beads. But my fingers aren't connecting with anything.

When memory strikes, it takes a second for the horror to settle in.

I loaned the bracelet to Brenna.

And then I broke up with her without getting it back. Fuck.

Oh fuck oh fuck oh fuck.

In the back of my mind, an angry voice is demanding to know why she hadn't contacted me in the three days since we saw each other to remind me she still has it. She knows how important it is to me and she couldn't be bothered to make a phone call? It wouldn't have even required seeing me. I could've sent Weston to pick it up.

But Mike Hollis said her heart was broken. And I'm the one who broke it. Of course she's not going out of her way to do me a solid.

Panic swirls in my gut, and I take a series of deep breaths. Force myself calm down. It's just a fucking bracelet. I don't need a *child's* bracelet to win this game. A bracelet didn't get us to the regionals. A bracelet didn't get me drafted by the Oilers. A bracelet didn't—

"Jake."

My head snaps toward the door. Hazel tentatively enters the room.

"You shouldn't be in here," I croak.

"I'll be quick, I promise. I…" She keeps walking, stopping when we're two feet apart. Her throat works as she gulps, several times from the look of it. Then she pulls something off her wrist and holds it up.

The wave of relief that crashes into me almost knocks me off my feet. I snatch the bracelet from her grasp. It takes all my willpower not to cradle it against me and start calling it my precious. But Jesus fucking Christ. That was a scare.

"I wasn't going to give this to you," Hazel tells me, and the shame in her tone makes me narrow my eyes at her.

"What the hell are you talking about? How did you even get this?"

"Brenna showed up and asked me to give it to you."

"Right now?"

Hazel slowly shakes her head. "Maybe thirty minutes ago?"

"You mean thirty minutes *before* we spoke outside that door?" Anger rises in my chest, burning my throat. "Are you kidding me, Hazel? You had that on your wrist when we were talking just now?"

"Yes, but—"

"And you didn't give it to me? You wished me luck and sent me away without fucking giving it to me?"

"Let me finish," she begs. "Please?"

Once again, I rely on willpower in order to force my trap shut. I'm going to let her finish, out of respect for a sixteen-year friendship. But I'm so furious my hands are trembling.

"I wasn't going to give it to you because then you would've found out that Brenna is here," Hazel whispers.

My heart beats faster. Not from anger this time, but at the notion that Brenna is here. Even after I broke her heart, she still drove all this way to return my good-luck charm.

"But then I realized not only would that make me the worst friend in the world, it would make me an unbelievably shitty person. Messing with your ritual to try to keep you away from her? Because I'm jealous of her?" Hazel avoids my incredulous gaze. "There'd be no coming back from that."

My stomach churns. This is not a conversation I want to be having right now. At least not with Hazel. Now that I know Brenna is somewhere in this arena, she's the only one I care to talk to.

"I've always had a thing for you," Hazel confesses.

Crap. Well, I can't leave *now*.

And her confession takes so much balls I can't help but admire her. "Hazel," I start, my tone rough.

"It's stupid, I know. But it's hard not to develop feelings for *the* Jake Connelly, you know?" A sad half-smile lifts one corner of her mouth. "And I'm well aware that you only see me as a friend, but I guess a part of me always thought it would be like one of those cheesy rom coms, where you woke up one day and realized I was the one you wanted all along. But that's not going to happen."

No, it won't.

I don't voice the confirmation, because I don't want to hurt her any more than she's clearly already hurting. But I know she sees the truth in my eyes. I don't feel a spark toward Hazel, only platonic love. Even if I weren't in love with somebody else, there could never be anything between us.

"I'm so sorry, Jake." Genuine remorse floods her expression. "You have every right to be pissed at me. But I hope the fact that I came back to return the bracelet, and to tell you that Brenna is here, might make up for me not returning it to you before. I messed up. I had a selfish moment, and I'm owning that." She stares down at the floor. "I don't want to lose your friendship."

"You won't."

Her shocked gaze flies to mine. "I won't?"

"Of course not." I sigh. "We've known each other forever, Hazel. I'm not going to throw away years of friendship because you screwed up. I accept your apology."

She slumps with relief.

"But if you're truly my friend, you'll make a sincere effort to get to know Brenna. I think you'd actually really like her. And if you don't, then fucking fake it." I tip my head in challenge. "If you were dating someone I didn't like, I'd fake it for you. I'd support you no matter what."

"I know you would. You're one of the best people I know." Hazel fumbles in her green canvas purse for her phone. "I know you forgot yours at home, but I can find her on social media and—"

"Who?"

"Brenna," Hazel says. "She came all this way to return your bracelet, and she gave it to me instead of giving it to you herself, which tells me there's trouble in paradise. And there's no way you're putting one skate on the ice until you fix whatever's wrong." She unlocks her password screen, her silver thumb rings clicking against the side of the case. "Is she on Facebook or Insta? You can DM her from my phone."

"We don't need social media. I have her number memorized."

"Really? You memorized her number?" I nod.

"Wow. I don't even have my own mother's number memorized."

I respond with an awkward shrug. "I wanted it to be in my brain in case I ever lost it."

Hazel goes quiet.

"What?" I say defensively.

"It's just…" She looks oddly impressed. "You really are in love, huh?"

"Yeah. I am."

41
BRENNA

Since it's sacrilege not to make use of a perfectly good pair of hockey tickets, Dad and I end up sticking around in Worcester. We're in the standing-room-only section of the arena, which happens to be near one of the cameras that are set up on the perimeter of the rink to capture and televise the game. I spot a cameraman in a HockeyNet jacket and wonder who Mulder sent to cover the game. Kip and Trevor don't report live, so Geoff Magnolia probably got the gig.

I know who Mulder *didn't* send: Georgia Barnes. I mean, come on. Vaginas and sports? The horror.

A lanky man in a suit approaches the cameraman, and I curse softly under my breath. Not softly enough, because Dad glances up from the email he was answering on his phone.

"What is it?"

"Geoff Magnolia," I grumble, nodding discreetly toward the cameras. "That's who HockeyNet assigned to cover this."

Like me, Dad also isn't a fan of Magnolia's reporting. He follows my gaze. "Huh. He got a haircut. Looks like shit."

Laughter bubbles in my throat. "Dad. Since when are you so snarky?"

"What? It's a shitty haircut."

"Meow."

"Can it, Brenna."

I watch as Magnolia converses with his cameraman. He uses a lot of hand gestures. It's distracting. Thankfully, he never does that on camera.

"You know what? Screw HockeyNet," I say. "I'm applying at ESPN this fall. They have a way better track record of hiring women. And if I intern there, that means I don't ever have to see Ed Mulder again. Or that tool over there."

I glance at Magnolia again, and oh my God—he's drinking coffee out of a straw. Or if not coffee, it's at least a hot drink, because steam is rising from the liquid.

"Ugh. I take it back. He's not a tool. Tools are actually useful. That man is not."

"And I'm snarky?" my father demands. "Take a good look in the mirror, Peaches."

"Can it, old man."

He howls with laughter, and then returns to his emails.

As I crane my neck trying to pick out any familiar faces in the stands, my phone rings. I peer down, register the unfamiliar number on the screen, and hit *ignore*.

Three seconds later, a text pops up.

Hey, it's Jake's friend Hazel. He gave me your number. He's
in the locker room and desperately needs to see you.

I frown at the message. I don't know why, but this feels like a trap. Like she's luring me into the locker room so she could... what? Beat me up with a hockey stick? I resist the urge to roll my eyes at myself. My paranoia is a bit absurd.

"Dad, hey, do you mind if I go talk to Jake for a minute?"

His head pops up from his phone. "How'd that happen?"

I hold up my own phone. "He says he wants to talk."

Dad thinks this over for a second. Then he shrugs. "Give him hell."

"Oh, I intend to."

"That's my girl." He pauses for another beat, and his tone becomes brusque. "If the outcome of this chat results in my daughter coming back here with a boyfriend, then tell that boyfriend he's invited to dinner tonight."

My jaw drops, but I don't question him or attempt to discuss this unexpected invitation, because I have no idea why Jake even wants to see me.

And why am I racing to see *him*, I ask myself a minute later, after I've burst through a second set of doors. My step stutters in the middle of the hallway.

Jake broke up with me. I shouldn't be running back to him so eagerly. And what if he's only summoning me to say thanks for returning his bracelet? That would be so humiliating. I don't need his gratitude. I need his...

His what?

I don't even know. I mean, my heart certainly knows what *it* wants. It wants Jake Connelly. But news flash—my heart is reckless and stupid. It doesn't look out for itself, which means I have to look out for it.

When I reach the locker room area, there isn't a security guard in sight. I'm not sure which door leads to the Harvard locker room, so like a total fool I call out, "Jake?"

One of the doors to my left immediately swings open. I half expect Hazel to be on the other side of it, but she's not. It's Jake, and his forest-green eyes soften at the sight of me.

"You came. I wasn't sure if you would." He opens the door wider so I can come in.

I follow him inside. The game doesn't start for another forty-five minutes, but it's still weird to see the locker room empty. The wide wooden lockers spanning the walls are neat and tidy, uniforms and padding hung up and waiting for Jake and his teammates.

"Where's your friend?" I ask when my gaze returns to his.

"In her seat, I assume. I'm sorry I had to text you from her phone, but I forgot mine at home."

"Ah. That's why you didn't respond to any of my messages about your bracelet." I nod at his wrist, relieved to see the familiar pink and purple beads. "I see you got it, though. Good."

"Almost didn't," he murmurs.

"What?"

"Nothing. It doesn't matter. We don't have a lot of time before the team arrives, so let's not waste it on a stupid bracelet."

My eyebrows fly up. "A stupid bracelet? You're talking about your good-luck charm here, Jakey. Show some respect."

A huge smile stretches across his handsome face.

"Why are you smiling like that?" I ask suspiciously.

"Sorry. I just missed hearing it."

"Hearing what?"

"Jakey." He shrugs adorably. "I'd gotten used to it. I don't even care if it's a jab. I'm digging it."

I take an awkward step backward. "Why did you ask me to come?"

"Because…" He hesitates, running a hand through his hair.

I'm slowly beginning to lose patience. "You broke up with me, Jake. Remember? You said you didn't want to see me anymore and that I was a distraction, and now you're dragging me to the locker room before such a crucial game? How is this not a distraction? What do you *want* from me?"

"You," he blurts out.

"Me, what?"

"That's what I want. I want you," he says simply.

I stare at him in disbelief. "You dumped me."

"I know, and I'm so fucking sorry. I was a moron. And I was selfish. And…" He swallows. "I was a coward, okay? No other way around it. I've always been selfish, but the one thing I've never been is a coward, and *that's* why I broke up with you. Because I was scared shitless. I've never been in a relationship before and I was feeling pressured."

"Pressured how?" I'm confused for a moment, until I realize a bleak truth. "Oh. I get it. I told you about the miscarriage and everything that happened, and…I became some sort of emotional burden for you—is that it?"

"What? No, not at all," he exclaims. "I promise, that's not it. I was happy when you opened up to me. I was waiting so long for you to do that, and then when you finally did, it was like…" His gaze softens again. "It felt good to be trusted, especially by you. I know you don't trust a lot of people."

"No," I say pointedly. "I don't."

"The pressure I felt was more about relationships in general. I was stressing over how we would make it work when I'm in Edmonton, how I could make you a priority, how we'd cope with not being able to see each other that much. I could list a bunch of other things, but it all boils down to…I had a panic attack." He sighs. "Men are stupid, remember?"

I can't help but smirk.

"*I* was stupid. And now I'm asking for your forgiveness." He hesitates. "And I'm asking you to give me another chance."

"Why would I do that?"

"Because I love you."

My heart expands in my chest, and for a moment I worry it might burst through my rib cage. Hearing those three words come out of Jake Connelly's beautiful mouth triggers a wave of emotion that I desperately try to suppress.

"You hurt me," I say softly.

This time, my vulnerability is not thrown back in my face. "I know I did. And you can't even imagine how awful I feel about that. But I can't change it. All I can say is that I'm sorry, and that I'll do everything in my power to never hurt you again."

I can't answer. My throat is too thick with emotion.

"If you want me to beg, I'll beg. If you want me to jump through hoops, bring them on. I'll spend every waking hour until I have to report to training camp proving to you how much you mean to me." His teeth dig into his lower lip. "Proving that I'm worthy of you."

I feel my own lips start to tremble and pray to God I don't cry. "Fucking hell, Jake."

"What?" His voice is hoarse.

"Nobody's ever said anything like that to me before." Not even Eric, in all the months and years he spent trying to win me back. Eric tossed out phrases like *I'm the one for you* and *you can't do this to me.* Not once did he offer to spend even a fraction of a second proving that *he* was worthy of *me.*

"Every word is the truth," Jake says simply. "I fucked up. I love you. And I want you back."

I swallow past the lump in my throat. "Even though I have another year left of college?"

He offers a half-smile. "My rookie season is going to be brutal, babe. Time-consuming. It'll probably be better for us if you're also busy, right?"

He has a point.

"We can make it work. If we truly want to be in a relationship, then we'll make that relationship work. The question is, do you want it?" He hesitates again. "Do you want me?"

The stark emotion contained in that one question robs me of breath. The words are so raw—*do you want me?* It's not the hour-long confession I gave the other night, but that doesn't make him any less exposed. All of his insecurities are revealed in his eyes, the hope, the regret, the fear that I might reject him. And, oddly enough, I also glimpse that familiar Connelly confidence. This man is even secure about being *insecure,* and damned if that doesn't make me love him even more.

"I want you." I clear my throat, because I sound like I've been chain-smoking for a week straight. "Of course I want you." I exhale in a fast burst. "I love you, Jake."

The last boy I said those words to chose himself over me, repeatedly, and without a second's thought.

But the man I'm saying them to now? I have faith that he'll always choose me, always choose *us*.

"I love you, too," he whispers, and the next thing I know he's kissing me and, oh my gosh, I missed this so much.

It's only been a few days, but it feels like years since Jake's warm lips were pressed up against mine. I loop my arms around his neck, kissing him back hungrily until his husky groan bounces off the locker room walls.

"Christ," he chokes out. "We gotta stop that. Now." He glances at his crotch. "Fuck. Too late."

I follow his gaze and laugh when I notice the massive erection straining behind his zipper. "Control yourself, Jakey. You're about to play hockey."

"Don't you know? Hockey players are passionate and aggressive," he says silkily.

"Ha. Right. I totally forgot." There's a big, dumb smile on my face, and it refuses to subside. I'm overflowing with happiness, a state of being that is completely foreign to me. I'm not sure I like it.

Nah.

I actually kind of love it.

"You should go," Jake says reluctantly. "The team'll be bursting in any second now. Are you staying for the game?"

I nod. "My dad's here, too."

"Seriously? Aw fuck, why'd you have to tell me that? Now I'll feel extra pressure to perform."

"Don't worry, Jakey. I speak from personal experience when I say I've got nothing but confidence in your ability to perform."

He winks. "Thanks, baby."

"Oh, and don't let this freak you out even more, but he wants to take us to dinner after the game."

"*Don't let this freak you out even more?*" Jake scrubs his hands over his face. "Jesus Christ. Just leave, babe. Leave now before you do any more damage."

"Love you," I say in a singsong voice on my way to the door.

"Love you too." He sighs from behind me.

That big-ass grin is still plastered to my face when I walk out, and a disgusting spring to my step carries me down the corridor, as if I'm a character in a Disney movie. Oh no. I'm in trouble. Badass Brenna Jensen isn't allowed to fall this hard for a guy.

It happened. Deal with it.

Yeah.

I guess this is my life now.

At the end of the hall, I turn the corner and my happy gait takes a bit of a stumble when I bump directly into Daryl Pedersen's bulky chest.

"Whoa there, Nelly," he says with a chuckle—which dies the second he recognizes me. "Brenna." His tone is careful now. "Here to cheer Connelly on, I suppose?"

"Yup. I came with my dad, actually." When his expression darkens, I try not to laugh. "We're both rooting for you today, Coach."

Although he's momentarily startled, he recovers quickly and gives me a smirk. "You can tell Chad I have no need for his support. Never have, never will."

"Still a sore loser after all these years, eh, Coach?"

His response is terse. "I'm not sure what you're insinuating, but—"

"I heard you tried to bang my mother and she shot you down," I cut in cheerfully. "And I'm not insinuating anything—I'm explicitly suggesting you were a sore loser back then, and you're a sore loser now." I shrug. "With that said, I'm still rooting for Harvard tonight. But that's because of Jake, of course. Not you."

Pedersen's eyes narrow so much they resemble two dark slits. "You're not like your mother," he says slowly. I can't tell if he's pleased or disheartened by that. "Marie was a sweet southern belle. You're... you're not like her at all."

I meet his disturbed gaze and offer a faint smile. "I guess I take after my father."

Then I continue down the hall, my legs moving in that obnoxiously bouncy gait I can't control, because my happy heart is calling all the shots, and all I want to do is get back to the ice and scream myself hoarse as I watch the man I love win his game.

EPILOGUE
BRENNA

ST. PAUL, MINNESOTA

THE LAST TIME I WENT TO THE FROZEN FOUR, IT WAS TO CHEER for my dad's all-star crew: Garrett Graham, Summer's brother Dean, and the two Johns—Logan and Tucker. And they won the whole damn thing. I was happy, of course, but nowhere near as ecstatic as I am during this Harvard versus Ohio State game.

The score is 3–1, Harvard. There are five minutes left. It only takes a second to score a goal, so yes, we don't have it in the bag. It's not a guaranteed win, and I'm not sitting here counting my chickens before they hatch. But I have a good feeling about it.

Beside me, Jake's parents, Lily and Rory Connelly, are cheering themselves hoarse. They're actually pretty fun to watch a hockey game with—Lily gasps any time anything happens, literally anything; Rory, after every hit, winces and proclaims, "Well, that's gonna hurt tomorrow." You can tell they're not huge hockey fans. They don't know much about the rules and they don't seem to care. But any time Jake has the puck, they're on their feet screaming their lungs out.

I wish Dad were here, but he's watching the game at home in Hastings. However, he did call in a favor and arrange for this private box for us, which means we have the best seats in the house...and lots of privacy for Jake's folks to cross-examine me.

During both intermissions, the questions came hard and fast.

Where did you meet Jake?

How long have you been together?

You know he's moving to Edmonton, right?

Do you think maybe you'll move there, too?

You could transfer schools, his mother had said, her expression so hopeful that I almost laughed.

When they turned their attention to the ice, I glanced at Jake's friend Hazel and asked, "Are they always like this?"

She smiled wryly, answering, "This is kind of a big deal for them. Jake's never had a real girlfriend."

Okay, fine, I'm not going to lie—it warms my heart that I'm the first girl to meet Jake's parents. Hazel doesn't count; they treat her like a daughter. And, I'll be honest, the girl's been making an effort. She's asked me about my classes, my interests, as if she genuinely wants to get to know me.

She doesn't like hockey, though, and that's always a strike. I still can't believe I'm watching the most important game in men's college hockey with three people *who don't like hockey*. Figure that one out. On the bright side, my dad has been texting all evening with his thoughts on the game, which is nice.

I like our relationship now. It's easy. And I haven't heard from Eric since the night we went to rescue him. He's barely even crossed my mind, in fact. I'm finally putting that part of my life behind me and focusing on what's in front of me.

And what's in front of me is incredible. It's Jake, traveling like lightning across the glossy surface of the ice. One minute he's at the center line with the puck, the next he's in front of the crease taking a shot.

"GOALLLLLLL!" yells the announcer.

The entire arena goes absolutely bananas. It's 4–1 now. Maybe I'm starting to count those chickens, after all. At least a couple of them. The eggs are cracking, anyway, and I can see a beak. Those chicks are coming, because it's 4–1 and Harvard's got this. My man's got this.

Jake's family is on their feet again, screaming. So am I. My phone buzzes about ten times in my pocket. It's probably my father. Or maybe Summer, who's also at home, watching the game with Fitz and the others, including Nate, who's my friend again. Hell, the texts could even be from Hollis. He's been very chatty with me since I saved his relationship with Rupi. They're officially together now, and he *really* seems to enjoy telling people he has a girlfriend.

Which makes me wonder if, like Jake, Hollis never had one before. Either way, I'm happy for him. Rupi is nuts, but in a good way.

The clock winds down. I watch it with pure joy stuck in my throat, in my chest, in my heart. Jake deserves this. He deserves to end his college career with such a major win. He played brilliantly tonight, and I know he's going to be equally brilliant in Edmonton.

As the buzzer goes off, the rest of Jake's teammates fly off the bench and swarm the ice, and it's pandemonium. The boys are overjoyed. Even Pedersen looks genuinely happy. Not in a smug "we won na-na-na-na-na-na" way. In this moment, I can tell Daryl Pedersen actually loves his players and this game. He might play it dirtier than most, but he loves it just like the rest of us.

My phone buzzes again. I finish hugging Jake's parents and then reach to check it. I assume it's from my dad, but it's a voice-mail alert. Which tells me the previous buzzing was a phone call. And either I'm hallucinating or that actually says *ESPN* on the caller display. Probably a telemarketer with one of those speeches—"Is your cable provider giving you all that ESPN has to offer?"

But a telemarketer wouldn't leave a message. Would they?

"Guys, excuse me for one sec." I touch Lily's arm and walk several feet away to check the message.

The moment the caller says her name, I almost faint.

"Brenna. Hi. It's Georgia Barnes. Sorry to call you on a Saturday evening, but I'm working late to organize my new office. I wanted to touch base with you now, because starting Monday I'll be absolutely swamped. I got your number from Mischa Yanikov, the stage manager at HockeyNet. But let's keep that between us, because I don't know if grabbing your number off your résumé and giving it to a competitor was all that kosher. But it'll be our little secret."

My heart starts beating faster. Why is Georgia Barnes calling me? And what does she mean she's at her new office? At ESPN? Does she work there now?

Her next sentence solves that mystery.

"Anyway, the press release hasn't gone out yet, but I've officially left HockeyNet. ESPN made me an offer and, let's just say I'd be stupid not to accept it. They're letting me hire my own assistant, and I'd love for you to come in and interview for the position. If you do get the job, I'm aware you're still in college, so obviously in the fall we would need to discuss a schedule that suits you better. Maybe this could be a work placement or—I'm getting ahead of myself. For all I know, you interview terribly and that's why Ed Mulder let you go. But I have a feeling that's not the case."

Her confident chuckle makes me smile.

"Anyway, give me a call when you get this." She recites her number. "I'd love to schedule an interview. I think you'd be a good fit for this position. All right. Talk soon. Take care."

The message ends and I stare at my phone in shock.

"Everything okay?" Hazel comes up beside me.

"It's fine." I shake my head a few times. "It's all good."

All good? No. It's better than I could ever imagine. I have an interview at ESPN to work as Georgia Barnes's assistant. And Jake just won the national championship. This is the greatest day of my life.

All I want to do now is get downstairs so that mine is the first face Jake sees when he exits the locker room. I'm officially his groupie. But that's okay, because he's *my* groupie. We root for each other. We're good for each other. And I can't wait to find out what the future holds for us.

Read on for a sneak peek into *The Play*, the next book in the bestselling Briar U series

1
HUNTER

THIS PARTY BLOWS.

I probably should have stayed at home, but these days "home" is like living on the set of a Kardashian reality show. Thanks to my three female roommates, it's estrogen overload over there.

Granted, there's a helluva lot of estrogen here at the Theta Beta Nu house, but it's the kind I'm allowed to be attracted to. My roommates are all in relationships, so I'm not allowed to touch them.

You're not allowed to touch any of these women either...

True. Because of my self-imposed abstinence, I'm not allowed to touch anyone, period.

Which raises the question—if a tree falls in the forest and you can't fuck anyone at the sorority-house party, is it still considered a party?

I curl my fingers around the red Solo cup that my friend and teammate Matt Anderson just planted in my hand. "Thanks," I mutter.

I take a sip and make a face. The beer tastes like water, although maybe that's a good thing. A nice incentive to not consume more than one. Morning skate isn't until ten a.m. tomorrow, but I was planning on showing up at the arena a couple hours early to work on my slapshot.

After last season's disastrous end, I vowed to make hockey my top priority. The new semester starts Monday, our first game is next week, and I'm feeling motivated. Briar didn't make it to the national championship last year and that's on me. This season will be different.

"What do you think about her?" Matt discreetly nods toward a cute girl in tiny boxer shorts and a pale pink camisole. She's not wearing a bra, and the outlines of her beaded nipples are visible beneath the silky material.

My mouth actually waters.

Did I mention this is a PJ party? Yup yup, I haven't had sex in nearly five months and I'm kicking off junior year at a party where every single woman in attendance is wearing next to nothing. I never claimed to be smart.

"She's smokin'," I tell Matt. "Go make a move."

"I would, but…" He lets out a grumbling sound. "She's checking *you* out."

"Well, I'm closed for business," I answer with a shrug. "Feel free to go over there and tell her that." I poke him good-naturedly on the arm. "I'm sure she'll view you as an adequate consolation prize."

"Ha! Fuck off. I'm nobody's second choice. If she's not dying to hook up with me, I'd way rather find someone who is. I don't need to compete for a woman's attention."

This is why I like Matt—he's competitive on the ice, but off of it he's really decent. I've been playing hockey my entire life, and I've had teammates who wouldn't even blink at stealing another guy's girl, or even worse, hooking up with her behind his back. I've played with guys who treat our hockey groupies as disposable, who've shared girls like Tic Tacs. Guys with zero respect and terrible judgment.

But at Briar, I'm fortunate to play with some stand-up dudes. Sure, no roster is without a douchebag or two, but for the most part my teammates are good guys.

"Yeah, I don't think it'll be too hard," I agree. "The brunette at two o'clock is already boning down with you in her head."

His brown eyes widen in appreciation as they land on the curvy girl in the short white nightie. Her cheeks flush when their gazes meet and then she smiles shyly and raises her cup in a silent toast.

Matt abandons me without a backward glance. I don't blame him.

The living room is packed with girls in lingerie and guys in Hugh Hefner pajamas. I hadn't known this was a theme event, so I'm in cargo shorts and a white T-shirt, and I'm good with that. Most of the dudes around me look ridiculous in their get-ups.

"Having a good time?" The music is blaring, but it's not loud enough that I don't hear the girl. The one Matt had originally been checking out.

"Yeah. Nice turnout." I shrug. "DJ is pretty good."

She sidles up closer. "I'm Gina."

"Hunter."

"I know who you are." Sympathy creeps into her voice. "I was there for the conference championship against Harvard, when that jerk broke your wrist. I can't believe he did that."

I can. I fucked his girlfriend.

But I keep that to myself. It's not like I did it intentionally, anyway. I had no clue who that girl was when I slept with her. Apparently she knew who *I* was, though. She wanted to get back at her boyfriend, but I didn't know that until he launched himself at me in the middle of the second-most important game of the season, the one that determines who goes to the Frozen Four, the *first*-most important game of a college season. The broken wrist was the result of a tackle to the ice. The Harvard asshole didn't intend to break it, but it happened, and just like that I was out of the game. And so was our team captain, Nate Rhodes, who was ejected for fighting while trying to defend me.

I snap myself out of the past. "It was a shitty way to end the season," I say.

Her hand finds its way onto my right biceps. My arms are looking huge these days, if I do say so myself. When you're not having sex, working out is imperative for your sanity.

"I'm sorry," Gina purrs. Her fingers gently glide over my bare skin, sending pinpricks of heat through my arm.

I almost groan out loud. Sweet fuck, I'm so horny that a woman caressing my *arm* is giving me a semi.

I know I should brush her hand off me, but it's been so long since I've been touched in a non-platonic way. At home my roommates are constantly pawing at me, but there's nothing sexual about it. Brenna likes to mockingly smack or pinch my ass whenever we pass each other in the hall, but that's not because she wants me. She's just an asshole.

"Want to go somewhere quiet and talk or something?" Gina suggests.

I've lived on this planet long enough to be able to decode what "talk or something" means in girl speak.

1) There won't be much talking.

2) There'll be a lot of "or something."

Gina couldn't have made this clearer if she were holding up a sign saying DO ME! She even licks her lips as she voices the question.

I know I should say no, but the idea of going home right now and jacking off in my bedroom while my roommates marathon old seasons of *The Hills* isn't too appealing. So I say, "Sure," and follow Gina out of the room.

We end up in a small den that contains a couch, a couple of bookshelves, and a desk against the far wall under a window. It's surprisingly empty. The party gods have taken pity on my celibate ass and provided us with the kind of dangerous privacy I should actively be avoiding. Instead, I'm on the couch and letting Gina kiss my neck.

Her satin camisole rubs my arm and it's almost pornographic how good the barely there friction feels. Everything is turning me on these days. I got a stiffy watching a YouTube ad for Tupperware the other day because the MILF in the ad was peeling a banana. Then she chopped it up into bits and placed the banana pieces in a plastic container and not even that horrific symbolism could dissuade me from jerking off to Banana Woman. Give me a few more months and I'll be fucking the apple pies my roommate Rupi bakes every Sunday.

"You smell so good." Gina inhales deeply, then exhales, her warm breath tickling my neck. Her lips latch on once more, a hot, wet brand against my neck.

She feels good in my lap. Her shapely thighs straddle mine, her satin-clad body warm and curvy. And I have to stop this.

I made a promise to myself, and to my team, although none of them asked me to do it and they all think I'm insane for even attempting abstinence. Matt flat-out stated he doesn't believe that me setting aside my sexual urges is going to impact our hockey games in the slightest. But I think it will, and for me it's a matter of principle. The guys voted me captain. I take that responsibility seriously, and I know from personal experience that I have the tendency to let women mess with my head. Screwing around got me a broken wrist last year. I'm not looking to repeat that.

"Gina, I—"

She cuts me off by pressing her lips to mine, and then we're kissing and my mind begins to spin. She tastes like beer and bubble gum. And her hair, which falls over one shoulder in a thick curtain of red curls, smells like apples. Mmmm, I want to eat her up.

Our tongues dance and the kiss grows deeper, hotter. My head keeps spinning as lust and unhappiness war inside me. I've lost all capability to think clearly. I'm so hard it hurts and Gina makes it worse by rubbing herself all over my crotch.

Thirty more seconds, I tell myself. Thirty more seconds and then I'll stop this from going any further.

"I want you so bad." Her lips are fused to my neck again, and then, *fuck*, her hand slides between us. She cups my cock over my shorts and I almost weep with pleasure. It's been so long since a hand that didn't belong to myself touched my dick. It feels criminally good.

"Gina, no," I groan, and it takes all my willpower to remove her hand. My cock protests by leaking precome all over the inside of my boxers.

Her cheeks are flushed red. Eyes glazed. "Why not?"

"I'm…taking a break from all that."

"From what?"

"Sex."

"What about it?"

"I'm going without."

"Without what?" She looks as confused as I am miserable.

"Without sex," I clarify glumly. "As in, I'm not having it for a while."

Her brows crash together. "But…why not?"

"It's a long story." I pause. "Actually, it's not a long story at all. I want to concentrate on hockey this year, and sex is too big of a distraction. That's pretty much it."

She pauses for a long beat. Then she touches my cheek and sweeps her thumb over the stubble on my jaw. She licks her lips, and I almost come in my pants.

"If you're worried that I'm going to want anything more, don't. I'm only looking for a one-night thing. My course load is insane this semester and I don't have time for relationships either."

"It's not a relationship issue," I try to explain. "It's sex in general. Once I have it, I want to keep having it. I get distracted and—"

She cuts me off again. "Fine, no sex. I'll just suck you off."

I nearly choke on my tongue. "Gina—"

"Don't worry, I'll get myself off while I'm doing it. Blowjobs turn me on so much."

This is torture.

Pure torture.

I swear, if the military needs any ideas on how to break someone? Give them a hard-up college guy, throw a hot chick on his lap, have her tell him how she wants nothing but no-strings sex and offer him blowjobs because it turns her on *so much*.

"I'm sorry," I manage to croak. Then I accomplish the even more difficult feat of easing her off my lap and getting to my feet. "I'm not in a good headspace for...any of this."

She stays seated, her head tipped back to stare at me. Her eyes are wide with incredulity and a touch of...I think it might be *sympathy*. For chrissake. Now I'm being pitied for my celibacy.

"I'm sorry," I say again. "And just so you know, you're the hottest girl at this party and my decision has nothing to do with you. I made myself a promise back in April and I want to keep it."

Gina chews on her bottom lip. Then, to my surprise, her expression takes on a glimmer of admiration. "I'm not going to lie," she says, "I'm kind of impressed. Not many guys could stand by that conviction in the face of my hotness."

"Not many guys are as stupid as I am."

Grinning, she hops to her feet. "Well, I guess I'll see you around, Hunter. I'd like to say I'll wait for you, but a girl has needs. And obviously they don't align with yours."

With a laugh, she saunters out of the den, and I watch her sexy ass sway with each step.

I rake both hands through my hair and then release a silent groan into my palms. I don't know if I should be proud of myself or kick my own ass for this ridiculous path I've chosen.

For the most part, it *has* helped keep me focused on hockey. I take out all my sexual frustration on the ice. I'm faster and stronger than I was last season, and there's almost a desperation in each shot that I snap at the net. The bullets hit their mark, almost as if in tribute to my suffering dick. An acknowledgment that his sacrifice must be honored.

It's only until the end of the season, I reassure myself. Seven more months, which will put me at one full year of celibacy once I cross the finish line. And then I'll reward myself with an entire summer of sex. A sex summer.

A dirty, decadent, endless sex summer...

Oh Christ. I'm so tired of fucking my own hand. Granted, I'm not helping my cause when I do idiotic things like opening myself up to temptation with gorgeous sorority girls.

For the first time in a long time, I'm dying for classes to start. Hopefully I'll have so much work this semester I'll be drowning in it. Homework, extra ice time, practice, and games—that's all I'm allowed to focus on. And definitely no more sorority parties.

Avoiding temptation is the only way to keep my head in the game and my dick in my pants.

ACKNOWLEDGMENTS

You guys. I had so much fun writing this book! The last time I enjoyed myself this much with a story, I was working on *The Deal* (which at the time was purely for my own enjoyment and not supposed to be published). Brenna and Jake really came alive for me, and their journey took me on a wild, emotional ride.

FYI—I took several liberties with the college hockey season in this book, extending the season as well as stretching it out a bit. I'm aware of when Division I teams play and how a season is organized, so these aren't errors but choices on my part :)

As usual, this book wouldn't be in your hands right now if it weren't for some awesome people:

Edie Danford, whose edits are not only top-notch, but make me laugh my butt off.

Sarina and Nikki, for beta reading and offering awesome notes.

Aquila Editing, for proofing this book. (I'm sorry for all the typos!)

Connor McCarthy, college hockey player who once again shared his expertise with me.

Nicole and Natasha, who I wouldn't survive without. Like, seriously.

Nina, my publicist, friend, and wifey. AKA, the best.

My agent, Kimberly Brower, for championing the Briar U series all over the globe.

The Bloom team for coming on board to bring the paperback to a whole new audience. My editor, Christa Désir, for knowing the significance of #family. Pam, Molly, Madison, Katie, and the rest of the marketing team. And of course Dom—publisher extraordinaire!

All my amazing author friends who shared this release and offered their love and support—you are the absolute best!

And as always, the bloggers, reviewers and readers who continue to spread the word about my books. I am so thankful for your love and kindness. You're the reason I keep writing these crazy stories. <3

ABOUT THE AUTHOR

A *New York Times*, *USA Today*, and *Wall Street Journal* bestselling author, Elle Kennedy grew up in the suburbs of Toronto, Ontario, and holds a BA in English from York University. From an early age, she knew she wanted to be a writer and actively began pursuing that dream when she was a teenager. She loves strong heroines and sexy alpha heroes, and just enough heat and danger to keep things interesting!

Elle loves to hear from her readers. Visit her website ellekennedy.com or sign up for her newsletter to receive updates about upcoming books and exclusive excerpts. You can also find her on Facebook (ElleKennedyAuthor), Instagram (@ElleKennedy33), or TikTok (@ElleKennedyAuthor).